THE
# KING
OF
# BONES
AND
# ASHES

ALSO BY J.D. HORN

## Witches of New Orleans

*The King of Bones and Ashes*
*The Book of the Unwinding* (forthcoming)
*The Final Days of Magic* (forthcoming)

## Witching Savannah

*The Line*
*The Source*
*The Void*
*Jilo*


*Shivaree*
*Pretty Enough to Catch Her: A Short Story*
*A Peculiar Paradise: A Short Story*
*One Bad Apple: A Short Story*
*Pitch: A Short Story*
*Phantasma: Stories* (contributor)

# THE KING OF BONES AND ASHES

A WITCHES OF
NEW ORLEANS
NOVEL

## J.D. HORN

47NORTH

Published by 47North, Seattle

www.apub.com

Amazon, the Amazon logo, and 47North are trademarks of Amazon.com, Inc., or its affiliates.

ISBN-13: 9781503954311 (hardcover)
ISBN-10: 1503954315 (hardcover)
ISBN-13: 9781542047104 (paperback)
ISBN-10: 1542047102 (paperback)

Cover design by Rex Bonomelli

Printed in the United States of America

*In loving memory of Duke Dunkirk Weissman, the best big black dog, and Sugar (yeah, that Sugar) Chloe Weissman, Kittycat Supreme. Your dads miss both of you.*

# PROLOGUE

*Monday, August 29, 2005*

Alice strained against the weight of the ancient powder-blue suitcase, its metal hinges cutting a shallow vein into the hardwood floor as she dragged it backward down the hall with a two-handed, white-knuckle grip. Inside the case she'd crowded every treasure she'd collected in her seven and a half years. Books and dolls, a battered music box, and a contraband cache of costume jewelry she wasn't allowed to wear outside the house, purchased at the French Market, though her imagination insisted it had been plundered from a pirate chest.

In the center of the booty, bound by a heavy silver frame, she'd secreted a picture she usually kept hidden in the false floor of the doll-house her uncle Vincent had built for her. She loved the photo, not only because it was the sole portrait she knew to exist of her immediate family—her father and her mother and both older brothers, Luc and Hugo—but also because her mother's gaze wasn't turned toward the camera. It rested on a miniature and only somewhat recognizable version of Alice herself, balanced between her father's hands on his knee. Her mother's hand rested on baby Alice's tiny leg.

Alice couldn't remember her mother.

"Are you ready then, love?" Daniel asked, materializing before her, hovering an inch or so above the stairhead. Alice couldn't bring herself to look him in the eye, focusing instead on the tan, brimmed cap that covered most of his red hair, then on the stained and dirty blues and greens and pinks of the petit-point flowers embroidered on his suspenders.

Daniel was bound to their house. There'd be no escape for him. Her father had promised her that Daniel would be all right, that he'd find a way to protect him, no matter what. But her father had also promised to keep her safe, to keep the whole of New Orleans safe.

Just hours ago, they'd all been so proud. So relieved. Her father's house had held a party atmosphere, with thirty or more weary, bedraggled witches cheering and congratulating each other on how deftly the Chanticleer Coven had coordinated the efforts of witches all around the city to divert Katrina. The storm should have hit the city dead on, but they, the brave witches of the Crescent City, had managed to slow its winds and nudge it just a bit east, far enough that the storm's path would cut through less populated areas. A case of champagne still sat on the kitchen counter, placed there in anticipation of the toasts they'd enjoy after besting Katrina, and, from the witches older than her father, duller reminiscences of having weathered Betsy before her. But Pontchartrain had pushed its way beyond its banks, and the levees had failed.

Her father always kept his word. Except when he didn't.

"I can't find Sugar," Alice said, moving on to a problem she could solve. "Anywhere," she added for emphasis. She'd received the tiny Devon rex as a birthday present from her aunt Fleur, and the cat and Daniel had taken an instant disliking to each other, Sugar arching and hissing whenever she sensed his presence.

"Not to worry. The pewter-coated terror yowled at me in the kitchen not five minutes ago." Daniel glanced down at her suitcase. "I'd help you carry your things down, it's only . . ." He let his hand pass through the newel post. "I've not been able to take full form of late."

Angry voices—Luc's, plus a few others Alice recognized as belonging to members of the coven. Loudest of all, her father's voice rumbled up like thunder, causing them both to peer downstairs in the direction of her father's study. Most of the words were spoken one over the other. Jumbled. Alice couldn't make out much of what was being said, though she did pick up on her own name, as well as that of her grandfather Celestin. It had been her father who'd spoken his name. Alice's father only ever referred to his own father as Celestin or, when he seemed to be feeling exceptionally piqued, as "that man."

Magic had been fading from the world since long before Alice was born into it, so in times of crisis all witches were called upon to put aside personal differences and form a type of collective to pool their energies. Even Alice had been recruited to try to weaken the storm, to shift its path, to help the levees hold. This morning, when it was still thought this effort would succeed, goodwill had reigned. But now the snatches of conversation Alice could understand told her that everyone was looking to lay the blame at someone else's feet, and she wasn't surprised to hear her father pointing the finger at "that man."

Alice liked her grandfather. He never treated her like a baby. He never shied away from topics the way her father and uncle did. He always answered her questions directly—although those direct responses were more often than not in French. If it weren't for her grandfather, Alice might never have learned of "the Dreaming Road," where witches give in to the intoxication of their own magic to escape their unhappy lives. Nor would she have known that her mother had chosen it over her.

"Shall I go fetch Hugo to help with your case?" Daniel said in a near whisper, as if he were afraid of drawing attention to himself.

Alice nodded, unable to speak, afraid what she might say if she did. Daniel faded away as quickly as he'd appeared.

A tardy flash of lightning tore through the gloom, and she turned, crossing to the large landing window and then rising up on her tiptoes to peer out. On the other side of the glass, a towering wall of muddy water spun counterclockwise just beyond the strip of green that stood between their street and the finger of water that had given their neighborhood, Bayou St. John, its name.

The water had risen so quickly. In minutes. The world had been drowned all around them, leaving their house and a few on either side an island protected by a levee of her father's failing magic. And even though the flooding had now leveled off behind her father's wards, this levee, too, would soon fall.

The swirling water reminded Alice of the color of the milky tea Daniel would pour himself, though never drink, each morning. Someone's white plastic lawn chair bobbed like a marshmallow on the water's surface before sinking back into the abyss, its legs straining to puncture the clear membrane of magic protecting the house. And then the chair was gone, dragged down and away by an unseen current.

It was mesmerizing, and Alice made a game of guessing the origins of the jetsam scraping the dam's cellophane-like wall. The blue trike that belonged to the little kid two doors down. A door—a red door—she didn't recognize offered the illusion of an escape, then popped up to the surface like a listing raft. A plastic pink flamingo from a garden on Mystery Street surfaced for only long enough to bob its head toward her. Two large gray garbage containers clung to each other in desperation as they spun around, the wheel of one caught in the hinge of its partner's lid. Alice caught the name of the corner store located a few blocks over painted on the side of one of the cans just before it lost its hold. She felt almost sad for it when its mate was washed away. A bubble of air belched up to the water's surface, bringing with it an explosive, colorful pattern similar to the millefiori paperweight on her grandfather's desk. Alice strained to make out the details, only then realizing a small school of paperbacks and DVDs had crested, their covers' bright colors floating on top of the water behind her father's magic dam. Alice wished she could turn into a mermaid and slip safely into this new kaleidoscope sea.

"Nicholas lied to you, you know." Alice spun around at the sound of Luc's words. She hadn't heard him approaching, and the sharpness of his tone worried her. He was her brother, but lately—always angry— he'd begun to feel like a stranger. He had a girlfriend now, and he spent most of his time with her. It was just as well. When he was home, it was nothing but yelling—Luc at their dad, their dad at Luc.

Luc had taken to calling their father by his given name, Nicholas.

Luc's girlfriend was a witch, too, but as far as Alice could guess, Evangeline was a different kind of witch, a kind her father and grandfather looked down on. Strange that Luc's girlfriend was the one thing her father and grandfather could agree on.

"The girl is talented, no doubt," she'd heard her father say to a coven member, "but lacks any pedigree."

To Alice, pedigree seemed an odd thing for a person to have. It was a quality one might use to describe Sugar, not a person. Evangeline and Luc had taken Alice out with them a few times since they'd begun seeing each other, mostly to the French Market, but once to a movie and once to City Park. She seemed nice enough to Alice. Maybe a little too anxious to make friends, but nice all the same.

Luc pushed his blue-black hair back from his inky eyes. "We're not packing to go to Grandfather's." Unlike Bayou St. John, the Garden District where their grandfather lived sat on the rim of the punchbowl New Orleans had become, high enough to escape the worst of the flooding. Bayou St. John and the Garden District were the extreme boundaries of Alice's world map, bolstered on each end by great dragons: one her father, the other her grandfather.

"He thought you'd be easier to manage if you didn't know the truth. If you thought you were going someplace familiar."

Hugo, younger than Luc but a world ahead of Alice, approached the landing from the hall, arriving in time to hear Luc's revelation. Hugo was seven years older than Alice, and back in the spring—she remembered the exact day she'd noticed, June 23—he had started looking more like a man than a boy. He resembled their father, nearly an exact copy, though with their mother's lighter coloring. Hugo was the opposite of Luc, who stood a good foot taller than their father, and whose dark eyes stared out from a face very like their mother's.

Alice turned to Hugo for verification of Luc's words.

Hugo nodded. "Father told me not to tell you. But I agree that you should know."

"We're evacuating," Luc said. "All of us. We're deserting New Orleans."

"What about Daniel?" she said. He'd been there to watch over her every day of her life. She couldn't bear the thought of leaving him here alone. "Will he be okay without us?"

"Nicholas doesn't care what happens to the people who get left behind," Luc said. Alice could feel the heat of his anger, an actual physical sensation, wafting off him. "No one in the coven does. And none of them give a damn about Daniel either." He leaned in close to whisper in her ear. "He isn't even real."

She pushed him away. "I don't believe you," she said, even if she wasn't quite sure which part of his statement she was contesting. Even though she sensed truth in his every word.

"Well, you will soon." Luc grabbed hold of her hand, whisking her off her feet and into his arms. The force behind the movement made her breath catch. But she stopped herself from crying out. He'd call her a crybaby. She didn't want him to call her a crybaby.

"Luc, knock it off," Hugo said, stretching to his full height, the action a silent and entirely ignored challenge.

She looked back at her suitcase, sitting there at the top of the steps, as Luc carried her down the hall. Hugo chased after them. Suddenly, they were climbing the tight, shadowy back stairs that led to the attic, the door to which their father usually kept sealed with both a protection spell and a heavy padlock. But the padlock lay forgotten on the floor, and the magical bans that had once fixed the door shut had been rendered useless. All magic, great and small, had been diverted by the united covens to aid their attempt to lessen Katrina's sting.

"We're not supposed to come up here," Alice said, her protest half-hearted at best. She knew her father had only permitted the attic to be opened to allow for the removal of a few objects considered too precious or dangerous to leave in the storm's path.

"No. But in an hour there may not be a 'here' to come." Luc shifted her so he could look into her eyes. "Don't you want to see what Nicholas has been hiding from you, from us, before it disappears?"

Father would be furious if he knew, but there was no use denying her desire. She nodded.

Hugo's silence was his consent.

Luc kicked the padlock against the wall, then opened the door and hefted her over the threshold. The electricity had failed forever ago, leaving the space in deep shadow, with only dim castoff light seeping in through the two dormer windows on the house's front. Still, she could tell the room was enormous, spanning the length and breadth of the house.

Luc set her on her feet and took her hand. The ceiling hung low enough that he had to duck as he tugged her to the farthest, darkest corner. He released her and snapped his fingers, causing a ball of light, about as bright as a candle, to form overhead. Until the crisis was over, they weren't supposed to use magic, not even a little. But it seemed that today was a day for breaking rules.

Despite never having breached this space, Alice knew this forlorn corner was where her father had hidden away everything belonging to their mother—at least everything he hadn't burned. She'd heard Luc and her father fight over the rightful ownership of what was left of their mother's possessions.

"Behind here," Luc said, and Hugo helped him push aside a stack of unlabeled cardboard boxes, a whiff of perfume rising from them. Their mother had left before Alice could walk, and memory, that fickle thing, had betrayed her—she wouldn't even know what her mother had looked like if not for that single image of the Marin family. And yet, this ghost of the once heady fragrance of sweet olive and gardenia came close to conjuring her mother's face.

Luc paused, seeming to have caught their mother's scent as well. But then his face hardened, and he whipped away a sheet that lay over a dozen or so canvases, exposing paintings Alice somehow knew to be her mother's work.

She would have liked to look more closely at each, but Luc flipped through them, slapping one against the other, taking no care to protect their mother's art. Alice caught a flash of what looked like an unfinished portrait of her grandfather, then Luc discovered the painting he'd been searching for, pulling it out from the others and turning it so she could have a better look. It was of Daniel, all right. The same cap. The same ginger hair poking out from beneath it. The same sweet but sad look in his eyes.

"Our Daniel believes himself to be a ghost, the unsettled spirit of a young Irishman who died during the construction of the New Basin Canal. But Daniel isn't a ghost. There never was a Daniel." Luc paused, maybe to give his revelation time to sink in, or maybe just to see if she'd flinch. She didn't. Luc seemed satisfied with her reaction. "He's a magic trick," he carried on, "a servitor spirit our parents conjured up to look after Hugo and me—so they didn't have to. Nicholas thought they had more important business to attend to, and mother, well, she did whatever he told her to do, like it or not. Until the day she stopped . . ." Luc's voice trailed off.

They stood for a few moments in total silence. "Mother," Hugo said, nodding to confirm Luc's story, "painted this to help Father visualize Daniel. She didn't want to. Father made her do it."

Luc looked up from the painting. "That's the first step, you see." His voice sounded scratchy now. "You give a servitor form, one that suggests the traits you'd like it to have, and then you imbue—you know what I mean by 'imbue'?" She shook her head, so he offered a different word. "You fill it with a sense of self. That's the glue that helps keep the entity intact. It works best if you give the servitor a tragic past, an injustice it can fixate on. Saddling your creation with a dark secret or two, something it's ashamed of, something it's afraid you'll learn, doesn't hurt either." Luc's light brightened, and he held the painting up, offering her a final look at it.

Alice studied the portrait, her mouth open, her heart pounding. Though she wanted to deny it, it all made sense. Whenever she asked Daniel what his childhood had been like, he couldn't remember the simplest things. Nothing. Not even if he'd gone to school. If he'd liked candy. If he'd had friends. He could rattle off some memories, mostly historical events, but the stories he told were always the same. Word for word. It was like he'd been given a list of facts to memorize. Facts that would fit what he believed to be true about himself, but nothing to show he'd actually had a life before joining their family.

Alice could feel that the Chanticleer Coven's magic was, at least for now, nearly exhausted, probably only enough left to ensure them safe passage out of the city. That Daniel still held together at all was testament to how deeply he believed the lie of his own existence.

"Nicholas would've probably let him fade away by now," Luc said, "but then you came along. And mother left . . ." He slid the painting

9

back in with the others and then flung the sheet back over them. He was rough when handling the paintings, acting as if they meant nothing to him. But if he didn't care about them at all, Alice realized, he wouldn't have bothered to offer even this flimsy protection.

He turned back toward her and Hugo, fixing her with his gaze. "You see, that's who our father is. This is what he does. He builds people up. Programs them to his liking, and when they stop being of use, he tosses them away without giving them another thought. Eventually you'll be one of the ones he throws away." His eyes shifted to Hugo. "You both will."

Alice wished she could defend her father, but Luc's words gave expression to something she'd always suspected. Always feared. Her father was loyal to no one but himself. He'd erased most if not all evidence of Alice's mother from the world, and while he allowed Alice to visit her grandfather, he rarely dealt with Celestin himself. She'd often heard him mock his own brother, her uncle Vincent, with Gabriel Prosper, the coven's second—but she'd also heard him curse Gabriel behind *his* back. She'd watched him pit coven members against each other in minor battles, then step in as peacemaker. "Then we should go. Go live with Grandfather."

Luc exchanged a silent look with Hugo before bursting into laughter. "Who do you think made Nicholas the way he is?"

She glanced at Hugo, who was biting his lip as if to hold back laughter of his own, then shifted her gaze to Luc. He stopped laughing and reached down to touch her cheek. "At least we've got each other, right?"

She bit her lip. Wanting to cry, but not wanting Luc to see it. She nodded.

Hugo took her hand. "We'll be leaving soon. You should head downstairs."

"Yes," Luc said, his voice suddenly bright, "before Father forgets you. Here, take this." He snapped his fingers, and the glowing orb he'd conjured floated down to her.

"Go on," Hugo said, "Luc and I have to talk, but I'll be down soon. I'll bring your case."

The light followed Alice as far as the foot of the attic stairs before it blinked out, leaving her with only her dark-adapted eyes to guide her. The voices below had quieted and grown fewer. She let her mind reach out, feel around to see who remained. Other than herself and her brothers, she sensed only her father and uncle.

Curious, she descended the stairway and crept down the hall toward her father's study. The door stood ajar, and bright streaks of light cut through the gloom of the darkened hall and raced up and down the wall across from the opening. Sugar sat by the wall, batting at the glints.

While Alice still sensed her father and uncle in the study, the hall had gone silent. She realized one of them—most likely her father—had placed a spell on the room to keep whatever they were discussing from being overheard. She craned her neck to spy through the opening, but all she could make out was the twinkle of the rhinestone-studded buckle on Aunt Fleur's vintage black crepe pumps. Her aunt was doing that thing again, where she was there, but not really—the same way she came to birthday parties or showed up for a few minutes on Christmas morning. That was why Alice hadn't picked up on her presence. Alice's grandfather told her the name for this gift was "astral projection," though Uncle Vincent always referred to it as "discount travel."

The scintillations on the wall shot up and dove again, synchronized to the impatient movement of Fleur's foot. The light the shoes were reflecting was probably hundreds of miles away, in her aunt's house. Any other day, Alice wouldn't have been able to resist barging in to ask her aunt, who wasn't really there, how the light playing off her shoe buckles could be in two places at once. She understood that her aunt appeared as a type of psychic projection, but this part of the puzzle didn't make sense to her.

For a moment Alice stood there, as mesmerized by the dancing glints on the wall as her cat was, but the sound of the front door creaking open caused her to look up. At first she thought it had to be the wind, that the door hadn't been pulled to properly after the other witches had left. But then she sensed a presence on the other side. A male presence. Sugar, too, stopped pawing at the wall and turned to face the foyer, curious as to the identity of the new arrival.

The door eased forward, inch by deliberate inch, until it stood wide open. Alice's eyes lied to her, telling her there was no one there, but her other senses insisted someone stood just beyond the threshold, beckoning her, inviting her to come out and play. She wondered if it could be a ghost, a real ghost, or another servitor spirit like Daniel, sent out by its master to brave the flood, but her instincts told her no. This visitor was something entirely different. And she wanted, no *needed*, to go out and meet him.

Alice understood—she felt the entity on the far side of the door warn her—that she mustn't be seen, or they'd stop her. They wouldn't let her join him.

She didn't hesitate even a single second. Scooping up the cat, she hurried past the doorway as silently as Sugar's anxious purring would allow. One of the magical wards her father had woven, now weakened by their fight against the hurricane, snapped, but it didn't matter. She needed to get to her visitor. Standing beneath the gallery, Alice reached out with her final spark of magic, already scanning her surroundings. Finally, she sensed him. But he'd pulled back. He now stood near the rotating wall of water. Eager to get to him, she stepped forward, moving out from beneath the gallery and onto the sidewalk.

Katrina had smelled salty as she chewed through the city, carrying the gulf in her grasp, but now the beach smell had faded. The air just smelled wet. The wind still blew strongly enough to whip up whitecaps on the water held back by magic, and even though the sky above the towering water still resembled the polished steel of their refrigerator door, directly overhead, within their circle of safety, the hot sun shone down from a patch of summer blue.

Sugar struggled out of Alice's grasp, her needle-sharp claws leaving fiery corkscrew tracks as she twined her way up the girl's arm. Alice watched the thin welts rise, but she felt no pain. She couldn't feel anything. An invisible barrier seemed to stand between her and all sensation—a barrier much like the clear membrane of magic her father had spun to hold the floodwaters at bay.

The cat paused once in her climb, one of her oversize peridot eyes winking at Alice in rage. Everyone in the Marin household knew better than to bring her outdoors. Even on the best of days, the world beyond her favorite sun-drenched windowsill was a strange and alien place. The feline fought her way to Alice's shoulder, where she perched and yowled in indignation at the sun overhead, unrecognized in its unfiltered state as the source of hours of golden pleasure. Then the cat fell silent, her head pivoting to the side as she stared at the exact spot where Alice had sensed their visitor. Sugar arched up, sinking her claws into Alice's flesh, and growled. Then, as if something had startled her, she jumped off her perch and bolted toward the house. Alice's eyes followed the cat as she tore across the lawn and disappeared inside.

The visitor wanted Alice to laugh, so she started laughing—great, rolling belly laughs, as if the cat's terror were the funniest thing she'd ever seen. Even though it wasn't. Even though she didn't want to. Even though she felt her own animal instincts kicking in. She struggled to free herself, to turn and run after Sugar, but she could not. She felt her feet moving forward, bringing her nearer and nearer the swirling wall of water.

Just behind the water's sheen, she caught sight of a bone-white Mardi Gras mask with wide and hollow eyes. As she drew closer, a series of bulges pushed out the surface of the water, five points pressing outward, forming a hand made from the water itself. It reached out to grasp her, its twin lunging at her from the other side. And then what she had thought to be a mask came to life, its lips pulling back, opening, exposing a razor-blade smile. She recognized the horrible face from the

13

stories her grandfather would tell her when she begged him to entertain her with ghost stories on rainy Sunday afternoons.

Babau Jean, John the Bogey.

Alice shook her head. Her grandfather's tales had turned to night terrors on occasion, and her father had always sworn to her this bogeyman didn't exist. That he was just a story.

Screams formed in her throat, but she couldn't make a sound, and when she tried to pull away, the cold, muddy hand closed around hers, holding her tight. It began drawing her in.

"Alice," she heard Uncle Vincent's anxious voice calling to her. "What are you doing over there? You know it isn't safe out here. Come back inside."

She couldn't answer. She couldn't take a step. All she could do was turn her head to look back at him over her shoulder.

Whatever he read in her eyes was enough. Vincent darted to her side, tugging her free from the hand's cold grip and up into his embrace. He didn't seem to see the hands made of the water, straining to snatch her away even as he carried her beyond their reach. He couldn't seem to sense the hatred in the empty black sockets where the monster's eyes should have been. "What . . . ?" he asked, giving her a puzzled look before she buried her head in his shoulder and gave in to sobs.

# ONE

**Present Day**

Evangeline brushed the cat aside without opening an eye. She'd been up till five a.m. closing the club, managing inventory, and then supervising the monthly deep cleaning, parts of which she'd done over again herself because the others' efforts had failed to match her standards. Once a month, she expected everyone at her club to pitch in, from barbacks to bouncers to the dancers who needed to remember to bring in practical shoes or quit bellyaching over having to mop floors barefoot or in nine-inch stilettos.

Third Monday of the month. All her employees complained about it, but she knew this monthly post-close maintenance was part of what made everyone feel they, too, shared a stake in Bonnes Nouvelles. And whenever anyone got pissy about rolling up their sleeves, Evangeline would remind the troublemaker that there were plenty of other clubs to work in. Ones that didn't offer medical and dental insurance, childcare assistance, and financial planning and support for education. Any employee who didn't see the value in what Evangeline was attempting—to raise everyone up together, to help them build financial security for themselves and their children, to give the dancers a life even after their boobs dropped and their asses sagged—well, Evangeline didn't want that kind of employee anyway.

She'd danced at the club to put herself through college, back when it was the Black Cat. Back when it was run by a sweat-stained, hirsute man-child who'd bought the club so he could live out a pubescent fantasy. He had packed it in two days after Katrina, claiming it was the storm driving him out, though Evangeline knew it was the work of running the club that had really scared him off. Five hundred dollars and a handshake later, Evangeline had taken over. Bonnes Nouvelles was hers, all hers—even its name a play on her own. She'd never get rich from running this place—in fact, most months breaking even was a crapshoot. This month was sure gonna be tight.

Nicholas could've provided the float she needed, but she sure as hell wasn't going to ask him. He said she was meant for better things, that running a strip joint was beneath her. What he really meant was that it was beneath *him*. He hated that she wouldn't give the club up, but she hated that he wouldn't give up leadership of his moribund coven. She guessed that made them even.

"No, no, no," Evangeline said as Sugar crawled back up onto her chest. "You know the rules: you want that nasty wet food, you gotta let Mama sleep till she's ready to get up. Otherwise it's kibble for you, missy." Sugar only weighed four pounds, and Evangeline was so worn out, she decided to go back to sleep and let her beloved cast-off cat perch wherever she wanted. She loved the furry terrorist. And what with the way the cat acted sometimes, the feline was damned lucky she did.

Sugar had been the one real constant in her life for over a decade now. The only thing left from the life she'd shared with Luc. The day after Katrina, Luc had brought the cat, a tiny, terrified refugee, to their apartment on Barracks Street. Alice and Luc's little brother, Hugo, had been shipped off to stay with their aunt for the school year, and Sugar had somehow been left behind. They'd always intended to return the cat to Alice, but one event had followed another, ending with the unimaginable. Shortly after his siblings returned home, Luc had put a gun to his head and left them all. Worse, he'd done the violent deed in front of his little sister.

That made Evangeline a castoff, too, just like her cat. But by her calculations, all that had happened around a thousand years ago, and the world had gone to hell and back and turned over on itself a few times since then, so who the hell cared anyway?

Luc sure didn't.

Sugar batted Evangeline's cheek. Twice. Evangeline peeled open one angry eye to see the cat's own olivine eyes staring back down at her with equal if not greater intensity.

"He's here?" she asked, letting the other eye spring open. The cat kneaded Evangeline's sheet. "Well, hell, I don't know. I didn't invite him." She pushed up on her elbows, causing Sugar to slip down to her stomach.

"No, I'm well aware you didn't invite him either." Sugar blinked one eye. "Yes, I did give him a key." She had given him a key. Years ago. Even though it was largely a symbolic gesture, as Nicholas Marin hadn't yet met a door that could keep him out. In all these years, he'd never once used it.

Sugar chattered. This cat sure knew how to hold a grudge.

"I'll see what he wants. And you watch your language, missy."

Evangeline shifted, swinging her feet out of bed and down to the floor. She was wearing one of the god-awful oversize Bonnes Nouvelles Bourbon Street T-shirts they stocked for the tourists—half of the people who bought them never even stepped all the way into the club. The shirt's front was graced by a scantily clad caricature of Evangeline herself, hanging from a pole, the back with the same image, smaller, along with the club's street address. She rationalized selling the cotton atrocities by turning the huge profit back into the business. Hell, at least the shirts were American- and union-made.

She caught a glimpse of herself in the mirror. She looked like hell. Her dark red hair was mussed, and not in the sexy way. She'd scrubbed her face clean of all makeup before she'd collapsed in bed all of three, no, two and a half hours ago. Her hazel eyes were puffy. But it didn't matter. She and Nicholas had grown past all pretense. They could be real with each other.

Her beloved cottage on St. Ann Street was Creole style, meaning there were no hallways. One room flowed into the next, so she didn't even have to step out of her bedroom to spy Nicholas, hunched over and head in hands, sitting at her kitchen table. She stepped into the kitchen, not speaking a word. Words so easily got in the way, especially when dealing with a prideful—no, that wasn't fair—a proud man like Nicholas. Evangeline visualized dismantling the wall she usually kept up to protect herself from her own empathic powers, dislodging just a brick or two from the mortar. She slid out a chair and sat down next to him.

Nicholas looked up, his eyes swollen and red. From crying? Unlikely. From drink. She could smell the stench of sweat and whiskey wafting off him. Without a doubt, he'd been wandering the French Quarter, working his way through the handful of clubs that never closed and were rarely cleaned. She suspected her house's proximity to the bars was the reason he'd found his way to her door.

Evangeline tapped into his feelings, trying to ease in, a dip of the toe to test the hot bath, but a wave of desperate and hopeless anger washed over her. She felt herself, her own psyche, spinning, sinking, being drowned in Nicholas's maelstrom of dark emotions. She pushed back, both physically and empathically, her hands held up in a protective stance.

He took no notice of her distress. He leaned back, smiling with his lips but not his eyes. Those eyes fell to her shirt. "I think of that night," he said, "often." The sunlight stole in through the window, lighting up the gray at his temples. "I saw you up there. Watched you gyrating. There you were, putting yourself on display, and at first I thought, 'This is what my son turned his back on me for.'" He reached out and touched the hand she still held, without consciously intending to, before her heart. He caressed and lowered it. A quiver played on his face as the false smile turned into a real one. "And then I looked into your eyes. For the first time ever, really. And I saw your intelligence. Your power. Your spirit."

Evangeline always felt a pang of guilt whenever she thought about how things had begun between her and Nicholas, just as she did every time son and father crossed her mind together, or in too quick a succession. Truth was, she'd been bereft of any spirit. Luc had only just killed himself, and she'd still been hurting, bad. It was the kind of hurt that could cripple you, or make you do something mean, something stupid—real stupid—like welcome your dead lover's father—a man who'd done nothing but look down on you, talk down to you—into your bed. Just to hurt the man who'd hurt you, and maybe to gain a little control over the man who thought you were beneath him. Maybe to convince yourself that you weren't beneath anyone. That you deserved loving, not leaving.

"I knew what you were thinking, what you were doing, from the second your eyes picked me out in the crowd," Nicholas continued. "I saw how badly you wanted, needed, to punish my son. And I guess I wanted to punish him, too."

It was true. It hadn't been her finest moment, not by a long shot. But somehow . . .

"But somehow from such a bitter seed," Nicholas's words echoed her thoughts—there really wasn't a single door that could keep him out—"love grew." He leaned in. His lips brushed her ear. "It's real, what we have. Isn't it?" He leaned back, his black eyes—so like Luc's—pleading with her.

Sugar pranced into the room, arching her back at the sight of him. But then she stopped and stared at him, her glassy green eyes blinking once, twice. Sugar leaped up on the table next to Nicholas and rubbed her head on his arm in a shocking expression of solidarity. He stared blankly at the cat, then reached out and began stroking her head and running his hand down her back. He caught Sugar in the crook of his other arm, and she responded by laying her head on his shoulder and purring.

Perhaps they'd arrived at the end of days after all.

She nodded. "Yes. It's real." She reached out to place her palm against his stubble-roughened cheek. "Nicholas, what is this all about? What's wrong?"

He grasped her hand, pressing it to his lips. His mouth twitched. His eyes widened in an expression that blended relief with disbelief. "The great Celestin Marin has at last departed this world." He drew in a breath and breathed it out.

"Oh, Nicholas," she said, "I'm so sorry . . ."

"Don't be ridiculous." He shook his head and lowered Sugar to the floor. The cat meowed in protest, then slunk away and found a patch of sun on the floor. Nicholas's face hardened. "Celestin has been in a coma for eight years, just hanging on in that hospital bed like a tick on a dead dog. He's been dead to the world for nearly a decade. He's been dead to me even longer. But still I have to pretend that I care."

His reddened eyes smoldered with a hatred Evangeline sensed he was trying to tamp down. "The coven is insisting we throw a commemoration ball in the old man's honor—a full-blown witches' ball the likes of which New Orleans hasn't seen in thirty or more years . . ." His words trailed off. "It's important, to the older members, at least. The kicker is that we only have a day to organize the thing. Son of a . . ." In spite of his apparent determination to maintain his composure, a tear brimmed in his eye and ran down his cheek. He dropped her hand and whisked the tear away.

Evangeline stood and leaned over him, wrapping her arms tightly around his shoulders. "Go ahead." She felt him shudder. "Let yourself cry." She sounded like a mother. She wondered if she would've made a good mother. It seemed less likely than ever now that she'd have the chance. Nicholas always pirouetted whenever she gave even the slightest of hints she wanted this with him.

She forced herself to focus on the moment, on his loss. "No matter how bad your relationship with him was, he was your father. You have to mourn him."

His face buried in her bosom, he started laughing. At least she had to think of it as laughter, even though the sound he made came out slow and sad. He pushed her back with gentle hands while raising his gaze to meet her own. "Oh, my love," he said, then laughed again. "It isn't my father I'm mourning. It's the loss of my children." A fresh anger ignited in his eyes. "And now that bastard's funeral is going to give him one last chance to rub my nose in just how badly I've failed them."

He peeled her arms from around him and slid his chair back from the table, the scuffing sound causing Sugar to stop licking her paw and stare at him. "How badly I've failed you . . . ," he said, and held up a hand to stop her from speaking. He stood and walked around her to the doorway separating the kitchen from the living room. He turned back. "I can't give you the life you want. I can't give you any more of myself than you already have." She knew what he meant, but he drove his point home anyway. "You've seen my luck with children," he said.

"What happened with Alice wasn't your fault . . ."

"But it is. You can't deny there's a pattern. My little girl. As mad as . . . well as mad as her mother. And hell, my mother, too. My oldest son. Dead. After trying to take my place. And Hugo"—a bitter laugh followed his younger son's name—"well, Hugo is doing everything he can to make sure the line ends with him."

"No, you're right." She nodded. "There is a pattern. And it points right to the Chanticleers," she said, spitting out the coven's name. "If it weren't for that damnable coven, you might have had a relationship with your father. Luc would still be here . . ."

"He'd still be here with you," Nicholas said. His tone felt like an accusation.

"He'd still be here with us," she said.

"That boy and his foolish challenge . . . ," Nicholas said.

She sensed he was trying to shift all blame off his own shoulders. "Like father, like son," she said, pinning his share back into place, "you both always put your pride first."

"I never suspected it would end as it did. Never," he said, turning away, shaking his head. "If I had . . . ," he said, looking back to her, steeling his spine. "Celestin encouraged him, you know. It was all about Celestin's damnable desire to get even with me. But Luc wasn't ready. I knew that. That's why I didn't step down. I was trying to save him from making the same mistake I made."

He had never before dared to say this to her. Evangeline had thought he respected her too much, but evidently not. She almost laughed as she studied his features, his expression a well-rehearsed blend of grief and stoicism. How many times, she wondered, had he repeated this rationalization? To others? To himself? "Is this the myth you've created to exculpate yourself?" She shook her head in disgust. "You may not be entirely at fault, but you're not blameless. Neither of us is. So lie to yourself if you need to, but don't lie to me."

His face lost its color, and he spun on his heel. She listened as his measured steps carried him across the living room. And then he was gone.

He didn't even have the decency to slam the door.

# TWO

The bell over the door clanged, announcing that the current had carried a fresh school of tourists down from Jackson Square to the shop's threshold. A burst of steamy air came in as a bit of the air-conditioned cool escaped. "Everything that gives, takes," her mother had once explained back when Lisette had still been willing—eager, even—to listen. With the mighty Mississippi flowing maybe a thousand or so feet to the east, rounding Algiers Point on its way to the Gulf, there was certain to be another force, though unseen, pushing back, trying to balance energies, a current that could snatch up deep-pocketed tourists and wash them away from the French Market and past the shop's door. That's how it worked, her mom had said, that's why her mother had chosen this spot on Chartres Street for Vèvè, her Voodoo supply shop that took its name from the symbols, seen from Lisette's perspective in reverse, painted on the windows. Her mother had believed it to be true, and there was a time before her mother's death, and before Katrina, when Lisette had believed it, too.

That time had long since passed.

A trio of white women, the same who had been milling about the store windows for going on five minutes, snapping cellphone pictures of the vèvès and debating whether they should risk a visit, entered. Lisette pretended to ignore the arrivals but sat up straight and—with a practiced air of mystery—took up her tarot deck and fanned the cards into an arc. She flipped one over and pretended to contemplate it, as if a randomly drawn cardboard cartoon could truly impart any worthwhile knowledge. By serendipity, the card was the three of cups, featuring the three dancers. Cursed by a liberal arts education, Lisette couldn't help but recognize them as the three Graces. She bit her lip to stop herself from smirking as she silently compared the three winsome goddesses to her patrons.

One of the women, a well-fed brunette wearing a print dashiki and cyan Bermuda shorts, struck Lisette as quite keen to come in and poke around, but her companions seemed agitated. A tall blonde, whose Persian-blue blouse bore traces of powdered sugar, made a show of humoring her friend, her air of amused forbearance revealing that she considered the obligatory visit to a Voodoo shop as much a part of a New Orleans vacation as beignets from Café Du Monde. Still, she remained near the door, her gaze turned toward the window, perhaps scanning the street for some real shopping opportunities. She fished a smartphone from her purse and began swiping away at its screen. "This is Chartres Street?" She pronounced Chartres like the name of the French cathedral city.

"Mmmhmmm," Lisette hummed, "but around here we say it like 'Charters,' and four blocks that way"—she pointed away from the river—"that street's 'Burgundy'"—she accented the word's second syllable, slipping into a bit of well-practiced tourist banter. "And if you really want to pass for native, call the grassy medians like on St. Charles and Esplanade 'neutral ground,' and don't you ever speak of this town as 'Nawlins.'" She offered the blonde a somewhat sincere smile, but the woman met her smile with a cool stare that seemed to question whether Lisette had suffered a sudden descent into madness.

"The Napoleon House . . . ," the blonde said, her inflection rising in pitch with each word. "It's that way?" She pointed in the direction of St. Louis Street.

"Yes, ma'am," Lisette said, "it is." She returned her gaze to the deck of cards, but continued to toss surreptitious glances at the blonde's cohorts.

"The symbols in the window," the brunette piped up, "do they have a meaning or are they just decorative?"

Most of the people who came into the shop, believers or mockers—it seemed that few ever fell into the realm of true skeptic—came for the Hollywood version of Voodoo. Lisette braced herself to deliver an elevator pitch introduction to the religion. She wondered why she still felt a compulsion to explain, to defend, to enlighten. To educate without biting the hand that feeds, rather than just offering up a bit of theater.

"Each symbol," she said, gazing into the woman's eyes, searching for what? Worthiness of her wasted breath? "Is a kind of pictogram used both to represent and to summon the loa . . ."

"The intercessory spirits," the brunette finished her explanation for her. Lisette rewarded the woman for not having referred to the loa as "gods" with a quiet nod and knowing glance, signaling that the woman could, in a safe and easily escapable manner, consider herself an initiate.

The woman began wandering around the shop, tracing a finger over the books and array of variegated candles, over the statues of loa in their natural and saintly guises, over premade potions with names like "Lover Come Back" and "Four Thieves," seeming to take stock of all around her. She came to a stop before the painting Lisette's son, Remy, had done—a reimagining of an old snapshot of the two of them as Erzulie Dantor and child, depicted with photographic precision in warm umbers and ochers, clothed in rich hues of red, indigo, and gold, and marked as an embodiment of the loa by two scars on her right cheek.

The third woman, a pasty, puffy creature with anxious ice-blue eyes, trailed behind her enthusiastic friend. First she followed her around the shop's periphery, then through its narrow aisles, her arms folded tightly across her chest, as if she were trying to make herself smaller to avoid coming into contact with any of the displayed wares.

In spite of the brunette's attempts to be respectful, the two were all stage whispers and stifled laughter as they passed the altar and caught sight of the erection sported by the grinning skull-faced statuette of Baron Samedi.

Lisette flipped another card, the tower, upright and looked up. "Quite the cigar, is it not?" she asked in an innocent tone, drawing their attention up to the cheroot clenched between Samedi's teeth.

Schoolgirl titters preceded the brunette's response. "Indeed it is." Her timid friend gazed down at her own shoes, but at least the baron had managed to bring a bit of color to her cheeks. Maybe Lisette was mistaken. Perhaps these trinkets held some magic after all.

Lisette had already had more than enough time to gauge each woman's interest, comfort level, and gullibility. She'd written off the sad, pale sister as a no sale, but the brunette who had instigated their visit, the most open of the three, she was a ready consumer of hygienically packaged cultural exploration. With her, Lisette at least stood a chance of selling a book on the life of Marie Laveau, one of the simpler, more declarative biographies that didn't attempt to delve too deeply into the many contradictions surrounding New Orleans's nearly sainted, frequently damned, Catholic Voodoo queen. With a touch of finesse, Lisette might add some jewelry, a silver vèvè pendant perhaps, to the woman's tab. Or maybe even a made-to-order gris-gris bag, though for that the client would have to be willing to open up about her desires within earshot of her companions. Though perhaps Lisette could sort that out on her own. For what—she focused her full attention on the trio's most zestful member—did this woman's secret heart yearn?

Lisette bit her tongue as her current best client disregarded the "Do Not Touch" sign above the altar, reaching out to trace a finger along the neck of an undrinkable bottle of crème de rose liqueur placed there ten years back as a sacrifice to Erzulie Freda. Of course. *Love. No, passion.* The words came to Lisette in her mother's voice.

Lisette no longer allowed herself to believe in the loa, but since she had been taught about them since infancy, their stories still resonated with her. Her subconscious dealt with the cognitive dissonance of her disbelief in the myths with her emotional attachment to them by moving the narrative into her dead mother's voice. At least that's what she'd been told by the one hundred and twenty dollars for a fifty-minute-hour therapist she'd consulted, until she decided—crazy or not—at those prices she'd have to learn to live with it. And she had.

She had.

The brunette's eyes sparkled as they caressed the other items on the altar. *Danger.* Lisette's mother's voice began whispering the ingredients she should place in the gris-gris bag—an odd combination to suggest, given that it would, if it actually worked, dampen the woman's chances of realizing her goal. Lisette shut out her mother's voice but still felt a pang of sadness for the brunette, who she suspected would have no more luck in attaining the desires of her heart than the weepy Erzulie Freda herself.

A pendant. A good-quality one at a fair price. One Lisette would wear herself. That's what she'd sell this woman. *Damn.* She knew better than to allow herself to feel empathy for customers. The weekly receipts suffered each time she did.

To balance it out, she'd send the blonde off with a Voodoo doll keychain, a souvenir for a coworker or underappreciated spouse, thirty-nine cents wholesale, seven ninety-five retail. It didn't matter that Voodoo dolls had no place in real Voodoo. The use of the poppet to harm or control another was the invention of European witchcraft, grafted on to her mother's religion by Hollywood. But now, in the public imagination, those dolls were inseparable from the faith.

"Soulange." The blonde shocked Lisette by speaking her mother's name. It took her a moment to realize the woman's eyes were focused on a placard advertising "Readings by Soulange" affixed to the wall behind her. "Is that you?"

Lisette smiled and nodded. The sign had been there for almost as long as she could remember, but she often let tourists believe that she was the once famed seer Soulange Simeon. It was partially done out of expediency, partially in imitation of the Laveau women, whose multiple generations of Maries had come close to building a myth of a single immortal woman. Perhaps one day her daughter, Manon, would choose to pick up the mantle and join in the game. "Would you like me to read the cards for you?" She reassembled the deck and held it out to the patron.

The blonde was tempted. Lisette could read the curiosity in her gray eyes. If she'd come into the shop on her own, she would've said yes, but then again, she would've never deigned to darken the door without her fellow Graces. "No," she lied as her friends awaited her answer. "It's just a pretty name."

Lisette smiled. "It is indeed."

Just over the blonde's shoulder, through the window, Lisette caught sight of a familiar head of closely cropped gray hair. Her father, Alcide Simeon, came weaving down the sidewalk, threading his way through the throng of tourists, stopping and bowing theatrically before a young girl, stepping into the street and ceding the sidewalk to her and her parents. The girl's father reached down and swooped the girl up into his arms as a car horn blared a warning at Alcide. The driver swerved around him, and he stepped backward onto the uneven sidewalk, stumbling but righting himself. The glint of something silver in his hands caught Lisette's eye.

Lisette's father did not take drugs. He did not touch drink. Always said he'd watched too many of his buddies lose it all down those roads. But here he was, stumbling toward the shop. Still, seeing her teetotalling father drunk was a lesser shock than the sight of the strange instrument he carried. Bessie was his "brass belle," the horn such a familiar sight that it seemed an extension of her father's hand. Seeing him with this new horn cradled in his hands made her feel like she'd caught him carrying on with a strange woman.

"You'll excuse me for a moment," she said without looking at the women. "You all just keep on looking around as much as you would like." She stepped around the counter and brushed past the blonde. She grasped the door handle, and, walking through the bell's protest, slipped out to the street.

She strode up to her father, whose lips tipped into a smile as he threw his arms wide to welcome her.

"There's my baby girl," he said. "I was just coming by to see you."

She stopped just beyond his reach, and his stupid, drunk glee faded—but only a touch. For the first time in her life, she felt ashamed of him. "Why are you all lit up?" she said, her hands on her hips, unintentionally mimicking her mother. "And what are you doing with that horn? That isn't yours."

"Oh, it's mine all right. I bought it special this morning." He raised it to his lips and ran up a quick scale, ending with a flourish.

She held her stance and narrowed her eyes. "Special for what?"

His head jerked and his eyes widened in genuine surprise. "You haven't heard?" He turned to a passing stranger. "She hasn't heard!"

She stepped forward and grabbed his forearm. "No, she has not heard," Lisette said, her words breathless, angry, "but she is standing right here in front of you, so maybe you should get busy with the telling."

He looked at her, his lips drawing into a thin line. Then his face loosened, and he began to laugh. "Celestin Marin," he said, his eyes twinkling, "is finally dead. Funeral's day after tomorrow." He winked at her. "Gonna be a band and all. This tin horn and I are gonna join in right before they cut the bastard's body loose," he said and laughed. "May end up a devil of a second line."

"Celestin wasn't a musician. Why would anyone throw him a jazz funeral?"

Her father didn't respond with words, but a wide smile crept across his lips.

"You did not . . ."

"I sure did. I arranged the whole thing. How the hell else do you think it could happen?" He wagged the offending horn at her. "Just rang up a few friends. Charles Delinois made up a little white lie for me about how Marin was a secret donor for years to a charity to keep music in schools, and how it's the least we can . . ."

"You lied to Vincent," Lisette cut him off, regretting it before she could draw her next breath. It was ridiculous. Even after twenty-five years, the mere thought of Vincent darn near took her breath away . . . like someone had kicked her hard in the gut. She loved her husband. She loved the family they'd made together. Still, it hurt to speak Vincent's name. It hurt like hell.

"Yeah. I reckon I did a bit," her father said, sobering, Lisette could only surmise, from having witnessed the expression on her face. "The boy ate the story right up. Seemed kind of hungry for any kind words about his *defan papa*."

"Vincent's a good man. You've got no reason . . ."

"Vincent's a Marin." Her father's jaw stiffened, the mirth in his eyes turning to hatred. "Reason enough."

"You were friends once, all of you. Mama and you and the Marins." She hoped her words would summon a happy memory for him, but he remained stock-still and silent. "All right," Lisette said. "So how about you tell me why. What do you get out of this parade?"

The smile returned to his face, but it had come back cold and cruel, making him look less like the father she knew and loved. He held the horn to his lips and blew a few bars of the "Cross Road Blues" before lowering the horn. "I'm gonna play that son of a bitch's soul right into hell."

Lisette felt her jaw drop. It took her a moment to find words. "What kind of fool nonsense are you talking?"

"It isn't nonsense," he said, clutching the trumpet to his chest. "You aren't the only one who learned a thing or two from your mother. Gonna use this horn to blow his soul straight to the lowest pit of hell, then I'm gonna toss it in the river. Make sure it never gets played again. Would be too dangerous to let it fall into innocent hands afterward."

Lisette raised her hands to her temples. She shook her head. This could not be happening. Her father really couldn't think himself capable of speeding another man's descent into the fiery pit. She'd come so close, so many times, to telling her father that she no longer believed. That she knew none of this, not the vèvès, not the candles, not the gris-gris bags—especially not the table of premade ones at the shop now marked down to $19.99 each—was real. She'd only held her tongue out of respect for him and her mother's memory.

Dropping her hands, Lisette glanced back over her shoulder at the shop. She almost gasped, sure she caught the image of her mother moving behind the vèvès painted on the windows. No, that could not be. It was just a creation of her mind—more fodder for her next therapy appointment. Blinking the apparition away, she turned back to her father. "Listen, Daddy, even if you could . . ." She stopped herself, choosing her words more carefully. "Even if you do know how to do what you're planning, what good would it do? What happened with Mama and Mrs. Marin was so long ago."

"Maybe to you, but not to me. To me, it still seems like yesterday."

"But, Daddy, Celestin didn't have anything more to do with it than you or I . . ."

"Oh, he had something to do with it all right. I know it." Tears brimmed in his eyes, and he pounded on his chest with his free hand. "I know it in here."

*What harm can it do?* Lisette thought. *Might even do him some good. Do all of us some good. Bury this damned animosity between the families once and for all.* Lisette looked up at him. Patted his chest. "All right, Daddy. You do what you need to do." She leaned in and kissed his cheek.

As she pulled back, she noticed his eyes were reddening. His bottom lip began to quiver. For a moment, she wondered if the storm had passed, but then he raised his chin, his expression hardening, defiance growing in his eyes. "You could help, you know."

She traced her hand down his arm. "No, Daddy," she said, turning, heading back toward the shop. "I really couldn't."

# THREE

Alice gazed out the window, its thick damask curtains framing the waves as they broke on the rocky beach below. She wanted to go down to the water's edge. Take advantage of as many hours of the summer sun as she could. But she'd been asked—in a manner that couldn't be refused—to remain in the great hall. Her doctors were reviewing her case. Again. There would be questions. Questions to be answered when she felt like it, questions to be evaded when she didn't. She wondered if her responses even mattered.

She no longer spoke of Babau Jean. She no longer insisted that the bogey had been controlling Luc, holding his hand, forcing him to pull the trigger. She pretended to no longer believe that what she'd witnessed was real. For years now, she had pretended to no longer believe in him at all.

But he was always waiting for her in her dreams, just beyond the edge of consciousness.

Her grandfather's stories about Babau Jean, the wondrous monster, had entranced her, but it had terrified her to see the creature in the common world. Until the day the levees fell, until she felt Babau Jean's cold grip around her wrist, she'd never understood that the children in her grandfather's stories would never return from their adventures.

After the bogey's attack, she'd pretended to believe her uncle Vincent's promise that the only thing threatening to run away with her was her imagination. And she had very nearly begun to believe it. The nine months she and Hugo had spent living with their Aunt Fleur had been an oasis of stilted normality. But she'd no sooner arrived home than she'd witnessed that beast murdering her brother.

Babau Jean had remained with her ever since.

She sat, hoping to appear composed, patient, her navy peacoat slung across her knees. A heavy coat in summer. She'd never truly accepted the need to bundle up in June, but it was never warm here. Not really. Wind whistled around the island day and night. Still, there was a difference between the kiss of the cool, damp summer air and the deathly bite of the winter gales. In winter, the beach was off-limits for residents. Here, it seemed winter could last forever.

As far removed as it could be from the mainland while still remaining an official part of the States, Sinclair Isle had a habit of being overlooked by mapmakers, and even satellites seemed to blink while surveying the earth below. On sunny days, lobster and crab boats would bob in plain sight of the island's inhabitants. For years, she had waved at the fishermen, an act of childish friendliness, a childish dream of rescue. But the men on the boats had never taken notice of the spindly girl shrieking "hello" from the shore of the fairly substantial landmass not even half a nautical mile away. One of the security guards had laughed at her antics, and it was he who had told her the truth—the island was cloaked, hidden from those who didn't need to know of its existence. If any uninvited guests came too close, they would be overcome by a sense of disorientation and foreboding that would not lift until they changed course.

The island had been cut off from the rest of the world to minimize disturbing outside influences. That's what her doctor had told her when she'd asked him. But it was a lie, and she knew it. Sinclair Isle was home to a psychiatric care facility, one that housed witches with emotional issues. Witches who were considered too dangerous to live without supervision.

There had been a dozen or so institutions like Sinclair scattered around the globe. But with magic failing, most of them, Sinclair included, were being phased out. Without magic, the inmates might still be disturbed, but they were no longer witches. The residents who were deemed safe enough to return to society would be shipped home, and the rest would be consolidated into one of the three hospitals that would remain open. Alice had watched, sometimes through this same window, as the other residents boarded the ferry and rode off over the rough sea.

There were no roads to speak of on the island. A simple single-lane path ran from the docks up to the great house, then snaked around the cottages, the private homes of the institution's medical and administrative staff. It ended at a copse of pines behind the dormitory that housed the maintenance workers and security officers. The area where the cottages sat had been off-limits to residents for most of the time Alice had been here, but as the staff and residents continued to dwindle—the institute moving toward closure—many rules had been relaxed.

She and Sabine, a girl near her own age who had become her only true friend, had dared to explore this forbidden kingdom together, the afternoon before Sabine was released. That had been at the end of March. A year ago.

Alice had been left alone to face another island winter.

She'd come to hate winter. She'd come to hate snow.

Snow—the first time she'd seen it—had fallen in New Orleans the Christmas Day before Katrina. She'd begged to be excused from the table, and in a rare turn of good nature, her father had agreed. They'd all gone out—her father, Luc, and Hugo. She had danced with Luc, spinning in wide, intoxicating circles. She'd laughed to see snowflakes dust his lashes. Her father and Hugo had pelted each other with heavy, wet balls. Even Daniel had ventured outside, as far as the magic would let him, to gaze up at the falling flakes. On the day, it had seemed miraculous, but she'd since learned nothing good had ever come from snow.

Alice had put a lot of thought into what she'd do if she ever got to leave. First on that list was burning her coat. She'd go to a place where the snow never came. She'd cut her hair. Short. She'd get a job in a café. One that sold books. She'd get a place of her own. She'd fix a flower box in the window, and a lock on the door, one to which she held the only key. She'd . . .

She'd heard nothing from Sabine, but that didn't mean Sabine hadn't tried to reach out to her. The institution did all it could to discourage former residents from reconnecting. Recidivism had, at some point, been shown to be higher among those who'd remained close with other former residents. Much better, the staff would say, to build a future-focused life.

Alice realized her foot was jiggling. She set her foot on the floor, pressing the sole of her shoe into the rug, trying not to seem impatient. If they sensed her impatience, they might put off talking to her, just to see how she would take the delay. The doctors, the nurses, they were always testing the residents. And now that there were fewer residents than ever, more of their attention fell on Alice.

She turned her own attention to the light the sun cast on the sea, the way it pierced the depths, creating a patch of translucent blue in the field of gray green. She traced the path of a wave with her eyes, willing the swell to rise higher, to crash harder against the shore, but to no effect. The same spell that hid the island turned it into a magical dead zone. The burst of energy would be picked up and registered, she knew. Her chart would show that she had once again attempted an act of magic, and that, once again, the ward over the island had diffused her effort.

"Alice," a man's voice said. She turned to see an unfamiliar face. That face wore the same placid smile she'd grown used to seeing from all of the staff at Sinclair. He was surprisingly young for a doctor. He wore a white coat. Not the usual attire for Sinclair staff. The orderlies wore scrubs, often beneath a heavy jacket or sweater, and the guards wore midnight-blue uniforms that reminded her of the New Orleans police, but the doctors and nurses tended to wear street clothes, not much different from the residents. Many of the familiar medical staff had moved on or been transferred. She'd gone through six primary doctors in the past five months. "Hello," the man said, then tapped the screen of one of the pads the medical staff carried around everywhere.

"You're new," she said. He looked back up at her. Really looked at her. She held his gaze and offered him a well-honed counterfeit of a Duchenne smile—one she knew to be convincing, and in some circumstances, disconcerting. No one expected to encounter true happiness in an inmate's eyes. "It's always so nice to see a new face around here." If the doctors here made a career of studying her, she had made a vocation of studying them. For them, it was a matter of professional curiosity. For Alice, it was a matter of survival. Perhaps not in the literal flesh and bone sense, but to save the spark of herself, the one she had brought with her to this place.

She allowed herself a glance at his wrist. The staff who did have magic wore a metal band engraved with a combination of sigils, occult symbols, that allowed them to access their magic even here on the island. They always seemed to be touching those bands, adjusting them as if they chafed. Maybe the new doctor wasn't a witch, or maybe his access to power had become so weakened—quiet observation and eaves-dropping led her to believe the rate and degree of magic's failure had been exponential over the last several months—he felt it wasn't worth the irritation.

"Yes, I am new here," he said. "My name is Dr. Parker." His head tilted to the side, a quick involuntary movement. His lips parted, then fell back into a smile. A genuine smile. For a moment, Alice felt a twinge of guilt. He seemed like a nice guy. But then she reminded herself that she couldn't trust anyone in this place, this new doctor included. "I've been brought in to assist Dr. Woodard." His face flushed, and he dropped his eyes.

"Dr. Woodard?" Alice said. She hadn't even laid eyes on him yet, but she'd heard his name from Sabine and others who had met with him before their release. He was the keeper of the key. And this interview, which she'd envisioned as another routine check-in with the everyday staff, was likely, at last, to be the formal review.

"Yes," the young doctor said. "He'd like to speak with you, if now's a good time."

"Of course," Alice said.

"Then, if you wouldn't mind . . . ," he said and motioned to a door at the far end of the great room. Alice rose from the bench where she'd sat. The doctor glanced back at her, gripping his pad between both hands—a nervous gesture—and pressing the screen to his chest. When their eyes met, he flushed once again. "You probably know better than I where the consultation rooms are," he said, though he still led the way.

"Yes," Alice said and nodded. Two wings flanked the central hall where she sat to watch the waves. Long before Alice had arrived on the island, an unsympathetic builder had carved a row of identical, sterile, windowless offices—the consultation rooms—from a single room in the ancient stone house's eastern wing. Private consultations were always held here. The only interesting feature in any of the drab, otherwise featureless rooms was the detailed pattern of sigils overhead. She didn't understand all of them, even after years of the residents' shared speculation as to their purpose, but she was well familiar with the room closest to the guard station. This room was known as "the bubble"—the one place on the island where a witch's access to magic wasn't dampened. She'd visited this room often in her early years. Had even spent several nights there so the doctors could perform a sleep study on her. They'd searched for Babau Jean, but he'd been too clever for them. She'd slept beneath his watchful gaze, but neither their machines nor their empaths could pick up on his presence. They'd taken the experiment to prove that he didn't exist except as a shadow in her mind.

Babau Jean had laughed in silence as he continued to move freely through the liminal spaces.

Dr. Parker led her past "the bubble," then surprised her by carrying on past the row of offices to a door at the far end of the hall, a door she had seen before but never *noticed*. It was painted gray and appeared to be made of reinforced metal. As she focused on it, she realized it was covered in another set of symbols, painted in the same shade but a different luster. You had to stand at a certain distance, and look at the door from a certain angle, to notice them. "An obscuration," she said aloud without realizing it.

Dr. Parker froze, his hand balled up and poised, ready to rap on the door. "Yes," he said, his smooth forehead bunching up, a line forming down its center. "You can see them? The sigils?"

Alice nodded. It was too late to fib. "For a second. I was just guessing. I mean, I've spent a lot of time in the consulting rooms, but I never noticed . . ."—she paused, looking for precision—"never *cared* to notice this door. Or wondered where it went."

He began to speak, but seemed to think better of it. He turned back to the door and knocked, then grasped the handle and opened it without awaiting a response. Alice intuited that if permission to enter hadn't been granted, the door wouldn't have budged. Parker entered first, then turned back. "Please," he said, holding the door open wide.

Alice was surprised to find a beautiful, light-filled library, a room she never would have imagined at the end of the sad hall. The south-facing wall was covered in windows with leaded diamond panes, the eastern and western walls were lined with floor-to-ceiling bookcases, and the ceiling soared overhead. A tall ladder leaned against one of the walls.

Books were everywhere. Some still on the shelves. Some laid out on two long mahogany tables. Others were wrapped, and in the process of being packed into sturdy crates. Alice forgot everything and began to wander around the periphery of the room. She approached the first table and let her fingers hover over the beautiful, rich covers. To think, this bounty had been so close all this time. She'd dreamed of such a place while wandering among the stacks of the residents' well-stocked but no-frills lending library devouring everything she could find about the home she'd lost. If she'd grown up in New Orleans, she, like most people, probably wouldn't have paid attention to the details of what was right before her. But New Orleans had been taken from her, so every detail felt precious. She probably knew more about the city's history and architecture than she would have if she'd finished growing up there.

Still, she sensed the books held in this library were never intended for general circulation. She could almost imagine the sparks of dying magic leaping up from their pages.

"The Sinclair House has always boasted an extensive and covetable collection," a masculine voice said. She looked up to find Dr. Parker standing next to another man. Older. Older than her father even. With closely cropped gray hair and piercing eyes. His bearing reminded her of that of the security guards, even though he was dressed in a royal-blue linen suit and a navy and burnt-orange tie. "One of the finest I personally have ever had the pleasure of perusing." Tiny crinkles formed at the edges of his eyes. "Of course, it's missing the one work that would complete it, but some argue the book we are lacking no longer exists. Maybe never even did. Though lore has it that it was last seen in New Orleans. Imagine, Alice, a legendary grimoire hidden right in your own backyard." There was such familiarity in his tone, yet she had never met this man—she was certain of it. He ignored her confused expression and focused on her hand, still hovering over one of the texts.

Dr. Parker rushed to speak, as if he wanted to insert himself in the conversation before it veered off in an unwanted direction. His eyes telegraphed a message of caution. "Alice, this is Dr. Woodard."

"Yes," the older doctor said, turning toward his colleague. "That will be all, Doctor." Woodard's left index finger slid up under his right sleeve. Alice caught a glimpse of metal.

"But . . ."

He stifled Parker's protest with a simple glance. The younger doctor nodded and exited.

Woodard turned back to Alice. "Go ahead," he said and nodded to her. She turned back to the table of books, narrowing her attention to one of them, and traced her finger over the fantastical image embossed in silver on its cover. A nude woman, bent, her back supporting a winged satyr's head and a bare-breasted, ram-headed female whose clawed arm held aloft a branch decorated with a stag's skull. "Austin Osman Spare," the man said. "Not merely a first edition, but a specially commissioned single printing. One of a kind. It's even signed."

"I've never seen anything quite like it," she said, daring to ease open the cover, "but it seems . . . familiar."

"It should," the man responded. "You've witnessed many examples of his work." He paused, seeming to want her to make the connection on her own.

She felt her finger point overhead, though she was thinking of the ceilings in the consulting rooms. "The sigils . . ."

"His design. Some done by his own hand." He nodded, anticipating her question. "Yes, he spent time here, though I'm not at liberty to discuss in what capacity." He leaned in. "But I do want you to understand that time spent at Sinclair can serve . . . *has* served . . . others as a source of inspiration." He smiled at her—that patented, bland Sinclair smile again—and motioned toward a desk by the library's back wall. "Let's sit, shall we?"

She let her hand brush the cover once more, reluctant to leave the book, then followed him. There were only two chairs, a large leather desk chair behind the desk and a smaller armchair before it. "Please," Woodard said, nodding at the armchair. He continued around the desk and stationed himself in the more intimidating seat behind it. He leaned forward and clasped his hands in an almost prayerful gesture. She slipped into the seat, putting herself in the direct line of his stare.

He studied her for a moment, then pushed back into his chair. "We received a call this morning from your Uncle Vincent. I'm sorry, Miss Marin, but I must inform you that your grandfather passed away last night."

"Oh," she said. She tried to remember her grandfather's face, but it didn't arise with ease. She felt nothing beyond the notion that she should feel something. "I should care more. I know," she said. She raised her eyes to meet his.

"A very honest answer from a very honest young woman." He turned a bit sideways and rested his left arm on the desktop. "His death, I understand, can hardly come as a surprise. He's been under the care of one of our clinics for years now.

"Your uncle has inquired as to whether you might be amenable to returning to New Orleans to attend the funeral." He began drumming his fingers.

The key word twisted in her mind. "Amenable?"

"You're twenty-one now. Of legal age to sign for your own release. I've reviewed your file, and we would have released you—*should* have released you—years ago. Only your father requested that we keep you on." He paused. "I should inform you that this was new information to your uncle, as well."

"I don't understand . . ."

*Eventually you'll be one of the ones he throws away.* They were her brother's words, spoken so many years ago in the darkened attic of their home.

"Nor do I," the doctor said, then sighed. "Understand your father's motives, that is. Though I'm afraid I understand far too well why the former head of this clinic acquiesced to his request." He leaned back again and folded his hands over his stomach. "Your father doesn't seem to want you anywhere near New Orleans, and he has very deep pockets." The doctor turned and pushed away from his desk. She watched as he crossed the room to the table of books she had admired. He reached down and touched one, easing open its cover. "In another age, you might have spent your whole life with us, Alice." He lowered his gaze, appearing to examine the tome beneath his fingers. "But with most of our clinics closing, I'm looking ahead to retirement. And lucky for you, your uncle and I have come to a mutually satisfactory understanding."

# FOUR

Bourbon Street was no place for modesty. Anything on display on Bonnes Nouvelles's stage could be seen from the sidewalk through the glass-paneled doors and windows that dominated the club's entrance. A free peek got folk to slow down. Then it was up to the dancers, who each took two shifts a night, standing at the door, flirting with the passersby, men and women—hell, a good bachelorette party could put the club in the black for a week—inviting the curious to enter. Chants of "Come on in! No cover!" caught the folk who'd come to the Quarter looking for what Bonnes Nouvelles had to offer. Cautious pairs of coworkers out for a good time in the Big Easy could be snagged with a friendly enticement. "Get on in here, handsome, and bring your friend" never failed to provoke a jocular argument over who was the looker and who was the friend. "Where y'all from?" would stop just about anybody, and a hand on the shoulder could guide them through the door.

Once people were over the threshold, Evangeline took it as a near-sacred duty to make sure the good times rolled hard but without incident. Keep roaming hands off the dancers, respect your neighbors, respect your hosts, and everybody's happy.

Reasonably priced drinks. Last call came at one thirty. Closing at two.

Most nights, the dancers would clear out right after the last patron, leaving Evangeline and the night's closing bartender and barback to get the place in order for the next day. On a typical night, the bartender or barback would then walk with her to the night depository at the bank on Royal, but about an hour ago Evangeline had sent the duo scurrying off together through the downpour to drop off the day's receipts. After all, a little show of trust went a long way toward building employee loyalty, though there was no denying it was a risk. Lou, the new barback, had just finished a year's probation for burglary, and Matt, tonight's bartender, was his cousin. Still, treat a person like a thief, and a thief for life they'll be. That's what she always said whenever anyone, usually Nicholas, questioned her habit of offering second, and sometimes third, chances.

The truth was that Evangeline knew a thing or two about stealing.

She hadn't been born a thief, but there were only so many ways a thirteen-year-old girl could support herself. That was how old she'd been the year her mother's sister witches had killed her dad, leaving her an orphan.

Her dad had been a bastard, all right, but between the drinking and the preaching, he had also worked—every now and then, at least. Enough to keep them in a rented two-bedroom, seafoam-green 1968 Van Dyke Villager mobile home with a view of the Pineville Procter & Gamble factory out the kitchen window. And there'd been enough to eat. Most days.

After her dad's murder, she had waited, packed up and sitting by the door, for the sheriff to come, figuring a demolished vehicle and her dad's battered body would garner some attention from law enforcement. But one day passed. Then two.

The factory called. That was it. A real nice man asked for her dad, then misinterpreted the long, hanging silence on the line before she replied that he wasn't home. He asked once more to speak to her dad. When she repeated her lie, he told her that he was sorry, but she should let her daddy know he'd had his last chance. He should come by for his final wages.

She walked over, cutting through the open fields, to pick up the check. She was sent to the business office, where a hefty woman with dyed red hair teased high enough to poke God in the eye sat behind a counter surrounded by gray, wall-mounted mail sorters. Before greeting Evangeline, the woman removed her purple-framed glasses, letting them hang against her bosom from the chain that secured them around her neck. Evangeline lied and said that her daddy had sent her. The woman excused herself, then returned with the check for her daddy and a cold Pepsi and honey bun for Evangeline. "You take care of yourself, sweetie," the woman said, and as Evangeline cashed the thirty-two dollar and seventy-four cent check at the corner store, she realized she was going to have to do just that.

She'd had a code of sorts, in those years she'd relied on thieving. Never take anything that looked like it might be irreplaceable, especially if it appeared to have sentimental value. She had kept a list of everything she'd ever stolen, including the addresses from which she'd stolen them. Stupid, she realized now—had she ever been caught for one crime, they could have nabbed her for the rest. But she'd promised herself she'd make restitution.

She'd graduated early, at sixteen, having earned a good scholarship to a college in New Orleans. Around that time, she'd begun dancing at the Black Cat to make up for the expenses her scholarship didn't cover. She'd lied about her age, of course, and gotten her hands on paperwork to back up the lie.

Just like that, her thieving days were over.

No one ever noticed her daddy had up and disappeared. She knew magic had helped with that. Insult, she reckoned, added to the injury already dealt him.

Though she still had that old list, people moved on, people died. After all this time, she could never just send a money order and an apology. Besides, she'd come to realize it was more than video game boxes and unattended coin jars she'd stolen. From many, she reckoned she'd stolen their peace of mind. Someday, she'd tear the list up—but not until she felt she'd done enough good in the world to make up for the pain she'd caused others.

Maybe helping her new bar guys get back on their feet was part of what she needed to do to balance the cosmic scales. Tonight, though, she found herself questioning the wisdom of sending those two particular boys out together with a full sack of cash.

She bit her lip as she crossed to the alarm keypad by the door. *What's done is done.* Anyway, experience had taught her that it was unlikely they'd steal the lot the first time out. If they were going to betray her, it was far more likely they'd start skimming a few weeks out, once they thought they'd earned her complete trust.

As if that day would ever come. Evangeline could count on her thumb and index finger the people who'd earned her complete trust. One was Nicholas; the other was her cat.

A streak of lightning cut down the length of Bourbon Street like a zipper opening, causing Evangeline to stop in her tracks, her hand hovering over the alarm's keypad. She began counting, waiting for the clap of thunder to tell her how far away the strike had hit. She hadn't made it to one when the panes in the door began to rattle. She approached the window, then leaned toward it with cupped hands so she could see past her own reflection and out to the street. Another flash of lightning shot overhead, higher, and—judging by the thunderclap—much farther away.

Evangeline released the breath she'd been holding and returned to the security keypad to punch in the code. The beeping countdown began, so she hit the lights, grabbed her keys, and scurried out, pulling the door to with a loud, satisfying click. Locks and alarms. Wasn't so long ago she would've relied on a magical ward to keep out anyone who meant harm. Now Evangeline tried not to use magic. At least in ways other witches might notice.

*Magic is fading. Magic is dying.* She heard it whenever she got around a group of witches. Truth was, Evangeline didn't have a clue what they meant. Her power was holding up just fine. Might have even gotten a bit stronger over the last couple of years. Still, she had the sense to keep her mouth shut. She hadn't even said anything to Nicholas.

Evangeline rubbed her thumb against her index finger, realizing her trust list had just been cut in half.

She turned to face up Bourbon Street, bracing herself for the walk home. The building's double balcony offered her a moment's protection from the worst of the deluge, but beyond its reach, the street had begun to flood, the gutter system failing to keep up with the generous sky. She sighed, then darted out from beneath the balcony and across St. Louis Street, slowing only when she reached the cover of the gallery belonging to the first building on the block. Dodging from one protective covering to another, she figured she could make it home only half-drowned.

On the sidewalk, she spotted the soaked remains of the hand-printed cardboard sign Reverend Bill, a tattered old street preacher, had been carrying all week, a sign that denounced Evangeline and foretold her eternal damnation. The old man, mostly harmless, mostly bald except for a wild white fringe, spent half his life stumbling drunk down Bourbon, the other half pointing his shaky finger at other people doing the same and decrying their sins. The whole damned road was lined with clubs like hers, but Reverend Bill targeted Bonnes Nouvelles twice as often as any of the others. As if she needed another wild-eyed, fire-and-brimstone preacher telling her she was hell bound—she'd heard enough of that from her dad before his death.

Looking down at the sign, she made a mental note to remind the reverend there was only one *z* in Jezebel. She crossed over Toulouse Street, weaving her way through a group of diehard revelers, then past

St. Peter, dreaming of a hot bath and bed. A few short hours of sleep before she had to go downtown to meet with the bank, see if they might extend a new line of credit.

"Ms. Caissy," a smooth, deep voice on the other side of Bourbon called out to her. Evangeline raised her eyes to see a large, beautiful, melting drag queen holding Nicholas's younger son Hugo by the scruff of his neck. "I believe this belongs to you." The drag queen's biceps bulged as she hefted Hugo up over her shoulder and then crossed the street, admirably managing her burden in sling-back, peep-toe pumps despite the flooding. "You better be glad I'm not wearing my best shoes," she groused in a deep baritone as she deposited Hugo on his feet next to Evangeline. Nicholas's son promptly swayed and dropped onto his bottom on the wet sidewalk. "Making me come out in this weather," the queen said in a polished alto, affecting in a heartbeat an exaggerated floral femininity worthy of any Tennessee Williams heroine. She lifted a long false nail and pointed to her own head. "You think these lace-fronts come cheap?"

"I think that one did," Hugo said, laughing. He drew his knees in and wrapped his arms around them.

"That is it." The towering queen fell silent for a moment, then started shaking her head as she built up steam. "You are banned. Banned from the bar. Banned for life. Banned for good."

Hugo looked up at the drag queen with a defiant smile. His eyes narrowed. "You all'd miss me too much." His voiced dropped. "*You'd* miss me too much."

The queen looked down her nose at Hugo, her outlined lips puckering like she'd just tasted something sour. "Two days. I don't want to see you around for two days, you hear me?" Hugo just kept staring up, smiling. Her eyes didn't change, but the pucker smoothed into the tiniest of smiles. "You'd better be glad you so damned pretty, boy." She looked up at Evangeline. "And you." She gave a slight nod of her wigged head. "You need to teach that one some manners."

"I don't see what I can . . . ," Evangeline began, but the drag queen had already stomped off, holding one acrylic-taloned hand up over her head as she walked away. Evangeline shifted her focus to Hugo.

"What have you taken?" she asked, looking down into his enlarged pupils. She grasped his chin and turned his face into the glow of a neon beer sign.

"I dunno," he said, laughing. "Something red, something blue," he nearly sang the words. "Something yellow. Maybe something purple, too. A whole rainbow"—he stretched out the word, rocking back as he did—"of feel good." Hugo indulged in many nights of decadence that would have killed a normal man. But he was, of course, far from normal. A witch's tolerance for drugs and booze was renowned, but sooner or later, if magic truly was fading, Hugo might just push his way past the limit.

"You can't keep living like this," Evangeline said. "You've got to pull it together." He stared up at her, offering her the same boyish charm that had worked on the drag queen. Too bad for him, his brother and father had immunized her against the self-serving charm of the Marin male.

She crossed her arms over her chest as a blast of wind whipped past them. "One of these nights . . . ," she said, her voice failing her as she wondered how much of Hugo's problem could be attributed to her habit of cleaning up after him.

"One of these nights, what?" he said, laughing, looking up with her with a sparkle in his blue eyes.

"One of these nights"—she forced the words to come—"I'm not going to stop. I'm just going to keep walking."

His brow lowered as the smile fell from his face. Tiny lines formed at the edge of his eyes. "That night isn't tonight, is it?"

She stood there for a moment, gazing down at him. She shook her head. "No. It isn't tonight."

"Good," he said, his face brightening, cockiness returning to his tone. "'Cause I'm not sure I can stand."

She crouched down beside him and hooked her arm around him. "On three?" she said, helping him balance more than rise once they arrived at that number.

"I love you, you know?" he said, weaving a bit as he did. "I mean really love you."

"Yeah, I know." She gave him a tight squeeze.

"Not like Father either. Not like Nicholas."

"Let's not talk about your dad right now. You just focus on not tripping, okay? You'd take us both down."

"Okay." He leaned in and surprised her with a kiss on the top of her head.

She had a flash of him as the gangly, sullen, love-starved teenager he'd been upon her first introduction to the family. He might be a grown man now, but to her he'd always be that kid. "You're not punishing Nicholas by doing these things to yourself," she said. "You're only hurting yourself . . . and me."

"I thought we weren't talking about Nicholas now."

"We're not," she said, tugging him forward, willing the rain to let up, surprised when it did. She hadn't intended to use magic.

"She's coming home. Our Alice. Vincent has set up a family reunion." Evangeline hadn't heard. Nicholas had always painted his daughter as being too fragile to leave the hospital. But before she could express her surprise, Hugo carried on. "I figure it'll only take a week or two before she's back in care." He laughed as if what he said were funny. "We're hard on our women, the Marins. Two end up in the nuthouse, and one takes to the Dreaming Road. Aunt Fleur was lucky. Celestin just bartered her to her husband for a chance at prestige and political clout." He looked down at her, nodding in drunken agreement with himself. "You're pretty damaged, too, you know." He plodded forward, weaving worse than before. "Even my mother had the sense to take off.

But not you. You bed Luc. He blows his brains out. Then you spend a decade screwing the guy who damaged him. Like it was nothing." He tossed the words out with such nonchalance. As if they held no weight. No sharp edges. "Where do you think you'll end up? Crazy or dead?"

She stopped in her tracks. She felt herself shaking, not from the damp, but from rage. She heard a sizzling, popping sound as one neon sign after another exploded, shooting sparks, making Bourbon Street light up like a burning sparkler. The display seemed to shock him to sobriety. She raised her hand to strike him, but he'd already braced himself for it. Hugo had gone through life braced. Pushing away those he loved as fast and as hard as he could, just so they could hurry up and hurt him. She laid her palm against his cheek, caressing it.

"I'm not your mama. I'm not gonna leave you," she said. "I'm not Nicholas either. I don't give a damn whose sheets you warm. I love you. Not in spite of who you are, but because of it." She grasped his hand and gave it a gentle tug. "You gonna behave yourself now?"

"Yeah," Hugo said. "At least for a couple of days."

She looked back up at him. "I'll take what I can get." She led him left, turning off Bourbon and onto St. Ann.

# FIVE

Alice was walking from her grandfather's home to her father's. She knew this to be true, even though the path leading between the houses was a long interior corridor rather than a five-mile trek cutting through the heart of the city's Central Business District. Even though the muffled roar of jet engines at the edge of her awareness protested that her actual body was soaring over the spinning earth at thirty thousand feet.

The corridor seemed more real than the jet. More tangible. More plausible. And so Alice carried on down the hall despite it being too dark for her to see. Flickering light glowed to life around her, as if in response to her complaint. Both sides of the hall were suddenly lined with gilded torch lamps shaped in the form of women, all in varying degrees of classical undress.

She recognized the golden *torchères* as belonging to Versailles's Galerie des Glaces, a place she had always dreamed of visiting, and instantly she became aware of the Hall of Mirrors' vaulted ceiling and tall rounded windows. For an instant, full light flooded through those windows, but it extinguished itself just as quickly, perhaps to justify the quivering play of shadows and candlelight.

It was ridiculous, of course. Even Alice's sleeping mind balked at a geography that would have Versailles's Galerie des Glaces running like a corridor linking two houses in New Orleans, but still she walked along.

Alice wondered that her footsteps made no sound as she continued down the wide hall's parquet floor, but the thought left her mind, for she suddenly heard Sabine's voice droning on behind her. She was reading aloud in English—a language Sabine understood but rarely spoke—from a guidebook, a passage about Charles Le Brun and the hall's 357 mirrors.

At the mention of the mirrors, Alice found herself staring into one, and though the looking glass offered a good faith reflection of her image, something told her it was designed to look deeper than the surface—that it was, perhaps, capable of seeing her unspoken desires.

Sabine's voice carried on directly behind her, but her friend's reflection didn't appear on the mirror. Alice looked back over her shoulder. Sabine wasn't there, and the hall fell silent.

Alice turned back to the mirror, her eyes fixed on their own reflection, while in the periphery of her vision, the hall around her changed, rounding itself into a perfect sphere. The mirrors cracked and then shattered, their jagged edges spinning smooth until she was surrounded by hundreds of round looking glasses. She remained fixed in place, but the mirrors revolved around her, a whizzing, buzzing movement that caused her reflection to tremble and blink, almost imperceptibly, in and out of existence. Each mirror took her measure, each offered her a different view, though the speed at which they moved was too great for her to consciously register a fraction of what she saw. Vistas arose and erased themselves, slowing, seeming to grow in precision as they honed the world around her in response to desires she might not without some discomfort avow as her own.

And then an image, incorporating some aspects of the hall and reimagining others, came into focus around her. It *claimed* her, making her part of the tableau. Women, some in corsets, others in antique-style lace nightgowns, each exquisite in her own way, stood immobile in the flickering light. Alice recognized them as her dreaming mind's reinterpretation of the *torchères*. One, a tall, commanding beauty with olive skin and lustrous black hair, stood before the room, naked except for an opulent, museum-quality necklace of diamonds and teardrop-cut emeralds. Her eyes shone greener than the precious stones she wore.

The flicker of the light stilled, and the women stirred as if they had stolen movement from the light. Their swaying, a dance full of a sensuous languor, demanded music.

A group of male musicians appeared beneath a gas-lit chandelier. The women's spirited dance quickly fell in time with the music. A muted trumpet sang out over the rest of the ensemble, the player's fingering hidden beneath a handkerchief draped over his hand. A trombone and clarinet teased and taunted the trumpet to more and more dangerous improvisations. A drummer tried to maintain the order, but it was the pianist who provided the underpinning, giving the others a home base to return to when their wanderings were done. The music moved along, begging the pianist—Alice intuited him to be the prisoner of strict classical training—to break free, but his style, though faultless, remained bound by precision.

The dance demanded music; the music called for an audience.

But the hall didn't transform itself into a theater. Instead it took the shape of a mirrored parlor, complete with a style of furnishing Alice would have expected to find in a Victorian-era gentlemen's club. The sight of wriggling along the walls alerted her to the presence of others, men, their features swallowed by shadow. They stepped forward one or two at a time, glancing around as if trying to spot their marks on a stage, and then took their places.

Soon a peppering of men, many in formal attire, most wealthy looking, filled the space. As one, they turned back to look at the mirrors. Their faceless reflections stepped through the glass, doubling their numbers in a blink, each reflection developing his own unique features as he emerged into the space. Soon the parlor was filled with men. Drinking. Smoking. Laughing. They approached the women and brushed up against them, grasping them roughly. Alice flushed with anger, astounded when the women looked on unaffected, some laughing. A few even groped the men back, then pulled them into the swaying mass of dancers undulating before the now outnumbered band.

Alice looked away, and her eyes fell on two men smirking at each other from their seats on opposite ends of a card table. Both were wearing black tie, but the man who sat between them had on a sweat-stained striped shirt, rolled up at the sleeves, and a straw hat pushed back on his head. He eyed the cards he held. Alice sensed that he was trying to maintain an air of sangfroid, but the pallor of his face broadcast his dismay.

Her eyes shifted to another man with a thick, bushy mustache and heavy, lethargic eyelids, reclined opposite the table on a divan. A mahogany wine table on three slender legs sat before him, a small lamp burning at its center. It struck Alice as strange that rather than brightening the room, the lamp seemed to swallow the light around it. A long metal pipe ending in a wolf's head with fierce ruby eyes dangled between the fingers of his left hand. He leaned forward, holding a tiny knob on the pipe's lower section over the lamp's low flame. Then he placed the pipe's other end to his lips and inhaled, his face tilting back as he exhaled a filament of cloying smoke that smelled of perfume gone off from age.

The man seemed to feel the weight of her stare, and he turned his face toward her. His tongue slid out to moisten his lower lip. "Alice," he said, but something about the way he spoke her name made it seem as if he had just imparted a word of great import. Her name combined welcome and warning, recognition and regret. He looked at her over the length of his pipe as he inhaled once more. He let the plume escape his lips, then his mouth curled into a smile. "What would your mother say if she were to see you here?" His gaze drifted upward, toward the ceiling, where Alice saw her own name trace itself, as if written by a living serpent of neon light, before flashing out.

The nude beauty circled the room, pausing before each of the men, longer before some than others, seeming to inspect them. Most of the men present looked old, in their thirties or even her father's age, but two younger men made their way to the center of the room, champagne flutes in hand. The beauty signaled to two of her sisters, who came and escorted the men to the foot of the stage.

It struck Alice that a stark dichotomy existed between the men in the hall. The musicians were all darker-skinned, the audience white. Unlike the men, divided by race, the women mingling there, like the beauty, appeared to be of Creole extraction, some darker, some fairer.

The beauty stopped beside the unlucky poker player and whispered in his ear. She kissed his ashen cheek, then laughed and undid her necklace, laying it atop the pile of cash at the center of the table before sauntering away.

She drew near Alice, reaching out and taking a glass of champagne from the silver tray Alice had only then realized she was holding.

"Alice, my girl, Miss Lulu doesn't pay you to stand around gaping," the beauty said. Alice looked down, surprised by the harsh contrast of her own dress's long black sleeves and the white apron she wore over it.

Suddenly lucid and aware that she was dreaming, Alice wondered if she should play along with the role her subconscious had assigned her or break character, but the other woman just held up a silencing finger as she turned back to the band.

The beauty passed a man who sat backward on a chair, his arms draped over the back. He seemed both part of the tableau surrounding him and removed from it. The beauty ran her fingers through his thick dark curls as she passed. He looked up, and she handed him the glass of champagne. She grasped his free hand, a shade darker than her own, tugging him up and forward to join the two young men in black tie, who now stood on the band's raised dais. Of course, there had been no raised platform before, but now the dream commanded it. The man shook his head, attempting to refuse both the champagne and the invitation, but the beauty took no heed. The dancers parted at their approach, leaving them a clear path.

The beauty deposited the curly-haired man beside his brethren. Next to the other two, whose features were handsome but bland, he stood out even more—his complexion a deeper tan than the beauty's, a strong brow, high cheekbones underscored by a day's growth of dark stubble, and bottomless black eyes outlined with the thickest lashes Alice had ever seen on a male. He had a thick Cupid's bow mouth. His features were too pretty for most men, but they only seemed to highlight the unaffected masculinity of his bearing. The more she focused on him, the more his companions paled in comparison. It struck Alice that even though she hadn't paid much attention to their appearance earlier, it seemed as if their features might have changed, grown less fine, their coloring mousier, to emphasize the contrast with him. The handsome man's eyes fell on Alice, fixed on her. He tilted his head to see around the crowd milling between them. He took a step forward, moving as if to leave the dais, but one of the other two young men reached out and draped an arm around his broad shoulders.

The beauty raised her hand, and the band—the entire room—fell silent. She stood still for a moment, letting her eyes graze every face in the room before speaking. "There's a lot of talk," she said, her voice as clear as if she were speaking directly in Alice's ear, "of the law shutting us down. Shutting us all down. Clearing Storyville clean out. All so you menfolk can have that silly little war you're just itching to have."

"Storyville," the word escaped Alice's lips as she connected the name Lulu to her surroundings. This, she realized, was Mahogany Hall, or at least her interpretation of Lulu White's renowned bordello. But Alice knew from her reading that Storyville, New Orleans's once famed and legally prescribed sixteen-block vice district, had been closed before the beginning of World War I, and Mahogany Hall razed after the end of the second. *Why*, she wondered, *would I have come here?*

"And what you menfolk want," the beauty continued, "you always get. But not," she paused and laughed, "before we womenfolk get what *we* want. Before we let you ship all the pretty young boys off to get killed, we're going to claim one as our own." She stepped back and gestured with a wide wave toward the three young men at her side. "Ladies," she called out, "I give you your candidates for Mahogany Hall's last king of Mardi Gras." She reached out and ran her fingers once again through the man's thick, dark curls. The beauty drew him nearer. "I know which one gets my vote." She placed a passionate, if practiced, kiss on his lips.

She released him, then accepted a shiny white object from one of her ladies in waiting. Stepping behind the swarthy man, she reached up around him to place an unadorned white Mardi Gras mask over his angelic features.

Alice knew him then. Babau Jean. He was always present. In all her dreams. She wondered how it was she had only recognized him when he wore his true face.

In the next breath, he stood before her. The room was silent, empty except for the two of them. He leaned in, the mask brushing her cheek as he whispered in her ear. "There's such beauty in darkness, Alice," he said, leaning back and taking her chin in his cool hand. "And such darkness in beauty." He lowered his hand, tracing a finger down her neck, letting it rest at the hollow of her throat. She felt her pulse throb beneath his touch. He leaned in, the cool bone china mask pressing a chaste kiss on her forehead. On the edge of her darkening awareness, she heard a woman's cry of distress. The voice was achingly familiar, and it reached in and stirred her earliest memories.

She knew it to be her mother's voice. Alice turned her head, searching for the source of the sound.

A child's wailing jolted Alice awake, her own reflection looking back at her from the plane's window, the night sky all around her.

# SIX

*Damned if I know. Damned if I know.* Fat raindrops struck her umbrella, the rhythmic sound triggering words in Lisette's mind that repeated themselves like a mantra until she finally relented—first mouthing them silently, then muttering them under her breath. The responses, she realized, came to her subconscious questions. How many mornings had she walked down this same street to pass another day in her mother's shop? How many more mornings would she revisit her steps?

The gas station paper coffee cup she held in her left hand was too hot. The wind tugged hard on her umbrella, straining her to the right. She paused beneath a gallery to trade hands, her eyes drifting up to a pigeon perched on the sharp spike of an old Romeo catcher, a vicious collection of hooks and barbs known to some as "Babau Jean's dentures"—originally fashioned to discourage suitors from shimmying up posts to reach their girls' rooms. *Go up a Romeo, come down a Juliette*— an old joke that may have once had some very real teeth to it. The catchers didn't pose much of a threat these days, but Lisette still walked around with a mental catalog of the contemporary hazards to her children, her son Remy more so than her daughter Manon.

Manon was two years older. And smarter. Maybe twice as smart. Not in terms of scholarship—Remy, he was a bright boy, could've been top of his class with a little more effort—but sure as hell when it came to the ways of the world. Her boy was fearless in the face of a world where having a little fear could be seen as a virtue.

Lisette's mother would've loaded Remy down with gris-gris to protect him. She wished she had her mother's faith. But no amount of brick dust on your front steps could keep a stray bullet from penetrating the wall as you slept. And no eye-opening spell was going to turn the world "woke" overnight. If such a thing were possible, the Widow Paris herself would've shifted the world in the right direction going on two centuries ago.

No, Lisette didn't share her mother's faith, not anymore. Still, the world being what it was didn't stop some folk from believing, and since Lisette and Isadore were still helping with tuition for both of their kids, she knew she should be grateful for that.

She took a sip of her coffee and was bracing herself to charge back out into the blustery weather when her phone began ringing. She propped her umbrella up against a storefront and fished in her coat pocket for the flip phone she'd been carrying since Manon was in eighth grade. For years, her girl had been mortified by the very existence of that phone—now, she'd matured enough not to care Lisette wasn't up to date so long as Manon herself had all the latest tech toys the world could not find a way to live without. Her daughter always went to Isadore for those things, knowing that her father would say yes long past the point at which Lisette herself would declare hell no.

Lisette squinted at the tiny caller ID and saw it was Manon herself ringing. She smiled at the thought that her girl was checking in, but the smile slipped away. The kids only ever texted these days. A voice call meant trouble.

She flipped the receiver open and pressed it to her ear. "What is it, baby?" she said, striving for a tone that blended the threat of severity with the promise of mercy.

She waited for a response. Waited too long. She started to pull the phone from her ear to see if the call had gotten disconnected when Manon finally spoke. "Mama," the tremble in her voice sent shivers down Lisette's spine, the two syllables of the word carrying the worst news in the world right up to her and laying it at her feet. "Mama, where are you?"

Lisette's shoulder brushed the wall. She dropped the paper cup, and it fell, sending a spray of hot brown liquid up on her leg. Lisette barely noticed. "What's wrong, girl? You okay?" Her breath came to her with difficulty. She felt the pulse in her neck.

"I'm fine, Mama . . ."

"Remy . . ."

"No, Mama. Remy's okay. Daddy, too. It's you I'm worried about."

Lisette felt the steel return to her spine. "Why're you worried about me?"

"I'm outside the shop. Somebody's . . ." Manon's words stopped. The sound of her breathing told Lisette that her daughter was choking back tears. "I thought you might be in there," she cried into the phone.

"It's okay, baby girl. It's okay. As long as you and your brother are okay, everything is right as rain . . ." Her eyes focused on the rain that had gone from a shower to a full-on downpour.

"Mama, you got to get on over here." There was a pause. "Some son of a bitch has trashed Vèvè. There's a goddamned swastika sprayed on the door. The windows . . . ," she began. Manon didn't have to finish for Lisette to know the windows were gone. In Lisette's mind's eye, she could see herself as a small child looking on as her own mother painted each of the vèvès by hand, precariously balanced on a step stool, and quizzed Lisette as she worked. Which mark belonged to which loa. What offering you should make to summon which spirit.

"Mama's on her way," Lisette said, only then realizing that she had already dashed out from beneath the gallery, forgetting her umbrella. "Are you safe?"

"Yeah. I think so."

"Don't think it. You get over to the café where there are people." Lisette heard only the sound of her own breathing as she bounded down St. Peter toward Chartres Street. "You hear me?"

"Yeah, Mama. I hear you, but what if he's in the café now? It could've been . . ."

"Anyone," she said, finishing her daughter's thought. Lisette's eyes scanned the people she passed, many of them turning to watch her as she dashed past them. Her eyes jumped from face to face. "It could've been anyone. But I sure don't think it was that gay boy who sells you those five-dollar lattes. Now get. And call your daddy."

She stepped off the curb and into a puddle. Her already wet shoes flooded.

She crossed against the light. A taxi blared its horn, and an angry male voice succeeded in demeaning her intelligence and her sex in just three syllables. She didn't care. She couldn't care.

Lisette could make out Manon's anxious face peering out through the corner café's window. Then her baby girl rushed out of the café and met her on the corner. Lisette threw her arms around her, pulling her in close. Manon was soaked to the bone. Shivering. Lisette realized that she was, too, but that didn't matter.

She gave Manon a tight squeeze, putting on her brave face before letting the girl lay eyes on her again. She glanced at her own blurred reflection in the café window. Her jaw was set, and her eyes looked full of fire. Good. She released Manon. "Show me," she said, taking her daughter's hand and leading her down Chartres.

She gritted her teeth, stifling the urge to cry out as they drew near. The scene was just as Manon had described it. "Wonder why the alarm didn't sound," she said, just to have something to say that wasn't a scream. She took her phone and dialed 911. She glanced around at the neighboring shops. All unharmed. Some were still dark. All seemed unnaturally quiet. Most didn't open till ten, but certainly someone had come in early. Someone must've seen the attack. "I wonder if anyone's called this in." She took a step, heard the crunch of glass. "Here," she held the phone out to Manon. "You talk to them. Tell them to come." She let the phone drop into her daughter's trembling hand. "Gonna be fine, girl." She crossed the street without looking, turning back so that she could take in the extent of the destruction. The windows were indeed all gone, except for one pane on the upper left. A dripping red swastika had been sprayed on the black door, with the words "Go back" above it and "to Africa" beneath it. At first her breath stuck in her throat, but then she started laughing, loud and hard.

Manon closed the phone and gazed at her. Lisette was pleased her daughter looked both ways before crossing, just like she'd taught her—didn't matter that it was a one-way street. "Police are on their way," Manon said. A siren screamed in agreement to her daughter's words. Manon took her hand. "You okay?"

Lisette caught her breath, only to start laughing even louder. She pointed at the defiled door, gasping. "They want us to go back to Africa."

Manon's worried eyes narrowed. "That type always does, but I don't see why it's so funny."

Lisette reached up to wipe away a tear, or maybe just a raindrop. "'Cause, baby girl, we're Creole. We didn't just come from Africa. We came from all the hell over."

# SEVEN

The rain had ended. The sun was burning high in the sky. Pothole puddles were boiling up into steam, making breathing a damned misery. Carver's dirty orange backpack rode his shoulders like a bitch as he struggled up Claiborne past Dumaine Street. His damp, graying tank top clung to his chest, chafing skin still tender from the tattoo he had gotten done last night.

Still, he was good.

He was worn out all right. But worn out in the good way. A smile came to his thin lips as he thought of it. As good as sex, it'd been. He'd damn near popped a load, busting up that shop. And son of a bitch if he hadn't gotten paid to do it. Hell, he would've done it for free just to watch that mulatto-looking bitch spinning around, crying for her mama. His mouth was dry. His lips stuck together as they parted to laugh at the thought of her.

He decided to stop and take off his shirt, wring out the sweat. It'd give him a chance to show off his new ink, a circle on his right pec, with the numbers fourteen and eighty-eight separated by twin bolts of lightning in the center. The tattooist had wanted to use red for the bolts, but Carver wanted to keep it real, so they'd stuck to black and gray—black numbers, gray circle and bolts.

Those who understood would understand. Those who didn't would soon have no choice but to learn.

He shrugged off the backpack and dropped it by his feet. He stepped on the strap, just to make sure no one would try to punk him and take off with it. He wasn't nobody's damn servant. Not anymore. He was a goddamned entrepreneur. And that backpack contained the beginning of his empire.

He'd taken the money he'd been paid for the shop job and traded it over on Perdido Street for a pack of pretty white powder—heroin mixed with fentanyl to give it a quick, hard kick. Least that's what he'd been promised. He knew enough to recognize the real thing, but he wasn't fool enough to try it himself to find out. That was where a lot of men went wrong—sampling the merchandise. When you went down that road, the sample size just kept getting bigger. Not him, though.

Be his product a weak-ass buzz or a ticket to the pearly gates, he did not give a good goddamn.

Carver had already cut that shit in half with cornstarch, and now he was gonna turn around and sell it for four, maybe five times as much as what he'd paid. And then he was gonna start all over again.

He slipped his shirt over his head, pulling the neck wide so it wouldn't snag on the freaky Voodoo necklace the old Garden District bitch had given him to wear while he did the job. The necklace was made up of bones, arranged by length. Twenty-seven of them. It didn't take a whole hell of a lot of imagination to see how they would fit together into a human hand. She'd claimed it'd let him do his work without getting noticed, without getting caught. He didn't believe in that hoodoo bullshit himself, but he liked the necklace. Liked the way it looked. The way it felt against his skin. The way it made him feel tougher. Stronger.

Figured he might as well keep it as a little lagniappe, now that he'd decided to move on.

In her words, it was his "utter lack of scruples," his willingness—eagerness, even—to break any and all rules, that had landed him the job as her driver. So it could hardly surprise her that he'd decided to leave without giving her notice, or that he'd taken a parting gift of his own selection with him. He figured she was gonna fire him anyway. He could smell it on her. She'd been acting pissy for weeks.

No skin off his ass. She'd been a bitch to work for. A total ballbuster. Still, Carver figured she wouldn't sic the cops on him for petty theft. First of all, she'd not want him to talk about the shop. Second, he may not have understood everything she was mixed up in, but he'd driven her around enough to know everywhere she liked to go—and that she wouldn't want anyone to know she'd been there.

He worked his shirt through the loophole of his jeans, then pulled on the backpack, the serrated edges of its black nylon straps burning like they were full-on metal mothers. He gritted his teeth and shifted the straps, but only succeeded in giving them fresh flesh to bite. "Son of a . . . ," he said, but his words fell away when he caught sight of the familiar "Tremé" in black and blue graffiti on a gray picket fence that ran alongside an apartment building on the other side of Claiborne. Some fool had marked over the neighborhood's name in a careless red scrawl. A new player, maybe? Carver squinted to make out what the tag said.

Babau Jean.

For an instant he was six, alone in a dark bathroom, screaming. His big brother laughing on the safe side of the door, holding the knob tight so he couldn't escape. Calling the bogeyman's name over and over. Yelling that Babau Jean was coming, and he would step right through the mirror to snatch Carver away.

Babau Jean. Bitch, please. Carver forced himself to laugh, but the sweat on his back had turned icy.

He could still taste his six-year-old self's fear. Carver had been so scared he'd pissed himself. In the goddamn bathroom. He remembered the shame. Remembered washing his pants in the tub so he wouldn't catch it from his mom. He'd still caught it, though. His brother had made sure to show her the damp trousers.

The six-year-old's embarrassment flared in a blink to a grown man's rage. He felt the ice turn to fire, thinking of the beatings his older brother had given him. The beatings he'd taken for the liar from their mom, who didn't really care who she punished so long as she could pass along her own bad day to one of her boys. He clenched his fists and gritted his teeth. Then he looked up at the wide blue sky hanging over his head and chuckled, thinking of his sorry punk of a brother now, up in Angola, the state pen, in his fourth year of twenty, getting turned out and traded for a new pair of sneakers, or maybe even just a pack of smokes, now that he wasn't as fresh.

Carver passed the stub end of Ursulines Avenue without noticing.

His eyes continued to scan the other side of Claiborne. Pilings, some faced with brick, others covered with bright street art—the kind the city liked, not the kind they painted over—supported the overpass that ran the length of this stretch of the street. A parking lot about the width of the overpass separated the lower street's eastbound and westbound lanes. There were five, maybe six guys wandering around the pilings and taking advantage of the shade the overpass provided. They looked rough and maybe homeless—the kind of guys who might not like his tats, if they got a better look at them.

On the corner of Esplanade, an old Negro woman sat on a green folding chair beside a large red cooler. A sign taped to the cooler's lid advertised "Water $1." She shielded her eyes as she took him in. "Nice cold water, here," she said, lifting the lid to show a dozen or so plastic bottles jammed down into the melting ice.

He reached down, but she slammed the lid closed. "One dollar," she said, her lips pursing as she looked up at him with cautious eyes.

He raised his hand up and ran it down his chest, letting it hover over the new tattoo.

The way she looked at him said that she did not give a single damn. "One dollar," she said.

He forced his hand deep into his pocket and pulled out a crumpled twenty. He dropped it in front of her. She bent over in her chair without ever taking her eyes off him. "I ain't got change for no twenty."

He grabbed the cooler's handles and raised it overhead, dumping its contents. "No need." He dropped the cooler back to the sidewalk before snatching up a bottle as it rolled away.

"What the hell is wrong with you, boy?" the old woman said, struggling up from her chair.

The guys he'd noticed a block back were watching him from beneath the shade of the overpass on the opposite side of the street. He took one of the necklace's bones between his thumb and forefinger. He wasn't scared of those sonsabitches. And there was a good chance some of these dusky shadows would be his first, maybe even best, customers. He zigzagged through oncoming traffic and walked right up to the nearest of them.

Rather than challenge him, the men cast nervous glances at him as he approached, then began slipping away, a couple east, a couple west. One whistling a warning that wasn't worth his spit—Carver wasn't spooked by this bunch of pussies—as he headed lakeside back into the Tremé.

Only one of the group didn't take off, some punk wearing a hoodie, hood up, despite the heat. He was hunched over in the overpass's deepest shadow, his back to Carver, using one of the pilings as support. *Damn junkie,* Carver thought, then wondered if he was a damn junkie with cash. "You need something, buddy?" he called out. "I got something good here for you. Something that'll fix whatever you got wrong with you."

The guy began shaking. At first Carver suspected a seizure, but soon the man's wild laughter echoed around him, drowning out the traffic noise, bouncing down off the concrete overhead, reaching around him and pulling him closer. Carver's next breath found him standing several feet closer than he had been, toe-to-toe with the man. He felt his pulse pounding in his neck. The man's face wasn't right. Too white. Too shiny. The freak was wearing a Mardi Gras mask. This had to be the bastard behind that Babau Jean tag.

Carver tried to pull away, but something held him in place. *No. There is no damned way.*

The man raised his hand, pointing at the necklace with one sharp nail. The necklace lifted, rising up and scraping the back of Carver's neck, tugging against him like it wanted to fly into the outstretched hand. The man slipped off the hood and leaned in, sniffing him like a dog, running his nose along the tender skin of Carver's neck, breathing him in. A moist tongue darted out and pressed itself against the point where Carver's blood pulsed. Carver felt a warm dampness running down his leg. The man—no, this was no man, it was a monster—leaned back, its hollow black eyes, eyes that had once stared back at Carver through a mirror in a darkened bathroom, focused on him, *recognized* him. The face—he knew it was a face now—moved like flesh, moved like no mask could, the mouth opening wide in laughter, exposing sharp, silver teeth like razor blades.

Then the laughter stopped.

Two hands reached forward, clasping the sides of Carver's face, caressing it, drawing him in as if for a kiss. Carver couldn't resist. He couldn't even move. All he could do was stare into the bottomless holes that sat where any normal man's eyes would have been. It pulled Carver's head forward and leaned in until their foreheads touched. Cool. Too cold to be alive. A foul smell, like a carcass rotting in swamp water, worked its way up Carver's nostrils, into his own skin.

It leaned back, its hands sliding forward until both thumbs met at the center of Carver's forehead. Two quick slices—each thumbnail like a scalpel—a full circle from forehead to just beneath his jaw, and Carver began screaming. Agony, then a wet sound he remembered from his uncle's taxidermy shop, and a shower of red. He wanted to pass out. Knew that by any rights he should. Knew that this monster was the only thing keeping him conscious.

It held up the flap of wet skin, examining it, turning it around and holding it before Carver's peeled eyes. Then it drew the flesh back, sliding it over its own blank face, holding it in place, smoothing it. As it did so, its body changed, shortening, thickening, becoming a mirror image of Carver's own. It lowered its hands and leaned in toward Carver, allowing him an eternity to stare at his own face, into his own eyes.

The creature stepped forward, looping its fingers around Carver's necklace. It gave the necklace one sharp tug, and then another, nearly yanking Carver off his feet, but the necklace stayed fixed around his neck. A cry of anger sounded from his double's lips. It caught hold of Carver's head with a rough grasp, tight enough that he heard the popping of fractured bone. His view twisted. There was a flash of light, and then came darkness.

# EIGHT

Evangeline stumbled through the house, pulling on one shoe, tilting her head to spy beneath the sofa for its mate. She spotted it across the room, then remembered the kick she'd given it last night as she made her way to the vodka. She didn't make a habit of drinking late, and she never drank alone—except when it was necessary.

Last night it had been necessary.

She'd managed to tug Hugo over the threshold and stretch him out on the sofa. She'd sat down across from him, watching him sleep, and thought of Nicholas and his children. And proceeded to drink herself into a stupor.

Hugo had been gone in the morning, along with a twenty from her wallet. Little son of a bitch had left an IOU with a smiley face on it.

She'd have a talk with him later. Probably on her way home from work tonight—after yet another bartender kicked him to the curb.

But there was no time to stew about it now. She had only fifteen minutes to make it to her meeting at the bank.

She snatched up the wayward shoe, balanced on one leg like a stork as she pulled it on, then headed back into the kitchen to grab her keys.

Sugar followed along, cutting figure eights around her legs, mewling. "Mama's gonna feed you in a second," Evangeline said. "It isn't like you're starving."

The cat started chattering—sharp staccato sounds the likes of which Evangeline had never heard her make. She stopped in her tracks and looked down at the cat.

"Well, yeah, sweetie. I know she's coming, but . . ."

The cat chattered again, cutting her off.

"She's here already?" she asked. Sugar's steady gaze served as the cat's reply. "No. I don't know how long Alice is going to be in town. You seem to know a whole hell of a lot more than I do."

A chirrup.

"I'll ask," Evangeline said, wondering if she really should. Sugar's large peridot eyes implored her to make good on her word. "I'll ask. I will. I'll ask Nicholas . . ."

The feline hissed at his name, and Evangeline held up her hands, signaling for her to stop. *Looks like the détente was short-lived.*

"I'm not going to the funeral."

Her head started pounding, and her mouth felt like she'd been chewing cotton balls. Even after a shower, she was still sweating alcohol. If she showed up at the bank now, she wouldn't stand a chance. She'd call the loan officer. Tell a white lie. Beg to reschedule to this afternoon, or better yet, tomorrow. She stepped around Sugar and went into the kitchen. Ignoring the cat, she took her time pouring herself a glass of cool water.

Sugar padded into the room and sat in its center.

"Because I haven't been invited," Evangeline said, irritated at being interrogated by her own pet. "Why? Maybe because I pissed him off." She scowled at the cat. "You were sitting right there sunning yourself, so don't pretend you didn't hear the whole damned thing." She held up a finger, like she'd just had a brilliant idea. "Or wait, maybe because Celestin hated me, and the whole world knows it." She dug a bottle of aspirin from the junk drawer and swallowed a couple of pills, draining her glass and setting it on the counter.

The damned funeral was tomorrow. And Nicholas didn't have time for her. She'd called. Twice.

She'd spent nearly a decade waiting for him to remove this armor. To expose his heart fully to her. She thought maybe, just maybe, yesterday had been the beginning of that. It was the rawest she'd ever seen him. But then he'd gone and made her angry, giving her that line of bull. And maybe she'd snapped back a little too hard, 'cause now he didn't want her. Not at the wake. Not at the funeral. Not at the ball. If he did, he would've already asked.

She'd hoped he'd see her as someone he could lean on, but she'd let her fool self forget. Nicholas Marin did not bend.

"Oh, yes, and thank you for reminding me. I'd forgotten my close personal relationship with the other Marin men." She shook her head. "You know that one is different," she said, speaking of Hugo. "It isn't like that with him." She grabbed her keys, then scanned the room for any sign of her phone. A meow. She stopped to glare at the cat. Sugar returned the glare.

"I don't know why Nicholas hasn't asked me to go with him. Maybe he's just waiting for me to say I want to." The cat made a sound that could only be meant to express disbelief. "No. I don't really think that's true either."

"Listen," she said, leaning over and offering a caress, but the cat had no intention of approaching her. Evangeline drew her hand back. "I just don't want you to be disappointed. Hurt. Alice left a long time ago. She was a little girl. She may not even remember you."

Sugar offered a simple declarative meow.

"Okay. Of course you're unforgettable, but it's been a long time. She may not feel the same way for you she did when you two were young." A blank stare. "I just mean, she may not love you like she did. But it's okay if she doesn't, 'cause I do." Sugar twitched her tail. "No,

I am not jealous . . . well, maybe I am. A little." Sugar padded closer, rubbing her cheek against Evangeline's leg. "All right. All right. I'll find a way. I'll reach out to her. But you've got to promise Mama you won't get . . ."

Two loud thumps hit overhead in quick succession.

"What the . . . ?"

Sugar arched her back, hissing.

Evangeline looked up. A heavy clawing, like an anchor being dragged across the roof, sounded from above, moving from the center to the side. Then came the tapping, a recurring rhythmic strike against the windowpane. It was coming from the old-style, multipaned French doors that opened out of her bedroom into the tiny walled-in garden behind the house. Those doors, and the ones in the guest room, were the only way to enter the garden. Anyone would have had to sneak through the house to get in there, or drop in . . . from the sky. The tapping grew louder. Like stones being pitched in waltz time—one, two, three, one, two, three—against the glass.

Then came the unmistakable sound of one of the panes shattering.

Sugar howled, and Evangeline shushed the cat. "Mama needs you to hide. Real good. Like you hide when you're mad at Mama. You hear?" The cat darted from the room.

Another pane smashed. She crept through the kitchen, edging up to her bedroom door, craning her neck to try to see what awaited her beyond the French doors. A movement near the bottom of the door caught her eye. A black bird—a raven, she realized—stood staring in at her. When she didn't move, it began tapping the pane with its beak.

"Come, half-witch, join us," she heard a woman's voice say, though to anyone else's ears it would have sounded like a rough *cruck, cruck, cruck, cruck*. Another pane smashed. The raven began to grow in size and morph into another shape as it cawed.

A living chimera now stood on the other side of the door, a creature with the head of a woman, her blonde hair long and flowing, and wings where arms should have been. She stood balanced on one foot. The other dark, scaly appendage reached in through the broken pane, flipped up the lock with its talons, and drew the door open.

Evangeline was repulsed and attracted in equal measure. These witches had killed her father. Left her alone in the world. Still she couldn't deny that their magic spoke to hers.

"You're not welcome here," Evangeline called out, walking like a somnambulist over shards and splinters of glass, a quarter pane snapping into smaller fragments beneath her heel.

She'd caught sight of her mother's sister witches, sometimes as women, sometimes in avian form, a few times over the years, but they'd always kept their distance, never approaching her, never speaking to her directly. She might have chalked up their occasional visits to bland curiosity, if she hadn't always sensed them trying her magic, sipping at it as a chef might sample a soup for readiness.

"Imagine," the chimera said, then turned back to address someone beyond Evangeline's field of vision, "her mother's own dear sisters not welcome." Evangeline watched as the wings transformed into pale arms, the claws below wriggled and then changed into normal human feet. Those feet turned away and disappeared into the garden. *Marceline*, the witch's name came to her.

"That's her daddy's doing," another voice said.

Evangeline stood at the door, doing her best to muster her courage. As she suspected, there were two others in the garden, the witches Margot and Mathilde. Somehow she could tell which was which, even in bird form, as surely as if she were looking on their human faces.

She had first learned their human features from an old daguerreotype her father had forced her to study—a precaution so she'd recognize them. That's how little he'd understood these witches. He may have known the names that went with the faces in those pictures, certain details Evangeline's mother had shared with him when the marriage had been new and happy, but he'd been completely ignorant of their magic. The very thing he feared. Bird form or human form, Evangeline needed no photo to identify them. She could feel their magic, savage and seductive, buzzing in her veins.

"You aren't my mother's sisters. Not by blood," she said, hoping she sounded unafraid, maybe even confident in her ability to protect herself. Despite her own protest, a part of her thought of these gruesome strangers as her mother's true sisters. Her own aunts. The pull of their shared magic made it seem somehow true.

The creature who'd broken the panes now stood at the edge of the brickwork garden, a full-fledged woman deadheading a potted plant. Marceline glanced back over her bare shoulder, smiling at Evangeline. "Blood may be sticky, but it makes a poor glue. We shared a stronger bond, your mother and we."

"You killed my father."

Marceline gave a slight shrug. "Your father needed killing."

Evangeline had a flash of her father, red-faced with fury, eyes bloodshot from drink, the day he had caught her working magic, a magic Evangeline hadn't even known she possessed. His rough hands had nearly choked her as he forced the ugly pendant her mother had worn until the day she died around Evangeline's neck. She could still feel the way the medallion had burned into her skin, glowing as it drained the magic from her. Her hand wrapped around her throat, halfway expecting to find the damned necklace still there. Like she'd never escaped its grasp, like she'd never escaped him. Evangeline felt only the pulse in her neck, a physical reminder to stay in the present, to face the danger currently before her. She took a step backward.

"And worse," came two caws from a large, though by all appearances natural black bird, its wing outstretched. It bent its head in toward the wing and started preening. This creature was Evangeline's mother's eldest "sister," Mathilde, though when it came to these witches, age was counted not in years, but in centuries. If what her father had told her was true, these women had been around to witness Andrew Jackson's defeat of the British navy.

"You'll forgive me, child," the second voice she'd heard spoke again. Its owner, Margot, crouched low, her arms spread out and feathered like wings, though ending in hand-like tips—trapped, it seemed, between human and avian forms. "Changing doesn't come as easily to me as it once did."

Margot forced herself up onto her somewhat human legs, then reached out and took Evangeline's hand, her grasp too strong to escape, and led her over the threshold into the tiny courtyard.

"She made that medallion, our Mireille," Marceline said, less reading Evangeline's thoughts than walking her back into the memory, reliving it with her. "Forged it herself, then let him place it around her neck on their wedding day. Only death . . . only death could release the clasp."

Evangeline remembered the night drive home with her father from the storefront meeting house he called a church. The sight of her father's weathered Bible on the seat between them. The rawness of her skin, chafed and red from three days of wearing her mother's heirloom. The rain was falling so hard Evangeline could no longer tell if a road still ran beneath the shroud of water. She remembered the sound of the windshield splintering as something hit it and rebounded off the car's hood. Her dad slammed on the brakes, and the pickup spun to face the opposite direction, the Bible flying from the seat down to his feet. The engine stalled, and her dad shifted to park. He looked at her, his eyes glassy with fear and drink. Evangeline leaned over to look through the passenger seat window. She could see nothing. Not an animal. Not a person. But instinct told her that whatever they had hit had been large.

She expected her father to get out of the truck to see what or whom they'd hit. But he didn't. Instead, he cranked the keys in the ignition again and again as the engine gurgled and sputtered, only to die a final death.

He grabbed the door handle, cursing, and nearly fell to the ground when the door opened. Once he found his footing, he walked around to the front of the truck, the headlights illuminating him as he strutted in one direction and then turned, though his image was obscured by the heavy rain and the cracked windshield and the building steam of Evangeline's own breath. He grasped his head between his hands, seemingly puzzled, before lowering them and peering up. Evangeline leaned forward and wiped the condensation from the windshield with her sleeve. At that exact moment, something large and black, blacker than the night itself, swooped down and lifted him, his scream lessening in volume as the distance between them grew. She sat there in shock, listening to her own throbbing heart. The next instant Evangeline caught a glimpse of her father falling through the headlight beams, followed by a wet popping sound as his body struck the pavement.

She couldn't remember what happened after that. She had screamed, she reckoned. She must have screamed. She wanted to scream now at the memory.

All she knew was when she came to, wandering dazed along the road, it was dawn, the rain had ended, and the necklace had disappeared.

"Why have you come?" Evangeline said, her voice coming out as a shout. Never, not once on any of their visits, including the one that had ended in her father's death, had they deigned to talk to her. She tugged her arm, once, twice. Finally her hand slipped from Margot's, though Margot's sharp nails left claw marks on her. She grasped the wounded hand with the other, pulling it to her chest.

Marceline drew near and held out her own hand. "May I?" she said. She placed her fingers, now very human looking, on the wrist of the scratched hand. Though Evangeline was shaking, she allowed her visitor to take her hand. Marceline waved her free hand over the deep scratches, the gesture erasing any evidence they'd ever been made. "There now, that's better, isn't it?"

"Why are you here?" Evangeline repeated herself, though this time her anxiety had faded. A part of her mind warned her that the witches were working against her, using their powers to make her more amenable to suggestion. She envisioned a curtain rising up around her, blocking them off, and as the curtain rose, she sensed their influence lessening. In a few moments, she felt more in control of her own thoughts, of her own emotions. Still, a tiny voice warned her, that very sensation might be an illusion. Perhaps they were letting her believe she had regained control. She allowed the curtain of energy to drop around her, and it blew outward, pushing her aunts back, their feet dragging along the stone pavers, tiny sparks shooting up from the points of contact.

"Very good, *ma chérie*," Marceline said, a sparkle of true pride in her eyes. "Your mother would have been proud."

"Don't lie to the child," Margot said. "She knows the truth well enough. Mireille would have been horrified."

"Thanks to the poison *he* put in her head," Mathilde cawed again from ground level.

Evangeline knew her parents' story all too well. How the swamp witch had fallen for the handsome preacher. How that love hadn't lasted long enough. How fear and loathing had set in. But by then, it had been too late—Evangeline's mother had the magical noose of her own making tied around her neck, and a child on the way.

"I don't want to discuss her," Evangeline said. "Not with you."

"If not with us, with whom?" Mathilde cawed.

"Enough history," Marceline said, again seeming to walk through Evangeline's thoughts. She leaned in, as though testing the viscosity of the air between them, then took a step closer. "We've come to offer you a proposition. A business proposition.

"We believe," she added, speaking up over Mathilde's croaking, "that Celestin Marin's death has created an opportunity, and you are in a unique position to help us—all of us, yourself included—profit from that opportunity."

"An opportunity for what?"

"To lay claim to something that, by rights, should have been ours long ago."

"The book," Mathilde said, or perhaps "The Book," for the reverent way the creature cawed the words was surely deserving of a capital letter. "*The Book of the Unwinding*."

Evangeline couldn't help herself. She started laughing. "You've got to be kidding me. It doesn't exist." These fool women thought she could help them get their claws into a fabled grimoire, a guidebook for the final days of magic. According to the myths, the witch who held the book would, in the end, control the last breath of magic and determine what was to come next. "*The Book of the Unwinding* is a fairy tale."

"It's no fairy tale. It's the reason we came to this country," Marceline said, her focus softening as if she were remembering younger, if not kinder, years. "We carried it here, the three of us and your mother, to this city, to the ends of the earth, to the convent they built here to contain it."

"The Ursuline Convent—" Evangeline began.

"You've never wondered"—Margot cut her off—"why the attic is fixed shut with nails blessed by the pope himself? What did you think they were keeping up there? Did you believe the stories about vampires?" She began cackling with laughter. Mathilde's black beak cracked open with raucous caws.

Marceline, cool as she appeared always to be, held up her hands, a signal for her sisters to calm themselves. "Those stories were created to frighten away the curious. Long ago. No one imagined we'd ever live in an age perverse enough that common men would run toward monsters." She held out her hand, offering it to Evangeline. Despite herself, whether it was her aunt's compelling magic or just her own desire for a sense of connection, Evangeline took it. She felt Marceline's hand tremble as it held hers, and then her aunt's ice-blue eyes widened in hopeful surprise. A smile rose to her lips. "You may not ever come to trust us. Not fully. But you must believe three things." She tightened her grasp on Evangeline's hand. "The Book is real. The Book has fallen into the wrong hands. And," she said, looking deep into Evangeline's eyes, "without your help, magic will be lost. Forever."

Evangeline yanked back her hand and burst out laughing. "And just exactly how do you think I can help you in your mission to save the fairies and unicorns?"

"Your lover's daughter, Alice," Margot said, moving toward her. "So fragile, really. So vulnerable. She'll need someone to watch over her."

Evangeline held out her hand, signaling the witch to come no closer. "Your concern for Alice is . . . unnerving."

"Oh, dear, you may take me at my word," Margot said. "We mean her no harm. None whatsoever." The words started in high singsong and ended in a croak, Margot already shifting back into avian form. "Just the opposite, in fact. She is very important to someone very important to us."

"I'm sure Nicholas will see to her well-being."

"Will he?" Mathilde said, focusing on a bug walking along the edge of the tile. "Like he did with his elder son?" She pecked down and bit into the insect.

"Yes," Margot added. "What was his name again?"

Evangeline refused to give her the satisfaction of a response.

"All we ask," Marceline said, again in that maddening voice of calm reason, "is that you find a way to watch over her, to protect her. I sense you have a maternal nature. We're only asking you to do something that comes to you naturally."

"Just keep an eye on her?" Evangeline hated that they'd gotten through to her, that the reminder of Luc's demise was enough to make her question if Alice might, indeed, need protection from her own father.

"Yes. Waking. Sleeping. Keep vigil over her."

"And just how do you suppose I do this?"

"Follow your heart. I'm sure you'll find a way." Marceline's human form fell away as if it were a burst balloon, and she reappeared as a raven already in midflight. A mad flapping of wings filled the small courtyard, and the three sisters were gone.

Evangeline turned to find Sugar standing on the threshold, winking one eye up at the sky. Suddenly aware of the broken glass, she scooped the cat up then carried her back into the kitchen.

The cat squirmed in her arms, freeing herself to perform a corkscrew leap that ended with a graceful landing on the counter.

"All right," Evangeline said, staring into the cat's intense eyes. "What do you think?" The cat sat perfectly still, like an alabaster statue of the goddess Bast, but her mind was churning. "Well, no. I don't understand either, but yes, I do think we should do something . . ."

*Guard. Watch. Protect.* Evangeline could hear the cat's mind struggling to express an unpracticed concept. *Man not man, smells of thunder.* The words came in a jumble. Sugar hissed at her own thought.

Evangeline's mind flashed to embroidered suspenders and ginger hair. "Of course," she said, reaching out and patting down the cat's bristling fur. "Daniel."

# NINE

An alarm sounded, and the machine rumbled to life. Alice watched as the mouth in the wall flicked its flayed black tongue and spat out first one case, then another, the carousel catching each and carrying them along, nearly identical bags festooned with only slightly less similar ribbons. Those standing around her—the strangers to whose destinies a common destination had, for the last few hours, bound her own—dove like hawks at the looping belt.

She was *home*, if New Orleans could still be called her home, but even the airport felt like a hostile, alien world. Her own magic prickled her skin—an odd, unfamiliar sensation after years of being cut off from it. The temptation to use it, to try even the smallest act, was seductive, but she feared the magic even more than she was drawn to it.

She had concluded years ago it was her use of power that somehow summoned Babau Jean.

It was a matter of simple deduction, really. She'd first encountered him after she'd nearly exhausted herself helping the coven divert the hurricane. In the months she and Hugo had subsequently spent at Aunt Fleur's house, they'd been forbidden to use magic—Fleur's husband found sorcery disconcerting, at least when it didn't directly benefit him. The entire time, there had been no sign of Babau Jean.

When she and Hugo had returned home—and returned also to magic—the bogey had resurfaced.

On Sinclair, where her magic had been denied to her, the demon had haunted her dreams, but here, in New Orleans, he had touched her. In the flesh. He had killed someone dear to her. Maybe she would have been better off, maybe they all would, if Vincent had left her on Sinclair . . .

The belt came to a screeching stop, and a collective groan rose up. Half the flight still stood vigil for their belongings, and the sighs and grumbles and muttered curses reminded Alice that she was not, as yet, home. Even here, surrounded by a group of impatient, foul-mouthed bridesmaids bedecked in matching and grammatically incorrect "Laissez Les Bon Temps Roulez" T-shirts and out-of-season Mardi Gras beads, she hadn't moved past that liminal space between where a traveler has been and where she's going. It served as a mundane metaphor, she decided, for the vegetative state her grandfather Celestin had lingered in for over eight years, with only a feeding tube and respirator anchoring him physically to this world.

Where had his spirit been while his body lay moldering in a private hospital? Had it been aware and trapped there in a moribund cell? On another plane? Perhaps it had been free to wander . . . Had he haunted as a ghost even before his body had finally given way? She shook her head to clear the thoughts, refocusing her mind on finishing the last leg of her trek.

She'd spoken to her uncle from the Portland airport. He'd promised to arrange for a driver to meet her here. Alice looked up, casting an eye over the car service employees, who held either paper signs or electronic pads displaying their intended passengers' names. Her shoulders dropped; none of those signs read "Marin." Vincent had most likely gotten distracted, wrapped up in the arrangements for her grandfather's memorial. Celestin would be going out in fine witch style—the typical period of mourning culminating in a grand witches' ball. A real one like New Orleans hadn't seen since before Alice was born.

The funeral itself was to be a New Orleans–style funeral with music serenading her grandfather's remains on the way to Précieux Sang Cemetery, and a second line joining in on the procession back to the funeral home. These "jazz funerals" were rare and usually reserved for actual musicians, but there could be nothing less, she reckoned, for the former head of the city's once most influential coven.

The flash of a memory struck her—she and her grandfather playing hide and seek among the tombs at Précieux Sang, the very cemetery where he was to be laid to rest in the family's oven-vault tomb—the area's renowned method of above-ground burial—which already held generations of Marins. Luc, too, must have been entombed there. Had his dry bones already been shifted to the *caveau*, the catch space at the bottom of the vault, to make room for the new resident?

Alice sensed a shadow.

"It is you, isn't it?" a reedy voice said. Alice felt an icy hand touch her wrist, and she turned to see a well-preserved woman whom she felt she should recognize, though she couldn't imagine why. It was almost as if her assailant—her subconscious fed her the word—were attempting to impress a feeling of familiarity upon her, to imprint a memory in her mind.

Of course. A witch. Welcome to New Orleans.

While Alice knew firsthand that witches lived everywhere, "The City That Care Forgot" enjoyed a greater concentration of magic workers than statistics would claim its general population should support.

"Delphine," the woman said, staring deeply into her eyes, her smile a tad too manic to instill the sense of ease she'd probably intended it to. For an instant, Delphine's image jerked and splintered, like a lost connection on a video call, and Alice caught sight of the ancient crone hiding behind a wall of cosmetic magic, her skin like fine vellum stretched tight. In the blink of an eye, the spell reassembled itself, its weaver seemingly unaware that it had, even for a split second, failed.

"Delphine Brodeur," the witch added her family name, very nearly jarring loose a true memory. The fragile voice, the icy touch—the witch couldn't hide these proofs of age, but to the naked eye she appeared at most a third—Alice estimated—her actual age. "I'm sorry, it's foolish of me to expect you to know who I am. I only recognized you because you bear such a striking resemblance to your mother." She paused, making a show of surveying Alice from head to toe. "Of course you don't have Astrid's coloring, but your features, my dear—you are your mother made over." Alice felt a jolt of pride mixed with shame. Her mother had been a beautiful woman, but everyone knew she'd deserted her family to take the Dreaming Road. The Brodeur woman, perhaps picking up on Alice's ambivalence regarding her mother, rushed on. "I'm a longtime friend of your grandfather . . . well, of your entire family, really."

"When last I saw you, you were . . ." She held her hand level perhaps three feet from the floor, allowing a more polished smile to finish her thought. "I sensed another . . . well, one of us, on the flight, but these days impressions are so vague, and your emotions didn't betray you." Alice said nothing. "It's only I would've expected to sense a stronger feeling of . . . bereavement." The statement, made with a calculated finesse, was intended to evoke a sense of guilt on Alice's part.

"Celestin," Alice said, choosing to use her grandfather's given name, "and I weren't estranged, but I haven't seen him since I was, well . . ." Alice flattened her hand and mimicked Delphine's earlier gesture. "And he's been incapacitated for so long. I have some good memories of my grandfather, but I mourned him years ago. His burial just feels like a formality," she said, turning inward, feeling ashamed in spite of herself. "Maybe when I lay eyes on the body . . ." Alice's words deserted her. She was struck by how easily this woman was working her emotions. Delphine had an agenda, but Alice couldn't imagine what it was.

"Of course, I didn't mean to be critical," Delphine lied. She tilted her head, reaching up to brush her dark bangs from her eyes. Like an act of sideshow prestidigitation, an imitation of regret appeared in Delphine's eyes as the hand passed before them. "Oh, look at me. I meant in fact to be of comfort, and I've come at it all wrong." Alice doubted if this woman ever made a false step. "It's only that I cut my own travels short so that I could attend Celestin's funeral—and the ball, of course. There was a time that we were close, your grandfather and I. Very close." She paused, a coy smile rising on her lips. "I don't mean to imply romantically, of course." Her tone and expression telegraphed the opposite sense of her words.

"He was so dedicated to your grandmother, after all. No, there were many women," her voice lowered, "witch and civilian, who hoped to fill the void in his heart after Laure's . . ."—she pretended to reach for the word—"'confinement,' but he remained loyal to her till her death. Your grandfather wasn't ever one to let go." She paused, her lips pursing. "Certainly he never let go of that grudge he held against the Perrault family. Blamed them, he did, for what happened to Laure." Her gaze lowered and took on a faraway, contemplative air. "But then Alcide lost his wife, too. Didn't he?" She looked up, curiosity playing in her eyes. "We never did learn what the two of them were up to, your grandmother and Soulange, to land the one in an institution and the other in her grave."

Another short burst of the buzzer and the belt lurched back to life, more suitcases spewing through the opening. A pale blue one caught Alice's eye, reminiscent of the one she'd packed as a child, intent on saving her treasures from Katrina, but it wasn't hers. "Would you mind"—Delphine wagged a finger at the very case that had attracted her attention—"grabbing that one for me? It isn't very heavy, but I'm so graceless at times." Alice nodded, sure that Delphine would topple over onto the belt if she tried to retrieve the luggage.

93

Alice reached out and clasped the case's handle, surprised by its weight when it tugged her forward. She caught the handle in both hands and gave a hard yank. It jumped off the belt and landed with a thud by her feet.

Delphine laughed at her struggle. "I'm sorry, *ma chère*. Perhaps I overestimated your strength." She leaned in, placing her glacial hand over Alice's own, still wrapped around the sturdy plastic handle. Alice released the case, recoiling from Delphine's touch, though the woman showed no sign of offense, or even that she'd perceived Alice's distaste. "Or perhaps I underestimated the weight of those bricks I packed in here."

She pulled her phone out of an expensive-looking clutch, glancing down at the screen. "I'm having to rely on a service, as my regular chauffeur is driving me to fire him." She smirked at the pun.

She winked at Alice, though the humor fled her face as she pursed her lips and turned her face toward the wall of liveried chauffeurs. Tell me, dear," she said, squinting. "Are any of those fellows looking for me?"

"Yes," Alice said, spotting the name Brodeur scrawled on a small dry-erase board. "That gentleman, there." She motioned in the driver's direction.

"A gentleman, you say?" Delphine's eyes twinkled with mischief. "What a shame." She raised her hand, waving the driver forward, then dropped her phone back into her bag.

He ambled in their direction, no sense of urgency in his pace. "Ma'am," he said, addressing the Brodeur woman. "Miss," he said with a slow nod to Alice. His large, pale hand caught hold of the blue case.

"We're not together," Alice hastened to say.

"But we may as well be. How do you plan to get home? May I offer you a lift?" She turned to the driver. "You can handle two women at once, can't you?" she said with a flirtatious toss of her hair.

He didn't rise to take the bait. "Same address, same price."

Alice noticed her own suitcase being pulled off the belt by a worker who then set it aside with the other unclaimed baggage. "That one's mine," she said, using the case as an excuse to pull away. "Thank you," she said, glancing back over her shoulder, "but I don't want to delay you."

"It's no bother, dear." Again she felt Delphine's cold, surprisingly steely grip. Alice turned back. "It would give us a chance to speak with greater privacy." She paused. "There's a matter I'd like to discuss with you." And now for the agenda. Alice jerked her arm away, no longer in the least worried about risking offense.

Delphine cast a wary glance at the driver. "Would you mind giving us a moment?"

"Of course," he said, nodding toward the exit. "I'll be waiting for you by that door." He seemed relieved to have been given permission to retreat. He scooped up the case as if it were filled with air and turned away. Delphine let a few moments pass, watching her chauffeur's retreating back, then turned to face Alice.

"It was really rather serendipitous, our meeting here," Delphine said. The crone took a step toward her, slicing away at the space Alice had managed to put between them. "I would have looked you up." She tilted her head, rounding her eyes in a parody of sorrow. "Some days after the funeral, of course, but before you skitter away again."

"I don't think . . ."

"It's a business proposition, really," Delphine cut her off. "Regarding your inheritance." Her face hardened; her eyes narrowed. "I'm speaking specifically, of course, of your relic."

"Oh, God," Alice pulled back. "I'm sure my family won't observe that hideous custom." A piece of dried flesh, an organ, a bit of bone. Parts of a witch that still held magic after death, at least until the ritual of dissipation that returned any residual magic to the realm from which it sprang. A Hand of Glory, a real one from a witch, not just a counterfeit one obtained by temporarily charging a hand amputated from an executed convict, had long commanded fortunes from non-witches. Alice had heard from others at Sinclair that now even witches were relying on relics and other forms of necromancy to bolster their failing powers, but this was the first time she'd ever been confronted with it.

"Oh, my dear. Everyone does it these days. Your grandfather certainly would," Delphine said, then smirked. "Your grandfather certainly did. You're going to find that he quite literally hid a few skeletons in his closet." She shook her head, her mien one of bewildered amusement. "Just look at the horror on your face. What good is it to let all that power go to waste, when there are so many in need? Think of it as recycling."

"No."

"You've been raised to get along without magic," Delphine insisted, refusing to accept Alice's response. "It would mean nothing to you, but to me it could prove invaluable."

"No," Alice repeated, moving to step around Delphine, but even as the witch's glamour flickered once again, revealing the crone underneath, she moved to block Alice's steps.

"You're being selfish." Her face flashed red as desperation turned to anger. Whether it was due to her age, her supposedly fragile mental state, or her sex—or perhaps all of those things—Alice intuited that the Brodeur woman had judged her to be the easiest touch in the family. Or maybe she'd already failed with the others? "Besides, I'm sure your father has been snipping off bits and pieces for years now. Pieces not noticed by the casual observer." A look of cruel glee rose in Delphine's eyes. "Remove the corpse's shoes. Pull off his socks. See if the old man has even a pinkie toe left to him. No, I bet your father has been at it for years." She held out her hand, her first and middle finger mimicking scissor blades. "This little piggy went to market." She brought the blades together. "Snip. This little piggy went to town." Again. "Snip."

Alice looked on in horror as the camouflaged hag carried on making cuts in the air and cackling. Those lingering in the area turned at the sound. Alice had never actually heard a witch's full-throated cackle before. It was this black-hearted screech that earned witches a bad reputation. For the first time it struck Alice that perhaps her father hadn't just cast her aside. Perhaps he'd been trying to protect her.

"There she is."

Alice turned at the sound of her Uncle Vincent's voice. He stood there, his black eyes sparkling. Vincent Marin couldn't have looked anything less like the typical depiction of a witch. He wore old blue jeans, battered flat-bottom boots, and a short-sleeved blue plaid shirt. A royal-blue ball cap covered his thick salt-and-pepper hair. He held one arm out to the side, an invitation for her to hurry into its crook, which she gladly accepted.

"Sorry, I meant to be here to catch you coming through security." His steely arm pulled her in, and she pressed her face against his chest. Of course, Uncle Vincent had come to see her home. He hadn't forgotten her after all. She could count on her fingers the number of times she'd seen her father since he'd sent her away. It was Vincent who visited, who video chatted with her at least once a week. Who had purchased her freedom.

"You're looking well, Delphine," Uncle Vincent said. When Alice glanced over her shoulder, she saw the older woman's face had transformed to a mask of beatific kindness. She turned back to look her uncle in the eye—and was happy for the glint of mischievousness she saw there. "See you again soon, Delphine." He released Alice from his embrace, but only after the older woman had begun making her way to the exit. "What was she after this time?"

A wave of exhaustion caught up with Alice. The evening ferry from the island, the ride to the airport, a late flight—they called it a "red eye"—to Charlotte, a transfer from Charlotte to New Orleans. An evil sorceress out to purchase her grandfather's bones. "A relic," she said and shuddered at the thought.

"Not surprised. Celestin Marin is dead, so the buzzards were bound to start circling." The corner of his mouth curled up. "You know they call a group of buzzards a 'wake.'" His half-hearted smile flatlined. "Fitting, 'cause we're heading to Celestin's wake, and you're going to get to lay your sweet eyes on the fattest buzzards of them all." He glanced down at his watch. "But first, you should brace yourself." He gave her a wink. "Fleur's asked me to collect your cousin Lucy, too. She should be landing any moment now."

# TEN

Cardboard boxes lined the back wall. The boxes contained salvageable stock. Items that hadn't been shattered or tattered or urinated on.

Two large gray garbage cans sat in the middle of the room, ready to be emptied into the bed of Isadore's pickup. Was gonna take six, maybe seven trips to the Gentilly dump before the mess got cleared out, and they were only just getting started.

It was hotter than hell, and Remy's tuneless whistling was starting to work her very last nerve. Lisette had shut off the air-conditioning since the window where her mother had painstakingly drawn the vèvès was now nothing more than a gaping hole with only a single pane, the upper right, still clinging to the remnants of its casing. No use trying to cool the whole of Chartres Street. Sweat dripped down her brow, and she wiped it away with the back of her glove.

Amidst the chaos of sorting and dumping, Lisette had managed to find a few silent moments, when Isadore was at the hardware store, when Manon was hovering by the counter of the corner café trying to charm a fellow who had no more interest in her than a frog has in spit curls, before Remy rolled out of bed and meandered—boy had too much of his grandfather Alcide in him for his own good—his way to the shop. In those moments, she had stood in the center of the damage, calling to her mother with a broken voice. There had been no response. There, in the silence, a sense of loss as deep and dark as what she'd experienced the day they found her mama's body out on Grunch Road had knocked her to her knees. Knocked her down so hard, she could barely breathe.

More than two decades after Lisette's mother's death, she finally seemed gone.

Vèvè was born on July fourth, 1976. Lisette had been small—four, going on five. They'd driven up, her mother and she, to City Park to pick up the keys from the building's owner, an elderly white man with a bent back and watery blue eyes, in a starched white shirt and wide red tie. Blond children—his grandchildren, Lisette now reckoned—had swarmed around him, calling for his attention, begging for coins to buy sno-balls from a passing vendor. The old man had been put out, Lisette remembered, about having to attend to business on the holiday, on a Sunday, no less. He'd dropped a few choice words in her mother's ear as his mottled hand dropped a large round ring with two keys into her hand.

Her mother had thanked the old man, apologized for interrupting his family picnic, and handed over the money order covering the first three month's rent. Then she'd announced, brooking no argument, that the money order was short for the three days she had been promised, but not granted, access. Lisette remembered it like it had happened yesterday—the tone in her mother's voice, the look in the old man's eyes. The building had changed hands a few times over the years, passing into the ownership of a limited liability acronym in 2008. Still, every time Lisette wrote the rent check, her imagination lent the old man's features to the faceless corporation.

Lisette didn't remember what type of business had been in the space before it became Vèvè. Maybe she'd never known. But the built-in shelving that framed the shop's tight aisles had already been in place. As soon as her mother unlocked the door, Lisette had burst in, running in wild circles through the aisles, slapping the shelves as she passed them. She'd kept this up until her frenetic activity had gotten the best of her mama's nerves, and then she'd been ordered to sit on a wooden footstool in the corner. Her mama had quizzed her on the loa—their likes and dislikes, their domains and how to seek their favor—as she set into those shelving units with lemon oil and soft cloths, polishing them until they glowed in the late-afternoon light.

Three of those shelves had now been utterly destroyed. Sledgehammered, or maybe just kicked, into kindling. Dark rectangles on the floor testified to where they'd once stood. Isadore and his employee, Santos, one of the Honduran guys who'd come to the city after Katrina and put down roots, had already carted the remains of two of them off in his truck to the dump in Gentilly. The third was still scattered, part of it filling one of the gray cans, the rest of it strewn across the floor.

Remy hunched over the second can, fishing through its contents, digging out shards of glass that had once been panes in the front window. He was placing some of the larger pieces, ones that still showed identifiable bits of vèvès, into a plastic tub she used to mix up the contents of the premade gris-gris bags.

"You be careful not to cut yourself," Lisette said. Remy was eighteen now. By legal standards a man, but she couldn't help but see him as her boy. Maybe she always would. "Last thing I need right now is to have to rush you off to emergency."

"Not gonna cut myself, Mama," he said, glancing up at her with the smile he'd been using to get out of trouble since he took his first step. Boy had the damned prettiest lashes she'd ever seen on a man. Pretty black eyes, too. Eyes he got from Alcide. He lowered a bit of glass into the tub, then ran his finger through his thick hair. Those dark curls were a gift from Alcide, too, and God knew he'd also gotten his way with women from his grandfather. Lisette's mother had always said she was probably the only woman who could've saved Alcide from himself. Seemed she was right: no other woman could compare to Soulange Simeon for the former Casanova. After losing her mother, Alcide had clung to his late wife's memory rather than remarrying.

Now Lisette looked at her own son, wondering if there was a young woman out there who'd be capable of doing the same for him. God knows, there seemed to be plenty of girls who wanted to try. Women loved artists. Had mad affairs with them. But then they'd go and marry the orthodontist instead. At least the smart ones would.

Isadore's truck pulled up in front of the shop. In place of the broken wood he'd hauled away, the back was stacked with sheets of plywood. He walked into the shop, then bit his tongue when he saw Remy digging through the trash cans. Isadore looked over at Lisette. She shrugged. There was nothing they could say now about their son that they hadn't been saying to each other since he was four. He was a good kid. A real good kid. Just hard to get focused.

Isadore turned and studied the opening where the windows had been. Loko's vèvè, the sole survivor, cast a shadow on his face, a fitting mark—Lisette decided, for a certified master arborist and owner of the city's most in-demand landscaping company. "Can you save that one?" she said.

"Of course," Isadore said, coming up and planting a kiss on her forehead. He nodded at Santos, who slid a ladder close to the opening and began to work the pane from its casing. He worked it side to side, with great care, until it slipped free. He handed it down to Isadore, who carried it over to Lisette.

"Maybe we can reuse it?"

"Maybe, but not likely," he said, stroking her arm in comfort. "The new window, it'll look like the old one, like it has separate panes, but it's gonna come as a single piece."

"I'll frame it then," she said and held it up toward the light flooding in through the opening. Seeing it as it had been, one last time. She lowered it and carried it behind the counter. She wrapped it up in the Bubble Wrap she used when fulfilling mail orders, then slid it into her purse.

"We're going to board the hole up now," Isadore said, leaning over the counter. He stood and patted Remy on the back, a silent signal to assist.

Lisette nodded, then turned and watched as Isadore and Remy held the first board in place so Santos could drill it into the wall. The scream of a drill filled the air as it sent screws chewing through wood, the wood blotting out the sun in revenge for its wounds. It all seemed terribly familiar somehow, like when they were preparing for Katrina, though now the boards weren't there to prevent damage, but rather to cover damage that had already been done. The men would cover the door next. Its safety glass hadn't been broken, but was filled with cracks and fissures. It, too, would have to be replaced.

A humming sound sent her gaze up to the overhead lights. She drew a breath and waited for Isadore and Santos to tackle the door, but to her surprise she heard the truck start up. She crossed to the door just in time to see it pull away. She could see the back of Remy's head between her husband's and Santos's. The three of them had taken off without even a word.

Across the way, Lisette caught sight of a new arrival, a woman a less critical eye might consider beautiful, but even from a distance, Lisette could read an odd mixture of entitlement and desperation in her features. She was of a certain age, although her hairstyle, with its thick, dark bangs falling almost to her eyes, suggested that she hoped to pass for younger.

The woman stood across Chartres, staring at the shop, her face partially obscured by shadow. She cast a glance to the right, then stepped into the street, coming toward Lisette. A brief shimmer, perhaps a prism of light caused by cracks in the safety glass, caught Lisette's eye. For an instant, the woman's face seemed transformed—her skin appearing so dry, so taut, that she put Lisette in mind of the mummy exhibit the art museum had hosted back before Katrina, when Manon was still small and fascinated by all things Egyptian.

The bells on the cathedral began ringing out the hour as Lisette opened the door, and the bell that still hung over the door joined the chorus—a discordant and drowned-out alert that was forgotten as the new arrival stepped over the threshold. Her presence filled the room as if she were its only rightful inhabitant.

"We're not open . . . ," Lisette began.

"Good afternoon," the woman said, tilting her head and brushing back her bangs. A coquettish gesture, which Lisette found charming in spite of the fact that she found no charm whatsoever in coquettishness. "Well, no," she said, "what a foolish thing to say." The woman's apologetic smile fell flat as she surveyed the wreckage. "I'm so sorry," she said.

"You're not to blame," Lisette heard herself saying, an automatic response that she felt she should make, that she wanted to make. Lisette struggled to understand the source of her visitor's charisma.

The woman shook her head. "What a terrible world we live in." She crossed behind Lisette, going over to examine the boxes lined up against the wall. "I've just purchased this building. Yesterday, as a matter of fact." She looked back and offered Lisette a benevolent smile. "I suppose that makes me your new landlady." Her eyes ran over the boxes of goods, then scanned the damage done to both Lisette's wares and the space itself. "Sentiment aside," she said, "how much is this all worth? Your entire stock? Any fixtures you personally own?" She looked back over her shoulder at Lisette. "Everything on display and anything else you might have set aside for the more, shall we say, discerning customer."

Lisette shook her head, half trying to clear it, half to signal her confusion. "I'm sorry. I don't understand."

"Then let me make myself clear, *ma chère*. How much would it take to get you to walk out of here right now with nothing but the clothes you are wearing and the shoes on your feet? To turn everything here over to me en bloc?"

"Even the mess?" Lisette said with a chuckle. Her eyes took the same path the woman's had, over the shop's few remaining goods, over the piles of broken merchandise, over the desecrated remains of her once cherished personal possessions—items she'd always sworn were not and never would be for sale.

"Even the mess," the woman said, her tone firm as she emphasized each word. She pointed down to the dark rectangles on the floor that marked the destroyed shelves' former positions. "I see something has already been taken," she said, crossing the floor and holding her hand out over the empty spaces. "The missing shelves don't matter to me, but not another splinter, not another shard should be removed."

Isadore understood Lisette's ambivalence toward this place. He'd told her countless times that if she wasn't happy, she should let go of Vèvè, sell the business, maybe even just shutter the doors and walk away. They could get by on his earnings. The thought had tempted her, even deeply once or twice, but with Manon finishing her business degree and Remy starting college this fall, intent on an MFA, she knew it would be a tight stretch without her income. At least that's the lie she had always told herself. Now she knew it was because it was here at Vèvè that she still felt connected to her mother. A connection that appeared to be broken.

What was the store worth if her mother had been banished from it? This strange woman was offering to take the burden off her hands— even the cleanup—despite Lisette having two years left on the latest three-year lease. Certainly the contract would've been transferred as part of any sale. It had always happened that way in the past. Lisette's common sense told her it made no sense. And then it did. "Ah, you just want us out of here." She thought of the "Go Back to Africa" message she'd spent the morning cleaning off the door, a door that was going to have to be replaced anyway. "Maybe Vèvè is gonna be a bit too much trouble for you. Gonna rent this space out to some nice dress shop, run by some nice white lady."

The woman stood taller and pulled her shoulders back, the picture of affront. "Oh, no. You couldn't be more wrong."

"Then why would you want it?" Even disregarding the damage done to Vèvè, there were at least four other shops like hers in the French Quarter's seventy-something square blocks, most of them clustered around its center of Orleans Street. And as much as it piqued Lisette's pride, even before the vandalism, her shop wasn't the Quarter's best—not by a long shot—though she remembered a time, back when it was under her mother's direction, when Vèvè had been the Vieux Carré's finest.

"Oh, my dear," the woman said, seeming to pluck Lisette's thoughts right from her mind, "it was a different time. You cannot blame yourself. The magic business just isn't what it used to be." Her tone carried an undercurrent of quiet sardonicism that Lisette intuited wasn't really aimed at her. "It's doubtful if Soulange could have held on any better than you have." Lisette noticed a tinge of reverence in the way the woman said her mother's name. This was, she sensed, a true believer. "But it's time you let go. Turn all of this"—she motioned around them, her shoulders drooping as if weighed down by the burden of what she witnessed there—"over to responsible hands. Someone who understands the true value of your mother's work. You've carried the weight of it long enough."

A glare—the sun reflecting off a passing auto? the flash of a tourist's camera?—caused Lisette's vision to blur. She reached up to rub her eyes, and as she pulled away her hand, she again witnessed a flash of taut dry skin, eyes sunk deep in cadaverous sockets, cheeks drawn in where teeth were missing. But Lisette's mind insisted it was only a trick of the light, and her eyes capitulated to this explanation. The next instant, the illusion resolved into the woman's utterly normal and arguably lovely features.

The woman seemed unaware of Lisette's momentary confusion, as she had turned her attention to digging something out of her alligator-skin clutch bag—a purse Lisette realized was worth multiples of her entire stock before the break-in, perhaps even as much as the balance remaining on her home's mortgage. "Really, my dear, just name your price," the woman said, producing a leather-covered checkbook. She reached in again and found an expensive-looking pen. She tilted her head and waited in silence for Lisette to respond. Lisette tried to focus, but her eyes kept returning to the bag's diamond-encrusted handle. A smile formed on the woman's lips. "Lovely, isn't it?" she said, holding it out for her to examine. "If we can come to terms on your establishment quickly, I'll toss it into the deal. A *petit* lagniappe, if you will."

The woman slipped the bag beneath her arm and turned her attention to filling out the check, squinting a bit as she wrote. She capped her pen, then bent the check back, tearing it from the book in a single precise movement. She held the inscribed check out for Lisette's inspection. Lisette's eyes darted from her own name on the "pay to the order of" line to the numerical representation of the amount being offered. She blinked. Five hundred thousand dollars. She nearly bowled backward at the sight.

"I'm sure," the woman said, tucking both pen and checkbook back into her bag, "you'll agree it's a generous offer. But I was an . . . admirer of your mother. She once helped me when no one else could. I feel I owe it to her to make sure you and yours are well taken care of." She reached out and grasped Lisette's hand. Her flesh felt cool, dry, paper thin. Lisette fought the urge to pull away, her mind flashing back to the image of that skeletal face the light had tricked her into seeing. "I can't truthfully say I was your mother's friend, but I would like to try to be yours."

Lisette stared at her, tongue-tied.

"Why don't you sleep on it?" the woman said. She tendered the check to Lisette. "Show this to your husband. Discuss it." She paused, a twinkle in her eye. "Put it under your pillow and see what sweet dreams may come." Lisette accepted the check from the woman's outstretched hand. "Just remember. This is for the whole kit and caboodle. Damaged or no. Not even an unbent paper clip should be missing from the inventory. Do you understand, *ma chère?*"

"Yes," Lisette said, even though she didn't understand a damn thing other than that this woman seemed to have far more money than sense. She nodded. "I do."

"Good," the woman said, a broad smile on her face. "Then I'll come back tomorrow . . . early . . . shall we say eight . . . for your decision." She turned and went to the exit, the bell sounding again as she opened the door. She cast a glance back over her shoulder at Lisette. "*À demain,*" she said and closed the door behind her.

"Everything that gives, takes," Lisette heard her mother's words once again, only this time it was she herself who had spoken them.

Lisette's eyes dropped to the check that she was now clutching with both hands. Written there on the signature line, in a measured, old-style French script, Lisette read the name Delphine Brodeur.

# ELEVEN

Lucy acquiesced to a quick squeeze from Vincent before offering Alice a cool "Is that all you brought?" It took Alice a moment to realize her cousin was referring to the small, black, wheeled bag Dr. Woodard had provided for her trip.

"Oh," Alice said, feeling her cheeks flush. The small case didn't just hold her clothes. It held every personal possession she'd been allowed to keep as an inmate at Sinclair. Half her life fit in that bag.

She was a good four years older than Lucy, but she felt so unsophisticated standing before her cousin. The younger girl towered over her, thanks to purple suede platform sandals, their gold piping glinting even in the artificial light. Alice caught a glimpse of red on the inside of the tall heel. Lucy wore a long-sleeved minidress in muted gold with a brocade top and mock neckline. The pleated skirt kicked up a bit with each self-assured step. Alice couldn't help but glance down at her own scuffed black flats, jeans, and deep-V T-shirt. The damned peacoat folded over her arm. She was certain her entire outfit cost multiples less than one of her cousin's shoes. "I'm only here for a few days . . . ," she said, embarrassed and trying to explain away the size of the suitcase.

"Then back to the loony bin?"

"No . . . ," Alice began. Vincent had promised to help get her established, here or anywhere she chose. Only she didn't know what she wanted. Now that she finally had her freedom, she found it vaguely terrifying. She had reason to believe she'd have some resources coming to her from Celestin's estate. But how far would that uncertain inheritance and the GED she'd picked up on Sinclair carry her? Would her father accept her if she decided she wanted to stay in New Orleans?

"Lucy," Vincent snapped at the girl, her name becoming a rebuke and a warning in two short, sharp syllables.

Lucy shrugged and tossed her straight blonde hair. She focused on Vincent, her face the picture of innocence. "You're the one who's always complaining that the family keeps too many secrets. That we never discuss things openly . . ."

"There's a difference . . ."

"Oh, please. Hypocrite much?" She turned to Alice. "See? Awkwardness over. We're already halfway to becoming best friends."

It struck Alice that Lucy was being sincere in spite of her abrasive manner. Lucy's eyes widened, and she growled in exasperation as she pulled her cell phone out of her purse, tapped the screen with an imperial-blue nail, and pressed the screen to her ear. "Yes, Mother. I am here." She lowered the phone and took an angry swipe at it. "That woman. She *knows* I'm here."

Lucy leaned toward Alice. "We have that pain-in-the-you-know-what witch mother-daughter psychic bonding thing, you know?" Her face went blank. "Or maybe you don't." She paused, seeming to consider the gravity of her faux pas, then raised her eyebrows. "Whoops. Sorry. More awkward. Thought we were done with that. Oh," she said on the heels of a sudden buzzing noise, pointing over Vincent's shoulder at one of the conveyor belts. "Those are mine." Four good-sized metal cases—titanium by the look of them—slid out onto the far belt. Lucy turned, scanning the people around them. "Where's the driver . . . ?"

Vincent smiled and bowed.

Lucy closed her eyes and sighed. "Tell me you didn't drive that old blue truck. I don't want my luggage being tossed around in the back like a pack of bucktoothed bayou hounds." She tossed a quick glance at Alice, then turned back to Vincent. "Does the azure embarrassment even have three seat belts?"

"Relax," Vincent said. "I left Bonny Blue at home." He smiled at Alice. "I brought my new toy."

"Will the glories of this day never cease?" Lucy said, crossing to the belt and smiling at a couple of awkward-looking young men who were busy shrugging on large, full backpacks. She pointed at her own cases looping back around. "Could you?" she said, her voice carrying like a stage whisper. As the guys stumbled over each other to catch the cases, she turned back to Alice, driving her unspoken point home by raising her eyebrows. Her expression collapsed into the most grateful of smiles as the young men set the cases at her feet. She called out to Vincent. "We're not far, are we?" But before Vincent could speak, she turned to the men. "You wouldn't mind, would you?" The two cast wary glances at each other, but Lucy reached up and grasped the nearest's bicep. "They're just stuffed full of clothes we're donating to charity. You know the one that helps unemployed single mothers find jobs?"

"Uh. Sure." The one she'd touched answered for his friend.

"You. Are. The. Best." She emphasized each word. Lucy leaned in and gave a little squeal and an even smaller squeeze. "You two go on," she said, releasing the volunteer, then patting him on the back. She waved at Vincent and Alice. "We'll catch up with you over there at the exit. My uncle can't walk too quickly." The men divvied up the cases, each taking one per hand, and began strolling to the door.

"You're going to hell," Vincent whispered as he and Alice drew near Lucy.

"Maybe, but not any time soon. Besides, I wasn't even really lying, just anticipating a future truth. Mother always gives my old clothes to that charity. Ridiculous, really," Lucy said, focusing on Alice. "I mean can you imagine wearing Chanel to interview for a job as a receptionist?" Her eyes drifted to the help she'd recruited—the two guys already growing impatient by the door. She waved at them. "But its goal appeals to people across the political spectrum, and Mother is nothing if not politically savvy." She wrapped her arm through Vincent's. "And you do like to work that leisurely Southern mosey of yours," she said, tugging him along. She looked back over her shoulder at Alice, who followed behind, dragging along her single case. "Coming?"

The highway from the airport dispirited Alice. Ugly, utilitarian. Billboards and office parks. Oversize department stores peeking around concrete sound barriers. It was ridiculous, of course, but she'd expected that somehow New Orleans would know her, that she'd feel a connection to the city—a welcoming—the second her feet touched earth. Instead, it was as if Alice and the city were facing off, each fixing the other with the same distrustful stare.

They rode along in Vincent's new toy. "A 1969 Boss 429," he'd said with pride in response to an inquiry from Lucy's ersatz porters.

"Yeah. Nice muscle," Lucy had said and rolled her eyes. Now she sat in the back seat, tapping away at her phone's screen. "Don't worry," she suddenly said. "It's like this everywhere. No matter what city you're traveling to, the airport road is the same." She'd only offered a few words since their departure from the airport, each a separate complaint, so it surprised Alice to hear her speak—even more so because she'd seemed to read her thoughts. She leaned forward between them. "Am I right?"

Vincent responded with a nod. A smile formed on his face as the road bent south, cutting through a cluster of cemeteries. "Feel a bit more like home now?" Right and left, there were mausoleums, miniature mansions, architectural revivals to hold the dead—Greek, Gothic, a peppering of Romanesque, a handful borrowing from ancient Egypt. Angels weeping, angels praying, angels ready to take flight. Pillars and crosses. Somewhere within, though it wasn't visible from the road, she remembered petting a statue of a faithful dog.

"Still not feeling it?" he said, turning to see her face. She shook her head. "Roll down your window."

"Or how about we don't?" Lucy protested.

"Just do it." Alice hoped to please them both by finding a compromise. She grabbed the crank and rolled the window down an inch or so. "All the way," her uncle insisted. Wind began to whip through the cabin, tousling Alice's hair. It felt wonderful, though Lucy didn't seem to appreciate the sensation.

"I am going to kill you both," Lucy shouted at them, leaning up between their seats.

"Shaking in my boots," he said, then reached over his shoulder with his left hand and nudged her back with two fingers pressed to her forehead. "What do you smell?" he said, barely audible over the rushing wind. "Close your eyes and breathe." He glanced at Lucy in the rearview mirror. "Hey, back there. You, too. What do you smell?"

Alice did as he told them to, though she doubted her cousin was playing along.

"Gas fumes," Lucy said.

"Beneath the fumes."

"Cheap fast food."

"Breakfast. Sorry. I was in a hurry to pick you two up. Go beneath that."

She chuckled. "Your awful cologne."

"Hey, watch it. I'm not wearing cologne. That's my natural musk."

"You should start wearing cologne," Alice dared. Her cousin burst into laughter, and when Alice winked open one eye to look at them, she caught Vincent sticking out his tongue at her. Lucy's eyes were closed.

"No. Really. Go deeper."

Alice relaxed and breathed deeply. And there it was. A kind of bass note scent. Sharp, hot, moist, green. Her eyes popped open.

"That's the smell of Mother Nature," Vincent said, his face beaming. "Waiting on the edge of New Orleans. Reminding us that our grant on this crescent of earth isn't permanent, and that she has plans to reclaim it." He paused. "Telling me that the only place on earth I belong is a place where no man in his right mind should be. It's in my blood, *ma chère*." He winked at her. "And like it or not, it's in your blood, too."

Alice expected a quick comeback from Lucy. It surprised her to see her cousin staring out the back window at the passing scenery, a look of yearning in her eye. Lucy sensed the weight of Alice's stare, and their eyes locked—but only for a moment. "Whatever," the younger girl said and turned her attention back to her phone. "Can we kill the wind tunnel now?" She made an impatient cranking motion with her hand. "The window?"

Alice nodded and rolled it up. She gazed out and tried to focus on the sights, but her thoughts kept returning to that horrible Brodeur woman. "Are we getting to that point? That we're dismembering our dead to distill an ounce of magic from their bones?"

Lucy sighed. "Really, must we?"

"Getting to that point?" Uncle Vincent said, ignoring Lucy, talking over her, not taking his eyes off the road. "No, my dear niece, we are at the point where such behavior, behavior we would've considered grotesque even a decade ago, has become the *norm*. Your father, he's been arguing with the rest of the coven over just that. He wants to entomb Celestin intact, but it seems that everyone wants their pound of flesh. And in this case I mean it literally. We've been taking turns sitting with the body, two at a time, your father, Fleur—she's here for real," he said, looking back at Lucy, "and she's in a real sour mood, so brace yourself"—he focused back on the road—"and I. But mostly Nicholas. He's doing his best to hold the ghouls at bay."

Alice felt sure her father's main interest in the matter was to avoid establishing a precedent. He was looking forward, to the day of his own interment. Alice felt a flash of guilt when she realized that she, too, was *looking forward* to that day.

"Nothing"—Vincent rolled down the window and spat—"like sitting through your own father's embalming, watching lifelong friends line up like vampires—like leeches—to get their share of his life's blood." He rolled up the window. "That was the compromise we came to with the coven."

Alice felt queasy. She reached out and turned up a vent so the air-conditioning blew in her face. The cool air alleviated her nausea somewhat, but she could still taste bile. "Would you?" she said. "Would you take a piece of Grandfather to augment your own magic?"

Vincent shook his head. "Me? No, *chérie*, I wouldn't. But I never had much power to begin with. I had to learn long ago how to make do without it. Not a drop of magic went toward building my business. Not a drop ever will. And this fine physique you're looking at?" He took his right hand off the wheel and patted his hard stomach. "What I didn't earn at a jobsite, I earned in the gym. A lot of witches, they never worked for a damned thing in their lives." He looked into the rearview and allowed a long enough pause for Lucy to reach up and slap his shoulder. "And now a lot of witches are losing their damned minds. Some of the smaller covens have lost members. And the solitaries, too—a number of them have," he hesitated, "gone, too." *Lost* and *gone* were vague words, but he didn't need to be more specific. Alice understood by his hesitancy alone that he meant these despondent witches had either committed suicide or packed up whatever magic they had left them and taken to the Dreaming Road, the place between dreaming and death that had long since claimed her mother.

"Me," he said with a glance in her direction, "if tomorrow's the day the last of magic dries up and disappears—well, on my own, I might not even notice."

Alice averted her eyes as they drew near the Superdome. She'd watched the old newsclips, seen the documentaries. The first night—the night Katrina passed over the city—she'd been safe, protected by a dome of magic that as a child she'd taken for granted as her birthright. But she was no longer a child. She'd read firsthand accounts of those who'd come to the arena seeking shelter and found themselves trapped in septic conditions. The number burgeoning from fifteen to thirty thousand people without food, without water, without functioning restroom facilities. No air-conditioning. No lights. Afraid of your neighbor. More afraid of the men who'd been tasked with maintaining order and the guns they carried. She'd read about it. She'd watched the news reports. But she hadn't experienced it, so there was no way she could truly understand. Alice didn't turn away out of horror, or out of respect for the thousands the storm had left dead and displaced, she turned away in shame.

"You shouldn't have left the city," Lucy said, surprising Alice by giving voice to her own thought. "When the city needed magic most, the witches all packed up and left."

Alice turned back and forced herself to focus on the arena, the sun lending a soft glow to its pale-bronze aluminum skin.

"Not all of us did, kiddo," Vincent said. He shifted gears and sped up, aiming the car toward the Carondelet Street exit.

"Maybe you didn't, but the others, like Father . . . ," Alice began.

"Yeah, your dad left, but only long enough to get you and Hugo settled at Fleur's. No, *ma chérie*, you two might be right about many of the witches in this town"—he reached over and tapped the tip of Alice's nose—"but you're wrong about your own family. Nicholas and

I. Your grandfather. Hell, even Luc. We were all right here, doing what little we could with what little we had left. I got to tell you," he said, shaking his head, "for a while after the storm, magic was mostly gone. It was like trying to strike a wet match. Me, I was good. I was used to making do without. But dear God, your grandfather"—he chuckled at the memory—"he was fit to be tied. Damned near apoplectic at points. Luc and Nicholas, they ended up having to work together for a while to raise a spark." He raised his eyebrows, shrugged his shoulders, and sighed. "I thought it would be good for them, maybe even help Luc work through some of his anger." He bit his lip, shook his head. "But I was wrong. If anything, forcing those two to cooperate was like tying two tigers together by the tail. It just got worse every day." He looked over at her. "You never spoke to Nicholas about any of this?"

"No," she said, slumping down in her seat. "Listen to you. Now you're talking like Father is some kind of saint." She didn't want to discuss her father's abandonment in front of Lucy. At least not before she could press him for answers herself. But still, hearing Vincent defend him felt like another betrayal.

"Oh, no. He's a total asshat, but he's my brother, so I can say that," he said as he downshifted and made a quick turn onto Calliope. His mouth pulled into a tight pucker. He reached over and grabbed Alice's hand, giving it a tight squeeze. It felt like an apology. Alice squeezed back.

He tapped the brake, then swung onto St. Charles. "But no matter what you know, or what you *think* you know, he's your father. Like it or not—admit it or not—how you see him affects how you view yourself. He's sure as hell not perfect, but for your own sake, you need to look for things in him you can love, things you can respect. And Nicholas Marin did not desert New Orleans. That's thing to respect number one." He held up a hand toward the street before them. "*Mesdames et Messieurs*, well, *Mam'selles* . . . I give you the world-famous St. Charles Avenue."

# TWELVE

Evangeline stood at Nicholas's door, glancing around, tossing a cautious look at the sky, eying even every damn squirrel with suspicion—who knew what forms the sisters might take next? She had no idea what her mother's sister witches were capable of. It struck her that she really had no idea what she herself was capable of either.

It was broad daylight, and she was hardly a stranger. But she still felt as if she shouldn't be here. At least not behind Nicholas's back. It felt like breaking and entering, and she had more than a little experience with the art of breaking and entering, so she should know.

She pressed the doorbell a second time, digging her feet into the welcome mat. She heard a muffled voice, intuition more than her ears telling her that the word she heard was "coming." Another moment, and the door opened.

"Oh," Daniel said, his mouth hanging open in surprise, "Ms. Caissy. Were you expected?"

Evangeline, too, felt surprised. She recognized the once familiar servitor spirit, but he had changed. The goofy hat and soiled floral suspenders were gone. He wore a trim-fitting plaid shirt, mostly blue with orange and white accents, paired with faded straight-leg jeans. His deep red hair looked as if it had been cropped short on the sides, though the top was just long enough to curl. He looked like just about any of the twenty-something guys wandering along Frenchmen Street might.

"Nicholas isn't at home," he offered in the face of her stunned silence.

"No," Evangeline said. "I knew that . . ."

He stood there, one eyebrow rising above the other, a confused smile surfacing on his lips. It was really, really hard sometimes to remember Daniel wasn't a real person, and that he never had been.

"Actually, I've come to see you," she said. "May I come in?"

"Of course," he stepped back and opened the door wide. "It's been . . . well, goodness, it's so hard to keep track of things on your time. I'm guessing two years?"

Evangeline did the math in her mind. It had been more than two years since she'd last visited Nicholas's house, even though it was an easy walk from her place to Bayou St. John. She had a brief flash of the argument that had led to her storming out of here. A stupid fight, really. At least on the surface. She'd suggested moving a couple of pieces of furniture. "Don't get too comfortable around here," Nicholas had said in reply. In return, she had reminded him just how hot a Cajun temper burns.

They'd made their peace over it. At least on the surface.

But her heart and her pride had both been bruised, and it had been enough to keep her away. The man and his damned walls. She felt herself starting to get pissed off all over again, just remembering.

Evangeline loved Nicholas. She did. Seemed most of the time, though, that she did more in spite of the man he showed himself to be than because of it.

She and Nicholas met occasionally at her house, but they more often chose neutral territory. Nicholas kept a condo in the French

Quarter for visitors he didn't necessarily want under his own roof. Most of the time, they went there.

*Visitors he didn't necessarily want . . .* And there it was again, that tiny, nagging voice telling her that Nicholas didn't really love her. That he loved the convenience of her. That he was wasting her life. That *she* was wasting her life. That it was way past time for them to move forward together or go their separate ways. That voice had been whispering in the back of her mind for at least five years, but now it was practically barking at her.

Daniel seemed to read something on her face—or maybe in her aura. Nicholas and Astrid had given him the ability to read auras so he could better understand when his charges were sick, or fibbing, or planning mischief. "But it is such a pleasure to see you again now." He offered Evangeline his hand and she took it. It felt so solid, so warm. And was that a pulse beneath his skin?

Evangeline offered him a sincere smile. "Thank you," she said, as he released her. "I guess this must be a rare occurrence for you—receiving a visitor of your own?"

He tilted his head, again seemingly confused, but then a look of childish excitement rose in his eyes. "Not anymore. Hugo gave me this Christmas last, or was it the one before that?" he said, pulling a smartphone from his pocket. He tapped the screen and held it out so she could examine the latest dating app. "Swipe left, swipe right?" He turned it back around and gazed down at the torso showing in the photo. "With abs like that," he said with a wink, "methinks we shall swipe right." He dragged his finger over the glass and then slipped the phone back into his pocket. He paused as if remembering something. "Not that it isn't special to receive a visit from you." He smiled. "How may I be of service?"

Evangeline felt her tongue poke out to lick her lip. This was her tell, Nicholas had taught her, the indication that she was about to tell a lie.

Instead, she shook her head. "I'm sorry, I shouldn't have come. I'm not even really sure why I'm here."

"Well, I don't share that problem. At least I didn't use to. I've grown more sympathetic with that particular quandary since my return."

"No," she said, "I don't mean in the grand scheme, I just mean *here* . . . to see you."

"Oh," he said, his voice smooth, unoffended. "Then if you don't mind"—he pressed his hands together as if in prayer—"I'm a bit preoccupied myself." His face began to beam. "Alice is coming home today"—he gestured down the hall—"and I'm a bit busy in the kitchen." The light in his eyes faded. "You know Nicholas is not the most effusive of men. I'm not sure what kind of welcome she'll receive from her father, so I thought perhaps a few treats . . ." A line of concern formed between his eyes. "Well, I just want my girl to know someone here is happy she is home."

Without thinking, Evangeline reached out and placed her hand on Daniel's shoulder. This man. This spirit. This magic trick with a pleasant attitude. No matter what he was—or wasn't—in actuality, it was clear he did love Alice. Perhaps more than even her own parents did. Yes. It was worrisome that she was acting on a request made by the sisters, but what harm could it do to speak to Daniel about keeping a special eye out for the girl?

"Alice's return was the reason I came to see you."

His look combined mistrust and hope. "You shouldn't worry that her return will upset the applecart between you and Nicholas. He's never been an attentive father, and I fear her visit may be quite short."

"No, no," Evangeline said, squeezing his shoulder, rock-hard muscle. It would seem Hugo had made a few modifications to things other than Daniel's wardrobe. "It's nothing like that," she said. "I want to make sure Alice's visit is successful. I'd like to see her come home. For good."

Daniel's slight pout flashed into a wide smile. "Follow through with me, please?" he said, turning and heading down the hall toward the kitchen. As Evangeline followed him, she caught the scents of vanilla and caramelized sugar in the air, though it struck her there was something else, too. Something she had sensed before in Daniel's presence, but hadn't really taken the time to consider. A trace of ozone, or was it petrichor? Sugar's image of "man not man, smells of thunder" struck her as an apt description for Daniel.

He raised his head then dashed into the kitchen, leaving the door flapping behind him. Evangeline pushed in to find him rescuing a batch of cookies from the oven. "Just made it," he said, using a spatula to slip the cookies onto a cooling rack. "Butterscotch chip," he said, then his forehead wrinkled. "I hope she still likes them."

"I'm sure she will," Evangeline said, coming closer and examining at least a dozen different varieties he'd already prepared, "or one of the score of others."

He shrugged, his face flushing. "I don't sleep. And Nicholas didn't come home last night, so . . ."

"It's a lovely gesture. I'm sure she'll be thrilled."

He pulled out a stool by the island. "Please, have a seat."

She did as he asked.

"May I get you something to drink? Coffee? Tea?" He held up a finger and turned, pacing over to the enormous stainless-steel standing freezer. He pulled out a vodka Evangeline quickly recognized by the graceful, almost feminine curve of the bottle's shoulder. "Hugo dropped by last night and deposited this here before slipping off to who knows where." He held the bottle up. "Would you like some? Or maybe you'd like to sample some of my baking?"

Evangeline started to refuse, but then remembered the day she'd been having—no to the line of credit, yes to an unkindness of ravens. "Yes," she said.

He raised an eyebrow. "Vodka? Cookies?"

"Both." She pointed at the plate of oatmeal raisin. "One of those, please. Alice never liked raisins."

Daniel's face pulled a tiny frown. "No. Of course she didn't." He slapped his forehead, seeming angry with himself. "I should've remembered." He grabbed the plate and strode toward the garbage can, then he put his foot on the pedal to open its lid.

"Hold on," Evangeline held up a hand in protest. "You set that plate right by me. I love raisins. And I'll take the rest back to the club. They'll be gone in no time."

He looked down at the plate as if the cookies themselves had betrayed him, but he did as she asked. "I should've remembered," he said. Even as he talked, he worked, filling a shot glass with ice-cold vodka.

"It's been a long time. Besides, I suspect she disliked them more on principal than due to the actual taste. Tastes change. *People* change. You need to prepare yourself for that. There may be very little left of the girl you knew." She bit into the lovely, still-warm cookie and washed it down with a sip of the alcohol. "But it's okay if she's changed. After all, you've changed."

"Well, yes," he said. "I have changed. That's the greatest advantage to learning everything you've ever believed about yourself to be a lie. If you survive the learning, it means you get to make whatever you would like of yourself." Evangeline held her tongue, unsure of how much Daniel had discovered about his true nature over the years.

"You needn't worry," he said, intuiting her line of thinking. "I know. I've had more than a few people tell me I'm not the real thing, but you know what?" he said. She felt sure the question was rhetorical. He refilled her glass, then poured one for himself. "I'm still here anyway." He held up the shot glass, and she clinked her own against it, then set hers down on the counter.

"I still can't leave the house. Oh, sure, I can venture out into the yard, but if I try to go any farther than the end of the walk, the next instant I'm snapped right back here. I don't even sense it coming. One moment, I'm heading toward the waterway, and the next I'm standing in the foyer, the closed door behind me." He shrugged. "Anyway, here I stand. No children to look after, and all the time in the world on my hands. So I started watching those cooking videos on the Internet. I've always had some basic skills, but I'd like to believe I've now become a very good cook. I can't really taste what I make, you know, I can only determine if it's safe for human consumption. But the dish always comes out looking like it does in the video, and I haven't managed to poison Hugo or his father yet." He looked at her through narrowed eyes. "Although the way they go after each other sometimes, I cannot say I haven't been tempted."

"You've developed a wicked streak, you," Evangeline said, prompting a smile.

"I'll take that as a compliment." He held up a finger, as if he'd just flashed on something. "Speaking of wicked, how is the Pewter Devil?" He reached over and plucked a strand of Sugar's fur from her shirt.

Evangeline laughed and took another sip. "She's as cranky as ever," she said and wagged a finger in his face, "but I love her, so watch what you say." He held up both hands in mock surrender. "Actually it was her idea for me to pay you a visit."

He took the glass from her hand and emptied it into the sink. "Sorry, but when a patron tells me her cat sent her, it's time to cut her off."

She could tell he was half joking—but only half. "Said the man who never was," she said.

"Touché," he said, though he didn't return her glass. "Have another cookie."

She leaned into the counter, wondering if her next question might offend him, if it were even possible to offend him. Perhaps Nicholas and Astrid hadn't built him that way. "How did you manage to return?"

"There was no 'manage' to it. I was here. Then I wasn't. Then I was. It was disconcerting at first."

"It took a while, though, right? It wasn't really a clean transition."

"Well, no. It actually took quite a long time. I've been here, fully realized for . . ." He squinted. "There's that troublesome time thing again. I've been back three years, though Hugo told me that he first noticed me 'lurking,' as he likes to say, as far back as eight years ago. He said I'd pop in, then fade out as quickly as I appeared, though I must admit I don't remember any of it. That's why I asked that Alice not be told that I was back. Until she needed to know. I'm still not sure I have my grapple planted firmly in this world."

"Eight years ago."

"Yes, around the time Celestin took his bad turn." He looked down at her. "The thought crossed my mind, too. That maybe he was giving me a boost of some kind, though I can't imagine how or why. I hadn't actually laid eyes on him since Mrs. Marin . . ." He cut himself short. "Nicholas bristles when I call her that. I'm to speak of her as Astrid, though he'd rather I'd not mention her at all." He gave a slight shrug. "Anyway, I hadn't seen Celestin since Astrid left us."

"The thing is"—Evangeline's thought was forming as she spoke it—maybe it was good Daniel had taken her glass after all—"and I don't mean to demean you in any way, but all over witches are yapping about magic disappearing. How is it that you just pop back into place . . . better, stronger even than you were before?"

"Don't think I haven't had the same thoughts," he said, seeming to grow excited, coming and sitting beside her. "I've tried to discuss them with Nicholas, but he always gives me a pat on the back and a 'Just happy you're here with me, old boy, and did you put starch in my underwear?'" He laughed. "Just between you and me, I might've done that once, but I was a bit out of practice with laundry, you know." He shrugged. "And when was the last time you tried to have a serious conversation with Hugo?"

Evangeline nodded. "Last night, in fact, but I know what you mean." She slipped another cookie off the plate and broke it in half, handing the smaller piece to Daniel. "So I guess you have a theory or two."

He stared at the cookie like it was an alien object, then popped it in his mouth. It struck her that she'd already forgotten he wasn't "real," and he either appreciated her forgetfulness, or he just didn't want to embarrass her. "I do," he said, a boyish grin appearing on his lips, "but one of them is about you."

"About me?"

"Yes. Although I guess it's less of a theory, and more of an observation."

"And what might that be?"

"Your magic hasn't faded." He shook his head when she opened her mouth to refute it, her reaction automatic. "No, don't bother to deny it. I can see it on you. Your aura, it's matured. The colors bleed more easily into each other now than they used to. You used to be much more careful, even punctilious . . ."

"I had to survive . . ."

"Oh, please, no. Don't think I'm judging you. I liked you then. I like you now." He gave a slight shrug and a chipper smile. "Like you said. People change, and that's okay." She hated having her own cheerful words turned back on her. "But"—he held up his hand and wiggled his fingers at her—"the sparks emanating from you are still the same colors: ice blue,"—he moved his hand to the left—"aqua, and I'm going to call those fuchsia, no cerise." He shook his head. "Anyway, they're the same colors, and they burn just as brightly as they did, back . . . well, way back when. You haven't lost any of your magic."

His eyes scanned her again, and she knew that he was still studying her aura. She felt a subtle tickle, a bit like walking through a spiderweb. Her hand rose, an involuntary motion, to brush the sensation away, but it lingered. "Graying, graying . . . ," he said. "Ah, you want to keep this fact a secret." His eyes widened just a bit as his head tilted. "You *have* kept it a secret. Even from Nicholas." The bright smile returned to his face. "Not to worry. Your secret is safe with me. I'm sure you have your reasons.

"So here I am," he said, "and there you are. And neither of us should be . . . at least not as we are."

Evangeline suddenly regretted the loss of her vodka.

"I've come," he said, "to think of magic like an animal's circulatory system. If a vein is blocked, old ones can be forced to carry more blood, and sometimes new veins are formed. I'm not sure *magic* is failing so much as the system that carries it." He pushed up from his stool. "May I show you something?"

"Of course," she said.

"I'll be right back," he said and hurried from the room. He mustn't have gone far, for he slipped back through the door within seconds. In his hand he held a thin, red, leather-bound book. He lay a towel down on the counter before her and sat the book on it, then offered her a pair of purple rubber gloves. She looked at him for a moment, uncertain. The book must be from Nicholas's private collection. At least, expensive; at most, priceless. And Nicholas was always so careful . . .

"Not allergic to latex, are you?"

"Maybe I shouldn't," she said. "This looks really old, and I don't want to risk harming it."

"Oh, no," Daniel said, shaking the gloves at her. "These aren't to protect the book. They're to protect you."

She looked up at him, pointing down at the thin volume. "What is this?"

"This," he said, tugging one of the gloves onto her hand, "is *The Lesser Key of Darkness*, and my intuition tells me it has something to do with me." His eyes widened, taking her in as if a light bulb had just flickered on in his head. "Something to do with the both of us, really. It's just hit me your visit today may be more than just a pleasant surprise."

# THIRTEEN

At first Alice noticed nothing but rundown buildings and fast-food restaurants, but soon the completely unromantic stretch began to give way. The steeple of a quaint white church rose up above the neighboring dry cleaner like a flower breaking through concrete. She remembered being driven along this road in the back of her grandfather's limo—how he would point at each of the street names and teach her about the Greek Muses from whom those names had been borrowed. He'd once made the driver take a detour to show her the stump of Urania Street, cut short by Felicity so that it didn't intersect with St. Charles like the streets named after Urania's sisters. "*Méfie-toi*," he'd said, shaking his finger playfully in her face, "*de ceux qui sont trop heureux.*"

"Beware those who are too happy," Vincent said as they crossed Felicity, speaking in English, but mimicking her grandfather's tone to perfection.

"How did you know . . . ," Alice began.

"Oh, please," Vincent said, "the old man said it damned near every time we drove through here. Good thing, too. Turns out the ladies," he cast her a sideways glance, "love a man who can tell his Clio from his Terpsichore."

Alice could practically hear her cousin's eyes roll.

"So you remember him?" Lucy said.

"Yes, bits and pieces. I used to spend every Sunday afternoon with him," Alice said, her mind drifting back to the clearest of her memories of the man. His soft, cold hand running over a skinned knee, healing it in an instant. "He was good to me."

Beautiful, older homes repurposed as storefronts began popping up between the newer construction. An odd building reminiscent of the Eiffel Tower loomed on the left-hand side of the street. A streetcar, painted a deep olive green and trimmed in a rusty red, rumbled up alongside them. She had ridden the St. Charles line with her grandfather a handful of times, more as a source of entertainment than for transportation. Most times they took the line down to Canal Street, then caught the same car back.

As the named streets gave way to the numbered, Vincent pointed back over his shoulder with a raised thumb. "Remember? Celestin's house is back that way, a couple of blocks riverside."

"Why can't you people just say north or south like everyone else in the normal world?" Lucy complained.

Alice smiled. She remembered. "It's because of the river," she said. "Lakeside" and "riverside" replaced the regular cardinal directions in those parts of the city where the bends of the Mississippi River rendered compass bearings useless. "Yes," Alice said, nodding to her uncle, "I remember. The house, at least. The general direction." She scanned the road for familiar landmarks. A thought surfaced. "I loved that house. It seemed so mysterious to me as a child." She shifted her gaze back to Vincent. "There's even a secret passage between Grandfather's bureau and the card room."

"Yeah, not so secret. The gap between the panels is like a mile wide," Lucy said, unimpressed.

Alice shrugged. "Whenever we played hide-and-seek, I hid there. And he always pretended to forget the passage was there."

"Lucy's right," Vincent said. "You can spot the panel that leads to that passage from across the room. Your dad's house, on the other hand, has a priest hole that got added when the city fell under American control. There was worry we'd face persecution from the Protestants. That priest hole is a work of art . . . and that's coming from a builder. If I wanted to hide something I didn't want anyone stumbling over, that's the first place I'd go." He shook his head and laughed. "I'm still trying to wrap my head around the fact that you played games . . . honest-to-God games . . . with Celestin." He seemed pleased by the thought.

"My only memory of him is being bounced on his knee," Lucy said, her tone bitter. "Happy, happy, sunshine. Right?" Alice and Vincent's eyes met in the rearview mirror as they looked back at Lucy, who stared at Alice through narrowed eyes. "Listen, I hate to disabuse you of any golden memories, but while Grandfather may have enjoyed playing *bon-papa*, he treated my mom like he owned her." Lucy sat slumped in her seat, glowering. "Don't pretend he treated you or Nicholas any better," she said accusingly, eyes now fixed on Vincent.

"No," Vincent said. "It isn't that. It's just for a second there you almost sounded like you care about Fleur."

"Yeah, well, let's keep that our little secret, okay?" She leaned forward and caught Alice's upper arm. "My parents' marriage was arranged, you know? Mom wasn't given a lot of choice in the matter, 'cause good old Granddad had ambitions of turning her into the next Jackie Kennedy. Minus the grassy knoll experience, of course. Fleur Marin Endicott. First Lady. Most men dream of their sons becoming president, but considering what Celestin had to work with . . ." She released her grip and slid back. "No offense, Uncle Vincent."

"None taken, Bad Seed."

"Yeah, cute," Lucy said. She grabbed the seat and pulled herself forward again, poking her head between them. "Are my parents getting divorced?"

"Why would you think that?"

"Well for starters, the senator," Lucy turned to Alice. "My mother always calls my dad 'the senator.' Sometimes even when she's talking to me. So weird, I know." Her gaze shifted to the side of Vincent's head. "'The senator' has remained in D.C. He isn't coming. Said Mother told him it wasn't necessary. Make of that what you will, but now with Celestin gone . . . well, let's just say when Fleur Marin promised 'till death do us part,' I don't think she was talking about her own or Dad's."

Alice wondered at the nonchalant way Lucy spoke of the dissolution of her parents' marriage.

"Come on." Lucy reached forward and slapped Vincent's shoulder. "If I'm right, I'm sure you know something."

"I know that Fleur has asked me to bring her a list of the city's best interior decorators." He offered the information in a cautious tone. "Seems that your mother's decided the family manse needs a little freshening up. Damn." Vincent said and swung right without signaling. "Sorry. That's where gossiping will get you. Almost missed the turn."

Alice didn't catch the street name, but they slowed as the car approached an impressive white Victorian with a single turret that rose above the gray mansard roof. The structure struck Alice as being everything a mortuary should be—the house's corners were edged with quoins, but its façade was otherwise void of any gingerbread or Eastlake ornamentation. The house was Second Empire, she guessed.

She realized just how many hours she'd spent in the library.

"Here we are," Vincent said, parking on the street rather than in the circular drive before the house.

Alice climbed out of the car and approached the building, wandering a bit to the side, where she caught sight of a double porch, supported by what appeared to be simplified Egyptian-style papyrus columns. Considering ancient Egypt's obsession with the funerary arts, the columns seemed a bit too on the nose for a mortuary, but this could be considered the architect's sole misstep. She looked back over her shoulder to find Vincent and Lucy staring at her in bafflement.

"Are you coming?" Vincent said, gesturing to the house next door—a simple, two-story, redbrick Colonial.

"Uh, yeah," she said, casting one more confused glance at the Victorian before rushing to catch up with her uncle at the Colonial's door.

Vincent pressed the doorbell, but Alice heard no sound in response. Lucy reached out to press it again, but he caught her hand. "It's silent. A little light flashes to tell 'em someone's at the door." Alice raised an eyebrow in question. "So the bell won't disturb the mourners."

A sense of surrealism fell on Alice as it struck her that the word "mourner" now applied to *her*.

The door eased open, and a slim, delicate man, shorter than Alice, greeted them. His porcelain skin was in stark contrast to his lusterless jet-black hair and his English-cut suit of the same severe color. An incongruous horseshoe mustache dominated his face. "Yes, Mr. Marin, welcome." The man's eyes fell on Alice, and he gave her a curt bow. "The Misses Marin and Endicott, I presume." He stepped back to allow their entrance.

"Yeah, Frank, this is my niece, Alice," Vincent said, placing his hand on her shoulder. "Nicholas's daughter." He paused. "The other one is Fleur's fault." Lucy pulled a face, but held her tongue. Alice could sense her cousin was uneasy in this place of death.

The mortician acknowledged Vincent's joke with a slight, noncommittal nod before shifting his focus to the girls. "So sorry to make your acquaintance under these sad circumstances," he said.

"Like he'd make my acquaintance under any other circumstance," Lucy muttered under her breath. Her harshness no doubt stemmed from her discomfort, but still Alice blanched with embarrassment.

If Frank heard Lucy, he chose to ignore her snide remark. He closed the door behind them, then turned. "Please follow me," he said, beckoning them with a cool smile and an outstretched hand, the fingers closing one by one onto the palm. As he led them down the hall, Vincent turned to wink at Alice and mimicked Frank's hand gesture.

"You're terrible," she mouthed, and he rewarded her with a smirk.

"Ladies' room?" Lucy called out, causing Frank to turn.

"Of course," he said, motioning to a door that had been left ajar at the end of the hall. A dim light shone from within.

"Sorry," Lucy said, addressing Alice. "I need a moment before diving into the shark tank. Want to come with? Do each other's hair? Talk about boys?"

"No," Alice said. Her refusal was too quick, too firm.

A knowing look rose in Lucy's eyes. Her expression was sympathetic, comforting. A silent promise to keep any secret. "Fine," Lucy said, with what Alice intuited was an affected harshness. "Have it your way," she said, pushing away from them and stomping down the hall. Lucy, Alice realized, was a consummate liar, and that simple fact made her trust her cousin with every fiber of her being.

Frank let Lucy pass, then motioned for Vincent and Alice to follow him. The ground floor appeared to consist of this foyer and four larger rooms set two by two along a wide hallway, though the stairs that ran up the right side of the hall concealed the entrance to one of them. Alice glanced over as they passed the front room, a parlor cum showroom, filled with a selection of coffins for purchase. The door opposite was closed, but a small brass plaque designated it as the "Office." Alice would hazard a guess that it had served the home's first owner as a formal dining room. The odor of cheap coffee, heated for too long, wafted down the hall, pointing the way to the kitchen. That left only the room with the occulted doorway, hidden behind the rise of the stairs. Frank led them to this very door. "The Viewing Room," he said in a manner that caused Alice to hear the capitals. He eased open the door and then stood back, waving for Alice to precede him. "A quick word, Mr. Marin?" he said, insinuating himself between her and Vincent. Her uncle nodded her forward.

Alice stepped over the threshold, then froze in her tracks. She'd expected to have a private moment to view her grandfather, speak with her father, and find her footing in this funerary mess, but although there was no sign of her father, the room was occupied by various members of the coven. She hesitated, feeling like an interloper.

The room was enormous, designed to hold a small army of mourners, larger than she would have guessed the house's footprint would allow. Still, her grandfather's matte silver casket sat not at the head of the room by the dais, but on the side. From her viewpoint, all Alice could see of him was the highly polished tips of black dress shoes. Alice forced away the image of the dreadful Brodeur woman and her mimed scissoring.

Two rows of formal Federal-style seating—a collection of vacant Hepplewhite shield-back chairs, and three occupied upholstered lolling chairs—were arranged in casual semicircles before the casket. Two settees with carved dolphin arms and paw feet stood between her and the chairs, creating a separate sitting area between the entrance and the visitation area. Both occupied, they had been positioned to face each other, and a low mahogany coffee table with the same animal motif sat between them. This little slip, a nod to contemporary convenience, was enough to tell Alice that although the furnishings were all very good, none of them were real. Low coffee tables like this had not existed before the early twentieth century. Just like pale Frank's sympathy, she surmised—genuine enough in appearance, yet only a reproduction of the real thing.

But even beyond revival furniture, the arrangement seemed odd. It struck Alice that rather than trying to provide any added comfort for the gathered mourners, the mortuary had come up with the layout to make the room seem less empty. She knew her grandfather had once been an important man, both in and beyond the circles of magic. It made her sad to think so few had come to pay their respects. Then again, perhaps her father had chosen to keep the entire affair small to keep vultures from the remains.

Alice was surprised to realize she knew everyone present. Though wizened, their features were familiar.

"Teleportation," said a sack of bones with stooped shoulders and frizzy red hair gone gray at the roots. Without context, the word rang out like an accusation. Alice recognized the speaker as Rose Gramont. Rose fell silent when she noticed Alice in the doorway. The witch grasped the head of her cane with both veiny hands and forced herself to a standing position. Her once, Alice knew from old photos, peaches and cream complexion, now saggy and mottled, flushed with excitement. Rose started advancing in a waltz of *step-step-cane* toward Alice.

"Of a kind, perhaps, but not in the true classical sense," a polished male baritone caviled. The witch must have spent years cultivating that patrician tone. Alice had only known him as Monsieur Jacques, though she'd never been sure if Jacques was his given or family name. When they were children, Hugo used to refer to him as "Monsieur Perruque," an allusion to the thick mat of steel-gray hair that sometimes failed to remain centered on his head. Monsieur Jacques took belated notice of Rose's excitement and turned to face the doorway.

"Astrid," Rose said, catching Alice by the arm and willing her forward, tugging on her, yet relying on her for support at the same time. Alice glanced back over her shoulder, surprised to find Vincent wasn't following. He had disappeared with pale Frank deeper into the shadows of the establishment.

"We were just discussing," Rose said, "which of Celestin's abilities we most admired." A devilish smile came to her lips. "Or should I say 'envied'?" The smile slipped from her lips, replaced by a furrowed brow and a distant gaze. "Though of course it wasn't Celestin who was capable of teleportation, was it? It was your mother-in-law, Laure." Her eyes glistened. "Now there was a witch to envy." She paused and sharpened her gaze. "You've changed . . ."

"This isn't Astrid." Guillaume—just-call-me-Guy—Brunet rose from one of the lolling chairs and rushed to Rose's side. Guy, who in his late thirties counted as the youngest of the elders, was the last member to have been accepted into the coven's ranks. "This is her daughter, Alice."

Rose tilted her head from side to side, examining Alice. "Oh," she said, at first sounding unconvinced, then nodded in apparent acceptance of Guy's words. "Of course. You must forgive me." She held her hand up by her head and shook it. "Things get so jumbled up in here of late."

Alice was aware that dementia was on the rise among older witches, another consequence of the world's waning magic. The condition struck some with greater speed and severity than others. Some of the residents of Sinclair had been sent there because of it. She smiled. "No problem," she said, placing her hand over Rose's and giving it what she hoped was a reassuring pat. She stopped and considered, thinking of Celestin's gifts—at least, the ones he had shared with her. "Grandfather could hold an old photo and carry you back into the moment it was taken. They were mostly frozen moments, but sometimes he could capture a few instants before. Never after . . ." She thought of the once cherished photo of her family, which she'd lost track of years before. How many times had she begged Celestin to take her back to that moment just one more time so she could stare into her mother's eyes?

"Your mother," Rose said. She leaned in and spoke in a stage whisper, "I never believed she went willingly."

Guy flushed and took hold of Rose's arm. "Come now, Rose. Not the time for old gossip." He tugged her away from Alice with great gentleness. "I'm sorry," he said, shifting his gaze to Alice. "So good to see you. So sorry for your loss."

Alice stood there dumbfounded. It took a moment to recover, but she gathered herself enough to nod and say, "Thank you." Guy nodded, then guided Rose away, easing her down into one of the upholstered chairs.

Alice forced herself to look past the gathered mourners, and toward her grandfather's casket.

Is this what they did? Sit around conjecturing? Making up stories so that they could better relish her family's misfortunes? The only thing worse than losing her mother to the Dreaming Road was the thought that her mother might not have had a choice in the matter. She began to make her way to the casket's side. She didn't look any of the other mourners in the eye for fear she might scream.

As she approached, a woman with long gray hair, a square jaw, and a sportsman's shoulders rose from one of the face-to-face settees, of which she'd been the sole occupant. Alice recognized her as Jeanette, whom Hugo had always jokingly called "The Ancient Wall of Jeanette." The settee groaned in relief, though the floorboards moaned as the imposing witch planted her full weight on them. She tilted her head back and sniffed the air, as if she were trying to catch scent of Alice's magic. For all Alice knew, Jeanette might be doing precisely that.

A pair of witches known as "les Jumeaux"—or "the Twins" when the phrase felt too awkward to slip into a mouthful of English—as if the two were a single unit without any independent existence, sat together on the second settee. The twins leaned in toward each other, perfectly mirroring each other's gestures as they pressed their temples together and linked hands. Though one was female and the other male, they were identical in every other way, their dress contrived to accentuate their great similarities and hide their small differences. They, too, had aged, though time seemed to have helped buff away any distinctions between them. Alice had neither opportunity nor desire to make a detailed study of the pair. Still, while passing them, her mind cataloged two noticeable variances—a slight coarseness to the male's skin, which he had attempted to erase with a theatrical-grade layer of foundation, and a marginal increase in the width of the female's hips. Alice surmised that the twins were communicating with each other in silence, their gaze locked on her as their temples remained pressed together.

As she passed them, Alice felt a tickle. A slight tingling. She realized the two were trying to work their way into her thoughts, though whether it was a mercenary effort or simply an act of psychic voyeurism, she couldn't say. She closed her eyes and drew a breath, forcing their energies out as she exhaled. She turned back over her shoulder to find the two of them staring back with wide, innocent eyes. Their attempt, weak and easily shrugged off, she intuited, came down to curiosity, maybe even boredom. The female twin shrugged and offered a wan smile in apology.

"The loss of Celestin . . . ," Julia Prosper, a striking woman with jet hair, large obsidian eyes, and hollow cheeks, said as she peered around Guy's shoulders, "is shared by us all." She circled around Guy. "Though, of course, your sorrow must be more acute, as you share blood." Her shoes made staccato taps as she stepped from the undoubtedly imitation Savonnerie carpet in the room's center onto the parquet.

"From what I hear, we all share his blood," Alice said, an unexpected flare of temper causing her to speak words she regretted the next instant. She could feel a wave of affronted hostility wash over her from all directions.

Julia's eyes flashed. The witch was petite, but still imposing as she drew up to Alice, only stopping when they were almost nose to nose. "And where do you find your magic?" With her head tilted to the side and her cheeks puffed out, impatient and hungry for any tasty tidbit, the woman reminded Alice of the puffins who visited Sinclair's rocky shore.

"This girl, she has magic," her tone turned sharp as she looked around Alice to Vincent, who was coming up behind his niece. "Abundant magic. You and your brother swore that the family would forgo any taking of relics."

"She has no need of relics." The voice, a man's, came from the far corner of the room. "She is a Marin witch. And feast or famine, the Marins have always enjoyed a surplus of magic. That's why a Marin has always been at the head of our coven." Alice went up on the balls of her feet to get a better view of the man who stood there, his face bathed in shadow. "Please forgive my rapacious sister. Envy is her defining characteristic." The words were spoken in the same tone a pleasantry would be delivered, but they carried a bite. Gabriel Prosper stepped into the light, pressing a tumbler to his lips as he did. When he lowered his glass, Alice could make out the ghost of a wry smile underlining a cool earnestness in his deep brown eyes. "And please forgive me as well, dear Alice. I would have . . . could have . . . never participated in the draining of Celestin's blood if we weren't all pressed up against the proverbial wall. He was more than a friend. I thought of him as a brother." Julia barked out a callous laugh, but Gabriel ignored her. "Perhaps you could speak to your father about allowing us a few keepsakes?" Alice grimaced at his euphemism for 'relic'. "Before we entomb Celestin in Précieux Sang, and his residual power is forever lost?"

Guy approached and planted himself between her and Julia. He spoke with a firm voice. "Don't let them pressure you."

"Oh, no," Julia said. "Let the gods forbid that a Marin feel pressured into acting in an unselfish manner." Gabriel approached and stood by his sister's side. Alice had no doubt that the rancor between them was real. She also had no doubt that—if the need arose—they could and would set their differences aside in a heartbeat. Brother and sister looked out for each other. Alice felt a twinge of jealousy at the thought.

"You're a fine pair of jackals." Alice turned at the sound of her father's voice. She felt cold, though her pulse quickened. She hadn't seen him in the flesh since his last visit to Sinclair, three years ago. He seemed somehow diminished. More compact. Less powerful. She realized she had grown, both in stature and magic. She shivered from the light touch of her neglected magic as it traced down her spine, tempting her to use it, to try herself by testing Nicholas.

"We're only saying . . . ," Julia began, but Gabriel's hand on her cut her off.

Her father approached them, looking down at her with tired eyes. He held out his hand, palm down. She felt she had no choice but to take it. It was cool, dry. He grasped her fingers, but only for a moment, then released her. "Good to see you, *ma chère*."

"Good to see you, too, Father." She was surprised that it was good to see him. A part of her had missed home so much. Longed to be near him.

A tiny spark flashed in his eyes, and the right corner of his mouth pulled up into a crooked smile. "Really, Alice. You're an adult now. Accountable for your own actions. You may as well call me Nicholas. Seems all my children do sooner or later."

"Oh," she said, taken aback, her heart tumbling into her stomach. In spite of Dr. Woodard's claim that her father had left her to wither on the island, she had hoped . . .

She had hoped. But his cold, fixed gaze underscored his cached message.

*Adult. Accountable for your actions.*

She had her explanation. Maybe he didn't believe in Babau Jean, but he blamed her—or her magic—for Luc's death. He'd given her a free pass because she'd been so young. He didn't love her. He feared her.

"Of course. Nicholas," she said.

"Where's Fleur?" Vincent said. "Did she leave?" His tone grew sharp.

"Yes," her father . . . Nicholas . . . said, then with an annoyed wave of his hand, "well, no. Fleur is in the office up front, availing herself of their computer." He held up his hand. "I've been with Celestin almost the entire time."

"Almost?"

"Nature called." Her father's lips pulled into a near snarl. "Shall we check the body? Perhaps go through the ladies' purses to see if they're attempting to smuggle out some soft bit?"

Her father's flippant tone made Alice wonder if Vincent had been giving his brother the credit for his own efforts to preserve the integrity of Celestin's remains. That Vincent wouldn't meet her gaze when she looked at him convinced her it was true.

"So," her father's head tilted as he turned his focus to Alice, "how long do you intend to visit with us?"

"Well, she isn't exactly visiting," Vincent said, "this is her home."

"Eight days," Alice blurted out the words. "Eight days," she repeated in a calmer tone.

"Good," Nicholas said, nodding his head. "You'll find your old room waiting for you," he said, and Alice instantly began replaying his words in her mind, scanning them for any touch of warmth, if not for the woman she was, at least for the girl she had been. "It's just as it was," he continued. "A bit ridiculous perhaps for the young woman you've grown into, but I'm sure you'll find a touch of nostalgia enjoyable . . . for a week or so. You'll be pleased to find an old friend waiting there for you."

Alice had opened her mouth to speak when she heard angry voices, those of her aunt and cousin, echoing down the hall. The door to the viewing room burst open, and Lucy stomped across the threshold.

"Have they caught you up yet?" Lucy said, catching sight of her. Anger simmered in her blue eyes.

"*Lucy.*" Aunt Fleur's voice came out sharp, a pin meant to burst Lucy's incipient—or was it ongoing?—tirade.

All a matter of perspective, Alice decided. "Caught up?"

"Seems that Mother has decided to divorce my dad, and she thinks . . ." Lucy looked back toward Fleur with a venomous gaze. "She thinks she's going to make me leave my friends, my school, my life, and move to this swamp."

"Well, in all fairness," Vincent said, "D.C. is a natural swamp, too, so—" His words stopped short when Lucy slapped both hands on her hips and glared at him. "I'm just saying you should give New Orleans a try."

Lucy's eyes widened in exasperation, and she shook her head. "Whatever." She raised her hands, palms held out, to Vincent. "It isn't going to happen." She turned on her mother. "You can stay here, but I'm going home to Dad."

"Sweetheart," Fleur said, her tone sad. She approached Lucy, leaned in. "Let's take a moment to talk about this. Really talk about it." She reached out for her daughter, but Lucy took a step back. "Just the two of us. In private. Please." No sign of acquiescence. "Please, dear, there are things you should know." Alice noticed that the Twins had scooted forward, literally sitting on the edge of their seat, feeding on the fiery emotional charge Lucy and Fleur had brought into the room with them. Seasoning it with the dregs of her own quietly bitter exchange with Nicholas. Rose, too, watched with a rapacious, lizard-like gleam in her eyes. They'd been denied their share of Celestin. Perhaps they felt this bit of psychic vampirism was their due. Still, Alice wished they would choke.

"No," Lucy said, with a toss of her blonde hair. "You can let this midlife crisis or whatever it is ruin your life if you want, but I'm not going to let it ruin mine. I'm going home. I'll stay for the funeral, but I'm leaving right after the ball."

"Your father doesn't want you," Fleur said, a long-unspoken truth that hung in the air, then came crashing down around them. Alice's gaze grazed Nicholas's face before darting away.

"I don't believe you."

"Sweetheart, I wouldn't say this to hurt you."

"No," Lucy said, shaking her head. "You're nuts. I'm going to call Dad. He'll set you straight."

Fleur rifled through her shoulder bag and produced a phone. "Here, use mine. He won't answer your number. He's not man enough." She paused, her shoulders slumping forward. "I'm no longer of use to him. He no longer needs the Marin money, and what magic I have left . . ." She seemed to remember herself, straightening her spine, raising her chin. "He wants his freedom, and he's left me to deal with the aftermath. I wanted to spare you, but if you need to hear it from him . . ." She tried to force the phone into Lucy's hands, but Lucy pulled her hand free from Fleur's grip, refusing to accept it. The girl took a step backward, then turned away.

The look on her face said she knew the truth, had known it for a while even, but didn't want to accept it.

"Your man has wronged you." Rose's voice broke the silence. She stood and began making her way forward, the spark in her eye intensifying with each thump of her cane. "It sounds to me like an old-fashioned cursing is in order."

"Oh, Rose," Fleur said, focusing on her daughter rather than the old witch. "Thank you, but that isn't necessary."

Lucy spun around to face them. The spark from Rose's eyes couldn't compare to the full conflagration that had bloomed in Lucy's. "Oh, yes," she said. "It is indeed necessary." She came forward and caught both Alice and Fleur by the hand. "But we Marin women can handle it all on our own."

# FOURTEEN

"I'm sorry, the what?" Evangeline said, tracing a gloved finger along the book's cover.

"Its full name is *The Lesser Key of Darkness*, though most refer to it simply as *The Lesser Key*."

"And if this is the 'lesser' key, that implies there's a 'greater' one."

Daniel nodded. "Yes. The . . ."

"No, wait," she said, holding up her other hand, "let me guess. *The Book of the Unwinding*."

"You've heard of it," he said, taking advantage of her gesture to tug the second glove on her upturned hand.

She looked at the glove. "Is this really necessary?"

"Look at it," Daniel insisted, pointing at the book. "Really look at it. See it with a witch's eyes."

Evangeline fought the urge to strip off the gloves and leave. The visit from the sisters, the fool's mission they'd manipulated her into accepting. If they had any interest in Alice's well-being, it was purely tangential to whatever they were really after. She'd been tricked. Hell, even Sugar had somehow been influenced, guided into thinking of a creature she'd despised since kittenhood.

Evangeline felt her blood pumping. It was one thing to mess with her, but another thing entirely for them to mess with her cat. Still, she let her eyes shift to the counter, peering at the book's edges and looking outward from them, seeing how the book interacted with its surroundings—examining it in negative space. Along the cover's red edges, she began to see tiny cilia, shadows reaching out. It struck her that this wasn't just a book, it was somehow a living entity, reaching out, sensing, testing those who held it in their hands, determining whom it might infect. She pulled back with such force, her stool rocked back.

Daniel reached out and righted her. "Not to worry. You're safe to handle the book. I don't think it can corrupt you," he said. "After all, I sense you've already visited dark places. And you . . . well, you're still you." He nodded at the gloves. "Those are just a precaution. They've been blessed. The cloth the book is sitting on has also been blessed."

She eyed her hands with suspicion. "Blessed by whom, exactly?"

"By me, of course. You don't think I just bought blessed gloves off the Internet, do you?"

"I suppose not."

"Though I did learn how to bless them myself from a video I watched online." His face was lit with pride.

"Of course you did," she said, then drew a deep breath, envisioning the purple rubber gloves changing into sleeves of white light. She opened the front cover on her exhale, then began flipping through. There was no title page, no mention of an author. A drawing. Pretty generic stuff, really, the all-seeing eye pierced by two crossed swords. The illustration reminded her of student tattoo work—heavy in ambition, light on execution. She glanced up at Daniel.

"A witch's eyes," he said.

She turned the page. Writing, symbols that looked like an uneasy marriage of runes and the Greek alphabet, dominated both pages. At the center of each page was an illumination.

"I believe you'll agree it's the Gothic alphabet," Daniel said. "Not that heavy-metal, rock-band script on word processors, but the real thing." He leaned in closer. "I find these characters interesting, as they served as a method of both transliteration and translation."

Unable to make heads or tails of the words, if they were words and not mere jumbles, Evangeline's eyes focused on the drawings. The left page showed a hand with the thumb pointing left, the right page another hand, its thumb pointing in the opposite direction.

"This text was obviously written long after the alphabet had fallen out of use."

"Obviously," Evangeline said, her attempt at sarcasm seeming to pass over Daniel's head. When he didn't react, she found it necessary to ask. "No, really, how could you know that?"

"Because the words aren't Gothic. They're English. Middle English, maybe, like pulp-fiction Chaucer, but if you look really closely . . . There," he said, letting his finger hover above a word. "That's 'metan' meaning 'to paint' or 'to dream,' and that's 'rode'"—a shift of the finger—"which is . . ."

"Yes, that one I got." She nodded. "When did you pick up Middle English?"

He waved his hand, a dismissive gesture. "Way back before the storm. When the boys were little." He looked down his nose at her. "I don't sleep. I thought we covered that."

"Sorry," she said, even though he didn't seem offended. It was more like it bored him to wait for her to catch up. "I guess we did."

"I've worked on translating a few pages, between batches." He glanced at the plate of cookies at her elbow. "It's something about a sojourn or a pilgrimage. A period of preparation."

"Preparation for what?"

Daniel shrugged. "I've not gotten too far, but it hasn't been explicitly stated in what I've decoded. It's almost like . . ."

"If you're reading this book, you should already know."

"Precisely, though I think it's safe to assume that as the lesser key, this book is the primer for the would-be student of the greater key."

She turned back to the book to study the images of the reversed hands. There was a symbol on the back of each of them. The hand on the left bore a mark that resembled a barred V. The one on the right showed something resembling a fat U. On instinct, she rotated the book upside down, so that the right hand, though downward facing, was on the right page, and the left hand on the left. It struck her at once that it was a very simple clue. The inverted V was an alpha; the U, an omega. She closed the book and turned it on its face, opening it instead from the back cover.

She felt a momentary flush of achievement before she realized the book was identical back to front. The same images and, she guessed, the same text. Still, she turned a few pages before giving up.

When she looked up, Daniel was smiling down at her. "Nice try, Nancy Drew."

She closed the book, flipped it back around, and stared down at the cover. After shooting a glance at Daniel, who seemed to be anticipating her next move, she balanced the book on its spine and let it open to what she assumed would be its most studied page. It cracked open close to, if not exactly at, the center. Here, there were no words, only an image of a man and a woman, the woman naked except for a necklace, the man also nude. The male figure carried a yoke on his shoulders, balancing a pair of pails. "Adam and Eve?" Evangeline wondered aloud.

"Possibly," Daniel said, "though the other images seem to draw on non-biblical mythologies. Going by the pictures alone, this work seems to be an amalgamation of several old mystery religions. You know, the ones proselytes had to go through an initiation ritual, face a symbolic death of some sort, to join. I suspect these two actually represent Inanna or Ishtar, the Queen of Heaven, and her consort, Damuzi, the King of Bones and Ashes."

Evangeline looked to him for an explanation.

"She represented Venus. And Damuzi, he . . . well, he died . . . a lot."

He motioned for her to turn the page, and she did—only to discover the center of each facing page featured the image of an ogre swallowing a child. The look in the monster's eye was so terrible, she flipped to the next page without prompting. A woman offered a sickle to a crouching man. The next featured a goddess riding on a chariot pulled by a lion. The following, the head of a young man wearing a conical cap. "Phrygian." She pointed to the picture. "Like Marie on French coins, right?"

"Yes, though based on the charioteer and her lion, I'm guessing that fair fellow is Attis." He reached out and grasped the book, using the towel he'd laid beneath it. "You could keep going, but I'll save you the displeasure." He folded the cloth around the book so that it was completely covered. "Other pictures, different mythologies. There's Uranus and Chronos. Chronos and Zeus. Isis and Osiris. Horus and Seth. There's even a golden ring and a dragon, though I'm guessing they have nothing to do with Tolkien." He smiled at his poor attempt at a joke.

"So what is this all about?"

"There are a few common themes I've picked up on. The struggle between generations, the sacrifice of fertility for power, a descent to the underworld." He grasped the thin volume between both hands. "My instincts tell me this is a guidebook." He held it so tightly his knuckles began to whiten. "A kind of 'how-to' with a built-in compass pointing the 'worthy' initiate to *The Book of the Unwinding*."

"Worthy?" she picked up on his tone when saying the word.

"I think that once a person's spirit, or mind, or soul—whatever you want to call it—has been darkened enough, *The Lesser Key* will lead him to the greater."

"Okay," Evangeline said, wondering why he'd whisked the book away so quickly, why he now held it so tight. "What haven't you told me? You said you thought this book was somehow connected to us."

"Yes," he said, lowering his gaze as if he were ashamed. "For me, the connection seems fairly clear."

"How so?"

"When I said I've translated a couple of pages, you may have inferred they fell toward the front of the book . . . or, in this case, the end. Same difference, really. But the pages I translated were closer to the center. They speak of a way of descending into the shadows, of slipping between dreaming and death by binding one's consciousness to a servitor spirit."

He placed the book in her hands. "Go to the center and flip back six pages." Evangeline did as he requested.

"All the other illustrations have been borrowed from ancient mythology, but I think you'll find the illumination on this page a bit more abstract in nature."

Evangeline focused on the picture, composed in deep red ink. It was a simple doodle that resembled a reversed question mark, its upper tip stretched into a long, curled tongue. Still, she could sense its power. "That's a sigil."

"Yes," Daniel said. "But not just any sigil." He blushed. "You'll excuse me." His expression took on the look of a shy schoolboy as he began unbuttoning his shirt. He opened his shirt and pointed to where a living man's heart would be. A gasp escaped her lips as she looked at the raised, reddened skin, the mark looking more like a brand than a tattoo, on his chest. "It's *my* sigil." She held the book up before him, the symbol in the book exactly the same in every way, even in scale, as Daniel's seal. "I used to hide it," he said, his expression graying, "back when I thought I was a 'real boy'—or at least the ghost of one. They used to brand criminals in the era I believed I was from. I thought I must have done something bad to earn it. I was ashamed. Afraid if

Nicholas and Astrid saw it, they wouldn't let me look after the children. Turns out they're the ones who marked me.

"I asked Nicholas about it. He told me it's meant to represent a shepherd's hook. A reasonable enough mark for a guardian of children. At least I thought so, until I found it in this book. A few pages away from a drawing of Damuzi. Evidently the King of Bones and Ashes has a day job. He's a shepherd."

"What does this all mean?"

Daniel shook his head. A tear fell from his eye. "I don't know. But I am afraid."

She wanted to take him into her arms and tell him it would be all right, but somehow she felt that would be a lie. "I'm sorry you're afraid," she said. That much was true.

He wiped away his tear, an embarrassed smile on his lips. "I wish I could say my fear wasn't self-centered, that I'm merely concerned for my family. But I'm afraid for myself. I fear that when I'm gone, really gone, I'll end in nothingness."

"We all do," Evangeline said. That, too, was true. The book began to feel heavy in her grasp. She wanted it gone. "So why do you think I share your connection to this book?"

"Go back two more pages."

Evangeline did so. In the center of the page was the image of a young man with a halo like rays of the sun. He rode a chariot being pulled by three rearing horses, his face a mask of panic—eyes wide, mouth crying out in terror. She recognized this image. "Phaeton."

"Yes," Daniel said, meeting her eyes. "The young usurper who attempted to take over his father's role and was executed for the chaos he created."

"But Luc killed himself . . ."

"There are still parallels to be drawn."

"How long has Nicholas owned this book?" she said, reaching back in her memory to a rainy Saturday she'd spent reading the myth. It was

Zeus, not Apollo, who'd punished the boy with death. Grandfather, not father.

Daniel's forehead scrunched up. "It doesn't belong to Nicholas." He took the book from her, once again using the cloth to protect his own hand.

"Then how did you get ahold of it?"

"I wanted to find a welcome home present for Alice. Not just some bit of junk off the Internet. Something that would hold real meaning for her . . ." He hesitated a bit too long, as if he feared his admission might get him into trouble.

"Daniel." She said his name in what she hoped was a firm, yet forgiving, maternal voice.

His eyes darted up to meet hers. "I sneaked into the attic. I thought she might like to have something that belonged to her mother."

# FIFTEEN

"There she is. There she is," Daniel said, rushing up to greet her before she could even close the door. "There's my little girl." He tugged her suitcase from her hand, wheeled it a bit to the side, and then grasped her upper arms with very solid, lifelike hands. He was glowing with delight, his eyes wide, his mouth twisted into the goofiest of smiles. If only her father could've reacted to her return with one tenth of this joy. Daniel looked her up and down. "But you're not a little one anymore, are you? All grown up now." Alice was surprised to see tears brimming in his eyes. "And I missed out on all the in-between."

Before she could form any words, he ushered her inside. "Come, come. It's the middle of the night." He raised his eyebrows and wiggled them—a gesture that had never failed to make her laugh as a child.

"It's only seven . . ."

"Ah, the witching hour, to be precise." She felt a smile lift up her lips. "You look tired. You must be tired." His head tilted to the side. "Or maybe you're hungry?"

Her stomach answered for her with a growl. She hadn't eaten since breakfast, a day and a half ago. He stuck his head through the still-open door. "Is it only just you? Not that you aren't enough," he quickly added. "I just assumed your father would be joining us. And perhaps Fleur and her spawn as well."

"No. Fleur and Nicholas," she stretched the name out to see if he'd react to her using it. He didn't. "They're staying with the body."

"Ah, yes," he said, grasping the handle of her case and heading down the hall, "the body." He deposited the case at the foot of the stairs. "I'll take that up for you later," he said, then shook his head. "I'm getting the most terrible sense of déjà vu, but a bit in reverse, if you know what I mean."

His comic expression caused her to laugh. She sensed he wanted her to be a little girl again, the little girl he'd cared for so long ago. And the truth was, she wanted the same thing—at least for a little while. He reached out to her, and she took his hand.

"Anything you'd like," he said. "Breakfast, dinner. You name it. I've become quite the chef in the last year. It's amazing the things you can learn from the Internet, I've even . . ."

"A year? That's how long you've been back? I've only just learned."

"No," he said, a guilty look in his eye, "a bit longer." He bit his lip, the way he always did when he had bad news to explain. "I asked that you not be told." He held up a hand to fend off any questions. "I found my way back," he said, "but I had no idea if I'd be able to stay. Still don't. Not really."

"But how did you?" Alice said, running her hand down his upper arm before leaning in for another hug. Her reunion with this artificial being, she realized, was as close as she'd ever come to feeling home. He leaned in and nuzzled her hair, seeming to breathe her in. Perhaps he felt the same way. "*How* did you find your way back?"

"Why?" he mumbled in her ear. "Are you looking for pointers?" She leaned back to find his eyes twinkling with humor—and kindness. He seemed to have read her feelings. Probably plastered on her face. "Looks like I might have cut closer to the truth than I'd intended," he said, but he didn't give her a chance to reply. "After you."

He held the kitchen door open for her, and Alice stepped over the threshold to discover the room held no resemblance to the one she remembered. A professional kitchen, all tile and metal and oversize appliances, had replaced the comfortable if shabby room where she used to have her breakfast.

"None of this," Daniel motioned around the room, seeming to want to avoid blame, "was done for me. Your father redid the place before I made it back. I understand it's the second renovation since Katrina. Just for show, I gather, but it's what inspired me to start learning. Seemed like a shame to let it just sit here, derelict and unloved."

She stopped at the sight of a dozen or so plastic bowls filled with cookies.

"I've done a little baking." He smiled. "Just for you." His face scrunched up in his customary look of fake seriousness. "After dinner."

He went to the center island and pulled out a stool. "Sit." She obeyed, watching him as he began opening and closing cabinets, foraging through the refrigerator. "I saw to it that we'd have a full larder for your visit. Since I can't get much past the yard, I'm stuck ordering on the computer to make groceries"—his use of the New Orleans vernacular pleased her—"so I can never be sure of the quality of produce till it arrives . . ."

"I'm sure it's all very good," she said, offering him a smile. "It was very sweet of you to think of me."

"I'm always thinking about my children. You, and Hugo." His expression softened. "And our Luc, too. I'll never forget my first." His face took on a look of determination. "First night back. Something special, I think." He raised a finger and wagged it at her. "I'm going to make you some shrimp calas."

"Or maybe just a sandwich?" she said.

He looked a little disappointed, but raised his hand in salute. "Whatever Mademoiselle de Pigwhistle, the Princess of Upper and Lower Paroisse, desires." He waited for her response, but she didn't know what to say.

"See?" he said, "I remembered." Alice smiled, though rather unconvincingly, she guessed, for the gleam left his eye. "Ah, but you didn't."

"I'm sorry . . ."

"Nothing to be sorry for, love. But wait," he said, seemingly happy to find a way to change the subject, "I almost forgot something, too. An old friend wants to see you."

"An old friend?" Alice shook her head. She'd been gone so long. She couldn't begin to imagine who it might be.

"Your cat," Daniel said. "Sugar said she wants to see you. Evangeline asked me to pass on the message. The furry fiend lives with her now."

"Sugar?" Alice said, another memory bubbling up. A gift-wrapped box with a bright red bow, walking across the floor under its own steam. Lifting the top to find a tiny speck of gray fur with viridescent saucer eyes and a pink dot of a nose. A kitten's meow that sounded a bit like a hurled obscenity. It had been love, at least on Alice's part, at first sight. "She *asked* to see me?"

"Well, from what I gather, it's more of a royal summons than a request," he said, bowing and scraping.

"But she *asked* . . ."

"Don't ask me," Daniel said, rising and shaking his head. "From what I gather, those swamp witches have a way with animals."

Alice hadn't heard the term "swamp witch" used by anyone other than her grandfather and her father, and then always in a derogatory tone. Alice was still trying to wrap her head around Lucy's update that her father had not only come to accept Evangeline, but to what? Love her? Even as a small child, Alice had understood that her father had felt a swamp witch wasn't good enough for his son. Maybe he had lower standards for himself?

A thought came to Alice. "She must be quite old now, poor thing."

"Well, you can never tell with that kind of witch . . . ," Daniel began.

"I mean Sugar," Alice said, laughing.

"Oh, well, yes, but I gather she's still healthy. Still feisty." He paused before the kitchen door. "She gave Hugo a good clawing a few months back. Seems she doesn't much approve of late-night gentleman callers. But then again, of late, Hugo hasn't been much of a gentleman."

"That bad?" Alice said. When she was first sent to Sinclair, Hugo had called every week. Then once a month. Then a couple of times a year. He'd visited Sinclair twice with Vincent and once with Nicholas. His final visit, he'd come on his own. A surprise, not linked to any other event like a birthday or Thanksgiving. But that had been years ago now. He felt almost as absent from her life as Luc did. He'd moved on without her. Just like her father had. Perhaps he'd even come to blame her, as Nicholas did, for Luc's death. Seemed the only ones who'd truly missed her were Daniel and a cat she was surprised to learn was still alive.

"I've found myself siding with your father," Daniel said, as if that alone should stand as a clear enough answer to her question. It did.

"So my father and Evangeline . . ."

"So your father and Evangeline. Took me by surprise, too. Keep in mind I missed a few episodes between Nicholas telling your brother she wasn't worthy of him, and your father deciding she was plenty good enough for himself." He shrugged. "She helps keep an eye on Hugo, and she makes your father as close to happy as I've ever seen him. She's a good person. I'm not going to tell you how you should feel about her, though I suspect your cat will. And considering how ferocious that little beast can be, it would be wise to obey."

Alice smiled. "I remember that even as a kitten she could be quite . . . convincing." An unconnected idea began to form in her mind. "You say you learned how to cook from watching videos on the Internet?"

"Yes, indeed, I did," he said. "It didn't take too long, it's all really just measuring . . ."

"Do you think," Alice said, "you could learn how to cut hair?"

He smiled and ran his hand through his own auburn curls. "You tell me. Just how short were you thinking?"

# SIXTEEN

Delphine cast a wary eye at the gathering dusk, then closed the curtain before the light of the room could transform the windowpane into a looking glass. She couldn't remember the last time she'd looked into an actual mirror. Perhaps it was only because she couldn't help but see through the glamour. Or maybe it was only tangentially related to her appearance. Perhaps she avoided her reflection because the lure of the Dreaming Road had grown too strong of late. It would be so easy to slip into the dream, letting go of all pain, forgetting every defeat.

Every breath was a matter of will, but not every battle had yet been lost. Celestin Marin was dead, and whatever spell he had used to hide the book was broken . . . or at least beginning to crack.

Delphine crossed the room and sat at her dressing table. She rearranged the collection of oils and creams spread across the tabletop, then opened a stone jar filled with a lavender-scented cream. She set its lid aside and dipped her fingers into the cool balm. After spreading the cream over her face, down her neck, and along her left arm, she took a soft towel and wiped herself clean. Next, she moved on to her right shoulder and arm. This was how she bathed now. Her skin was far too thin and sensitive to bear a jet of water. She feared that a soak in a hot tub might cause her skin to slough off like a snake's, though unlike the lucky reptile, she wouldn't have a new skin waiting beneath the old.

The cleansing process would be easier if she could bear to look at herself. Delphine had painted over the mirrors in her own bathroom and covered the one at her dressing table with a shawl. She'd heard others complain it was a hard, cruel world, even in this modern and supposedly enlightened age, once a woman's looks faded. Delphine had witnessed the birth of the cotton gin. Even to her own eyes she'd long appeared a ghoul.

She hated her cleansing regime, the touch of her own withered skin. How old was she now? If she hadn't been robbed, if the witches who had called themselves her guardians hadn't drained so much of her power, that question might not have mattered as much. Still, a tyrannical part of her mind insisted on doing the math. Delphine was pushing three hundred years.

They were out there, as near as near can be, "the sisters," as her former mistresses insisted on calling themselves, even though they didn't share a drop of blood among them. Delphine could feel them, smell them even. Margot still carried the smell of a fresh earthen grave, and Marceline the funerary scent of mums. Mathilde had once carried a light, albeit cloying, air of myrrh, though of late she smelled only of pee. The fourth, Mireille, the youngest of the quartet, though the first to die, had smelled of honey.

It was this sweet and familiar scent, tinged with a hint of orange flower, that had wafted above Bourbon Street's regular morning musk of piss and beer and street washers' detergent, and led Delphine to discover Mireille's daughter in the French Quarter. The girl was right out there in the open, living the most ordinary of lives, seemingly ignorant of her heritage, of the power that was her birthright. Delphine made a mental note, after settling up accounts with Soulange's daughter in the morning, to pass by Evangeline's charming establishment. Determine if the young woman, so similar in appearance to Mireille, could feel the change that had come with Celestin Marin's death. Or perhaps she'd felt a tug all along, consciously or not. That could explain why such a beautiful and powerful girl would choose to warm the sheets of the Marin men, *fils et père*, rather than searching out a more suitable mate. One who didn't suffer from the inner demons that seemed to torment the Marins.

There was a connection, Delphine was sure of it. Mireille's breaking away, marrying, giving birth, dying . . . Somehow her decision to forsake magic had left *The Book of the Unwinding* vulnerable and allowed it to fall into the Marin family's hands. Delphine had last felt the tug of the book when Laure Marin and Soulange Simeon landed in their bit of trouble. With Celestin's dying breath, she felt the book's renewed call.

And this time she would be the witch to answer it.

She would retrieve the book. She would breathe magic's last dying gasp into herself, nursing it until it was ready to be reborn in her image. And then, well then, she would light the greatest pyre ever seen—and every degraded witch who refused to kneel before her would feed the flames. A smile rose to her cracked lips. She hoped with all her will that the sisters would be able to hold on long enough, live long enough to see that day. She'd force them to kneel before her. Beg her pardon. Then she would take them apart piece by piece, letting them watch as she used their limbs as kindling, placing them into the lowest level of the fire.

Other witches, Delphine included, were scrambling, sinking their claws into any scrap of magic they could find, some going so far as to pulverize their own cut locks of hair and fingernail trimmings for use in unguents and incense. She'd hoped to charm Celestin's granddaughter out of a bit of the old man. The girl was a proper little prig, but—she felt it in her aching bones—no madder than the average witch. That the Marins could afford to waste Celestin's residual power just proved they counted on having another, deeper well to tap into. This confirmation was far more valuable than a bit of the dead witch's giblets. It made the morning she'd spent at the airport awaiting the girl's arrival well worth the time.

Laure's madness. Soulange's death. Nicholas Marin wresting control of the coven from his father—then, when challenged for dominance by his own son, taking both the boy's life and his love. There was a link between each seemingly unrelated event. Everyone else was playing checkers, trying to jump over each other, but the Marins, they had been playing the long game all along, and until now, their only true opponents had been each other.

Delphine lay her hand on a thin volume bound in red-stained pigskin, one of the handful of known extant copies of *The Lesser Key*, a tract reputed by those without discernment to be a heavily censored and intentionally obscured edition of *The Book of the Unwinding*. The volume touched her back, filling her mind with lovely dark images of standing above the apocalypse, surveying the destruction.

Copies of *The Lesser Key* had never existed in large quantity, and the greater part of those had long ago been put to the fire. Now the remaining copies floated around the world, the ugly gems of indiscriminate collections, each still commanding a small fortune whenever death or desperation brought one to the auction block. Delphine had stolen this copy more than a century ago, out from under the nose of a befuddled widower, a man Delphine had helped acquire his widower status. On the surface, the tract seemed to be a standard enough grimoire, illuminated by a medieval hand as skilled as any contemporary third grader. It held none of the power of the greater work, though she somehow felt closer to *The Book of the Unwinding* with the key in her possession. Like the way a tuning fork when struck can cause its corresponding piano string to vibrate, the two held the same frequency.

She had spent the afternoon poring over *The Lesser Key*'s parchment pages, trying to glean any information that might help her take final possession of the actual book. So far, she'd seen such little progress that she questioned whether it had been worth the trouble she'd taken to locate it among her belongings. But then she felt a flash of insight and wondered how she had never made a connection before. Mireille's daughter. Her dalliances with the Marin men . . .

She needed to determine whether Mireille's girl posed an opportunity or a threat. Cultivating an opportunity would require finesse on Delphine's part, and perhaps more time than she had. Dispatching a threat would only call for swift and deadly surprise. Delphine would prepare for either alternative. Perhaps Mireille's daughter would live to see another new moon. Perhaps she wouldn't.

Either way, she'd deal with the Marin family, regain the book, and then death would finally claim each of the sisters—perhaps in a single stroke if Delphine was feeling merciful, or perhaps one by agonizing one so that those who remained would suffer the loss of their sisters before their own painful demise. Delphine suspected the latter.

That three of these witches still lived had long piqued her. That they could still walk freely in the world without having to hide their decrepitude infuriated her. They had somehow found the secret to holding back the hands of time, drawing the life force from others—who knew how many before Delphine, who knew how many after. What Delphine did know was that she had been a special find for them, a witch with a supernaturally long lifespan—a renewable battery of sorts. That's why they'd taken her in and kept her close for a hundred years.

Delphine had long suspected that she owed her orphan status to the sister witches. They'd visited her parents three times to discuss Delphine's future before her father's death, and once again afterward, just a month before her mother passed. Delphine hadn't learned of her own powers, the magic these women had fed off, until decades later.

And decades more crawled past before she found herself skilled and lucky enough to break free of them.

Delphine had come with them to America in 1752, although it hadn't been America then—it had still been Nouvelle-France. She'd turned thirteen the month before she set sail with her guardians, the four witches tasked with transporting a secret cargo, a book about the size of a psalter, from the Old World to the New. The book was *Le Livre du Déroulage*, or *The Book of the Unwinding*, as it had come to be known since English had become the lingua franca of magic and business and just about everything else. It contained the fevered scribblings of the mad monk Theodosius, a fifteenth-century Cathar apologist and practitioner of dark magic, excommunicated and imprisoned in the bowels of the Vatican itself for attempting to popularize his own non-canonical vision the apocalypse. "Unwinding" had always struck Delphine as an imperfect translation for "*déroulage*," whose meaning came closer to "unrolling" or even "peeling." Peeling certainly matched the legend of the book's creation, as Theodosius, incarcerated with neither ink nor parchment so his visions and prophesies might die with him, was said to have removed his own skin, which the Devil himself renewed each night, to create vellum, severed his own left index finger so that its bone might be used as stylus, and collected his own blood in a depression of his cell's stone floor to use as ink.

Still "unwinding" had a better ring to it than "peeling," and in the end, Delphine reckoned everything came down to marketing.

The four witches had posed, with the blessing of Pope Benedict himself, as Ursuline Sisters. Delphine, an orphan who worked without pay for the women, an *engagée* if not an outright slave, came in the guise of a novice nun. It was Delphine who had carried the first pope-blessed nails across the seas, in a pouch worn around her neck. The sisters were not allowed to lay a hand on the pouch for fear the blessing would be corrupted.

That Benedict would be complicit in such subterfuge spoke of his desire to move the Book beyond the reach of even his most trusted advisers. There must have been a great seductiveness to Theodosius's eschatology, powerful enough to topple St. Peter's heir himself. And while *The Book of the Unwinding* couldn't be destroyed, proving itself impervious even to fire, it might be forgotten. That he would entrust such a duty to the sisters, reviled sorceresses, spoke of his desire not to stain any innocent souls—other, evidently, than Delphine's own—in the process.

That the sisters had agreed to participate spoke to their desperation.

They'd had little choice but to cooperate. The Church had captured them and bound their magic. A date of execution had been set. In return for delivering the book to the end of the earth and securing it in the newly rebuilt convent's attic, in a thought-to-be impenetrable vault that would open only when the four sisters could no longer practice magic, the pope offered them their lives, their freedom, and the restoration of their magic.

And so the pope had kicked the problem down the road for what must have seemed an eternity to him. Delphine had borne witness to every sunrise of Benedict's eternity. Certainly when the pact was made, none, not even Mireille herself, could have foreseen herself turning away from magic, lovesick for a storefront preacher and contrite for her sins. Nor could anyone have ever foreseen an alliance between Soulange Simeon and Laure Marin.

Delphine clutched *The Lesser Key*, focusing. She tried to understand, but no new flashes of insight came to her. She sighed and slipped the tract into the pocket of her robe.

There was a connection between *The Book of the Unwinding* and that damned shop Vèvè. She felt it. The call of the Book echoed in its walls. For that, she'd purchased the building, offered an exorbitant bribe to soften Soulange's daughter's conscience. Hell, she would have spent her very last dime to secure the store and its contents. She gritted her teeth as she thought of her fool of a man, Carver. She'd paid him to commit a little light vandalism, just enough to help make Soulange's daughter uneasy, not damn near destroy the shop. If she learned he had damaged anything of use, anything she needed, anything that might point her to the Book, she would do a little *déroulage* of her own when she got her hands on him.

He hadn't answered her calls or responded to her messages. Perhaps *she* had been the fool. He'd demanded five thousand dollars for the job on Vèvè. She hadn't thought twice about parting ways with such a small sum, but now she realized it must have seemed like all the money in the world to a man such as Carver. For a brief moment, he would feel rich, though he was probably off somewhere now, drinking or drugging or whoring his way through his windfall. She'd just as soon not gaze at his pinched face and rodent's eyes ever again, except for the necklace she had loaned him, one that had the special power of turning away unwanted attention. She sent out a call to the necklace, a summons its possessor wouldn't be able to resist. Carver, or anyone else to whom he may have traded it, would feel compelled to return it to her.

At one time, she wouldn't have given the purloined bauble a single thought. But she relied on it more than ever, now that her own magic was failing her, now that it had become a burden to maintain the glamour that hid her true grotesque appearance.


Three loud booms, one on the heels of the other, worse than thunder—couldn't be thunder, thunder wouldn't have set the protection wards glowing—shook Delphine's house hard enough to jostle the items on her dressing table. The wards were purchased, not magic of her own making, and she watched with fading hope as the ward hanging on the wall before her evanesced and died. Her house had just been bombarded, three strikes of magic stronger than Delphine had experienced in going on twenty years. Below, she heard the click of the exterior door being unlocked, followed by a long, slow creak as it was eased open, a haunted-house effect intended, she felt sure, to frighten her.

*Save it for the tourists*, she thought, putting on a brave front for herself. A woman, even a witch, didn't survive for centuries with a faint heart, especially in these parts.

Delphine had anticipated the sisters and was surprised to sense a strong, masculine presence. The sound of footsteps, deliberate, proprietary, as if the true master of the house had returned, resonated on the ground floor. Delphine's heart pounded in a mixture of indignation and adrenaline, the ancient call to fight or flight. Still, her first instinct was to whip her wig off the headstand and place it on her head. Glamours always worked with less effort if the right props were used. There was an intruder, one with strong magic on his side, but she was too worried about seeing the truth of what she'd become reflected in his eyes to fret about his intentions. The eyes of others were the only mirrors she couldn't cover, couldn't paint over.

The footsteps continued for thirty seconds or so, then fell silent.

"Delphine," a familiar voice called her name. "You best come on down now. You won't like what happens if you make me come up there for you."

The damned whelp. Delphine felt herself flush with rage, followed fast by confusion. That had been real magic she'd just felt. *Strong* magic. And the necklace Carver Roy had stolen from her, though once a potent relic, had long lost any of its great magic. He could never have used it to batter his way in. Besides, the fool Carver knew nothing of magic. Though perhaps he had met someone who did.

It didn't take a mastermind to put the pieces together—the sisters.

She tightened the belt of her robe, slid her feet into her nonskid slippers. She stood, placing her hand on the vanity to help herself rise.

She focused on the image of herself she wanted to project. One faithful to how she had appeared long ago, the image she still half expected to find looking back at her whenever she found herself before a reflective surface.

She made her way, taking her time not only because she didn't want Carver to think he scared her, but also because it took her time these days, period. If she failed to obtain the Book, she'd soon have to give up her upstairs bedroom. The stairs were becoming too difficult to navigate. When she reached the landing, she could see the light spilling from her sitting room out into the hall. Seemed that the little bastard felt confident enough to make himself at home.

She eased her way down, one hand clutching the banister as she did. Once she reached the hall, she forced her shuffling feet to step lightly as she traveled along the hall. She concentrated on appearing, on being young, vibrant, and in control. She steeled herself before stepping into the pool of light.

She looked through the open doorway into her sitting room, where Carver indeed sat, a glass of her best whiskey in one hand, the necklace he'd stolen in the other. "*La main de gloire*," he said, "the hand of glory, is a corruption, you know, of *mandragore*, the common mandrake." Delphine realized there was something different, something wrong about him. His energy had changed. The Carver she knew could never be called lucid, let alone erudite in the history of magic. No, in spite of his appearance, the man before her was not the twitch-nosed white rabbit she'd employed. She was looking into the face of Carver Roy, but something different was looking back at her. Something dangerous. She startled at the realization, but forced herself to recover, to slow her breathing, to calm her pulse.

"The mandrake whose roots aren't shaped like a man, that doesn't issue a lethal scream as you rip it from the earth, and that is of absolutely no value when it comes to real magic," her visitor said. "But that simple error in transcription—*mandragore* to *main de gloire*—led to the discovery of a way to capture a witch's magic." He held the necklace out before her and shook it so that the bones rattled. "The relic."

He tossed the necklace at her. She reached out to catch it, but it fell through her fingers to land at her feet. The strand that had held the bones together for two hundred years snapped, and the bones skidded along the parquet. "Who are you?" she said, taking a step back, feeling one of the bones grind to powder beneath her tread.

He stood, dropping the tumbler to the floor. He reached over his head, his fingers curling beneath his chin, digging into the skin there. Then, as if its face were only a simple mask, it peeled the flesh away, holding the flap of skin up for Delphine to see. But she paid the skin no heed—her eyes darted from the blood-rouged, white enamel face beneath Carver's to the horrible black holes where the creature's own eyes should be. Freed from his disguise, he began to grow, Carver's compact, muscular form stretching out into a tall, gangly, almost skeletal creature. A sound like the whisk, whisk, whisk of a knife being sharpened drew her attention to his mouth, where jagged bits of metal formed razor-blade teeth.

"I wonder," those horrible lips formed the words, "how many such trinkets I'll be able to make out of you."

The room around Delphine darkened and brightened twice. Her knees weakened. She realized she was on the verge of fainting. She tried to brace herself, her hand brushing over the pocket holding *The Lesser Key* as she did. A spark shot up her fingers, and she snapped to full awareness. Reaching out, she pointed at him with a finger of her trembling hand. "I know who you are. Who you really are."

The creature lunged at her, and she spun around, nearly falling but catching herself. A part of her mind told her that he was playing with her. That he was only letting her believe she might escape him, just so he could watch her, a pitiful, ancient creature who had lived many more lifetimes than anyone should, struggle out into the hall in her nonslip slippers. Still, she ran as fast as her feet would carry her, intent on reaching the door.

She latched onto the doorknob, yanked the door wide, and fled out into the twilight.

She heard a screeching overhead and looked up. Above her, two quickly descending shadows.

A fiery pain shot through her as sharp hooks—*no, not hooks, talons,* the part of her mind that was still functioning corrected her—pierced her shoulders. She heard the flapping of large wings, and she reached out for, but failed to grasp, her falling wig as she was whisked up into the darkening sky.

# SEVENTEEN

"Cursing is dark magic. The darkest," Fleur said, leading them up Decatur Street, past the old Mint and into the Marigny.

Fleur walked a few strides ahead, her usually pinned-up hair down, breezes from the river lifting it, giving it a wild, untamed air. Her movements were smooth. Fluid. Predatory. It seemed as if she might take to the night sky at any moment.

Alice walked beside Lucy, who in spite of the ridiculous appliqué bee on her backpack, seemed diminished, muted, in her athletic trainers and gray T-shirt. But it was more than the change of wardrobe. The beams of a passing car illuminated the apprehension in her cousin's down-turned eyes.

"I'm tired," Lucy said. "Why are you dragging us all over the stupid French Quarter in the middle of the night?"

"We left the Vieux Carré when we crossed Esplanade," Alice said. "This is the Marigny. It was once part of the de Marigny plantation. Its last owner, Bernard, introduced the game of craps to America."

"Thank you, Miss NOLA," Lucy said, glaring at her. "And speaking of craps, do you have any other information I couldn't give one about?"

"Well, the French Quarter. Its architecture is actually Spanish."

Lucy's jaw dropped and her eyes opened wide. "Oh, my God . . ."

"I'm sorry. I just had a lot of time to read. Sinclair had a good library, and they'd order anything . . ."

"We're hunting," Fleur cut her off, eyes fixed on Lucy. "You're the one who wants to lay a curse. This is where a good curse starts," she said, her voice hard, sounding indifferent to her usually coddled daughter's complaints.

"Hunting for what?" Alice said, feeling uneasy for the first time. When Fleur and Lucy showed up unannounced at her father's door, going out on an adventure with them had seemed a lark. Daniel had even packed snacks for her to take along, though she had left the brown paper bag beside a sleeping man whose cardboard sign said he was hungry.

"Back when I was a girl, a small girl," Fleur said, "younger than either of you two, a strong witch could still kill a man with just a needle and a poppet made from his handkerchief. But a curse, a true curse that's going to settle in and last, that took something more even then. You'll soon see, but you needn't worry. This is Lucy's spell. You're just along for the ride."

It was almost two a.m., but a couple of wiry young men–brothers, most likely—with dirty blond hair and similar rakish features, stood outside a closed tattoo shop singing about another lonely night in Cajun French. One of the boys took his hand off the keys of his accordion just long enough to point at a hat on the ground. A sign next to it read "Natchitoches or Beer." He smiled, winked, but never stopped singing. Alice shrugged and smiled back. She didn't have even a coin to offer. Still, she would've liked to stop and listen for a while, but Fleur carried right on past.

"They're witches," Lucy said, glancing back at them. At that moment the duo began a new tune, the words "*Chère* Alice" reaching Alice's ears just as Fleur spoke.

"Weak ones," Fleur said, "but then again, aren't we all, these days?" She nodded at a woman who shuffled past them, her entire world packed into a deep, four-wheeled metal cart. "How about her?" Then she pursed her lips and narrowed her eyes. "Poor dear has faced enough in her life. Besides, I think we need a male. What do you think?" she said, addressing Lucy. "This is your spell. Would you prefer a fresh gutter punk or a seasoned freight hopper? Or maybe we should aim higher on the food chain? How about an inebriated businessman?" They stopped across the street from a galleried, two-story Creole structure that sat dwarfed by its neighbor—an unlovely multistory pile of white bricks. "One of these fine fellows, perhaps?" She waved at a couple of red-faced and thick-waisted middle-aged men who stumbled out of an establishment housed in the older, shorter building. The men both wore khakis. Alice could imagine them coaching a Little League team, or maybe attending a dance recital.

Lucy remained silent.

"Pick one," Fleur said, snarling at Lucy. "It's your curse. Your blood to spill. You have to choose."

"Blood . . . ?" Alice began.

"Don't be obtuse, Alice," Fleur said. "Of course we're speaking of murder. A curse, a true curse, calls for the spilling of blood. That's what I've been trying to explain to your cousin. Even in better days, a curse wasn't something a witch could just will into existence. So pick one."

Alice began to perspire and felt sick to her stomach. Was Fleur being serious? The severe set of her aunt's features made her fear the worst. Alice considered calling out to the men. Warning them away. But she felt her throat tighten, and she couldn't tell if she was being muzzled by her own fear or Fleur's magic.

"I don't care," Lucy said, her eyes refusing to single out either man. "Does it even matter which?"

"Of course it does. This is magic. Everything matters."

The men stood there, acting confused, seemingly besotted with Fleur. One of them waved and then began to weave across Frenchmen toward them.

"You're beautiful," he yelled from the middle of the street.

Alice felt her pulse quicken.

"And deadly," Fleur called back, laughing. "No. I don't think they're quite what we're looking for." She raised her hand, wiggled a finger in a circle. The man stopped in his tracks and turned back toward his friend, a taxi pulling up as if on cue. The men got in, but they turned, their eyes fixed on Fleur until the car was out of sight.

Only then did Alice realize she'd been holding her breath. She exhaled, hoping the men's departure signaled the end of their macabre outing.

"If we're going to do this, really do this," Fleur said, "then we have to make sure the sacrifice we pick is perfectly suitable." She began walking again.

"But we aren't going to hurt anyone. Not really," Alice said, finding her voice.

Her aunt ignored her. "Like calls to like," she said, her tone pedagogic. "The sacrifice should share the characteristics you hate most in your intended victim." She stopped and turned back to Lucy. "Who is the man you want to curse?"

"You of all people should know."

"Oh, I know. I know, my dear, but you're the one working the spell." She wrapped her arms around herself. "Your father. Who is he really?"

"I don't understand."

"What is his defining characteristic?"

"He's selfish," Lucy said through gritted teeth.

"Yes, my dear, but we all are." Fleur turned away, unimpressed. "Who is he at his deepest level? What is his greatest flaw?" She picked up her pace, leading them over Royal Street and past the nondescript Washington Square, whose gates had been locked since before sunset.

"He pretends to care about people . . . ," Lucy said, chasing after her mother.

"Yes?"

"He talks about helping people, but he just takes advantage of their problems to build himself up. All he cares about is getting more power and prestige for himself."

Fleur stopped dead in her tracks and looked back and laughed, a rough cackle. Alice could swear her aunt lifted a few inches off the ground.

"Oh, yes," Fleur said after she regained her composure. "We are out here seeking a sacrifice because your father's private face doesn't match his public one."

"Yes. He's a hypocrite."

"Great," she said, excitement building in her voice. "A hypocrite. I can work with that." She held out both hands, and a tiny light, a will-o'-the-wisp no larger than the head of a pin, lifted from her palms and drifted in front of them, leading them down Frenchmen, then back toward the city once it reached Dauphine. They followed the light over Touro Street, where it came to rest over an elderly man, bald except for a greasy white fringe, who sat sprawled back on a bench that belonged to a closed corner café, his open mouth snoring. A glass bottle peeked out from a paper bag at his feet, and a strip of cardboard, half covered by his dirty, full-length wool overcoat—a garment no one with a place to lay his head would be wearing in this weather—showed the misspelled name of Jezebel.

"I think we have a winner," Fleur said, looking down at the old man. "I do hope it won't take long to sober him up. We'll need him to be fully awake, fully aware, to participate in our little endeavor. It's important he feels fear." She held out her hand, and the light returned to her grasp. She held the spark out to Lucy. "Here, darling, touch it.

Taste it. Does this man's sin feel like your father's? Is this man hypocrite enough to make it worth the trouble of slitting his throat? I mean, if not, we'll be wasting our time."

Lucy backed away, refusing to let the light touch her.

Alice wondered. If she had the chance to curse Nicholas, to punish him for deserting her, for believing that she could've killed Luc, would she turn away or would she grasp this spark? If she dug deep enough, would she find the darkness that might allow her to end this vagrant?

Fleur shook her head. "But I need to know why you're so intent on cursing your father."

"You know why I'm cursing him," Lucy said, her hands on her hips, defiant. "Because of how he's used you."

Fleur's head tilted; her eyes widened. A silent challenge.

"Because of the way he's used me," Lucy said. "He trots me out for photo ops. To show what a family man he is. His great moral fiber. But we both know he's been screwing his assistant. And she's not even really that much older than me. And . . ."

"And?" Fleur pushed her to finish. "Yes? Say it." Fleur stood almost nose to nose with Lucy. She leaned in. "I know you know. I've tried to hide it from you for as long as I could, but I know you know. You always know."

"She's pregnant," Lucy said, her voice turning into a shriek. "He's going to marry her. He's leaving us for her. For them. He always talks about the sanctity of marriage, the permanence of family, but . . ."

"He's a hypocrite?"

"Yes."

*Yes.* Alice responded silently, thinking of her own father.

"And you hate him?"

"Yes."

*Yes.* Alice's heart agreed.

"And this man, as miserable as he may be, he should die to salve your broken heart?"

Lucy made no response.

Alice's inner voice hesitated. She stifled it before it could respond, fearful of the choice she might make if she were standing in Lucy's shoes.

"I need to know," Fleur said. "Is this what you want? Is this who you are?"

Lucy's eyes filled with tears. "I don't want to hurt him. I don't want to hurt anybody."

Fleur pulled Lucy into a tight embrace. "I know you don't."

"I'm just so angry."

"Of course you are. I'm angry, too." Fleur looked up over Lucy's shoulder at Alice. "We're all angry, my dear. We're all hurting. And we're all scared, because we don't know what to expect next." She took Lucy's chin in her hand and lifted it. "You said you want the Marin women to work magic together." She held her other hand out to Alice, who hesitated, unsure, but when Fleur waved her forward, she took a cautious step toward her aunt. Fleur reached out and caught hold of Alice, pulling her in. She wrapped one arm around each of the girls. "How about we fix what's been too long broken? How about you two help me begin to mend this family?"

Lucy looked at Alice and began laughing through her tears. "Couldn't we just take Alice shopping first?"

Alice smiled at her cousin. At her aunt. She laughed along with them. She wanted to believe healing was possible.

But Alice knew some things were too broken to fix.

# EIGHTEEN

"You're gonna burn a hole clear through that check if you keep staring at it," Isadore said, skepticism evident in his voice. "And you should know rubber stinks when it burns."

"The check is good," Lisette said, folding it once again. She'd done this enough times to put a sharp crease down its center. She needed to handle it more carefully, lest she rip it in half by accident. "The offer is good."

"Oh, it's good, all right," he said, leaning over the counter. "Too good. Too good to be real." Lisette didn't respond. At least not verbally. She pursed her lips and looked down her nose at him with one eyebrow raised. They'd been married going on twenty-five years now, and this well-practiced expression would tell Isadore that if he hadn't already crossed the line, he was getting close to it.

He got her message loud and clear. He shrugged, then his shoulders relaxed. "Ah, honey, you know there are a lot of crazy folk in this here town. That woman is just one more."

Isadore had already made his point.

As per Delphine's edict, they hadn't removed a thing from the shop. Still, seven gray plastic industrial-sized trash cans, the kind on wheels, were lined up beneath the boarded-up windows. Three large green ones, like Isadore's guys used to haul away yard debris, sat before the counter. They were all filled. Filled and waiting. Waiting for her to come to her senses and realize no one in their right mind was going to drop a half million dollars on Voodoo doll key chains and urine-scented garbage.

Remy, squatting in front of the nearest shelf, looked up at them through bleary eyes. This was the earliest the boy had gotten up since he got handed his diploma six weeks earlier. Curiosity about the Brodeur woman's offer had driven him to tumble out of bed and dress himself. Lisette decided to reward him by putting him to work. She looked at him and flicked her finger at the shelves. "You just keep stocking," she said. "When that box is empty, you got a dozen more." She glanced over at what he'd put out so far. "Go on, spread things out a bit. Make it look like we got something in here."

"Come on," Isadore said, his tone soft, playful. He reached over and laid his hand on her hand that held the check.

Lisette held her tongue, but leaned back a little. She hit the "No Sale" button on the register, an item their vandal—odd that she had begun to think of him as "their vandal"—had left untouched, and slid the check beneath the cash drawer. She pushed it closed.

"If that woman is buying the place, I don't see why I got to . . . ," Remy began.

Lisette held up a single finger, and the boy fell dumb.

"You ask yourself, why so much?" Isadore picked up the same tune he'd been singing since last night. "Why for this place? It isn't special . . ." Lisette's narrowed eyes cut him off. "It isn't special to anyone but us, I mean. There are, what, six stores pretty darned near just like this one within spitting distance. But you're telling me you believe she bought this whole building just so she could get her hands on this little shop."

"I never said that. I said *she said* she'd bought the building *and* she wants the shop. And before you ask, I already called the property management company to ask about the sale of the building. They don't open till nine."

"Why does she want what's in this particular one?"

"I told you a thousand times," Lisette said, knowing it sounded less true with each repetition. "She said she owed Mama a favor. She wants to breathe new life into the place. And help us at the same time."

Remy stood and made a show of turning over the empty box before slouching to the back wall to pick up a full one. "Oh, yeah. You got it so tough," Lisette said.

"And you believe her?" Isadore came up to her, offering her the same dopey smile he used whenever he wanted to make up after a fight. And this time they hadn't even been fighting. Not really. "Come on, girl. The woman even wants this?" He waved a hand at the jammed full waste cans.

"I don't know. I was up all night asking myself the same thing."

"I know. Your rolling around kept me up all night, too."

"So you snore while you're awake now, do you?"

Isadore laughed, a hearty, throaty laugh that made it easy for them to be friends, even if their romance had matured enough to take a little work. "I'm just saying. This place isn't special to anyone but us." He held up a hand to fend off her response. "But it is very special to us." He looked deeply into her eyes. "If that check is good. If the offer is real. Are you really okay with turning your mama's legacy over to this woman without understanding what it is she plans to do with it?"

"I'm sure it's what Mama would've wanted," she said, trying to make it sound like she believed her own words. She waited, hoping her mother would chime in with a firm confirmation or denial. Lisette told herself she wanted an out. An easy out. One that would add something to her children's future, not just detract from it like shuttering the shop would do. That money would more than pay for Remy's college, and graduate school, too, if he wanted to go. And they could fund a new business for Manon. Of course, they'd have to call it a loan, or Manon wouldn't take it, but . . .

Remy opened a box of statuettes that had somehow managed to survive. Lisette was trying to repair Papa Legba, who'd lost both his cigars, with rubber cement. She wouldn't be able to sell the damaged figurine, but she'd add it to the new altar. She watched as he unpacked three identical busts of Marie Laveau, two Saint Michaels, a Saint Barbara, and a figurine of the Marassa twins. The three Marassa twins, whose torsos shared a single lower body—the loa of truth.

The truth . . .

The truth was that Lisette didn't know if she could stand to be here without her mother at her side.

"It's what Soulange would have wanted," Isadore said, stretching out each word to convey his disbelief. He shook his head and laughed. "Yeah, girl, you just keep on telling yourself that. 'Cause me, I grew up coming in and out of this shop, and I'm not so sure myself your mama would've been okay with it. Not at all."

The bells of the cathedral began pealing, announcing the hour.

"Well, we'll know soon enough if this offer of yours is on the up and up," Isadore said, turning and crossing to peek through the spy hole he'd cut in the plywood covering the door. He looked back over his shoulder at her. "Better brace yourself."

"Is it her?" Lisette said, a sinking feeling in the pit of her stomach.

"No. It's Alcide." Isadore's face assumed a near-comical expression, and he shrugged. "He's got that new horn with him."

Isadore stepped away from the door and crossed the room to her. He knew better than to try to hold her, or stand before her. He did what she needed him to do. He stood by her side.

Remy slunk up behind them.

The bell over the door clanged as Lisette's father entered the shop. He stumbled over the threshold and looked around the place as if he'd never set eyes on it before. In some ways, he hadn't. It had been changed by the violence, and then by the proffered deal. It felt less theirs. Her father shrugged his shoulders and turned to Lisette. "Well, where is she, then? This woman who's gonna take this place off your ingrate hands?"

Lisette felt her face flush hot. His words echoed her own feelings toward herself. This shop had been her last real link to her mama. And her guilt didn't just stem from thoughts of her mother. It was as if she were being disloyal to the shop itself. Her family had lived here, with sleeping bags and a camping stove, taking sponge baths in the tiny washroom, for two months after Katrina. Their block in the Tremé had only seen a few inches, maybe a foot, of floodwater, but the roof of their house had been ripped damned near off. No amount of blue tarp would've made the place livable. And no amount of intimidation—she'd even resorted to threats of hoodoo—or money was going to get the few roofers left in the city to fix things any faster than they had a mind to.

"She isn't here," Lisette said. "Yet." She decided to change the subject before he could start in. "You," she said, treading up to him, placing her hands on her hips, doing her best to imitate her mother, "smell like a damned brewery."

He raised a hand and waved her back. "You aren't your mama, girl. Don't you even try . . ."

"And you aren't my mama, either," she said, happy to feel the sap of her anger rising. "What are you doing? Running around with that horn of yours, talking hoodoo. Making a fool out of yourself."

"I'm no fool."

"Not a natural one. But you're sure making yourself look like one. What do you think your grandson thinks about all this nonsense?" She looked back at Remy.

Her boy's eyes went wide and he started stuttering. He threw up both hands and shook his head. "Oh, hell, no. You leave me out of this."

"Don't you swear at your mama," Alcide snapped at him. Then, turning to her, he said, "You leave the boy the hell out of this." He wagged the trumpet at her—and seemed baffled to find the instrument in his hand. "You come on, boy," he said, looking past her at Remy. "You come with me. We got time before the big show. There are things," he said, making an effort not to slur his words and failing. "I need to make sure you know. Things I'm not sure your mama is gonna wanna teach you."

Remy looked to her for guidance. She and Isadore shared an entire conversation with only two quick, silent expressions, the way that only people who really knew each other, who really loved each other could.

"Yeah, you go on with your grandpa," she said.

"Okay," Remy muttered. "Just don't yell at me if you gotta come bail us out." He went to his grandfather and looked back. It struck her once again how much her son resembled her father. So much more than he resembled either of his parents.

"Where we going?" Remy asked her father.

He winked at the boy, making good and damned sure Lisette could see the devil in his eyes. "You'll see, my boy, you'll see." He put that horn to his lips and blew a fast reveille before crossing to the door. He gestured for the boy to open the door, and at the sound of the bell started blowing "When the Saints Go Marching In." Remy tossed another confused look back at them, then followed his grandfather out the door.

"Would you . . . ," Lisette addressed Isadore, "will you follow them? Make sure Dad doesn't get himself too worked up? Or both of them into trouble?" There were a million reasons to worry about her dad that had nothing to do with magic.

Isadore nodded. "Of course." He cast his eyes around the shop. "What about the Brodeur woman? You don't want me around when she shows up?"

Lisette shook her head, then went up on her tiptoes to plant a kiss on his cheek. She wrapped her arms around herself. Somehow, without knowing how she knew, she knew. "Ms. Brodeur isn't coming."

# NINETEEN

Alice's first full memory was of riding on her Uncle Vincent's shoulders as he walked along, keeping pace with the rearguard of a jazz funeral. They weren't official guests—or maybe mourners was the correct word—at least she didn't think so. Their participation, as she remembered it, felt more haphazard, like they had stumbled on the parade, and through curiosity or perhaps the contagion of sentiment, got swept up in it. She couldn't remember her father being there, but she had flashes of a boy's face—Hugo's face. Hugo had reached up and given her foot a squeeze. She had begun crying. Not because Hugo had upset her, but because she'd been overwhelmed, by the crowd, by the mournful music. By her big brother's tender touch.

The current scene was eerie in its similarity. Only today, the whole family was there—at least the surviving members. And it was her grandfather's remains in the ancient black enameled hearse. Unlike the funeral in her memory, today there were no tears.

A pair of white horses pulled the glass-sided hearse along, snaking in a zigzag to extend the six-and-a-half-block direct route from the funeral home to the entrance of Précieux Sang Cemetery into a ridiculous twelve-block parade route. Her father had suggested it was a matter of noblesse oblige since the musicians involved had wanted to honor Celestin for his contributions to their community.

Uncle Vincent walked beside Alice, and Lucy followed a step behind, the soles of her black satin flats slapping the pavement with as much vehemence as the horses' shoes, even as their crystal buckles captured the sunlight and transformed it into a blinding weapon. Hugo, hidden behind the darkest of sunglasses, hungover, or maybe still even a bit under the influence of something, dragged alongside their cousin. Another disappointing reunion. Even present, Hugo seemed somehow absent.

Nicholas and Fleur were ten or fifteen yards ahead of them in the procession, Celestin's eldest and youngest children following directly behind the hearse. It was an odd and unexpected sight to see the two hold hands as they followed Celestin's coffin. This was the first show of affection Alice had witnessed between them, though they may have been close, she realized, when they were younger, perhaps before their mother's crisis.

Alice had often wondered about the nature of her grandmother's illness, whether it was hereditary or situational in nature. It had struck her grandmother. Everyone thought it had struck her. She couldn't help but wonder if they were right. Could it be something in the makeup of the Marin women? Did the males, too, carry its seed?

The band marching behind them changed to a new tune, one Alice felt she should recognize but could not place. Slow. Mournful. She felt her pace slow to match its tempo.

"You three have to promise me," Vincent said, speaking up over the hymn. "When my time comes, there'll be none of this nonsense. Promise me you'll cremate me, then dump my ashes in the river at the end of St. Ann on Mardi Gras."

Alice took a moment, trying to decide if he was serious.

"People do that?" Lucy said, sounding a bit skeptical, but ready to catalog yet another example of idiosyncratic behavior on the part of the city's residents.

"Of course people do," he said, a wide grin splitting his face. "As you young folk like to say, 'It's a thing.' Been going on for, what, like forty years now."

"So an ancient tribal custom, then?" Lucy said, with just a touch of sarcasm.

"Precisely," he said, then the humor faded from his eyes. "'Course since they wouldn't be placed in Précieux Sang, the coven would want to perform a dissolution ritual on my ashes . . ."

"Fire wouldn't be enough?" Alice wondered aloud.

"Seems like it should be," Vincent said, "but then you got folk like your new friend Delphine. She'd find a way to strain the last touch of magic out of the dust." He chuckled. "Reconstituted me. Just add water."

Alice grimaced at the thought.

"I'm just saying," he said, picking up on her disapproval, "some of these witches are getting downright desperate."

Hugo slid his glasses down the bridge of his nose and glanced behind them, casting the musicians an evil glance. He raised his hand and snapped his fingers. "There," he said. "That's better." The musicians carried on playing, unaware that Hugo had just turned down their volume.

He adjusted his glasses, then nodded toward Nicholas and Fleur. "I reckon if it doesn't kill them, we might just survive, too." He surprised Alice by grasping her hand. His hand felt clammy and cool in hers. He leaned down and kissed the top of her head.

A nascent hope caused her to catch her breath. Maybe Hugo wasn't lost to her after all. Maybe his heart hadn't been poisoned, at least against her.

"It grew out of the AIDS crisis," Hugo said. "The whole St. Ann ashes in the river thing."

"You think I didn't know that?" Vincent said, irritation in his tone. "You've read about it. Heard about it. They were my friends."

"I know you're one of the good guys," Hugo said, reaching up with his free hand and grabbing Vincent's shoulder. "I was just explaining things to the prodigal sister."

Alice wondered if that's how Hugo really thought of her. "Prodigal" implied someone had given her a choice. She'd had no choice about leaving, and very little about returning either. She had felt she owed it to Vincent, who at least wanted her to come home.

Mixed grumbling caused Alice to glance over her shoulder at the remnants of the coven, once dozens strong, who straggled along behind them. Alice had counted eight of the aging witches during the service, held in the same room at the mortuary as the viewing had been. Six of those witches now followed them.

"The Prospers aren't coming?" she said.

"No," Vincent said. "Julia and Gabriel are in charge of tomorrow's ball in honor of Celestin. Not much time to pull everything off, with the new moon tomorrow."

"Doesn't it seem a bit odd," Lucy said, "to throw a big party to honor the only person who can't attend?"

"What seems odd is that you're complaining. I thought you liked formal events."

"I do, when the guest list doesn't read like the human passenger list on Noah's ark—short, ancient, and mostly family."

"No," Vincent said, "the whole region is buzzing with excitement." He winked at Alice. "Every witch with a walker is gonna be there."

"Glorious," Lucy said.

"But it is," Alice said. "An odd custom, I mean. To throw a ball to honor a dead dignitary on the first new moon after their death."

"Not if you scrape off the bull," Hugo said. "These things never had anything to do with honoring anybody. And don't believe the bit about how they're a peace offering to other covens either. They're an opportunity to make a show of strength, simple as that."

"You're such a cynic," Vincent said. "This is hardly a show of power. It's more like one last hurrah for a way of life that's ending. It's unlikely any of us will see another." Alice cast another look back at the older witches, and her uncle leaned in, speaking into her ear. "Not many of us left anymore. We're a dying breed."

More like a species that was going extinct. Even Hugo was nearing thirty. Alice and Lucy aside, there were no young members of the coven anymore, and Alice wasn't sure if she and her cousin even counted. They were included because they were Celestin's blood relations, but the truth was, Alice suspected Lucy had no magic. Her uncle, the senator, had rarely been home in the nine months she'd spent with her aunt's family, so she did not remember him well. Still, she suspected he wouldn't have been so quick to cut ties to his daughter had she been in possession of power that might benefit him, new child on the way or no.

"The older witches you knew—the ones I always thought of as old, anyway—beat your grandfather into Précieux Sang," Vincent said. Alice knew most witches from New Orleans ended up there sooner or later. "I think trying to fend off Katrina took more out of them than any of us thought it would." Vincent shook his head. "But for the past five years or so, more and more of us are just . . ." He motioned with an upturned thumb, like he was trying to hitchhike. "The Dreaming Road. At least that's what people say has happened to them."

"You think otherwise?"

At first Vincent shrugged, but then nodded in the direction of the cemetery. "When someone dies, we bury them, but these witches who've left for the Dreaming Road, what happens to their bodies?"

"I don't know. I never gave it much thought," she lied. As a child she had spent many nights imagining finding her mother's sleeping form, waking her. Rescuing her. She had come to realize that it was only a fantasy. Besides—Alice's mind flashed on Babau Jean—she knew that dreams aren't so easily escaped.

"Sure, the magic will keep you going for a while, but once you stop eating, drinking . . . ," Vincent said, his words building on her own thoughts. "We may be witches, but we're still human. It was one thing back when a move to the Dreaming Road was a rare occurrence, but given the number of witches that have supposedly gone down it, it's odd no bodies have turned up."

"I'd just hide out in one of the cemeteries," Hugo said. "Find a family who'd died out, and climb right in with them. Hang on for as long as the magic held." It bothered Alice to hear he had a plan. It seemed like he had at least begun to think it through.

"You wouldn't last long in one of those. It can get up to two hundred degrees inside there. That's how they work." He winked at Hugo. "You'd be a pile of bones and pixie dust in no time."

"How very droll, dear uncle," he said, putting on an affronted air, though Alice could hear the amusement in his voice.

Vincent looked around at Alice. "Your friend Delphine," he said, pausing, seeming to give her a chance to catch up.

It didn't take long. "You think she's using the bodies for relics?"

He nodded. "She's both desperate and entrepreneurial. And if it isn't her, it's someone like her."

"Wait," Hugo said, removing his sunglasses and stopping in his tracks, seeming to forget they were part of a procession. "You're saying the people who've gone missing haven't taken to the Dreaming Road. That they've been . . ."

"Harvested," the word spilled out of Alice's mouth. She shuddered.

"Yes," Vincent said. "Everyone has their head buried in the sand, or up their . . ." He cut himself short. "But I'm going to take advantage of the ball to bend a few ears. Share my suspicions beyond our own coven.

Of course it would help if I had something other than a rumble in my gut to use as evidence."

"Do you think that's what happened to mother?" Alice said, surprised by the dark fantasy that began to spin itself behind her eyes. The thought was horrifying, but it was almost . . . comforting, too. It would mean she hadn't left by choice.

"No," Vincent said. Then more firmly, with an air of calming certainty, "No. Of course not." He paused. "Listen. Put it out of your mind. I've spoken to Nicholas, and he thinks I'm nuts. The truth will out itself, but it's nothing for you to worry about. I should've just kept my stupid mouth shut."

They walked on in silence. Alice tried to shake the gruesome image of her mother's body being carved up into tiny, marketable pieces.

Every few feet Fleur would look back and focus on Lucy, an encouraging smile on her lips, a warm, loving look in her eyes.

"Ugh. God," Lucy muttered under her breath. Alice looked over to find her cousin grimacing from behind the gray lenses of her sunglasses. Tiny flowers, each of their petals a precious stone, glinted at her temples. "I think I've allowed her a bit too much mother-daughter bonding. If I don't do something to tick her off soon, she is going to drive me nuts." Her shielded eyes pointed at Alice. "No offense." Before Alice could even register if she should be offended, Lucy had turned to Hugo. "You seem pretty good at alienating parents. Any suggestions?"

"Sleeping with men has worked well for me, though I doubt it'll have the same impact in your case." Lucy grabbed Hugo's arm and leaned in, pressing her head to his shoulder. They were close, Alice realized. They cared for each other. She felt a pang of jealousy.

"Probably not." Lucy tugged off her sunglasses and, squinting, held them out to Alice. "Here, try these on. I want to see how they look on you."

Alice slipped them on, the uneven pavement beneath her nearly causing her to trip. Vincent caught her arm. "I got you."

She leaned on Vincent's arm as she looked back to face her cousin. She didn't really need his support, but it felt good to know it was there.

"Exactly as I thought. They look better on you." She nodded. "Keep them."

"But didn't you just guilt Fleur into buying those for you this morning?" Hugo said, grabbing the frames of his own glasses as Lucy tried to snatch them away.

"Yeah. She'll be a bit annoyed with me. It isn't much, but it's a start."

Alice felt her heart sink at Lucy's words. For a moment she had thought the gesture a sign of affection. Now she realized she was just a tool in one of Lucy's campaigns to annoy and aggrieve. Alice removed the glasses and held them out to her cousin.

"Oh, don't give me that look," Lucy said, holding her palm up to refuse the glasses. "*A*, They do suit you. *B*, I do want you to have them. *C*, I really do like you. And *D*, it will irritate Fleur." She tossed her head back in summation. "It's the modern world, Alice. A woman has to multitask."

A protest, in the form of a loud cough, came from one of the coven members behind them. Alice slipped the glasses back on and cast a quick glance over her shoulder. The line of dour faces behind her made it impossible to say which gray-haired adherent had made the complaint. She caught sight of Lucy rolling her eyes. Alice mouthed the word "sorry," then turned back.

They made another and, Alice hoped, final right and then began proceeding down Dryades Street.

A man with hair as silver as the trumpet he held stood at the corner. A member of the band, Alice surmised, come to join in for the happier tunes to be played as they returned from the cemetery. She didn't much blame him. If she'd been in the band, she would've skipped the dirge portion as well. As the hearse reached him, he lifted the horn to his lips and began to add discordant, staccato notes to the music the other musicians had begun a block back. The notes he played were devoid of any grace, and the way they meandered through the hymn struck Alice as disrespectful. Sacrilegious.

Unholy.

Such antiquated concepts, but no other words seemed to fit. This nice-looking older gentleman seemed intent on inflicting harm, though to whom or why she couldn't even hazard a guess. The atmosphere around them thickened until Alice felt like she was treading water rather than walking on solid ground. The carriage's wheels began to creak, and though the horses strained against it, the vehicle slowed to a dead stop right before the trumpeter.

A young man approached him from the side, moving slowly, like a mime walking against the wind. There was something about this younger man that struck Alice as familiar. The hairs on the back of her neck began to tingle. She removed her new shades and craned to get a better look at him, but could only make out the back of his head. His hair was so black it shone blue in the bright morning light.

"Come on, Grandpa," he said. He reached out for the silver-haired man's instrument, but the older hand slapped the younger away.

"Alcide," Vincent said, advancing with effort on the older man. "What are you doing here, my friend?" Alice turned to her father to see if he'd join Vincent, back him up. But Nicholas stood there, watching the scene but not engaging in it, confused, ineffectual. She felt disgusted by him and focused back on the trumpeter.

This Alcide looked out at her uncle through narrowed, angry eyes, but he never stopped playing, even after all the other musicians had fallen silent. The tune, if it could be called a tune, rang out over the street, high and sharp, winding and sinking. "'Cause," Vincent continued, "I'm not quite sure what you're up to, but I don't think you really know either. You can feel it, can't you? I know I can. It's wrong, whatever you're doing here. It's gonna change you." Alcide stopped playing and lowered the horn, his gaze shifting from Vincent to the horn he held in his trembling hand and then back again. "I'm a good man," he said.

"Yes, sir, you are," Vincent said. "Always have been."

"I'm not going to let Celestin take that away from me, too," he said, turning to Alice almost like he was looking for her assent.

"No, sir," Vincent said. "Nobody can take that away from you."

Another man, this one around her uncle's age, came forward and took the trumpet from Alcide's grasp. The newcomer paused a moment before Vincent—the two seeming to take each other's measure—then the stranger shook his head and wrapped his arm around Alcide's shoulders. "Come on. Let's get you back home."

"What the hell was that about?" Hugo said, lowering his sunglasses.

"Damned if I know," Lucy replied.

The three men passed, the youngest offering them an embarrassed smile, though his gaze seemed to linger longer on Lucy than on Alice or Hugo.

That sense of déjà vu surged back. Alice *knew* him. She was certain, though she couldn't place him. Then she felt her knees begin to buckle.

The sparkling black eyes. The thick lashes. The Cupid's bow lips. The image of a naked beauty covering his features with a white porcelain mask.

The hearse pulled forward, and the band began to play. Hugo clasped her hand and tugged her along.

# TWENTY

Three hundred and seventy dollars for a black, mock-neck, hand-kerchief-hem dress—"marked way down," the clerk had said with a knowing smile, as if Evangeline had just negotiated to purchase a soiled kitchen towel, and even that rag was still too good for her. It had damned near killed her to ask him to put half on her credit card—her balance now just twenty dollars south of its maximum limit—and accept the rest with cash. Seventy-five dollars with tip for a visit to the blowout bar for a double strand crown braid—one of the few nice styles her rebellious hair might hold in this humidity—and another forty-eight for a mani-pedi so her feet wouldn't look like hooves in her new ninety-dollar, French-soled, open-toed flats. Twelve dollars more for a car from Magazine Street to Précieux Sang Cemetery. She eyed her discount-store gray beaded handbag with suspicion, worried it wouldn't pass muster, but dammit, she'd squeezed the turnip dry. She didn't even know how she was going to manage to pay electric at her house this month.

And all this because of a three-word text from Nicholas. *I need you.*

So here she was, more or less crashing Celestin Marin's funeral. The message had been cryptic enough that she had no idea if Nicholas truly wanted her here, but he had reached out, and she wasn't going to spend another day on the wrong side of the wall he used to compartmentalize his relationship with her from the one he had with his family.

She felt the sting of her own hypocrisy. She'd told Nicholas, and Luc before him, partial truths about herself, but she'd always let them believe she was the child of a preacher and a back-bayou practitioner of natural magic. A swamp witch, as Nicholas always used to say back in those days when he'd enjoyed disparaging her to his son. She'd never owned up to the witch her mother had been before her fall, and she certainly never mentioned her mother's sister witches. Not to Luc. Not to Nicholas. Not to anyone.

But the time had come. If she could manage to pull him aside, even for a moment, she would warn him about the sisters, alert him to their interest in Alice. Later—together—they could connect the dots between his daughter and the book the witches thought was theirs. Attending the funeral was, she felt certain, the right thing to do.

Still, she didn't want to embarrass Nicholas. Worse, she didn't want to embarrass herself. She'd be good and goddamned before she gave his sister Fleur a chance to look down on her.

In her imagination, Evangeline had already shrugged off, with infinite grace, a thousand different digs aimed at her by "Mrs. the Senator," as she and Nicholas often spoke of Fleur in jest. He would hold Evangeline in his arms and enumerate the ways she was too good for Fleur, rather than the other way around.

As the car pulled close to the cemetery, Evangeline caught sight of a decent-sized brass band milling about in the street outside the cemetery's gate. "You can turn right here and pull over," she said.

"Précieux Sang," the driver said as she followed the suggestion, though she was watching Evangeline's face rather than where they were going. Nathalie's—Evangeline remembered the app had said the driver's name was Nathalie—eyes had spent more time checking her out in the rearview mirror than they had on the road. "When I was little, this place scared the shit out of me. My brother used to tell me this here is where Babau Jean lived. Used to dare me to walk by this place alone and call his name three times."

"Funny. I always heard he lived out on Grunch Road."

"There ain't no Grunch Road," Nathalie said. "At least not anymore. Probably never was. I went to the library once. Looked at old maps trying to find it." Evangeline wasn't about to argue the point.

Nathalie shifted to park and turned back toward Evangeline. "Wish I could let this one be on me, but they've already charged your card." Evangeline did the math in her mind. That meant her card was now eight dollars south of its limit. If Nicholas wasn't happy to see her, she could very well be walking home. "I'm sorry for your loss."

Evangeline shook her head, laughing. "Don't be," she said, "I hated the son of a bitch." Nathalie cringed, seemingly shocked by her candor. Evangeline silently cursed herself. "I didn't really. Hate him," she lied. "It was just always so . . . complicated."

"So he was family, then?" Nathalie said.

"Of a sort," Evangeline replied. "Thank you." She clutched her purse and prepared to make her exit.

"I know you, don't I?" Nathalie said, snatching up her phone and confirming Evangeline's name. "Evangeline Caissy . . ." She tapped the air with her index finger. "You dance at that club on Bourbon." She smiled and nodded, seemingly pleased with having made the connection. "Bonnes Nouvelles. Am I right?"

"Used to dance," Evangeline said, grasping the door handle. "Now I'm just management." She smiled and opened the door. "It's a play on my name, you know," she volunteered. "They both mean 'good news.'"

"If you say so," Nathalie said, the corner of her mouth curling up. "I'll take you at your word on that bit. I used to drop by the club from time to time. After Katrina. Back when you all had the live musicians working."

"Yeah, strangely enough, those were good times. Kind of." It was true. There was a brief, very brief, period of intense camaraderie after the storm, when even the big musicians would play the clubs on Bourbon Street. Back then, they were happy to find any gig at all. Now, half of them wouldn't be caught dead playing on Bourbon. Just as well—the younger dancers didn't want any of that "old jazz stuff" anyway. They only wanted what you could find on the radio. And hell, the tourists plain didn't care, as long as they had a cold plastic grenade in their hand and a hot dancer to watch.

"Yeah, kind of a shame," Nathalie said. "Haven't been there in a long time. Place just doesn't seem as welcoming," she slowed the word down, hinting at a deeper meaning, "as it did before the tourists came back in force. Not that I'm complaining they're back."

Evangeline leaned forward. "We are just as welcoming"—Evangeline, too, slowed down the word—"as ever. Always will be as long as I'm around. You come back. You'll see."

"I'll do that," she said, then tapped the wheel. "You got a ride home afterwards? I could hang out. Take you anywhere you'd like. There's a new bar in the Marigny that does a great happy—"

Evangeline pursed her lips in fake disapproval. "Are you flirting with me?"

"Well, maybe . . ."

"At a funeral . . ."

Nathalie smiled and shrugged. "Hey, I figured wrong place, and probably wrong team, but you can't blame a girl for trying." Her eyelids lowered, and her lips pulled down into a disapproving frown. "You aren't here for no funeral. You're here for some guy, aren't you?" she said, but Nathalie didn't give her a chance to respond. "Well, whoever he is, he ain't good enough for you."

Evangeline winked. "Tell me something I don't know." She closed the door and lifted a hand in farewell as Nathalie pulled away. Part of her wanted to chase after the car. Get right back in and ride away. She had never been to a witch funeral before. If she'd attended her own mother's funeral, she had done it wearing diapers, and she doubted that her father had allowed much more than a good "ashes to ashes, dust to dust" anyway. She hadn't gone to Luc's. A part of her regretted it now, but she had refused to mourn him alongside those she considered complicit in his death. The tomb where Celestin was being interred also held Luc's bones. She'd come here once or twice in the early days after Luc's death, but at least seven years had passed since she'd stepped through Précieux Sang's gates. She wished she'd brought a flower with her. Not for Celestin, but for Luc.

"Miss Evangeline," she heard her name being called from across the street. She looked up to see a man wrapped in a brass sousaphone.

"Well, Charlie Ferrand, speak of the devil," Evangeline said, allowing his greeting to serve as an impetus to cross. After an awkward attempt at a hug, she went up on her toes and placed a kiss on his cheek. "I was just talking with my ride about how you and your buddies didn't use to be too good to play my club."

"Ah, don't be that way," he said and gave her a smile that said he knew any slight Evangeline might have felt had already been forgiven. "You here for the funeral?" he said. "Friend of the family?" She could read the trepidation in his eyes. She nodded. "Damnedest thing I've ever seen." He leaned in as best as the brass he wore would allow him to whisper in her ear. "Alcide Simeon set this gig up, but just between you and me, I think he's lost his damned mind."

Evangeline knew this Alcide fellow, but not well. He'd played the club a few times with Charlie's regular gang, but his daughter Lisette enjoyed far greater notoriety in her circles. Evangeline spent a good amount of time steering her employees away from the worthless gris-gris bags the woman sold in her store. She'd encountered Lisette herself a couple of times, once bobbing and weaving out of each other's way around a crowded Jackson Square, and again up in the Tremé when Evangeline went to check up on a dancer who'd missed two shifts without sending word. Both times Evangeline had to throw up a wall to protect herself from the woman's crushing awareness of being a fraud. The odd thing was that it took a bit of power to affect Evangeline so deeply. As far as Evangeline could tell, the only thing that was keeping Lisette from being the real deal was Lisette herself. 'Course that wasn't exactly the kind of advice a person could walk up and give to a stranger on the street.

"Alcide," Charlie said, "he showed up late, blew some shit that sounded like a rooster getting his neck wrung, then went off with his son-in-law and grandson. Left without a word to any of us after all of the fuss he made to get us here." He nodded around the rest of the band to demonstrate whom he meant by "us." "Those folk in there, they are one funny bunch . . ." He stopped himself. "Sorry there, girl, didn't mean any offense, but you got to admit . . ."

Evangeline shook her head. "None taken."

"Good," he said, then craned his neck to get a better look through a small opening in the cemetery's gates. "They don't want us in there." He pointed toward the gate that was being guarded by a solid, square crone with long gray hair hanging out beneath a floppy black sun hat. Evangeline recognized the woman as a member of Nicholas's coven, but she didn't know her by name.

"See, they done closed the place off. Left their pit bull there at the gate." Evangeline could sense his apprehension in spite of his swagger. Précieux Sang had a reputation, and so did the people who did their burying there. "They've been in there a while, but it's been pretty darned quiet." Evangeline suspected the witches had performed some type of concealment spell to keep out prying eyes and deafen eavesdropping ears. Their decision to close the gate and post a guard told Evangeline they weren't entirely confident their spell would hold. Even the high-and-mighty witches of the Chanticleer Coven were struggling. Evangeline knew it to be true, but to see it with her own eyes still made an impression.

Charlie looked up at the sun like he was checking a watch. "They've been at it for 'bout twenty minutes, so I reckon if you want to pay your respects, you should go see how long a chain they got her on."

"Thanks, Charlie," she said. "See you later?"

"Sure thing, but not for long. Second we get back to the funeral home, I'm gonna leave you to enjoy the pleasure of your friends' company"—he cast a wary glance at the guardian of the gate—"on your own."

"Understood." She headed toward the gate. "Stop by the club sometime. Old time's sake, right?" He nodded and made an exaggerated show of trying to give her a bow, trapped as he was inside his horn. She blew him a kiss over her shoulder.

The guardian advanced toward her as she drew near the gate. Evangeline recognized the woman, but could only come up with the descriptive part of Hugo's less-than-charitable nickname for her. These people. This coven. So important to Nicholas, but to Evangeline they were virtual strangers. Nicholas didn't like mixing work with . . . well, whatever she was to him. The witch's eyes locked with hers, and Evangeline felt tendrils of magic prod at her private thoughts.

"I don't think so," Evangeline said, and slammed a mental curtain down, pinching the guardian's psychic fingers as she did so. The older woman's gray eyes widened in surprise, and she jumped a good foot back. *Damn.* Evangeline had just drawn the kind of attention to herself she'd been trying to avoid. Some of these witches were getting desperate enough to let loose with some real crazy.

The guardian began what felt like a magical pat down instead. Evangeline decided it was better not to shrug this off. She'd already showed the Chanticleers more of her hand than she'd intended by refusing to let the witch read her intent.

The guardian stepped aside to let her pass, and Evangeline only just managed to choke back a thank you. While she didn't wish to be interpreted as a threat, either by this woman or anyone else in the coven, she also didn't want anyone thinking she owed them anything.

The second she stepped through the gate, the concealment spell fell away. She could hear singing, yes singing, coming from the diagonal far end of the cemetery. Not much of a surprise. It was the Chanticleer Coven's penchant for song over regular chanting that lay behind their name. The use of melodies, passed down over the generations, was unusual, but effective. As a solitary witch, her magic depended on the strength of her will, the rightness of her goal, and, more often than not, dumb luck. The work of coven witches seemed to depend on how well they could blend their wills together. Nicholas had explained that the Chanticleers used song to bind their intentions together, to move together into an altered state of consciousness. In what he described as a "communal hypnagogic state"—leave it to Nicholas to use such words—they could touch the level of the astral, from which everyday reality flows, and use their coordinated lucid dreaming to influence the concrete world.

Maybe one reason singing worked for them was it provided an audible measure of how well they were performing together. Evangeline had a nice voice. She and Nicholas had even tried once to work magic together this way, but it didn't come naturally to her. Truth was, she didn't like giving up control of her power, and any collaboration was a loss of control. No, this magical glee club wasn't for her. She'd never played well with others.

Evangeline crept across the gravel path, positioning herself beside the row of wall tombs that ran the length of the cemetery's eastern wall. Tradition held that an entombed body shouldn't be disturbed for a year and a day, so a second death in a family required use of a temporary vault. Wall tombs, like these, were used for that purpose, and also for those, like herself, who had no family to be buried with. She'd tried once to use a spell to find her mother's resting place, but she came up with multiple sites, a few of them moving, shifting across the map. She suspected the sister witches had somehow obscured the location, though she couldn't imagine why.

Her position offered her a semi-obscured view of the coven, gathered in a circle around the Marin family tomb. They seemed caught up, mesmerized even, by the task they were fulfilling. She craned her neck, then went up on her tiptoes to get a better view. There was Nicholas, his back to her. Then her eyes landed on the profile of a young woman with chestnut-brown hair in a pixie cut. In her face, Evangeline could see the lines of the young Alice she had known, though in truth, she recognized her from photos Vincent had shared with her. Strange, really, that Alice's uncle seemed to take more pride in the young woman than her own father did.

A delicate man with snowy skin and a brush of matte-black hair was hovering near the rear of the assembly. He took notice of her arrival, his eyes zeroing in on her, and broke away from the group. Hands clasped together in front of him, he approached her with a mournful pace appropriate to the occasion. Evangeline found herself focusing on his ridiculous mustache, a paean to masculinity written across such delicate features.

"Quite a sight to behold, is it not?" he said. "So many of the Chanticleers working in union with such a sense of purpose." Evangeline estimated that her arrival had brought the number of mourners to around a dozen, but who was she going to believe, this fellow or her lying eyes? "A shame, of course," he continued, "that it should be on such a sad occasion. Oh, forgive me." He gave a slight bow, then rose. "My name is Frank, Frank Demagnan." Evangeline of course recognized the family name. The Demagnans, though not witches themselves, had handled the interments of generations of New Orleans's witches. He offered her his hand. She took it, surprised by how cool and dry it felt against her own damp palm.

"Evangeline . . ."

"Oh, Ms. Caissy, you require no introduction." He released her hand. "It was the wish of the coven to limit attendance, but I must admit I was surprised that you, one of this parish's preeminent independent witches, weren't present earlier at the memorial service. Especially given your intimate connections to the family."

For a split second, Evangeline felt flattered. No. Validated. This guy was good. Considering his family's business, he was probably the product of generations of intentional breeding, aimed at creating someone sensitive to the others' feelings. She sensed that he wasn't an empath, that he couldn't feel the emotions of others like she did—but that same awareness told her that he could *read* emotions, even slight variations. That made him dangerous. "Well, I wasn't Celestin's favorite person," she said, performing a careful ballet of quietly throwing up a shield while appearing to share a vulnerable side. "And, in truth, he wasn't mine."

"Still, you've chosen to set aside any old rancor and join us in laying him to rest." He glanced at the coven, then leaned in, whispering in her ear as if they were conspiring together. "I enjoyed more than a passing acquaintance with the deceased. I'm sure the responsibility for any ill will between the two of you lays entirely at his clay feet. But, of course, you will attend the ball? We've seen nothing like it here in, goodness, over thirty years. I am, of course, thrilled to have been invited at all, but you will without a doubt be the queen, if you choose to grace us with your presence."

Frank fell silent as the coven's voices rose and fell. There were no words, only sound, harmonic dissonance surrendering to consonance.

A smile crossed Frank's bloodless lips, as the melody the Chanticleers had been singing swung on a single note and morphed into a different melody altogether. "The last movement," he said, brushing imaginary lint from his suitcoat. "It's a shame you came late. The first part of the ritual, 'the calling of the blood,' was quite moving. Haven't seen it performed with such clarity since I was a child." He paused, seeming to consider. "The family has forgone the taking of relics," he said, as if this were unusual. Perhaps, in these days, it was. He grasped his hands behind his back and faced the mourners, standing at what Evangeline thought of as "funeral attention." "Such a great family. Though so many tragedies. The last family interment . . ." He seemed to search for the name.

"Luc," Evangeline said, then felt herself flush. He'd tricked her into saying her dead lover's name to get a reading on her feelings for him.

"Yes," he said, twisting to catch a better look at her. "It goes against nature for the young to pass before their elders. And what goes against nature, weakens magic."

"Really?" she said, stifling a burst of anger, though she wasn't sure at whom it was aimed—this obsequious ghoul, or Nicholas, or maybe even Luc himself. She realized this was the reason Nicholas had excluded her from the services. He understood better than anyone just how fresh and immediate her pain still was. "I've come to wonder if magic has anything at all to do with what is natural."

"Well, of course, you would know better than I," he said, looking at her as if she had just fallen from the sky, "but that is what I've always heard." His gaze turned back to the coven. Their voices reached a sudden crescendo, then fell to a low drone. "You may want to brace yourself."

Before she could even ask what he meant, the last of Celestin Marin's magic broke over her like a cold wave, taking her breath and forcing her to brace herself against one of the tombs, hot to the touch in the afternoon sun. What was left of his power had been returned to its source. Evangeline righted herself.

"You'll forgive me," Frank said, "but duty calls." He gave her a curt bow, then followed the fading melody to where the Marins and the remnants of the Chanticleers stood. He knelt by the tomb to retrieve a tree branch—looked like sweet olive to her—and began circling the tomb counterclockwise, making sweeping movements with a branch. That, Evangeline decided, had to be a symbolic gesture, closing out the ritual rather than serving any actual purpose.

The witches began to unwind from each other, almost as if they were just then reawakening to the awareness of themselves as individuals. Lucy, who Evangeline recognized by her proximity and facial resemblance to Fleur, broke away first. Evangeline intuited she had only been playing along, not contributing to the magic. Evangeline didn't like to guess who had magic and who didn't, but these days it was growing hard not to notice.

Lucy tapped Alice on the shoulder and pointed at Evangeline.

Alice looked over, her expression at first cool, removed. For a moment, Evangeline's heart jumped to her throat. Her mental vision of Alice was of the little girl she and Luc used to take to the French Market. They'd never really been close, but she'd hoped Alice would have fond memories of her. The gravel crunched beneath Alice's feet as she approached. Evangeline tried to tap into her, wanting to know what to expect, but she couldn't. She couldn't find her way into Alice's feelings. Then, before she could process that fact—she could usually read anyone she wanted—Alice came to a stop directly before her. Evangeline found herself struggling between the urges to fight or flee.

Without a word, Alice wrapped her arms tightly around her and planted a kiss on her cheek. Evangeline squeezed her back. They stood there, rocking back and forth in each other's arms.

"That was so weird," Alice whispered into her ear, "working magic with the coven. They're powerless. Or as good as. I think Nicholas was carrying most of them." She leaned back and looked Evangeline in the eye. "It's so good to see you."

The sound of crunching gravel caused Evangeline to look up. Alice stepped back, but didn't release her hand. "I saw that dress yesterday," Lucy said as she approached, Fleur following on her heels. "From the sales rack of that store on Magazine, right? I find the sales rack is usually the best place to find out what not to purchase."

Alice tightened her grip on Evangeline's hand. "You look beautiful."

"Yes," Fleur said, the words addressing Evangeline, but the pointed tone an obvious message to Lucy. "You do look lovely. And I'm afraid my daughter hasn't learned that it takes a special woman to pull off some looks. If that dress was found on a sales rack, it's only because most women could never do it justice. But you certainly do. May I?" Fleur reached out to touch the skirt's fabric. "Lovely." Lucy gave her mother a sour look and wandered farther along the wall tombs lining the edge of the cemetery.

Fleur let her gaze linger on her daughter for a good moment before her eyes drifted back to Evangeline. "Well, my dear, I am so glad you chose to join us. At least now we can all stop pretending that you aren't part of the family." Fleur reached out and ran her soft hand down Evangeline's upper arm. "We're having a small get-together at Father's house now. You will join us, won't you?"

Evangeline cast a quick glance over Fleur's shoulder at Nicholas, who was approaching. His face was a stony mask, but his eyes betrayed him—despite the text he'd sent her, he was surprised at her presence. Vincent walked at his side, keeping pace with him. His face wore a wide smile.

"You," Fleur's words reclaimed her attention, "belong in the picture, regardless of how the puzzle piece fits."

It was all too confusing. Nicholas's coldness, Fleur's warmth. Evangeline began to wonder if she'd allowed Nicholas to turn his sister into a kind of Babau Jean to keep her at a comfortable distance. *Well, damn,* she thought to herself as the possibility suddenly struck her as a likelihood. "Yes," she said, "I'd very much like that. I know your father didn't think much of me . . ."

Fleur's shoulders lifted, then dropped as she let loose a full-throated laugh. "I don't think Father thought much of any of us. Yet here we are, and there he is." She gestured toward the grave.

"Mom?" Lucy's voice called. She sounded anxious. Her eyes were fixed on the wall tombs, but she was backing away from them. "Mom?" she said again, now seemingly close to panic. "There's something in there." She held out a shaking hand. "There's something *alive* in there."

"Step away," Nicholas called, rushing past them and heading toward his niece.

Vincent followed his brother. "Probably just an animal. A squirrel or something. These old tombs, not all of them are well maintained—"

A sound as loud as a crack of thunder drowned him out. Lucy screamed as the front of one of the tombs shattered, pieces of it tumbling to the ground in chunks. A moaning. An unfocused, guttural grunt sounded from the crevice, and something inside began to move. Fleur rushed away, wrapping her arms around Lucy and pulling her back.

Alice stepped forward, toward the tomb, pulling Evangeline along as she did. Evangeline dug her heels in as she began to pick up on the tendrils of darkness reaching out of the opening. Appendages appeared first—withered arms, Evangeline realized—their tips stitched together with rough twine to form rounded stumps where the hands had been amputated. The top of a head emerged, its leathery mottled skin crowned with only a few wisps of gray hair, and then the rest of it followed, its beak of a nose rising as if to sniff the wind. Open sockets showed that the eyes had been taken. The pitiful creature, for Evangeline had begun to pick up chords of its agony, dragged itself along, inching its way toward freedom, unaware it was about to topple from the tomb. An elbow went over the edge, and the creature's mouth opened, keening a wild and tongueless cry as it began to slide from the opening. It landed on the broken stones below, and Evangeline heard the sound of bones fracturing, saw sharp ends of bone poking out through patches of paper-thin skin. Still, it writhed on the ground, trying to force its way up.

Evangeline could now see it was a woman, or what was left of a woman. She tried to force herself to think of what lay struggling at her feet as a "her" rather than an it, but when she looked at it, she couldn't shake the image of a June bug struggling to break free of its casing. She opened herself, just a little, just enough to try to understand that she was indeed witnessing the suffering of a fellow human, but regretted doing so before she could draw another breath. The feelings and images that washed over her . . .

They weren't of the woman's own suffering, but of her insatiable desire to torture those who'd done this to her in even worse ways than they'd tormented her. It was only hatred, bottomless and undying, that kept this creature alive. Evangeline tugged at Alice, trying to pull her back, but the girl released her grasp and approached the woman. Evangeline felt a cry of fear, of disgust, form in her own throat, shocked as Alice reached out and laid her hand on the woman's forehead.

"It's all right," Alice said. "We'll help you."

Evangeline could not begin to imagine what any of them could do. How could Alice not sense that the woman was too far gone?

A sound caught between a snarl and a scream sounded from the woman's gaping mouth. The few teeth left in her mouth chomped together as her head jerked from side to side. She strained, trying to bite Alice—then, failing to connect, she tried to drag herself free of Alice's touch.

Nicholas grabbed his daughter's arms, pulling her away with a hard, rough tug. Alice was flung backward. She took a few stumbling steps before Vincent caught her and pulled her into his arms, placing his hand over her head and forcing her to look away.

Evangeline felt her own eyes drawn back to the sight that Vincent was trying to spare his niece from witnessing. Nicholas now squatted by the woman's writhing form, the largest chunk of the broken tomb clasped between his hands. He hesitated, but only for a moment, then brought the stone down with full force against the woman's temple.

Evangeline heard a crack as the woman's skull splintered and broke open like an eggshell.

Nicholas dropped the stone, then stared down in horror at his own hands, spattered with brownish blood and whitish bits of brain. He fell back, wiping his hands on the ground. His eyes rose and locked on hers, and she only had an instant to wonder if she'd ever be able to look at him again without reliving this moment. Then a shadow passing overhead drew her eyes to two jet-colored ravens swooping in and perching atop the cemetery wall.

# TWENTY-ONE

Surreal. That's what it was.

Twenty minutes earlier, Alice had watched her father and uncle scrape up what was left of Delphine Brodeur. They'd returned her remains to the very tomb she'd tumbled from, the coven joining their magic together to repair the broken and blood-spattered stone of its seal.

Now, catering assistants in crisp white uniforms circulated through the ornate great room of her grandfather's house, offering the civilians—non-witch neighbors and, Fleur had earlier informed her, important members of the non-magical community—tiny bites and strong drinks. Alice, caught up in the servers' wake, followed them from the great room into the library, where the guests' expensive floral perfumes clashed with each other, overriding the scent of the old, decaying books. It gave her some much-needed comfort to trace her finger along their spines.

Nicholas had gone home to wash off the splatter from Delphine. Vincent had gone to collect Gabriel and Julia. But the non-magical mourners gathered around her didn't seem the least bit surprised by the conspicuous absence of Celestin's sons. Alice got the sense that after generations of living in the midst of the Marin family, they'd all been taught not to be surprised by anything. Just grab a cocktail and enjoy the ride.

Still, Fleur—impressed, she'd said, by Alice's ability to keep calm—had deputized her to help represent the family, at least until Nicholas and Vincent arrived. Alice slipped from room to room, acknowledging the condolences offered by stranger after stranger, all of whom seemed to recognize her, though their ability to do so could, perhaps, be credited to the process of elimination. Under circumstances that even approached normality, Alice felt sure that Fleur would have leaned on her own daughter to assist with hosting duties. But Lucy had been reduced to a shaking, sobbing six-year-old by the horrific scene at the cemetery.

Pale Frank hovered at the edge of the party, still scandalized that the once great Delphine Brodeur should have received such an ignominious and anonymous interment. Strangely, he didn't seem the least bit concerned about how the living woman might have ended up tortured then sealed in a tomb at Précieux Sang, but now that she was well and truly dead, he seemed to feel a responsibility toward her. Earlier, in the cemetery, even as Frank offered her father a monogrammed handkerchief to wipe stray bits of Delphine from his hands, he had extracted a promise that the united covens would return soon to offer up their proper respects to her.

"The elders of the coven," her father's euphemism for the only remaining members with whom Alice didn't share blood, were in a panic. Their drawn and ashen faces in the cemetery had testified to that fact. As they circled around the tomb debating whether the ball should be canceled, and how best to alert the other covens to what had just happened, Alice had been surprised to hear even "the Ancient Wall of Jeanette" speak of her childhood memories of Delphine Brodeur. The sturdy sergeant at arms had expressed shock that the once great witch had been brought low in such a horrible fashion. To Alice, it seemed impossible Delphine could have been a dominant figure as far back as, and evidently long before, Jeanette's childhood. Then again, her husk of a body had resembled nothing better than an unwrapped mummy.

Upon arrival at her grandfather's house, the elders had pushed their way through the civilians, sequestering themselves behind the door of the delicate oval-shaped salon that had once served as a ladies' card room. Father . . . no, Nicholas had pressed Hugo into service, charging him with keeping an eye on the elders. He even mandated, much to Hugo's delight, that he employ his pharmaceutical knowledge and bartending skills to keep the old guard from coming entirely undone.

Hugo had leaned in, a wicked smile on his lips and a twinkle in his eyes, to whisper in Alice's ear. "I always wanted to have my own coven to play with." Then he'd reached into his pocket and slipped out a small plastic pouch filled with white powder. "A few toots of this fairy dust, and even 'Mr. Perruque' will let down his hair." The smile had slipped away as he slid the envelope back into his pocket. "Most definitely not for you."


Her father's act had been a mercy killing. Alice kept trying to convince herself of that. Nicholas had weighed Delphine's chances of recovering, of returning to a normal life—whatever a normal life might have been for Delphine—before bringing the stone down on her skull, extinguishing her final spark. Vincent had caught hold of her and tried to prevent her from witnessing the incident, but she'd slipped out of his embrace. She'd seen Nicholas's face. Watched his expression as he killed the woman. It had been a look of disgust, not compassion.

Alice realized she'd lost track of Evangeline in the chaos. Had she made it to the event? Perhaps she'd simply divorced herself from the proceedings and taken off home. Alice wouldn't blame her if she had. Given her choice, she'd claim as many of these books as she could carry and leave, never to come back.

Alice had yearned to return to this place—*home*—for so long. The way these witches were scrambling for the merest wisps of magic, leeching the dregs out of each other's remains, made her feel sick, soiled. A moment of clarity washed over her. Unlike the elders, unlike her father, she wasn't defined by—refused to be defined by—her magic. She couldn't be a part of what these witches were doing to each other, piling horror on top of horror.

"Alice, dear." Fleur's voice wrested her out of her thoughts. She looked up to see her aunt waving her forward with one hand. Alice drew near, but a stranger was offering her aunt an expression of sympathy, so she hovered slightly to the side. The woman caught sight of Alice on the periphery and turned to face her.

"Oh, our little Alice," the woman said with what seemed a heartfelt familiarity, though Alice couldn't place her. "It's so good to see you again, even under such circumstances." The woman released Fleur and grasped Alice's upper arm. "Before you take off again, I do hope you'll come for tea. Tell me all about your boarding school experiences. My son and his wife are considering boarding school for my granddaughter, and your insights would be most appreciated."

Alice almost laughed. Of course the magical community was aware of what had happened, of where she'd been. But the civilians would've required a cover story. Wouldn't do for them to know she'd been locked up in an asylum. Locked up just as her grandmother had been. They probably didn't know that her grandmother had gone mad either. There must've been another myth created to explain away her absence. Couldn't risk the stain of weakness on the Marin family name.

Alice's eyes flashed on Fleur, who gave a slight shrug. *Tell them. Tell them all. Tell them everything,* Fleur's expression said. "Your father would like that," Fleur said, her tone explaining that the lie fell at his feet. Of course it did. They stood there, eyes locked together long enough for the moment to pass. Alice would play along with the lie.

"You should join the others, dear," Fleur added. "Your father and Vincent want to speak to us all about tomorrow's plans." A nod in the direction of the oval room. "Just knock twice."

Alice nodded. "Yes," she said and smiled at the woman who still clutched her upper arm. "Excuse me."

The woman lowered her hand. "You will stop by?"

Alice smiled. "Yes, of course. Thank you." She turned and plastered an insipid smile on her lips, making her way down the hall, past tight packs of guests, their condolences sliding off her like water.

When she turned the knob of the door to the oval room, a shock like a strong burst of static electricity caused her to give a slight yelp. She drew her hand back, staring at the knob as if it had intentionally set out to shock her. Then she remembered her aunt's instruction. She knocked twice and tapped the knob with a single finger. This time the door opened at her touch.

She slipped inside, reaching back to shut the door behind her.

Rose Gramont took notice of her entrance, pushing up from her seat and shuffling along at an angle that prevented Alice from slipping past her. "Oh, Astrid," she said, "I am so relieved you're here. I was worried about you." She caught hold of Alice's arm with her free hand, her grip icy but as strong as a vise. "Certainly you've heard what's happened to Delphine." She froze, her watery eyes opening wide. "Oh, Astrid. Your hair. What have you done to your lovely hair?" Rose started snatching at her, a piercing wail escaping her lips.

"Rose," Guy, who seemed to have appointed himself the addled witch's keeper, jumped up to rush to her side. "Rose," he said again, pulling her hands down and drawing her into a tight embrace. He looked at Alice, his features hardening. "What did you do? What did you say to her?" His tone was severe. "You should know how upsetting this day has been for her."

"But I didn't—" Alice began, but Guy had already turned and begun leading Rose away.

"It's okay," he said, running his hand down the back of Rose's hair, like she was a girl and he her father.

To Alice's relief, Lucy caught her eye and gestured furiously for Alice to join her beside the bar.

"Okay, what the serious hell was that?" Lucy said, looking like she was doing her best to appear unshaken, though still trembling. If the day had been hard on anyone, Alice decided, it had been her cousin.

"It's okay. It was nothing. Ms. Gramont got a bit confused." Alice glanced over at the old woman, who kept looking back at her, eying her with suspicion. "Again," she added, as she turned away.

A double tap landed on the door, and Alice looked back to see Fleur approaching them. Her aunt took one look at Lucy and snatched the half-full glass of red wine from her hand. Instead of setting it aside, as Alice had expected her to do, she refilled it at the bar and handed it back to her daughter.

"Martini. Dry. Twist," she said, addressing the command to Hugo.

"Well, all right," he said with a large smile. He held out his pack of white powder to her. "A little candy to go with that?"

Fleur cast a guilty sideways glance at Lucy. "You know I don't mess with the serious stuff."

Hugo placed his hand over his heart and assumed an expression of mock horror. "No, of course not. What was I thinking?" His look of shock deflated, and he gave Alice a quick wink. He poured a line of powder onto the bar, then bent over and snorted it up. He made a show of running his tongue around behind his closed lips, then slipped the packet back in his jacket. He turned to Fleur. "Up?"

"Of course. We may be sacrificing each other for power, but I still choose to hold on to the illusion we're civilized."

He mixed gin and a touch of vermouth in a stem glass, then grated off a sliver of lemon peel.

"Join me, Alice?" Fleur said, taking a seat at the bar.

"I don't know," Alice said. She had been, from time to time at Sinclair, allowed wine with dinner or the occasional hard cider, but her gut told her today wasn't the day to take off the training wheels. "I think maybe I should keep a clear head."

"Suit yourself," Fleur said, taking a very ladylike but effective sip of her drink.

"You'll probably be the only one of us with one," Hugo said. "A clear head, that is."

Alice glanced over at Guy, who was still doing his best to calm Rose. "I don't think you should give her any more of your 'candy.'"

Hugo laughed. "Oh, dear sister of mine," he said, leaning over the bar. "She's pokey all on her own without any help from me."

Fleur had somehow managed to finish her drink. She handed the glass to Hugo. "Another," she said. "Make it fast; I can feel Nicholas and Vincent arriving."

"Vincent," Hugo said, "may have to rethink his theory about Delphine's involvement in the relic trade."

"I don't know," Fleur said, tapping the rim of her empty glass. "Delphine is most definitely involved in the relic trade, or at least parts of her are."

Hugo laughed, refilling the glass, this time measuring with much less precision than he'd made a show of doing the first time.

Lucy looked up at her mother, a combination of surprise, pride, and disgust dancing across her face. "Was that really necessary to say?"

Fleur raised her glass in salute. "Drink up, dear. And welcome to New Orleans."

The Twins sat nearly shoulder to shoulder in the far end of the room at a small card table—a piece, Alice suspected, of the room's original furniture. The two were sharing a single glass of red wine. Monsieur Jacques sat across from them, holding up a small stemware glass to the light, examining the green liquid inside it.

"Absinthe?" Fleur said, a note of surprise in her voice.

"Crème de menthe," Hugo replied with a shudder. He shifted his focus to Alice. "Straight, no candy." He looked at the elderly man with utter contempt.

Jeanette paced along the row of curved windows, stopping every few passes and peering out as if she were expecting an arrival. Alice remembered the view was that of an interior courtyard, a small nod to Creole influence here in the American sector. Perhaps Jeanette had determined this was the most likely entry point should someone try to breach the room, and she was just being a good soldier. Guy guided Rose over to Jeanette, seeming to place the frail woman in the care of the stronger one, and then looked in Alice's direction—taking in Celestin's gathered offspring. Straightening his shoulders, he crossed the room to join them.

He focused first on Alice. "I do apologize," he said, his head bowing a bit as he spoke. "I knew you hadn't intentionally done anything to upset Rose. I guess I'm more on edge than I thought."

"It's all right," Alice said.

"Sazerac?" Hugo said.

Guy nodded. "How did you know?"

Hugo reached under the bar and pulled out a bottle of cognac. "It's New Orleans. There's bound to be one Sazerac man in any crowd," he said, whisking through the preparation like it was a well-practiced dance. He poured one for Guy, one for himself. "Sometimes, two." He pushed a glass across the bar to Guy, letting their fingertips touch.

Guy blushed.

"Can you ever not flirt?" Lucy said, glaring at Hugo.

"And she's back, folks," Hugo responded. Then he nodded in the direction of Rose, who hovered by the window, seemingly ready to take flight were she not pinned by the crook of Jeanette's strong arm. "Too bad we can't say the same for her."

Guy's hand hovered near the glass for a moment, not touching it. Then his fingers darted in and snatched it up, seemingly either fearful of or perhaps hopeful for another brush with Hugo. "I think the shock may have been too much for her," he said, then took a deep drink. "Hell, I think the shock may have been too much for me."

As if on cue, Rose slipped from Jeanette's grasp and rushed forward, pounding her cane into the Ferahan Sarouk carpet. "It *is* you, Astrid," she said, waving the finger of her free hand at Alice. "Tell them," she said, crossing to her with surprising speed. "Tell them," she said again, tilting her head as she examined Alice's face.

When Alice, tongue-tied, failed to respond, the old witch pounded down her cane and turned to address the others. "We spoke together. Just this morning." She looked back at Alice, tears brimming the red rims of her pale eyes. "You told me how lovely it was to see me again."

The whole room was so focused on Alice, Alice seemed to be the only one to notice the knock on the door.

"Everything all right in here?" Gabriel Prosper asked as he entered, his sister Julia following nearly on his heels, a look of absolute joy, or perhaps accomplishment, on her face.

Vincent came in behind them, his face drawn, gray.

Fleur stood, pushing her way around both Alice and Rose. "Where's Nicholas? I thought he was going to address the coven. Formally," she added, seeming to react to something she read in Vincent's eyes.

"Nicholas has asked me to speak on his behalf," Gabriel said, pressing his well-manicured hands together. "Rose, dear, perhaps you would like to sit?" He nodded at Guy, smiling as the younger witch took charge, once again, of the senile one—leading her to a chair at the table shared by the Twins and Monsieur Jacques.

Vincent joined the family at the bar. He held up a hand and shook his head in response to Hugo's silent inquiry, then slipped his arm over Alice's shoulder. The smile he gave her didn't reach his eyes, but he pulled her close and placed a kiss on her temple.

"What is this about?" Fleur said, addressing her brother and Gabriel with a single question.

Vincent began to speak, but he cut himself off and turned his attention to Gabriel, indicating they should do the same.

Gabriel cast a glance at his sister, who came to stand beside him, beaming as she took hold of his hand. She nodded at him.

Gabriel cleared his throat, then smiled broadly. "Nicholas has stepped down as the head of the coven." He paused. "It is with great humility that I now accept that role."

# TWENTY-TWO

Evangeline opened the door before Nicholas could knock. She had sensed him coming, preceded by a cloud of resentment and anger, fear and needing, at least fifteen minutes ago. He was freshly showered, his suit gone—hopefully burned—and replaced with faded jeans and a white button-down. His still-damp hair had more gray in it than on his last visit. Maybe even more gray than there had been earlier today.

She pushed a vodka lime into his hand. "If ever there was a day for day drinking, this is sure as hell it," she said, turning away from him. Evangeline herself was on her second, maybe third round. Easier to lose count some days than others. "Close the door behind you." She wondered for the thousandth time whether she should lead with her feelings about watching him bash in an old woman's brains, or with her shame over the certainty that it was her own mother's cohorts who had tortured and entombed Delphine in the first place?

She went and sat cross-legged—after jumping over her threshold like a panicked deer, she'd shed the dress and changed into cutoff shorts and an oversize white T-shirt—in her thrift-shop upholstered club chair, leaving the sofa all to Nicholas. The low coffee table formed a barrier between them. She needed that space.

Nicholas seemed to get the message. Staring into his drink, he set it down on a Saints-logo coaster without taking a sip. He collapsed backward onto the sofa, rubbing his hands together as if he were trying to warm them. Finally, he raised his eyes to meet hers. "It's broken," he said, then fell silent.

"What's broken?" She heard her own voice crack.

"The whole damned world," he said.

She took a sip of her own drink, but said nothing. She leaned forward, wondering if she should go to him, but she feared if she did, he might never say the words she sensed he wanted to say. A sinking feeling hit her stomach. All this talk about what was wrong in the world was bound to spiral inward, toward the specifics of what was wrong with Nicholas's life—and at the center of that, she felt sure, was bound to be everything he felt was wrong between the two of them.

"I've stepped down as the head of the coven," he said, looking up at her, smiling. The warmth didn't reach his eyes, which were full of pain. "Just like you always wanted me to."

She felt her temper flare. "You didn't do it for me," she said, her tone coming out harsh, accusatory. She shifted, turning a bit to the side, a movement that was both a signal and a shield.

"No," he said, shaking his head. "I didn't do it for you. I should have. Years ago. But I didn't."

"Then why? Why now?"

"Sometimes things get so damaged, so broken," he said, "you've got to throw it all away. Start over."

"Wow. Great way not to answer my question."

"I was asked to step down," he said, his face flushing red. "Asked," he repeated the word with irony. "I was . . . *told* to step down. Told that I've lost the confidence of the coven. Told that it's time to hand over the reins." He looked out into the distance, as if he were contemplating a landscape Evangeline couldn't see. "It's almost as if they blame me for their own failing powers." He shrugged, his gaze sharpening as he returned to the room. "Who knows, maybe Celestin would have found a way to hold on." His head tilted. "Perhaps Luc could have."

"They can't simply make you step aside. They have to challenge you. Like Luc did. You defeated him, after all." She let herself once again feel the fullness of the old loss, the bitterness she'd tried so long to set aside.

"There will be no challenge, formal or otherwise," he said, anger flashing in his eyes. "I've been offered a 'compromise.' Gabriel and Julia. They've learned things. Things about me. About my family. Things I just couldn't bear to let them gossip about." He held his hands out, palms up.

Of course. It had been his pride that had driven him to step down—not concern for his family, not his feelings for her. How could it have been otherwise? She didn't know what to say. She didn't know how to comfort him. She didn't know if she *wanted* to comfort him.

He glanced around the room, almost like he was looking for an escape, then his moist, reddening eyes settled on her. "I've told you that I can't give you the life you want. But we can't go on the way we have been."

There it was. Evangeline imagined that she heard the heavy sky crash down around them. "Yes, that does seem to be familiar territory."

Sugar padded into the room, then stopped, flashing them a comical wide-eyed look, as if surprised to find them there. She turned and fled back to the bedroom. Nicholas's eyes followed her as she made her retreat.

"So this is it then? You've given up the coven. You're breaking up with me. Make it all one big clean slate?" she snapped. He sat there in silence, focusing on her legs, looking at her and not looking at her at the same time. The awkwardness made her temper start to spark again. "Come on," she taunted, wanting to provoke him, wanting him to give her a reason to haul off and slap him into next week, "just spit it out. It's not me. It's you. It's—"

Nicholas's shoulders slumped forward. He rose and crossed to Evangeline, then sat before her on the coffee table. "I'm not breaking up with you. I'm just finally getting around to telling you the truth." He reached out, grasping the sides of her knees between his hands. "Though once I do, I suspect you might choose to break it off on your own." He bowed his head. "There are things you don't know. Things I myself don't understand. Ways I myself have been betrayed—"

"I've never betrayed you."

"No," he said, glancing up and flashing a smile at her. "You're a liar and a thief, and you let that hotheaded Cajun temper of yours get the best of you," he said, holding up a hand to stop her from protesting. She had no intention of protesting. What he said was true. "But somehow," he said, reaching out to take her hand, "you're still the most trustworthy human being I have ever met." He kissed her hand, then took it between both of his, caressing it. "No. I'm not speaking of you."

"Astrid, then."

He laughed. "Well, yes, Astrid, too. But no . . ." He hesitated, biting his lip. "You're impatient, you know." She tugged back her hand, folding her arms over her chest. His eyes narrowed, and his lips pulled into a tight smile. "See, I told you."

She almost snapped at him, but then she'd be playing his game—he was simply buying time.

He really did believe that what he was about to tell her would cause her to end things with him.

"Tell me," she said, turning back to him, taking his hand.

He leaned back, almost pulling away, but he stopped just short. "My mother may have been a complete and utter madwoman," he said, "but she was a talented witch." His gaze softened, his mind seeming to reel back to a memory. "Perhaps she wasn't quite a modern-day Medea, but she was willing to make certain . . . sacrifices." He closed his eyes, seemingly incapable of facing her reaction. "Soulange Simeon. Herself. Me." He held her hand up to his forehead. "And the damnedest thing is I never knew why."

Evangeline was long acquainted with the rumors that Laure Marin had tricked the Voodoo priestess out to old Grunch Road and killed her, and she'd heard dozens of wild conjectures as to why, each exponentially stranger than the last. But until this moment, she'd never suspected that Nicholas had suffered any harm from the incident beyond having to bear the disgrace of a psychologically damaged mother. "I don't understand," Evangeline said, leaning in. "What did your mother do to you?"

His eyes shot up to meet hers. "I can't give you children. I am incapable of fathering children. And no magic, no science can help the situation."

Evangeline laughed from shock. "That's ridiculous. You had three children with Astrid."

"No," he said, the word a forceful exhalation. "No," he said again, this time his voice soft. Wounded. "I had two children with Astrid." His eyes rose to meet hers. "I had two sons. But Alice . . . She isn't mine." He pushed back, rising. His face pale with rage. "And God help me, I hate her because of it. I can't bear the sight of her."

He stepped back, staring down at her, seeming to read something in her eyes that she herself hadn't even consciously registered yet. She felt a wave of nausea wash over her as the thought she'd been denying pushed its way to the surface. Nicholas, she realized, had been willing to make a sacrifice of his own.

"But it isn't the only reason you don't want her here, is it?" She rose and began backing away from him.

He rushed forward, reaching out to her, but she threw up both hands, ready to blast him with any magic she could muster and, failing that, fight him with her bare knuckles.

He stopped, seemingly surprised—no, shocked. He looked her up and down. "I guess we're done here then?"

Evangeline held her fighting pose. She nodded. "Yes, I believe we are."

He nodded, then turned, crossing the front room and leaving the front door open to the street as he exited.

# TWENTY-THREE

Technically the corner of Badine and Canal fell into the French Quarter, and the Vieux Carré was tourist central, but Lucy couldn't imagine what was so special about the masked freak who stood performing magic tricks beneath the twin palms at the intersection of the two streets. She could barely maneuver her shopping bags through the gathered crowd.

Lucy had had less than zero desire—no, really—to waste the morning at Celestin's house listening to the Chanticleers' joints creak as they independently and as a single body lost their shit over what had happened yesterday at the cemetery. She had no magic, never had, so she was more than happy to take a pass.

Besides, she'd taken a peek into the little black bag of horrors her cousin Alice called a suitcase, and no number of cartoon mice could make any of the garments crammed into it work for a formal occasion. So she had volunteered—rather graciously, she reflected—to go shopping for an ensemble for Alice to wear to the ball. Of course, she didn't really know what Alice's style was, but after all the time she'd spent in the asylum, chances were Alice didn't either. Lucy had decided to treat her cousin's wardrobe as a clean slate.

For the ball, she'd picked out a black, sleeveless V-neck jumpsuit and, since Alice probably hadn't walked around in heels at the looney bin, a pair of flats. Not just any flats, of course—these were suede and crystal studded, with a pointed toe. For a bit of sparkle, she'd chosen a sterling-silver choker with a variety of semiprecious stones. Nothing too garish, nothing too girly for her hard-to-pinpoint cousin.

She smiled, pleased with herself—Alice was going to stand out, and stand out in a way she would love. The suit would fit her cousin like a glove. After all, eyeballing a woman's true size was kind of Lucy's super-power. She had realized, a bit late, that maybe she should've offered to take Alice along, but hell, she wasn't a saint. Besides, the shopping trip provided her with an excellent cover for a few other clandestine activities.

A cry of appreciation rose up around her as the street magician continued to *amaze* and *astound*. She glanced over and decided he was either a basketball player in nine-inch stiletto heels or wearing stilts. His undecorated Mardi Gras mask glinted in the sun, sending a dark trace through her vision in spite of the new sunglasses she'd just purchased as a reward to replace the ones she'd given Alice. She blinked.

Maybe she was just being paranoid—watching a mutilated crone tumble out of a wall grave would set anyone on edge—but it felt like the black holes of his mask were following her as she struggled upstream through the pack of slack-jawed tourists.

First she had to maneuver the full, heavy bags past a wall of gym-rat guys dressed to impress in "Sun's Out, Guns Out" tank tops or tight "Southern Decadence" T-shirts. She grimaced as she dodged one sweaty, hirsute shoulder, biting her tongue to keep herself from offering to set up a crowdfunding page to raise the money to pay for electrolysis.

The throng was enthralled, impervious to calls of "pardon" and "excuse me," so she'd given up on politeness long before she came up behind a pair of middle-aged women wearing overloaded stretch pants and the most god-awful T-shirts Lucy had ever seen—one lime, one neon salmon, both with a cartoon stripper hanging sideways from a pole. Lucy paused behind the women, offering up a moment of silence for the cotton that had died to make their shirts, then pushed between them, her bags banging back against the women's shins.

A collective gasp of surprise floated up from the crowd.

Lucy might've been curious enough to stop and watch a trick or two, despite the weird feeling the performer had given her, but she heard the *Natchez*'s calliope blowing ragtime music. However much she wanted to hate it, the music conjured images of hot-day cherry sno-balls with Uncle Vincent in Woldenberg Park. Then she remembered he'd taken her out because her parents had been in the middle of a real dustup. She slid her new sunglasses down and squinted in the calliope's direction. Maybe she hated the music after all.

She glanced down at her phone. It was a bit after two, and she'd promised to be at the ferry landing twenty minutes ago. She kept walking, but she didn't pick up her pace. She hit the phone screen. Two old and until now ignored messages from her mother. "Have a good time." Then "Be sure to use your father's card," followed by two smiley faces. She sighed, regretting ever having taught that woman about emojis.

Another gasp, followed by a flock of "what the hells," sounded from behind her. She stopped in midstride to glance back. The freak had disappeared into thin air. His audience milled around, looking stupidly at each other, laughing. A little boy began to cry.

Okay. She was impressed. At least enough that she'd stop and watch a bit, the next time she passed him.

She kept one eye on the ground, guarding the heels of her shoes, as she crossed the train tracks at an angle. There he was. She spotted Remy sitting on the steps of the ferry terminal. He rose as she approached, standing at attention and raising a silver trumpet to his lips. The sound that came out of that poor horn made her laugh, really laugh, just as she knew he'd hoped it would.

She loved him, or thought she might, though Lucy knew herself well enough to know the long distance and the forbidden aspect of their relationship had made it more interesting. Would she feel the same way about him if they could simply be together?

He lowered the horn and came down the steps to join her, drawing her into his arms and kissing her. Electricity caused her hands to release their grip on the bags, which tumbled to the ground. He laughed and kissed her again, then scooped the handles of both heavy bags into one large hand. Yes, she decided, she would still feel the same way.

It took Lucy a moment to collect herself. She stared up into his entrancing—yes, that was the word for it—entrancing eyes. She could have stood there forever, or at least until her feet started to hurt, staring up at him, but he held the silver trumpet out for her to examine. "Here it is, the horn of hell."

His expression turned serious again, more serious than she'd seen it in a long time, though admittedly, they hadn't had a lot of time to call long. They'd met two years back. Flirted. Figured out that a family feud, years in the making, sat between them. Fell in love. All in a two-week visit.

Last year, she'd shocked her mother by asking to spend her summer break in New Orleans. In the end, she'd gotten six weeks here, half of the time in the Garden District under Vincent's supervision, the second half in Bayou St. John, in Nicholas's house—less under his supervision than under Hugo's bad influence. Hugo was the only one who knew about her and Remy. He had helped them spend time together, but it kind of bothered her that he'd seemed more motivated by the thought of sticking it to his dad than the pure pleasure of helping her. Still, gift horse. Mouth.

Now it wasn't just a visit. Now she was going to be stuck living here. That meant changing schools. Missing friends. But . . . he leaned in and kissed her again . . . hello, silver lining.

*Silver.* As he leaned back, a glint from the horn caught her eye. She reached out to touch it, but pulled back without knowing exactly why.

After the funeral, she had texted Remy—texted him with a level of *what the hell* unlike any *what the hell* she'd ever known before. He'd explained his grandfather's nutty plan.

"Seriously, what is wrong with your grandfather?" She regretted her choice of words, the harshness of her tone. She'd only intended to ask if he were sick, but she'd spent half her life building up her sarcasm muscle, and, well, the sun was out . . .

"I guess he still blames your lunatic grandmother for killing mine," Remy said.

From anyone else, this answer would've provoked a nuclear response. But Remy stared down at her, and she up at him. He wrapped the arm that held the trumpet around her. "I mean, we all know she didn't do it herself, but he thinks she was the reason Grandma was out on Grunch Road the night she died." He gave her a squeeze, then bent over and placed a kiss on the top of her head.

"To be honest, though, I think Grandpa is slipping a bit. I mean, this is a perfectly good trumpet. We could clean this thing up, give it to a kid to practice on. But the old guy is freaking out. Made me promise to drop it halfway between here and Algiers."

Lucy looked at the horn. It looked normal enough to her, but knowing what Mr. Simeon had planned to do with it still creeped her out.

"The truly weird bit is that Dad told me to do as he asked. I mean, I told him I'd take it to school or something, and he pretty much jumped down my throat. He's on edge with Grandpa and the shop, but . . ."

"I think he's right. Bad juju and all that."

He looked down at her, releasing her from the crook of his arm. His beautiful lips turned downward. "Listen to you. Juju. It's like you really believe in this stuff. This is just a metal tube with a few valves. No matter who blows it, it isn't going to send anyone's soul to hell."

"The way you play it, it might," she said, hoping to erase his frown.

It worked. He smiled. "You ready?" he said, already leading her back up the stairs to the terminal. She nodded. "Good, 'cause we already missed one ferry."

She narrowed her eyes and gave him a dirty look, but he just laughed.

He led her down the long, white hall. Anywhere in the civilized world, the terminal would've been brushed up a bit, passed off as industrial chic, but leave it to her ancestral home to settle for nothing but exposed rivets and painted commandments that promised—if followed—to ensure everyone's safety and enjoyment.

A couple pushing bikes slid past them, heading toward the ferry's lower-level entrance, but Remy led her to the upper level. He sat down her bags and slipped the horn under his left arm as he fished a wad of singles from his pocket. He presented four dollars to the fare taker, then scooped up her shopping. There were a couple of seating areas that, although open to the wind, provided shelter from the sun. "Over there," she said and nodded, making a beeline to a group of plastic chairs. It was hot, her shoes were killing her, and in spite of being here with Remy, something about this little jaunt to Algiers was not sitting well with her.

Remy sat the bags down between them, then took the chair beside her. She noticed the way his knees poked up in the chair—funny, when she had to sit forward in it so that her feet touched the deck. "Seems a bit of a shame, really," he said, turning the horn in his hands.

The breeze blew her hair into her face. She reached up to brush it back.

"It isn't cursed," he said. "It isn't tainted."

She didn't contradict him, but she regarded the trumpet with suspicion.

"You don't believe in this magic stuff do you?" he said.

"You don't?" she asked.

"You're the only magic I need." His eyes twinkled.

Her eyes rolled. "Smooth. Real smooth." She pretended his words didn't have precisely the effect he'd intended.

"I'm sorry, you know," he said.

"For what?"

"For Grandpa showing up and acting the fool. Interrupting your grandfather's funeral like he did."

"Don't worry about it," she said, leaning over to kiss his cheek. "It only got weirder from there."

"What? Your cousin? Alice?"

Lucy shook her head and laughed. "No, she's very sweet, actually. A bit fragile. I mean, I half expect her to go all *Glass Menagerie* at any moment, but . . ."

"But . . ."

"Nothing. She's fine. It's the rest of the family that's nuts."

"Present company excepted, I hope."

She turned without finishing the thought to find her uncle Vincent smirking at her. *Oh, sh* . . . In a flash she calculated her next move—*offense best defense, shame the devil,* or *look innocent and lie.* The white ball bounced around the roulette wheel, then fell into place. "Are you following me?" she said, turning on him. "What do you think gives you the right . . ."

"I dunno. Love? Concern? An avuncular sense of duty?" he said, assuming the same tone of false outrage. "Or maybe I'm not following you at all." He nodded at Remy. "Maybe I'm following him."

"Me?" Remy said, his eyes widening.

"Maybe his dad phoned me and asked me to make sure the task got done and got done right." The ferry's engines kicked in. Vincent shouted to be heard over the noise. "And maybe finding you here was just a perk of the job."

"My dad? Phoned you?" Remy seemed fixated on the idea. The ferry pulled forward and swung out into the river.

"Yes," Vincent said. "Your dad. Phoned me." He held out his hand. "Give me the horn."

Remy hesitated, flashing Lucy a confused look. "It's just . . ."

"It's just your dad has always hated me. I know. But maybe your dad has decided it's time for us all to put the past in the past. Move on." Vincent turned to face Lucy, a smirk on his lips, as he yanked the trumpet out of Remy's hand. "Looks like none too soon for your sake. Now. An honest answer. How long has this . . . ," he said, waving the horn at them in a wide circle, "been going on?"

Lucy looked at Remy, and he at her.

"A while," she finally said.

Vincent's lips pursed. He shrugged. "Fair enough." He turned to Remy. "There's history here, you know. History that means your parents might not be comfortable with your relationship."

"I thought we were putting the past in the past," Lucy said.

"This is an awful lot of past to shift all at once," Vincent said, never taking his eyes off Remy. He held out his palm toward her, seeming to anticipate her protest. "I'm not saying you should put an end to it, but I do think you may want to keep this to yourselves for a while. Let things settle down a bit." He swung his palm around and patted Remy's shoulder. "Then figure out how to break it to them. Very gently." Vincent turned back to face her. "If that's an acceptable solution to Miss Capulet here."

The wind came across the ferry at what must've been gale force. Her hair was whipping all around her, stinging her face. She must've looked like a frigging Medusa to Remy. She reached up to catch her hair and pull it back. "You won't say anything to Mom?" she said, hating how her voice squeaked up into little-girl range at the end of the sentence, hoping that the roar of the engines would cover it.

"Not a word. Not till you're ready. Or she finds out because of your own carelessness. I'm good at keeping secrets. You, not so much."

"I'm not keeping any secrets." Lucy felt her face flush. "Any other secrets."

Vincent smiled. "All right." He wagged the horn under her nose. "This looks like as good a place as any. Shall we?"

She glanced back at the shore, surprised that even though it didn't feel like the ferry was moving all that quickly, they had, in fact, cut across a good portion of the river.

Vincent glanced around the deck. Most of the other passengers were looking back at the city's shrinking skyline. "Over there," he said, nodding toward the Algiers side. The ride was smooth, but she still teetered a bit on her shoes as she pushed up from the chair. Remy reached out and caught her shoulder, steadying her. He grabbed both bags in one hand, then wrapped his arm around her shoulders.

He looked down at her, his expression a bit uncertain. As they drew near the railing, Vincent gave one final glance around, then flung the trumpet out into the Mississippi. Lucy took a step forward, her eye on the silver horn as it spun through the air, the sun glinting off it one last time between now and doomsday.

Remy shifted. It felt like Lucy's heel caught on something. Or maybe one of the bags had hit her behind the knee. She felt Remy's arm slide off her back, even as his hand connected with her shoulder. She tumbled forward, seeming to soar toward the railing, as if she, too, had been flung, but Vincent turned back and caught her hand just as her other hand caught hold of the railing. For a split second, it still felt like there was a pressure willing her forward. Maybe she was just being paranoid—the thought came to her after she managed to right herself, after her heart stopped pounding in her ears—but watching a mutilated crone tumble out of a wall grave could set anyone on edge.

# TWENTY-FOUR

Evangeline sat on the edge of her bed, staring out the French doors that opened onto her courtyard. A scent Evangeline had come to notice more often all around New Orleans, sharp and green and savage, wafted through the open door.

Outside, piece by piece, link by link, the golden necklace that she had not seen since the night of her father's death was raining down on the brick patio. Each link sang out as it bounced and fell again. Each link found its mate. They were reuniting, the necklace rebuilding itself before her eyes.

The pieces, they were coming together all right, and it was breaking her heart. Evangeline had seen it all in a moment. The cold black hatred Nicholas felt for the girl he'd called daughter. The calm reason Evangeline had witnessed in Alice's eyes.

Alice wasn't sick.

She wasn't crazy.

She had been punished for more than half her life for the crime of speaking the truth.

A raven swooped in, dropping the quarter-sized medallion into her upturned, waiting palm. The sight filled her with memories of the few days she'd spent with this necklace as a yoke around her neck, burning, draining her magic, stealing her power—put there by her own father in his fear.

Marceline landed before her, growing, her feathers already receding, her long blonde hair jetting out. In no time, she was in full human form. Evangeline suspected the speed with which Marceline now shifted form had been boosted by magic harvested from that wretched Brodeur woman. No. She didn't suspect. She knew. Evangeline couldn't allow herself the luxury of denial. She was bargaining with a devil. But it would take a devil's power to do what she must.

Marceline came and sat beside her. Evangeline wondered which was her true form—the graceful, lovely blonde at her side, or the black-winged bird. Maybe both. Maybe neither. Perhaps she had another face, a truer face, that Evangeline hadn't yet seen.

"I'm pleased you called out to us," Marceline said, her voice cool, calming.

Evangeline sensed the witch was working her mojo, making it easier for Evangeline to bear her presence. Evangeline chuckled to herself. She'd already done her own medicating. Two screwdrivers counted as breakfast, right? "You've come alone," she said, turning the abhorrent coin over in her hand.

"Yes, I thought it best to come without my abrasive sisters. You're coming around to the truth," she said, slowing her speech, letting her hand rest close to, but not touching, Evangeline's own, "but you are still a scared little rabbit."

"I know it was you who sent me the message from Nicholas."

"We wanted you to see. We needed you to know the truth. About Nicholas. The things he's capable of."

"Let's not pretend you give a damn about the truth," Evangeline said, holding up her hand. The links of the rejoined gold chain streaked into her upturned palm with a soft *shink* sound. "Or about me." She hated this piece of jewelry, what it had meant to her mother, what it had meant to her. Once the medallion was fixed on both sides to the chain, it would reactivate. Anyone whose neck it had managed to find itself around would be caught in a noose that blocked the flow of magic through them. "I know you three were responsible for that abomination." She shook her head in disgust. "What did Delphine Brodeur ever do to deserve such a thing?"

"No," Marceline said, "let's don't pretend." She reached up and touched Evangeline's hair. Evangeline didn't resist. The touch felt comforting, and counterfeit or no, she could use all the comfort she could get. "But I do care for you. As much as my long-atrophied heart can."

Marceline paused, studying her features. She knew Marceline was trying to determine how far she could go without losing her. Marceline needn't worry. Evangeline was prepared to follow her around as many bends as it took to arrive at the truth. "I did love your mother, too. After a fashion. We called each other "sister" long before we came to this country as Ursuline nuns.

"And as far as Delphine is concerned, she was the closest thing to a daughter I have ever known," Marceline fixed Evangeline with her gaze, daring her to open herself up, to use her empathic abilities to weigh the truth of Marceline's words. But Evangeline was no fool. "You must know we weren't responsible for the harm done to poor, poor Delphine. We cannot even enter Précieux Sang. The united covens long ago put a ward over the spot. The wall where you saw Margot and me is as far as we can penetrate."

"Or maybe the ward has failed. Maybe you can flit right in," Evangeline said, not yet willing to make the leap she intuited the other witch wanted her to make, though suspicion had nettled her even before her visitor had come.

Marceline laughed. "Oh, my dear, I assure you. I never 'flit.'"

"Why were you there at all, if not to check out your handiwork?"

"To see to your safety."

"Oh, really?" Evangeline said.

"Yes, really. I care for you. I do." Marceline focused on the coin in Evangeline's hand. "If I didn't care for you, that yoke would still be around your neck."

"You are such a liar."

"I haven't lied to you, *chérie*. My truths may not be to your taste, but I have never lied to you."

"Death," Evangeline said, shaking the chain. "You said only death could open its clasp."

Marceline leaned back, raising her chin, studying Evangeline. "Perhaps there's an emergency escape, or"—she reached out with one hand, caressing, Evangeline felt, her very aura—"or perhaps I killed you."

The words unsnapped something inside her, and the memories came flooding back. Clambering out of the cab of her father's truck. Seeing the splatter where his skull had cracked open like an egg against the pavement. A screech from above. Looking up as a winged beast swooped down on her. Running. Running. Tumbling forward at the exact moment talons caught hold of her, sweeping her up into the sky.

Dropping. Dropping. The thin finger of black, muddy water coming closer. Screaming. Struggling against baptism. Trying to fight back. Trying to move her hands. Trying to strike out. The flapping of wings as she dipped beneath the surface. Burning lungs. How could cold water burn? Blackness.

An injunction to forget.

Evangeline jumped up, turning to face the creature she had invited into her home.

Marceline clasped her hands together in an entreaty. "Half-witch, we killed him, but not for what he did to your mother. She went into his bed, under his hand, of her own free will. He met his fate because he took away what should have been ours. *You.*"

"Me?"

"Your mother bargained with us for her release from the blood oath she made to us." Marceline nodded. "You were to join us the day your magic came to you. You were to take her place. But he put your mother's trinket around your neck."

Evangeline shook her head. She supposed she should be terrified, but she was too damn angry. "You killed my father to get your claws on me. You drowned me—"

"We brought you back—"

"You drowned me to remove my mother's amulet." She flung the coin and chain at Marceline's bare feet. A spark rose as it struck. "And then you deserted me. Left me to raise myself."

"You've done okay. Maybe even better than you would have done growing up pumicing the callouses from Mathilde's feet." Marceline smiled and gave a slight shrug, seemingly incapable of feeling guilt or even regret. But then her mirth fell away, her expression turning serious. "You were too much him, half-witch."

"I'm nothing like my father."

Marceline said nothing. She responded by raising her eyebrow, tilting her head. Then her eyes dropped to the coin and chain at her feet. "You should know. Water won't work again," Marceline said. "The medallion has an intelligence. It knows when it's been cheated. It won't allow itself to be tricked a second time." She knelt, keeping her eyes on Evangeline, and picked up both medallion and chain. Rising, she threaded the chain through one of the talisman's clasps. "How do you plan on using this?"

"To protect Alice. Just like you asked me to," Evangeline said as her mind turned to Nicholas. The lies he'd told about Alice, just to keep her locked up where he'd never have to see her. Where she could never betray his secret.

The crumbs he had tossed Hugo. Never good enough.

The years she'd wasted.

Marceline's eyes narrowed in pleasure, like she'd just tasted something delicious. "Protection, you say?" She sniffed the air and smiled. "It smells more like revenge."

Evangeline wished she could deny it, but now she knew. Revenge was in order.

"A few members of the Chanticleer Coven," Evangeline said, "Rose Gramont, Gabriel Prosper and his sister, another couple who've since passed . . . they were there when Luc Marin was killed . . . when Luc was murdered. Alice was there, too. She saw it happen." She reached out her hand to accept the talisman and chain. "The adults, they said Luc killed himself. But Alice . . ." Evangeline looked down at that coin, the last of her mother's magic, examining the old script engraved on it—older, it seemed, than even the damnable Gothic Daniel had shown her. "Alice said she saw a force behind Luc." Alice had claimed to see some force driving Luc to put that gun to his head and pull the trigger, but Evangeline could no longer allow herself the luxury of believing it had been Luc's own wounded pride. "She claimed Babau Jean killed him."

"Well, Babau Jean has always delighted in revealing himself to children."

"But Babau Jean isn't real. Nicholas said . . ." Evangeline caught herself. She was speaking with a buck-naked witch who'd flown into her room in the form of a raven. She'd put on two pounds overnight eating cookies baked by a servitor spirit. And still, she had accepted at face value Nicholas's claim that Babau Jean was a figment of the collective imagination.

"Oh, I assure you," Marceline said. "He's real enough. At least when he wishes to be." She paused, studying Evangeline's expression. "Or when one with enough power wishes him to be."

Alice had claimed Babau Jean was following her everywhere. Day and night. Terrified, she'd begun using her magic to strike out. And so

Nicholas had sent her off to molder on that faraway island. Evangeline bit her lip, nodding to herself. Feeling the weight of the conclusion she had reached. "I believe Alice saw something. And I believe it was something so terrible she couldn't allow herself to see it. Not without a filter."

"You believe Alice saw her father murder Luc."

Evangeline's heart skipped at the words. She began nodding. She felt numb, but her numbness had nothing to do with Marceline's intervention. It came with the knowledge she'd been giving herself to the man who'd killed Luc. For years. She had allowed herself to love Luc's killer. "Yes. But she couldn't stand it, so her mind told her she saw Babau Jean do it."

"Perhaps the mask and the true identity are one."

"I don't understand."

"Perhaps her father and Babau Jean are one, or are at least in the process of becoming one."

Evangeline shook her head. She was in no mood for puzzles right now. "What in the hell are you talking about?"

Marceline smiled. "I planted a seed," she said and glanced around the room, seemingly searching for something. "In your pet's mind." Marceline's focus sharpened. "Not an easy act. She is a willful creature."

"Daniel," Evangeline said. "You made her remember Daniel." She'd already guessed as much. It had felt too convenient for the cat to suddenly remember her old foe on the heels of the sisters' visit.

"Guilty as charged," she said and purred, an imitation accurate enough to bring Sugar to the door. The cat took one look at Marceline and yowled, casting a warning glance at Evangeline, then tore back into the kitchen. "Guilty," Marceline said, "even where I haven't been charged."

Marceline rose and went to a nightstand, tugging open the drawer and tossing out its contents—a collection of letters, including an unused recommendation from a professor for a graduate school application. She fished out a strip of photo booth snapshots of Evangeline's parents—her sole inheritance from them aside from the talisman and her own flesh and blood. Marceline had known exactly where to find the strip, almost as if she'd seen it there before. Evangeline felt her skin crawl at the thought that this creature might have come in secret, her presence veiled even from Sugar, to riffle through her private affairs. Marceline regarded the pictures, her disgust evident. She held the photos up, seeming to compare the two faces to Evangeline's own. "Too much him," she said.

"Why Daniel?" Evangeline said, doing her best to maintain focus.

Marceline dropped the photo carelessly back into the drawer. "Can you really not hear it? *The Book of the Unwinding* calling?"

"What does your book have to do with Daniel?" Evangeline insisted.

"He showed you *The Lesser Key*," she said. "Don't try to dissimulate. I can smell it on you."

"Yes. He showed me. How did you know he even had access to it?"

"*The Lesser Key* resonates along with its master, *The Book of the Unwinding*. Theodosius's lesser work explains how to *earn* the greater. I know where every single extant copy of *The Lesser Key* is. Every single one."

Her expression turned beatific, a saint of the darkness. "Your Daniel, he has the mark, does he not? The mark of *The Lesser Key*?"

Evangeline held her tongue, but Marceline seemed to intuit the truth. "He was created to walk between worlds. To open a lock that couldn't be opened solely from either side. Your Nicholas created him . . . or rather he made his wife create him. So he could wear him. Like an envelope. No"—she held up her hand—"like a diving suit." She nodded at her own simile. "Man joined to spirit. The only way to travel to the underworld and return."

"The underworld?"

Marceline looked at Evangeline as if she were a natural-born fool. "What do you think lies at the other end of the Dreaming Road, *ma chérie*? The underworld, the afterworld, the great beyond." Her eyes flashed with humor. "Perhaps even the Elysian Fields." She laughed. "Oh, *ma fille*, it was no coincidence that the Book brought itself to New Orleans. The Book called out to the world, and the Crescent City bent its spine like a willing lover to receive it. Why do you think death is so ever-present here?

"It was all anticipated. It was all foreseen. The prophecies of the twilight of magic, the ascendance of *The Book of the Unwinding*. In the final days of magic, the hiding of the Book between worlds." She held out her hands as if she were handing something precious to Evangeline, beseeching her to hear, to believe. "The Book," she said, "has been waiting. Waiting so long for its time."

"And Nicholas?" Evangeline asked, returning to the matter central to her own heart.

"Nicholas, he knew of the prophecies. He believed . . . believes himself to be the inheritor of the last breath of magic."

Evangeline shook her head.

"The final breath of magic will issue from the Book itself. The witch who holds the last bit of magic will determine what comes next. I believe your Nicholas plans to mold magic in his own image. But to do so, he'll have to make a couple of sacrifices."

"Sacrifices?"

"The girl Alice. The boy Hugo." She looked at Evangeline with something that came close to sympathy, as if she couldn't muster true sympathy, but cared enough to counterfeit the real thing. "Luc has already been disposed of, but the King of Bones and Ashes, my dear, must be entirely without progeny."

Evangeline's mind flashed to the image at the center of *The Lesser Key*. The King of Bones and Ashes. The Queen of Heaven. Inanna and Damuzi.

"Astrid loved her children," Marceline continued. "She never wanted to be Nicholas's queen, so she escaped the only way she knew how. She took to the Dreaming Road. She left him with Daniel, a hobbled knight, and deprived him of his queen.

"I believe Nicholas found Babau Jean while he was searching the Dreaming Road for Astrid. Your Daniel is a well-mannered parlor trick, but Babau Jean is perhaps the strongest servitor spirit ever created. A far better vessel than anything Astrid, powerful witch that she was, could have created. I believe your Nicholas latched onto Babau Jean. But he still needs his Inanna. His queen. A strong, beautiful witch, capable of both darkness and light, to pull him back from the beyond." She traced a cold finger down Evangeline's cheek.

"You must realize Luc's death wasn't about punishing him." Marceline dropped her hand to her side. "Not entirely. Nor was it only about removing an obstacle between himself and the Book. No, *ma chérie*, it was about Nicholas claiming you as his new queen."

Evangeline felt cold and hot at the same time, her own heart turning toward murder. She grasped the chain in her clenched fist, reassuring herself—no, this fate, being broken, powerless, would be a much more satisfying punishment.

"As long as his children live, he can't get his hands on the Book," Marceline said. "We told you that Alice was important to someone important to us. You, *ma jolie*, are the one to whom she is important."

"But Alice isn't his daughter. Not really."

An amused glimmer rose in Marceline's eye. "Nicholas told you that?"

Evangeline nodded, though Marceline's tone had already set her to doubting.

"And you believed him, did you?" Marceline tapped the side of her nose. "Seems to me that a man capable of murdering one child would have no trouble denying another—if it suited his purposes to do so."

Marceline cast a look back down at the photos from the drawer. She smiled. "You say you're nothing like your father." Evangeline watched as Marceline fell away, transforming once again into avian form. "But your father," she said, taking wing, "he used the necklace for revenge, too."

# TWENTY-FIVE

Today was Vèvè's not quite so grand reopening, but tomorrow was St. John's Eve, and in keeping with her mother's practice, Lisette would close the shop for the holiday. Anyone serious about Voodoo would be getting together for a drumming, or maybe gathering—clad all in white—over by Magnolia Bridge for a head washing. Even those folk who didn't partake in public ceremonies would be home making offerings of cigars or candy and white rum on an altar dedicated to the Widow Paris. Lisette hated to lose out on the tourist trade, but it was her mother's way.

Lisette had kept the shop open late, as she always did the day before the holiday. She did so to allow extra time for true believers, most Lisette's parents' age, to come together and reminisce. Even last year, a number of them had claimed to remember congregating by bonfires on the banks of Lake Pontchartrain where it meets the Bayou St. John, a mathematical improbability if not an outright impossibility, even for those with the grayest hair. Lisette had listened and smiled as she always did when the old folk spoke of old times, *les temps jadis*.

Not challenging the veracity of these cherished memories was a little lagniappe she offered these elderly clients.

This year the longer hours served a more mercenary purpose—she hoped to bring in a few extra dollars to help cover the insurance deductible. Maybe catch up a bit on tomorrow's loss.

Isadore had wanted to come keep an eye on things, keep an eye on her, but she had refused. He had two days of work to catch up on, and the late twilight would give him and Remy a chance to finish some jobs he'd let slide. Lisette would be all right—had to be all right—on her own. If not, she was letting the Aryan-wannabe bastard win. Still, Lisette had not argued when Isadore insisted he'd come by to pick her up at ten.

Manon had offered to find someone to fill in for her at the hotel, claiming Lisette might need extra help on the register, but her daughter had already missed out on one night of wages this week. She'd said no. Besides, she knew what had motivated the offer. Manon had been studying Krav Maga, and Lisette knew her daughter was just itching to give the son of a bitch who had wrecked the shop a taste of what she'd been learning. She reminded Manon, just to show her that she wasn't fooling anyone, that it was unlikely the vandal would return so soon. If he planned to come back for another go, he'd wait till the repairs were further along.

In the end, it didn't matter that Lisette had been left there alone. Holiday or no, Vèvè had hardly been overwhelmed with business. In fact, this year, not a soul had ventured in. She'd given up an hour ago, flipping the "*Ouvert*" sign over to "*Fermé*" and turning the lock. It looked like none of the old folk had any interest in coming out, preferring their slippers and the glow of a television screen to reminiscing about dancing by firelight.

Or maybe they had just moved beyond what Vèvè had to offer.

*Love. Success. Sexual prowess.* The things Lisette promised to sell were a young person's dreams. Maybe the old guard, feeling the aches in their bones and lint in their pockets, had figured out that they weren't going to get much further in life than they already had, no matter how many candles they lit. Maybe they'd lost faith, too—or they'd realized that *she* had.

Or perhaps in spite of the large "We're Open during Repairs" sign Remy had spray painted this morning, they'd been put off by the plywood covering the windows and the whole of the door except for a six-by-three-inch spy hole. A damned masterpiece the sign was, a testament to the indifference of the Ghede loa to both the slings and arrows of life and the crowbar of some cowardly white supremacist. Maman Brigitte herself stood in its center, swallowing shards of the broken vèvè windowpanes Remy had rescued from the garbage bin and incorporated into his art. Manon, who rarely praised her little brother to his face—*gotta keep the little prince humble*, she always said—had wrapped her arms around him as she stood there taking his work in.

"You're going to be somebody," she had said.

"Already am," he'd answered with mock affront.

"Yes, you are," Manon had said, and planted a kiss on his cheek. Seeing the two of them like that, bending but not breaking, had convinced Lisette that no matter how loud people got, how nasty, her family would survive. Hell, they would thrive.

Lisette looked around the now quiet shop. "You saw them, didn't you, Mama?" She scanned the dim corners, pricked up her ears. Waiting. Hoping. "You saw them, your grandbabies pulling together to get this place back in shape." She stood, stock still. No response came.

The door rattled, causing Lisette to startle.

She cast a glance at the clock. It had just gone nine. Maybe Remy's assistance had helped his dad catch up quicker, or perhaps Manon had slipped out from the hotel on her break? She stood, intending to investigate, but then the fear slipped in. What if the man who'd done this— the vandal who'd desecrated the altar built by her mother's hands, who wanted to erase her and her family from this country, if not from the whole damned world—what if he'd returned?

There was a loud rap on the door. Did criminals knock? She eased her way out from behind the counter and took two quick steps toward the door. She slowed as the lights dimmed once, twice, then returned to normal. The knock was repeated with greater insistence.

"Coming," she called, wondering if there had been a power surge.

Reaching the door, she stationed herself to the side of the spy hole and lifted up on her toes to peek through the hole Isadore had cut, two inches too high, in the plywood. The eyes peering back at her through the gathering shadows were the last she'd expected to see. She rolled back on her heels, wondering if it were possible to pretend she wasn't in.

"Lisette," a voice she hadn't even heard in over a decade called through the slight opening. "It's me. Vincent. Vincent Marin," he added, as if it were necessary. As if she wouldn't recognize the man she had come so close to marrying unless he mentioned the family name that had almost been her own. "Can I come in? Talk with you a bit?"

For a moment her mouth went dry. She didn't need him here. Certainly not now. She sure as hell didn't need Isadore finding them here together. Her husband didn't have a jealous bone in his body, except when it came to this man. She considered telling Vincent the shop was closed. That he'd have to come back. Then she realized just how stupid she'd feel turning him away. She cast another glance at the clock. Better to hear him out—and then get him out.

"Just a moment," she said, reaching to open the lock. She heard the click, then stepped back, pushing the door out. Vincent's hand reached in, tugging the door to him. He stood there on the threshold, a strip of rose sky darkened overhead, the building opposite in shadow.

"I'm real sorry about Celestin," she said, blocking his way.

His lips curled into a smile. "Well, Alcide sure wasn't."

There was a pause. Too long to pretend she wasn't thrown by the nearness of him. This was the closest she'd been to him since the night she'd sent him away, more than two decades before.

Vincent's face had filled out, and laugh lines had long since become permanent creases. His curly black hair, now cropped short, had gone salt and pepper. But none of these changes came as a surprise. She had spent twenty years now scrutinizing photos of him on the society page or accompanying news stories about his construction company, cataloging all the ways in which he'd changed. She felt a sinking feeling that he, too, was probably examining her, comparing some idealized version of her to the woman she'd slowed and thickened into.

She'd aged. Hell, they both had.

But he was as handsome as ever. And he wasn't just some inky newsprint or computer glare now—he was here in the flesh, and that made a difference. She felt the blood rise to her cheeks, remembering some *temps jadis* of her own.

"Yeah. About that," she said, finding her voice, forcing those memories back into the past. She loved her husband. And she was enough of a realist to know she no longer loved Vincent. She no longer even knew him. Not really. What she loved was the memory of the two of them, young and together. She loved the memory of herself at twenty. "I'm sorry about that, too. I should've done more to stop him. I know . . ."

Her mind flashed on her father's silver horn. How much did Vincent understand about her father's intentions?

Vincent held up his hands, shook his head. "No need to apologize. I'm not here for that. Besides, I think Alcide's blues solo might've helped him bury some of the old animosity. And that's a good thing." His eyes twinkled. "'Cause I'm not sure our families are quite through with each other yet."

Lisette shook her head, confused.

"I took a little ferry ride today with your son and his date."

"Date?"

"Fleur's daughter, Lucy. You should've seen the way Remy was looking at my niece," Vincent said. "And the way she was looking right back. Seems like history is about to repeat itself."

History. A poor choice of words, she thought. The story of their families was not one she'd care to hear retold. "I, I," Lisette stuttered. "Remy didn't mention . . ."

"A young man didn't tell his mother he's been sprung by a pretty girl?" Vincent said. "Imagine that." He smiled again. A big, warm smile that promised her things between them were all right. That maybe even the whole damned world was all right. "May I?" he said, and only then did Lisette realize she hadn't yet allowed him to enter.

She returned his smile. "Yes. Of course." She stepped back, giving him room to pass her.

He hadn't ventured inside since before her mother's death. She gave him a chance to take it all in, allow the ghost of how it used to be fade into her slapped-together attempt at recovery. She cast a guilty glance at the sad altar she'd set up for Erzulie, an old card table she'd pulled from her garage and covered with a cheap pink sateen sheet. She'd stopped off at the convenience store on her way in and picked up a plastic-sheathed bouquet of drooping pink roses and a six-pack of pink frosted mini-cupcakes, two of which had served as her breakfast. A couple of white candles she kept beneath the counter in case of a power outage completed the offering. It was a lazy offering, but then again, Erzulie was a lazy loa.

Vincent wandered around, looking at the makeshift displays, casting his eyes over the reclaimed merchandise, the few bits and bobs that hadn't suffered damage, mostly mass-produced plastic souvenirs, but also dozens of books. The shelves where the books had been lined up had for some reason been left untouched.

"I heard about what happened here," he said. "I wanted to see if there was anything I could do to help." He paused. "You know my crew could get this place cleaned up in no time."

"I don't think we could afford you."

His shoulders dropped. "Gratis. No charge. Take this place down to its bones, if you'd like." He raised a hand and pointed around at the tight aisles, the high, battered built-ins that gave the shop the feel of a maze. "Give the old place a better flow." He nodded at the wasted space against the back wall, sacrificed to a stairway to nowhere. The upper floor had been given a separate entrance forty years ago or more. "Free that up. Make it better in here than it was before." It was funny. Until the break-in, Lisette had considered this space as integral, inviolate. Vincent's desire to break down and rebuild, even in an attempt to help, felt almost like a second act of violence. "I'll even cover the materials," he said, turning his gaze up to the "Readings by Soulange" sign. Lisette thanked whatever force in the universe had caused the vandal to overlook it.

"I loved your mother, too," he added.

The word "too" hung in the air and attached itself to the rest of his sentence. It changed the whole thing from an expression of affection for her mama, to a declaration of love for her. Then there was the way his gaze sharpened on her. The way his nostrils flared. They served as witness to the fact that his feelings were not entirely a thing of the past. "Let me do this for her." He took a step closer. "Let me do this for you."

Though he stood at a safe, respectful distance, he was leaning in almost imperceptibly, and there was a slight twitch in the thick muscles of his arms, as if he were readying himself to open them wide, if only. If only she would take that first step.

Lisette shook her head. "I don't think we could *afford* you."

He nodded, then he crossed before her and went behind the counter, looking up at the "Readings by Soulange" sign.

"They were such great friends, our mothers," he said, tracing her mother's name with his finger. "Mother would've never hurt Soulange."

She felt a pang of guilt, even though she had nothing to feel guilty about. "I never said she did."

"No," he said, "but I know it's what you think. Or at least you did at the time." There, in his gravelly voice, buried beneath the hurt, Lisette uncovered a layer of anger. He grasped the edges of the sign, and for a moment, Lisette feared she might lose this last bit of her mother, too. But he only straightened the plaque before lowering his hands.

Lisette's mama had taken the St. Charles streetcar to the Garden District to meet up with Laure Marin that day. The two women had been scheming about something for weeks. But while Lisette had assumed the two were meddling, planning to apply joint pressure to get Lisette to agree to the big wedding they both wanted, she'd never suspected they were involved in something truly dangerous. Somehow the two had ended up miles away, out on Grunch Road in East New Orleans. That's where the police had found them—her mama dead, and Laure Marin, her hair gone white as snow, mumbling some bullshit about Babau Jean.

She'd held on to her mother's faith, perhaps more out of loyalty than true conviction, at least until Katrina. That wave of universal suffering had crashed over her city and washed away what was left of her faith in magic, but, still, it was Laure's story about Babau Jean that had put the first crack in her levee. Lisette might never learn what happened out there, but even on the day she'd felt pretty damned sure the bogey-man hadn't killed her mama.

"I don't know what I thought at the time. It was so long ago," she said. "And I know even less what I think about it now."

"But you must have some idea. Or at least a theory. What do you think they were getting up to?" Vincent looked back over his shoulder at her. "I know you were in too much pain to talk about it back when it happened," he said, his lips quivering up into a sad smile. "Hell, you didn't want to talk at all. At least not to me."

It was strange that whenever Lisette thought of the days surrounding her mother's death, she remembered them in black and white like some old movie. Her therapist thought it was a sign she was trying to repress the memories by making them seem less real, and there was no denying it hurt like hell to go back to those days.

"I'm sorry," he said. He must have read her pain on her face. "I meant to help make things better, not stir up old ghosts."

Lisette listened, waiting. That should've been her mother's cue—or at least the cue for the voice in her head—to speak. To make some dry comment. She . . . *it* remained silent.

"But I've always wondered," Vincent continued. "Did Soulange share anything with you?"

She shook her head. "No, Mama didn't tell me anything," Lisette said, which was true enough, even if it felt like a lie. Her mother had said nothing to her while living, but since then, her mother—or at least the voice in her head that *sounded* like her mother—had told her not to grieve her death, that between Laure and herself, she'd been the luckier of the two. "I don't know what they got themselves into." She forced herself to pause. To regain control before speaking again. "I've come to understand," she said, weighing her words, "that our mothers both had vivid imaginations, what with their talk of spirits and spells." She felt sure this would put a lid on the subject, but Vincent seemed even more intrigued.

"What spirits? What types of spells?" He leaned forward as he asked.

"I don't know. I don't remember." She wondered at his earnestness. "It's all nonsense anyway."

His expression changed. His head tilted forward, his lips pulled together, his eyebrows moved in toward each other and up. He looked like the textbook picture of concern. "You don't believe?"

"Oh, Vincent," she said, and laughed at his serious expression. "There's no magic in this world. Not real magic."

He turned and came around the counter, then reached back and grasped the edge of it. "Well, there's certainly much less of it than there used to be." He looked down the bridge of his nose at her. Expectant.

Waiting, it seemed, for her to acknowledge his words. As if he were part of a secret society, and he expected a response that would show she, too, was in the know.

She drew a breath, shaking her head, intending to offer some platitude about gilded memories.

"You seem so sure—"

"No," she cut him off. "I'm not sure about anything." It surprised her that a grown man, a man who built things out of stone and steel, could still be caught up in childish fantasy. But he'd grown up hearing the same stories she had, and for him, she could tell, they were as good as gospel. She'd lived long enough to know you can neither argue nor embarrass a man out of his beliefs.

"Delphine Brodeur."

Her mouth fell open, shocked as she was to hear the woman's name on Vincent's lips.

"She believed," he said—and his choice of the past tense struck her. "She came here looking for magic. Real magic. Strong magic," he said.

"I sensed that she's a true believer, but how the hell did you know about—"

"Was," he said. "Was a true believer. She's no longer with us," he said, answering one question, raising a thousand others. "You know, she was sniffing around here," he continued before she could ask them, "a long time before she ever poked her nose in. She believed you had something invaluable. Something you inherited from Soulange. Something that rightfully belongs to me."

Lisette's eyes darted around the shop. "There's nothing special here. Nothing she couldn't have found in any of the other Voodoo shops in the Quarter."

"She thought there was. She was certain of it. That was why she sent her man Carver to bust the place up. To spook you into selling." He paused, one eyebrow rising. "Not that Carver didn't enjoy his work."

The shock made her knees weaken. She reached out and caught hold of a shelf, bracing herself. She thought of the broken windows, the mostly misspelled racist scrawls, obscure combinations of symbols and numbers, the meaning of which she had intuited even though she'd never encountered them before. That damned swastika.

The way the bitch had looked her right in the eye and called herself a friend. "Delphine was behind this?"

"You look surprised," he said. "You shouldn't be. Delphine never considered herself a racist—might've even protested if anyone had called her on it—but she sure had no trouble aligning herself with them. She wound her man Carver up and set him loose. On her own, she might not have ended up where her man did, turning a simple act of intimidation into a hate crime. But she knew where he'd take this, and she was fine with it as long as it served her purpose."

Lisette sensed movement and heard the heavy tread of Vincent's work boots as he came closer. Soon, he stood directly before her. She felt the temperature of the room drop, though it had been hot in there most of the day since she'd cut back on the air-conditioning to save on the electric bill. She wrapped her arms around herself, surprised to see her own breath form a mist. "But they've paid a price. They've both been punished."

"How could you know? How could you know any of this?"

"Because I'm the one who punished them."

"I think you'd better go." Lisette lowered her eyes, not wanting to see the strange glint that had risen in his.

Vincent nodded, but he didn't move. Instead he leaned back, looking at her through narrowed eyes. "Do you really know nothing of the Book? Of your mother's actions?" She recognized his tone, a cautioning incredulity. She'd used it enough when her children were young. When she knew they were hiding something, dissimulating, and she wanted to coax the truth out of them before they strayed into a full-fledged lie.

"I don't know," she began, shaking her head.

He looked down on her. Considering her. "All right," he said, the warmth returning to his voice. "I believe you."

The door opened, and her eyes darted toward the sound, expecting to find Isadore there. Relieved before she saw him. But instead of her husband, she saw the brunette woman, the one who'd visited the shop with her friends the day before the break-in. She held a thin red book.

"I told you that you were wasting time," the brunette said, addressing, Lisette soon realized, Vincent. "The fool knows nothing." She raised her hand in the air, moving the book she held in a widening spiral. "Nothing."

A large black bird—a raven? a crow?—swooped in over the woman's head. A second bobbed up on the floor behind her, struggling on unsteady legs. It flapped its wings and bounded to the reconstructed altar, where it pecked away at the remaining convenience-store sweets Lisette had put out as a quick and easy offering for Erzulie.

"I sense a blood lock," the brunette said, raising both eyebrows, then turned her gaze on Lisette.

"A death to seal," the bird sang, hopping up and down on one foot. "A death to open."

The first bird stationed itself in front of the door, and it began to grow, to shift, before Lisette's wondering eyes—its feathers flattening first into flesh-like scales, then smoothing into fair skin. Ice-blue eyes shone from behind a flattening beak. Blond hair jetted up like water from a fountain, then fell around a now normal-looking woman's naked shoulders. The cool blonde. The brunette's friend.

At the sight, Lisette felt a sense of serenity descend upon her. The vandalism. It hadn't triggered a breakthrough; it'd brought on a breakdown. But that was okay. If she was mad, if she had hit rock bottom, she'd be able to start clawing her way back up.

"Blood like hers," the brunette said, nodding toward Lisette. She clapped her hands in happy anticipation. "She should certainly fit the lock. If her mother's death created the seal, then none better than hers to break it."

"No, sisters," the fair woman said, holding up both hands, now quite human, and kneading the air. Her eyes focused, and she walked over to the altar, a small smile rising to her lips. "It's more complex than that." She swooped her arm across the folding table, brushing the bird, the candles, and the remaining crumbs to the ground. The raven cawed angrily, and even pecked at the blonde's hand, but the woman disregarded its displeasure. "This one, she's of no use to us." She grasped the edges of the table, yanked it up into the air, and flung it to the far end of the shop. "But there is one here who is," she said, running her hands around the now-empty space, a space once held by her mother's true altar. She turned to face Vincent. "The spirit of the Simeon woman. She's here. She's hiding, but I can feel her."

Lisette's eyes darted around the room. She didn't see her mother. She didn't feel her.

"Soulange," Vincent said. "Of course. She's the piece of the puzzle Delphine sensed was hidden here." He spun around, his eyes wide, wild. "Well, come on, you bitch. Come out, come out, wherever you are."

His challenge was met with silence.

"All right, then." Vincent sighed, and reached out to touch Lisette. He took her chin in his hand and forced her eyes to meet his. "When I took his heart, I never expected to feel his pain." His grip tightened, squeezing her chin like a vice. "This will hurt me more than it hurts you," he said, "at least if you don't struggle." He raised his hand, forcing her up on her toes.

"What the hell is wrong with you?" she gritted the words out from between her teeth.

His hand slid down, catching her throat in large calloused fingers. She grasped the first weapon she could reach, one of the few unbroken statuettes, a figurine of the Marassa twins, the three torsos sharing a single lower body. She reached back and swung it as hard as she could.

It shattered as it connected with Vincent's temple, a sharp point lacerating his cheek, the skin peeling away in a flap. It must have hurt like hell, but he didn't cry out. He released her, catching at the flap of skin, pressing it back into place.

*There should be more blood.* The words drifted through her mind unbidden. The women dove at her, but Vincent held out his other hand, warning them off, stopping them.

He grunted, growled—the sounds coming out of him were not human. He lowered his hand, and the flap of skin fell again. His hand reached up, impatient, and caught hold of it, pulling it up and out. Lisette felt her stomach begin to churn as Vincent's face peeled away to reveal a pale white mask. She watched in disbelief as the man before her grew taller, Vincent's thick muscles lengthening, growing thinner. This . . . this *creature* tossed aside the mushy flesh that had once been Vincent's face. The bird hopped over and began pecking away at it.

Lisette forced down the taste of bile. She began backing away, grasping the shard of the statuette with both hands, swinging it in a wild zigzag.

The pale creature glided across the room without taking a single step. He held out his hand to Lisette, and her paltry weapon crumbled to dust.

"You have brought this," the creature said, though his voice was no longer Vincent's baritone, but a shrill, whispery whine, "on yourself." She felt herself caught up in the air, her arms and legs shooting out like an X, then he began pulling her apart, her fingernails loosening first. She heard herself screaming.

A wall of fire, blue like the tips of a gas jet, instantly shot up between her and the monster. Lisette tumbled to the ground. When she lifted her eyes, she saw the monster was backing away, a figure, blue like the fire—a part of the fire—advancing on him. The women and their bird fled from the fire, screeching as if they themselves were being burned.

Lisette heard words. Powerful words. A chanting. Her mother's voice.

"Mama?" she said as the creature who'd attacked her seemed to grow smaller, sliding backward—not so much out of the shop as into another space that shrunk around him until it closed and disappeared.

The fire turned toward her . . . and *spoke*. "All right, girl," her mother's voice said. "Are you ready to listen to me now?"

# TWENTY-SIX

Lisette didn't know what the hell to think.

The hot blue flames faded, leaving Lisette's mother standing there as clear as day. She rushed to her mother and threw her arms around her, only for Soulange to evaporate like a wisp of smoke.

"It doesn't work like that, baby," her mother's voice sounded around her. Lisette watched as her mother's image reassembled itself. She looked, Lisette realized, exactly as she had the last time Lisette had seen her alive. "You want something to hold, you've got to give me a *chwal* to ride. You should know that. Or have you forgotten everything I taught you?"

"No, Mama," Lisette said, thrilled to be in her mother's presence, no matter how impalpable, but still burning with a sense of shame. "I haven't forgotten anything."

"No, you just stopped believing in it."

Lisette froze, looking into the eyes she'd longed to see for so long. "Yeah, Mama. I did."

"I don't fault you, my sweet girl." She shook her head. "Not one bit. In your shoes I might've done the same."

"Why have you never shown yourself to me before?"

One eyebrow raised, an expression Lisette well remembered. It meant her mother was about to put her in her place. "Would that have helped? Really? When I felt you losing your faith after the storm, I did what I could to let you know I was still here, trying to guide you. I talked to you, but would you listen? No. You went running off to some psychiatrist to yammer about what a bad mother I was to you."

"Oh, Mama, no," Lisette said, reaching out to touch her mother, remembering herself the instant before her hand passed through the phantasm. "I never said anything like that. I never said you were a bad mother. Never." She said the word with conviction. A small smile rose on her mother's lips. "It's only I thought I was losing my damned mind."

"And me popping up in your mirror while you brushed your teeth would've helped with that?"

It felt like a storm cloud hung between them for a moment, but then they both burst out laughing.

"No, I reckon it wouldn't have." Lisette became aware that she could see the shelves through the lower half of her mother's body. And there, only a few feet from where she stood, was the ruined flesh that had once been Vincent's face. She wrapped her arms around herself, meager protection against the chill that ran down her spine. "I still think I might be ready to howl at the moon."

"No, my girl, no. The whole world is going mad, but you have not. You have to believe that, or you're never going to make it through what comes next." Her mother's image blinked out for a moment. "I need to show you something." The words filled the air before her image was fully restored. "You still trust your mama?" she asked.

"Always," Lisette said. "And forever."

Her mother's eyes twinkled, Lisette hoped with pride, as she held a hand out to her. Lisette hesitated. "Go on."

Lisette reached out and took the hand, surprised to feel it was solid, warm. "How?" she began, confused that her mother's hand hadn't dissolved in her grasp. But then her eyes focused on her surroundings. The shop was gone, replaced by some swanky reception hall. She looked at her mother in wonder.

Her mother drew her into her arms, giving her a tight squeeze. Lisette wanted the moment to last forever, but her mother placed a kiss on her forehead and then released her. "We don't have long here, my girl. And there's a lot you have to learn."

"What is this place?" Lisette asked.

"Well, there's the place it appears to be, and then there's the place it is." As Soulange spoke, a man wearing a striped shirt and a straw hat appeared over her shoulder. The man doffed his hat, then raised a pistol to his temple. He pulled the trigger. Lisette gasped, but the man disappeared the next instant.

"He isn't real, sweetie. At least not in the way you're used to. Only the dreamer is real." She motioned to a sofa—no, a divan—half hidden by shadow. A man with a thick mustache lay back on it, seemingly lost in a fitful dream.

A beautiful woman, naked except for a resplendent emerald necklace, appeared before them. "Lisette, my girl, Miss Lulu doesn't pay you to stand around gaping," the beauty said. Then she, too, blinked out of existence.

"Miss Lulu?" Lisette said.

"Lulu White, *ma chère*," her mother said, wrapping an arm over her shoulders. "Mahogany Hall. Storyville. It was special to him. It was his last bastion in the living world. He has preserved its image here. Welcome, my girl, to the Dreaming Road, the space lost between dreaming and death."

Her mother seemed at ease in this place, but then again her mama had a bit less to lose. Lisette glanced around the room, hoping that it lay a tad closer to dreaming than it did to death. "Who is this 'he' you're talking about?" Lisette asked, then glanced over at the man on the divan. "That man?"

"No, that is only the dreamer. The latest dreamer. They come and go. Replaced like light bulbs when they burn out." Her mother leaned in, whispering in her ear. "'He' is Babau Jean."

In spite of everything, Lisette found herself turning to her mother in disbelief. "Babau Jean," she said, laughing. She flashed back to sleepovers—standing before the mirror in a darkened bath, shining a flashlight up from beneath her chin. Her friends laughing and squealing behind the door, daring her to say his name for the third and damning time. "You're telling me the bogeyman is real."

"He's real, except when he isn't."

"Yeah, you're making a hell of a lot of sense."

"You"—her mother looked down her nose at her—"had better watch your tone, missy. Now you need to shut your mouth and open your mind." Lisette felt a sense of bereavement as her mother's arms slid off her shoulders. But then her mama grasped her hand, and the pain went away. Her mother gave her a slight tug, leading her across the room to the formal painting of a man Lisette felt she should know.

Lisette reached up with her free hand, her finger hovering above the nameplate affixed to the portrait's heavy frame. "Dr. Joseph Dupas," she read the name aloud. The tinkling notes of a music box began to play a familiar, though nearly forgotten, tune at the mention of his name. "Beautiful Dreamer," the name of the song came to her.

"The greatest witch New Orleans has ever known," her mother said. "Though in truth he wasn't a natural witch at all. He was a pharmacist. Or at least what passed for one back before the Civil War. The pharmacy he ran was not far from where Vèvè is now."

"Yes, of course," Lisette said, "I know the place." She had passed by the establishment a million times or more. Waves of darkness seemed to emanate from the painting, and she felt a chill in her hand, as if that darkness were reaching for her. She stepped back, dropping her hand to her side.

"He used to carry on experiments. Some of them scientific, others occult. All of them evil. He hurt people. People who had no means of fighting back."

Lisette stared into his dark, disinterested eyes, trying to understand how a man with such a bland expression could be capable of such acts. His features were utterly unremarkable. Forgettable, even. They seemed to flee her mind the second she looked away.

"Then came the war, and all its death," her mother said. "'Course New Orleans fell early on and didn't face the destruction a lot of other places did, but a lot of sons and husbands had gone and gotten themselves killed. Left behind a whole cotillion of brokenhearted women, they did, women who would do just about anything to forget their pain, and, lucky for him, the good doctor discovered a way to turn their pain into power.

"Back then they put opium in everything. Cough drops, baby formulas, even the products for a lady's time." She gave a curt nod. "You know what I mean."

"You're dead, mama. And I'm menopausal. You can say 'period.'"

"Between the grieving and the drugs," she said, ignoring Lisette, "the doctor's patients started experiencing odd things, things that shouldn't happen. Levitation. Apports. Apparitions. Keep in mind, these weren't witches. They were just ordinary women. And just like any man would, Dupas first wrote it off as hysteria. Till one of his patient's 'hallucinations,' a furry little creature with a human face and hands, followed him home. Then he realized he was onto something. He took one of the women, the one who seemed to experience the most intense activity. Started hypnotizing her before letting her slip all the way into her opium dreams. He figured out the connection between dreaming and magic, and how to change waking reality by carving his will deeply enough into the dreaming. It didn't take long for him to figure out that by getting these women to actively participate, he could build up magical energy for his own use.

"He created a servitor spirit. This spirit, his ability was to mimic the men the women had lost. And that, my dear, was how Babau Jean was born. 'Course they didn't know him as such. 'The Beautiful Dreamer,' they called him, after the song. In their dreaming, they could have back their husbands, their lost sons. And these women, they sunk everything they had into spending their whole damn lives in the dreaming.

"Then these women started dying. Some from the drugs. The stronger ones from age. And the government finally reined in the sale of opiates. Dupas himself, well, he died, too. From syphilis, they say. By any rights, the servitor he created should have faded away. But he kept going. Found his way along with the drug trade into Storyville. The working girls, they loved him. He could be any man they wanted, any lover they dreamed of.

"But then Storyville closed. Folks' dreams turned to terror, to war. And the Beautiful Dreamer changed with them. Denied the sweet opium dreams of brokenhearted working girls and wealthy socialites, he learned to feed from darker fare. War and more war. New drugs. Psychedelics. He turned from an angel of light to a creature of nightmare. Here. In this place on the Dreaming Road he remembers what he used to be."

"But I wasn't dreaming," Lisette objected. "If this is his happy place, then what in the hell was he doing wearing Vincent's face, with his hands around my neck? And what is this damned book he's looking for?"

"He's found a way to walk in the waking world as well, not just in dreams. But in the waking world his impersonations require . . . a few props."

Props, indeed. He'd taken Vincent's identity. He must have taken Vincent's life along with it. Lisette found herself wishing that just once she would've had the nerve to go to the man, the real man, not the monster masquerading as him, so they could make peace, real peace, with each other.

*His family*, the thought struck her. She'd have to tell the Marins. But would they believe her or would they think she'd just taken her time exacting revenge?

"He's coming," her mother said, her voice urgent. "This is his domain. I may not be able to defeat him here."

Lisette froze, realizing she might not even live through this night to face the Marins.

"Follow me," her mother said, and Lisette found herself standing before a door that hadn't been there a moment before. Her mother grasped the handle, a horned devil with a lolling tongue, and opened it by pressing the tongue. She stepped through and held the door open. Lisette cast a glance back over her shoulder at the salon as a band struck up a jaunty tune. She caught a glimpse of men in evening dress pressing themselves against mostly naked women. "Come," her mother said.

Lisette stepped over the threshold, and her mother closed the door behind her. The door shimmered and then disappeared without a trace. Lisette turned around to discover a darkened, significantly less pleasant world. Her feet were planted on a deserted dirt lane. Oaks and a handful of scraggly pines surrounded them. The moon hid her mother's face, but light pollution from the west left only a scattering of stars to wink down. They were east of the city, she guessed. She turned a full circle, her heart sinking as recognition set in. "No," she said. "No. No. No," she said until the word choked her.

They stood at the end of Grunch Road.

"It's all right, my girl. Nothing bad is gonna happen here. Not tonight, at least." Her mother reached out for her, but her hand passed straight through her. "Back on this side of the veil."

"So I can't feel your touch here, but that dream creature can strangle me?"

Her mother took a few steps away, losing clarity and fading, merging with the shadows. "All the strange things you've ever heard about this place"—her voice came from the darkness—"are true. And the reason why is that good old Grunch Road is one of the points where the waking world connects to the Dreaming Road. That's why we were here that night, Laure Marin and I. We came here to hide something." Her mother fell silent, leaving nothing but the sound of the wind blowing through the trees.

"Mama?" Lisette called, fearing she'd already lost her mother again.

"I'm here, my girl. I'm here," she said, her voice thin, whisper-like. "We came to hide a grimoire. An evil book that should've never been scratched into existence. *The Book of the Unwinding*.

"We tucked it between worlds, locking it in a state of flux, where it can be reached neither from the waking world nor the dreaming. From daylight or death. It's simultaneously everywhere and nowhere."

Lisette sensed Soulange was fading even further, but somehow she felt the waning was her mother's own doing.

"What are you not telling me, Mama? That witch spoke of a blood lock."

Another silence. Lisette heard a heavy truck rolling along on the nearby highway.

"Such a feat—bending, folding one reality over another, securing it—requires sacrifice."

"You?"

"Yes," the word came to her as if from a great distance. "And Laure. And Nicholas. And you."

"What do you mean?"

"It took more than a simple blood lock," she said.

"Simple." Lisette balked at her words.

"Yes, simple," she said, insisting on the word. "There's no act simpler than brutality, and there's no magic easier than the shedding of blood. Murder was the first act of magic." A blur flitted before Lisette's eyes, but failed to take full form.

"This took more than blood. The working called for a fourfold sacrifice. A loss of life. A loss of mind. A loss of fertility. A loss of love. Between us, Laure and I, we drew lots. I"—the voice came through with more determination—"was the luckier. I cannot imagine the hell Laure woke to. We were at peace with our own fates, but we had to involve our children. You were my only child. Laure had three, but she picked her eldest son Nicholas because he already had two sons. It didn't seem such a great loss for him to become sterile."

"But he has a daughter, too."

"Does he?" her mother's voice asked, though it was no question.

"I see," Lisette said. "And the loss of love?" She laughed as she finished the question. "Here I thought you two were trying to plan our wedding. Not tear us apart."

"You found love with Isadore." Her mother's figure flashed before her eyes, a burst of angry defensiveness bringing her momentarily back.

"Yes, Mama. After Isadore put me back together."

"But you love him. You've been happy with him." There was a pleading in her mother's voice.

"Yes." She nodded in the darkness to once again invisible eyes. "Yes. I've been happy. I just wish I could've had a choice."

"Do you think we wanted this? Any of this?" A pillar of blue flame shot up from the ground. "We had no choice."

"No choice? Really? Tell me, Mama, was it worth it? Was it worth you and Laure giving up your lives, deserting your families just to hide some dime-store magic book from the bogeyman?"

"Yes," her mother said, the flames burning even more brightly, illuminating the world around Lisette. Low to the ground, eyes glinted red in the light. Lisette feared they belonged to alligators until she realized they might belong to something worse. "But *The Book of the Unwinding* is no simple collection of magic tricks. And we didn't give our lives to hide it from Babau Jean. We sacrificed everything to hide it from her daughter-in-law, Astrid."

# TWENTY-SEVEN

"It's a church," Lucy said, sounding annoyed, as their limousine negoti-ated a turn up the narrow Bywater street.

Bywater was part of the "sliver by the river" that had, along with the Marigny, the Vieux Carré, and the Garden District, escaped most of the flood damage from Katrina. Alice could tell Lucy was feeling snappish, so she kept that bit of information to herself.

A line of cars, some even longer and more ostentatious than their own, snaked up the street, making progress slow. Each car seemed to be stopping directly in front of their destination; each guest seemed to want to take their sweet time alighting. On her own, Alice would have slipped out and walked the few blocks, but none of her fellow passen-gers made a move to disembark.

"Deconsecrated about a billion years ago," Hugo replied.

"That's what I mean. A deconsecrated church," Lucy said. "Could they have found a more clichéd location?"

Alice wished her uncle had taken the car with them, though she was relieved that Nicholas had not. Vincent had texted Fleur to say he'd be arriving shortly. And no one, not even Daniel, had heard from Nicholas since he'd been relieved as head of the Chanticleers.

"And what's up with all the Hollywood?" Lucy turned toward Alice, holding her cell phone out like an imaginary microphone. "Tell me, Miss Marin. Who"—she stretched the word out into a vocal fry—"are you wearing?" She winked. "You look pretty, by the way. Love the new hair." For a moment, they seemed to bond, but it was fleeting. Lucy immediately turned her attention back to her phone.

"Celestin was small-town royalty," Hugo said, shifting, seemingly on the lookout for something. "The king is dead. Long live the king."

"I wouldn't look for too much symbolism in the choice of venue, honey," Fleur said, giving her makeup a quick check in her compact mirror. Gold, square, studded, it had probably been a gift or a rescued castoff from Lucy. "Julia told me this was the space available on short notice. Something about a canceled wedding. With only a few days' warning, she and Gabriel couldn't be too picky."

"Wow," Hugo said, "aren't you just falling right in line with the new regime?"

"I'm not 'falling in line' with anything. The whole thing is ridiculous, if you ask me. I don't have a clue why Gabriel would have cared enough to spring a coup now."

"He's securing his place in history," Alice said. It seemed so obvious. She leaned against her seat, the better to take in her angled view of the building's battered twin towers, their silver-capped tops pinned to the night sky by searchlights. "He may have taken over a disintegrating kingdom, but he'll be the last king." Her own words almost triggered a memory—men playing poker, emeralds, sickly-sweet smoke—but it escaped her grasp the second she focused on it. Her forearms prickled up into gooseflesh.

"You okay?" Hugo asked.

She smiled and rubbed away the bumps. "Yes. Just a chill. The air-conditioning is on a bit high."

"Well," Fleur said, a worried look coming to her eyes, "I think this party is a good thing. People are nervous. With witches on a kind of power brownout, and with elders like Delphine being harvested for relics—"

"Yeah. About that. Have you two had 'the talk' yet?" Hugo said.

Fleur cast a nervous glance at Lucy, then flashed her eyes at Hugo. *Drop it.* The message was loud and clear.

He shook his head from side to side, his eyes comically wide. *I'm not the one who brought it up.*

"God. The two of you," Lucy said. "I know enough to walk the line between being careless and paranoid. I may not have any power, but someone might try to get to one of you through me. I get it. I'm not stupid, and I'm not blind."

"Unlike Miss Royal Wedding over there," Hugo said, nodding toward a middle-aged woman maneuvering her immense headdress out of a car a few places ahead in line. "I think she mistook a toilet seat for a fascinator."

"I don't think it's that bad," Lucy said, leaning over him to get a better look.

"Ugh. I disown you as a cousin."

"Please, you just wish it came in a size big enough to fit your fat head."

The two of them burst out laughing. Alice smiled. She wished she had the ability to toy with her brother and her cousin the way they did with each other. But it was over the next instant, and the same bored look washed over Lucy's features.

"We could've just held it at Celestin's house," Lucy said. Alice noticed she had picked up the others' habit of referring to their grandfather by his given name. "It's big enough."

"Big enough, yes, but you've never been to one of these events." She mirrored one of Lucy's own exaggerated expressions. "Witches and alcohol. If something doesn't get singed, it wasn't a good party." She reached over and patted Lucy's hand. "Come on. You might even have fun."

"Yeah," she said, "real likely at this nonagenarian prom."

"Nah," Hugo said, "together, you and Alice bring down the average guest age to around eighty-seven."

"You could've invited someone, you know," Fleur said.

"And whom exactly would I have invited to this fete?"

"Well," Fleur said, the slight hint of a smile on her lips. "Perhaps the boy you were carrying on a silent conversation with outside Précieux Sang."

"I wasn't having a conversation of any kind with any boy."

Alice couldn't resist. She examined her cousin, trying to identify her "tell."

"No? Because it sure seemed . . ."

"I barely know Remy," she said.

It was her eyes, Alice realized. She always looked right at you when telling the lie, but in the moment before, her focus wandered, a bit up and to the right.

"You know him well enough to know his name," Fleur said with a knowing air. "And your level of annoyance tells me there are sparks, even if there isn't a fire yet." She inspected her makeup once more. "Though as your mother and friend I should tell you that Remy not only looks like Alcide did at that age, but from what I hear, he gets around just like his grandfather did, too." She dropped her mirror back into her purse and smiled brightly. "And Alcide Simeon is still a legend around this town."

"Yeah, you right," Hugo said, dropping into New Orleans vernacular. He laughed as Lucy gave him a withering glance. He shook his head. "It isn't my fault. You're the one who's slipping." He turned, almost pressing his nose to the window, scanning the people mounting the narrow granite steps.

"I'm just saying the whole thing is a ridiculous bother." Lucy returned to her original theme in what Alice guessed was an attempt to turn the conversation.

"It's a tradition," Fleur said, allowing Lucy to slip the knot, if only for the evening. "A way of keeping the peace. There was a time when a death could spell a territorial war."

"Yeah, maybe way back in the when," Lucy said, pulling a face. "You know, when there was any turf to fight over. Besides, it really isn't our turf to protect anymore, is it?"

Their car came to a full stop just a bit past the entrance, alongside what seemed an incongruous wooden fence. A moment later Alice's door opened. She hesitated, looking out at the line of those entering the affair. "It's okay, Alice," her Aunt Fleur assured her. "We'll be right behind you."

"Don't mind the knives," Lucy said. Alice turned back. Her cousin shrugged. "What else is family for if not to stab you in the back?"

"Lucy," Fleur said, her tone full of stern warning.

"I'm just kidding. Relax."

Alice slipped out the door and went over to the fence, stopping just short of leaning back against it, so she could examine the church's exterior without blocking anyone's path. The building's white facade declared it the abandoned offspring of Baroque architecture and Germanic restraint. On the upper facade, niches, far too narrow to house the statues that might grace a Gothic cousin, made an imperfect effort to preserve the symmetry of the three nearly identical doors on its lower level. The trio of weathered doors still held the memory of sky-blue emulsion.

For Alice it was love at first sight. She would come back tomorrow. See it again in natural light.

"Perhaps if *you* would relax," Fleur's voice preceded her as she exited the car, leading the others to join Alice by the fence, "you might have a bit of fun. I certainly intend to." The words still hung in the air as a tall man with a square jaw and a V-shaped torso approached her. "Eli." Fleur offered him her arm. "It has been far too long."

"Good evening," this Eli greeted them all, as he offered Fleur his arm.

Fleur placed her hand over his forearm. "See you all inside," she said and risked one final triumphant look back at them. "Don't dawdle," she said, her voice bright and carefree.

Lucy watched with her jaw hanging open as Eli escorted her mother through the center door.

"Damn. Looks like Auntie F has scored," Hugo said.

"I just . . . don't even want to think—"

"Oh, look," Hugo said, cutting Lucy off, "there's *my* date." He raised his hand and waved, much to Alice's surprise, at Evangeline, who had just turned the corner on foot, coming from the opposite direction. She looked beautiful, if self-conscious, facing into the headlights of the line of disgorging vehicles.

"Wow," Lucy said, a wooden expression on her face, "I like that dress even better the second time around." Alice recognized it as the same dress Evangeline had worn yesterday to the cemetery. "Hope she got the brain splatter cleaned off. I had to toss the shoes I was—"

"Shut up," Hugo said, his anger real and obvious.

"Geesh," Lucy said, pretending not to be hurt by his tone. "Getting a little testy, there, aren't you?"

"It's only some people haven't always had everything handed to them."

"No," Lucy said. "I guess you were born lucky." She paused, presumably to ensure her words had hit home. "Come on. What's up with you inviting your dad's girlfriend, who was, wait, let me check my diary"—she flipped her finger through air, turning the pages of an imaginary book—"your brother's girlfriend first. What? Is she so irresistible to the Marin men, she's turned you? God, Alice will be falling for her next," she said, the comment casual, offhanded. Her eyes flashed to Alice—a sincere, though silent, apology.

"I don't think I'm her type," Alice said. She and Lucy focused on each other for a moment, then they both started laughing.

Hugo gave them both the stink eye, but then his eyes widened, as a truth, her truth, began to dawn on him. "Oh," he said, then "oh" again.

Evangeline began walking their way, but Lucy gave Hugo a shove. "Go on," she said. "You have fun with Jocasta. Antigone and I will hang."

"Yeah, thanks," he said, already walking away. "Say hello to your new dad for me."

"I hate you."

Hugo turned to blow a kiss in their direction, then headed off to meet Evangeline.

"Oh. My. God," Lucy said, whipping around to face her. "I am such a total asshat. You must literally hate me."

"No," Alice smiled. "Not at all. I'm glad Hugo knows." She focused on Lucy. Her cousin was this odd combination of weary worldliness and green immaturity. Somewhere behind the expensive clothes and sharp tongue was a good person. A scared person, but a good person. "I'm glad you know." Alice looked toward Hugo, who already seemed caught up in a conversation with Evangeline. "Is it ever real, between you and Hugo, the . . . ," Alice searched for the right word, then settled for "acrimony?"

"Always, a little. But never. You'll get the hang of it. I'm being nice to you now. But once we're friends for real . . . watch out."

"This," Alice said with a tinge of seriousness, "is what you consider nice?"

"See, you're already learning," Lucy said, then took her hand. "Come on, cuz, let's make the rounds, then we'll go find some real fun."

Lucy tugged, but Alice held her ground. "I don't think you should see Remy anymore," she said, the words escaping her before she realized what she was saying.

Alice expected an explosion, but Lucy stopped and looked deeply into her eyes. "Why do you say that?" No anger. No angst. Just a simple question.

Alice wanted to speak of her vision of Mahogany Hall, of the beautiful young man she'd seen there. She didn't know how to begin without sounding as crazy as Nicholas had always led the rest of the family to believe she was. "It's only a feeling."

Lucy scanned her face, seeming to search for a bit of missing information. "You're lying. I can always tell," she said, her voice calm. "You're lying about the why. But you're not lying about being concerned." She paused, as if considering how to proceed. "We'll talk about it later. Okay?"

Alice nodded.

An elderly couple, a study in stiffness, made their way from their car. A black and red strapless brocade gown had swallowed the tan, leathery skin of the nearly skeletal woman, and Alice suspected her face would have fallen into a ring of wrinkles if not held back by the tight chignon in her gray hair. Her partner, still dapper in black tie, held her arm, and they both meandered toward the cousins, the man bumping into Lucy.

"Pardon," the man said.

The woman turned to them. "So sorry . . . for your loss." She paused. "Please let me express condolences on behalf of the entire Silverbell Coven." She held out a deeply spotted hand, dominated by what appeared to be a six- or maybe even seven-carat emerald-cut diamond. Alice couldn't get a clear view of the stone, but she sensed a tiny glamour had been set on it.

In what seemed to be an out-of-character level of geniality, Lucy took the woman's hand. "The Chanticleer Coven is pleased to accept your gracious expression of sympathy." The two leaned in and brushed each other's cheeks with tiny air kisses that came close but failed to make actual contact. Lucy released the woman's hand, and the couple smiled at them before turning to negotiate the granite steps—the gentleman grasping the railing, the woman clutching his arm.

"The Silverbell Coven?" Alice asked. She remembered many of the names of the witch clans, but this one seemed unfamiliar.

"The *entire* Silverbell Coven. Right there. You're looking at the last of them."

"You were very diplomatic."

"They seem sweet. No need to hurt their feelings," Lucy said. "Besides, I wanted to get a better look at that rock. It's a legendary stone. Cursed and all."

Alice said nothing, but Lucy must have read the truth in her eyes.

"It's paste, isn't it?" She seemed sincerely sad. "But if you can see it, then . . ."

"Others will, too."

"They've probably been forced to sell the real one, and they're just trying to keep up appearances." A line formed between Lucy's eyes. "It really is over, isn't it? The magic. The wealth. The power."

"Yes, I believe it is. Will you miss it?"

"It's not like I ever had much power myself, but I'll miss the benefits of being magic adjacent." She looked up. "This may be the very last witches' ball we'll ever have the chance to attend."

"Could be."

Lucy took her arm, clutching it in imitation of the bejeweled crone and her mate. They began to climb the stairs to the entrance. "I'll still spend all evening making fun of people."

"I wouldn't have expected anything less."

# TWENTY-EIGHT

"Serendipitous," Lisette said, staring at her own reflection in the passenger-side window, an imperfect mirror. She could see the darkness that lay behind her own eyes. She looked away, struck by the realization that perhaps the window was her perfect mirror.

"Serendipitous," the driver, a sturdy young woman with short blonde hair and a quick smile, repeated the word. "That's what my papa would call a ten-dollar word." She laughed. "I guess I'd just say it was lucky I was passing."

"Yes," Lisette forced what she hoped looked like a sincere smile. She was grateful, beyond grateful, that the kind young woman had spotted her emerging from the tree line along the highway and had been gracious enough to pull over and offer her a ride. But the part of her that could truly appreciate this gesture was sequestered in the back of her mind, screaming in abject terror. No, better to fake it for now.

Lisette's gaze drifted up to the rearview mirror for the umpteenth time. Her mother's face, impassive, immobile as a photo, stared back from the backseat.

"I don't usually come out this way, but I was talking with a fare earlier—"

"Fare?" Lisette asked, feeling panicked. She didn't have a dime on her.

The woman nodded, glancing over. "Yes, ma'am, I've been driving part-time to help make the frazzled ends meet, or at least see each other waving. I work as a customs protection officer," she paused, seemingly waiting for Lisette to demand an explanation of the title. When Lisette didn't say a word—she couldn't—the woman continued. "All the risk, none of the weapons. That's what it means." Lisette nodded, her eyes traveling once again to the reflection of her mother's features. "It's private, though. Not official police work or anything like that." She signaled and pulled around a slow car. "My hours got cut a couple weeks back." She leaned in a bit. "So much for that great America we got promised."

"I'm sorry, I don't have any money . . ."

"Oh, no, ma'am," the driver raised her right hand, but only for a moment. It fell right back to two o'clock on the wheel. "You don't owe me anything. God put me out here to help you." Another flash of her bright smile.

*A decent person.* Lisette heard her mother's words. She turned, a reflex, to glance over her shoulder. *I raised you better than that. Thank the nice woman. Ask the nice woman her name.*

"I'm so sorry," Lisette said. "It's only I've had a bit of a shock."

"I can see that, ma'am, but I didn't want to pry."

"You are a good person. A real good person," Lisette said, then worried she sounded like she was stroking a dog. "Thank you for your kindness. I do sincerely appreciate it."

"We gotta look out for each other," she said. Lisette could tell this woman truly meant it.

*Name?*

"Yes," Lisette said. "I'm sorry, I don't think I caught your name."

"Nathalie. Nathalie Boudreau. Anyway, like I was saying, I don't usually come out this way, especially at night, but you know how when you get an idea stuck in your craw?" Lisette held her tongue, assuming the question was rhetorical. It was. "Well, the rider I had yesterday, you might know her if you're from around the Quarter—Evangeline from Bonnes Nouvelles—I dropped her over at Précieux Sang. Now, I live not a stone's throw from Odd Fellows Rest, so I know cemeteries, but I got to tell you Précieux Sang, well, that place just gives me the willies. I was telling Evangeline about how my brother used to pick on me about Babau Jean when we were kids, and she mentioned Grunch Road, and, well . . ." Lisette stiffened at the name of the road. Nathalie shrugged. "I never believed it existed—Grunch Road, that is—but Evangeline, she seemed convinced it does, or at least did. Back before Katrina, maybe. So I spent all afternoon today looking at the satellite photos, and dip me in honey and feed me to the bears, I thought I saw a portion of a cut-off old lane somewhere in the area near where I spotted you ladies. Not much light out there to see anything this late, but I work the next three days straight—not that I'm not grateful for the work—but, well, I know myself, and by the time I'm off again, I'll have moved on to something else. Figured I had nothing else to do tonight, so . . ."

Something in the stream of words finally got processed by Lisette's overwhelmed mind. "Ladies?"

"Why yes, ma'am," Nathalie grinned and nodded up at the rearview mirror. "I'm sorry, maybe I should've said something earlier, but you weren't alone out there."

Lisette tugged her seatbelt out so she could turn fully to face her mother. She turned back to Nathalie. "You see her?"

"Well, yes, ma'am. It's only I didn't know if you did. And you seemed real upset, and you don't know me, so I didn't want to scare you by going all Shyamalan on you. But you don't need to be frightened." Nathalie focused on Lisette's mother's face in the mirror. "She seems like a real nice lady. Pretty. Looks something like you, so I'm guessing it's your mama or maybe your big sister."

"You can see her?" Lisette repeated herself, unsure as to how many more surprises she could take in one night.

*I thought we'd covered that.* Lisette saw a smirk form on her mother's lips.

"Yes, ma'am, I can, indeed." Nathalie glanced over at her, a gentle seriousness in her gaze. "If you want, I can try to talk to her for you. See what she wants."

"No, no," Lisette said, "I think I already know that."

Nathalie nodded. "All right then," she said, her voice calm, respectful. "So you said you were headed to the Tremé?"

"Yes," Lisette said.

*No*, her mother said at the same time. *Bywater.*

Nathalie visibly reacted to the words. So, she could hear her, too. At least when her mama wanted to be heard.

"I could take you to either," Nathalie said, casting a nervous look at Lisette and then in the mirror at her mother, "or both." She added quickly, "Whatever you ladies want."

Lisette turned back toward her mother. "Now why in the hell would you want to go to Bywater?" She waited, but her mother had fallen silent once again. As still and as dumb as a mannequin.

*We have a party to attend. And you watch your tone.*

"Party?"

Nathalie gave her a nervous, questioning side-glance. "So Bywater?"

"I have a shop in the Quarter. On Chartres. You can drop us there," she said, then—remembering herself—added, "please."

Nathalie's eyes widened in excitement. She wagged a finger first at Lisette, then back at her mother. "Vèvè. And you, you're Madame Soulange Simeon," she said, her voice going up in pitch. She slapped her hand on the wheel. "Man, I can't believe it." Nathalie seemed more star-struck than a teenager at a pop concert. "It is such an honor, ma'am," she said, her eyes fixed on the mirror. Lisette looked back to see a satisfied smile on her mother's lips.

"I'm pleased to drop you ladies off at your store, but I got to tell you, when I was a girl, Vèvè used to scare me half to death. I'd walk two blocks out of my way to avoid all those faces looking out at me from the windows."

"Faces?" Lisette said, surprised. "There are no faces in the window."

"Well, no, ma'am, if you say there aren't, I'm sure you're right. It's your place and all. It's just I always used to see faces, a dozen or more, looking out at me every time I passed."

"There's nothing—was nothing," Lisette corrected herself, "in the windows, other than the vèvès themselves."

*She's right.* Her mother's voice rang like a bell. *You spent your whole life looking at those vèvès, but you never learned to* see *them. This Nathalie, she has the sight. You see the symbols, but she sees the loa.* She fell silent, but only for a moment. *You should try to be more like Nathalie.*

"Ah, ma'am," Nathalie said, "that's real sweet of you to say, but your daughter here is something special. I can tell—"

"Bywater," Lisette said.

"I'm sorry?" Nathalie looked over at her with a confused expression.

"Please drop us in Bywater." She pointed back over her shoulder. "She'll tell you where."

# TWENTY-NINE

"Did you bring it?" Hugo said.

Evangeline looked into his beautiful, pale-blue eyes, but all she could see there was the mirror of her own rage. She nodded.

"It's time to take this bastard down."

"Have you seen him?"

"No. Not yet. But he'll be here. The vanquished king come to foment discord while speaking of reconciliation. He had Daniel lay out his tuxedo."

"It's odd, though, isn't it?" she said, still trying to process the news that Gabriel Prosper had unseated Nicholas. "Magic is dying. The Chanticleers are mostly dead. Why would Gabriel Prosper challenge Nicholas now?" Something about his timing, about the sisters' arrival, about Daniel finding *The Lesser Key*, all one right after the other, didn't set right. It seemed like everything was being orchestrated.

She grasped her handbag, its beads biting into her fingers. She could feel the weight of the necklace, the weight of the entire world, riding in it. Had she allowed herself to be manipulated? Were they all, even Nicholas, just being moved about like pieces on a chessboard?

"Alice has a theory as good as any," Hugo said, wrapping his arm around her shoulders, maneuvering her toward the entrance. "The last king hits the history books."

Evangeline shook her head. "Maybe. I don't know."

He stopped, looking down at her. "You chickening out?"

"No," she said. She still felt Nicholas's guilt not only in her heart, but all the way down to the pit of her stomach. "It's time for Nicholas to answer for what he's done. And the more public his punishment, the better."

"Agreed."

He led her to the entrance, pausing to pat the head of a statue of Asmodeus that had been placed there, and then fell in behind her as they came to the leftmost of the three doors. It was evident from her first glance that magic had been used to enhance the venue, the footprint of the church having expanded to equal that of any of the great cathedrals. That bit didn't surprise Evangeline in the slightest. What did surprise her was the number, even at this early hour, of those in attendance. Evangeline hadn't realized there were this many witches left in the region, let alone New Orleans proper.

Hugo must have been struck by the same idea. He grabbed hold of her elbow and began counting off, "One, two, three, four, five, six," pointing at individual guests as he did. Then he turned her toward the other side of the hall. "One, two, three" was as far as he got this time.

"They're copies of each other. They aren't real." She turned, surveying those present. A good two-thirds of the guests appeared to be filler entities, smiling dumbly, shifting in predictable patterns.

Hugo laughed. "Looks like the new king is worried about low attendance at his inauguration." Hugo scanned the crowd. "Most of the people who are really here are probably too blind to notice."

"But this really isn't about him, is it?" Evangeline said. "It's about Celestin."

Hugo snorted. "Yeah. Right." He offered her his arm. "Shall we?"

She took his arm, catching her bag between both hands as he led her into the now enormous space.

A band, an incredible one, played on a stage built into the enhanced church's chancel. Dirty, bluesy ragtime that might have spun completely off its center were it not for the cautious shepherding of the ensemble's pianist. Evangeline had heard a lot of bands blowing before, but the players in this group seemed to predict one another's next turn as if they'd been performing together for a hundred years. The music made Evangeline wish this were a normal party. The tapping of Hugo's foot told her it was having a similar effect on him.

Fleur passed by, dancing with a man Evangeline didn't recognize. She laughed as he spun her past, a sloshing glass of champagne in one hand. "Come on, you two," Fleur shouted at them. "Don't let the new king catch you scowling." She laughed again, her eyes wide, mirthless.

"Okay," Hugo said, his eyes following Fleur and her date. "That bitch is up to something."

"So is this one," Evangeline said, reminding them both to focus. "I still don't see Nicholas."

Hugo turned a full circle. "Nor do I," he said.

Evangeline did her best to ignore the distractions, the artifice of the conjured guests, the preternaturally polished music, the expanded hall that seemed to reach farther back the more it was examined. She began picking out the faces she knew. Alice and her cousin Lucy were circling. The younger girl's finger was darting around the room, pointing to individual guests. Evangeline reckoned the cousins were just now making the same discovery she and Hugo had made earlier.

Even from a distance, and across the noise, Evangeline could sense Alice growing uneasy. "Maybe it wasn't the best idea to subject Alice to this," she said, leaning in to Hugo so she could speak without having to yell.

Hugo turned and looked at the girls. "Not to worry. Lucy's going to make sure she and Alice have been seen by anyone who might care, then the two of them are sneaking out to the clubs. Lucy's got this."

"Fleur's okay with this?" she said, not sure why she felt it was any of her business.

"It was her idea."

Evangeline turned, scanning the crowd for Fleur and her partner, only to find they'd drifted away from the dance floor and out of sight. Maybe she was up to something after all.

A tuxedo-wearing male witch from the Chanticleers passed by, an ancient crone with frazzled dyed red hair leaning alternately on his arm and her cane. The woman seemed a fragile collection of bones, bound in gray tulle and sequins.

"Guy and Rose," she said as she put names to faces.

"Yes, indeed," Hugo said.

Rose took note of Evangeline's interest and nodded at her, a wide and somewhat witless smile on her lips. Guy paused, eying Hugo, his expression telegraphing a satisfied sense of contempt.

Hugo blew him a kiss. "He's happy that Gabriel has taken the reins," he said, "in case you didn't catch that from his leer."

Another witch who'd been at the cemetery, the sturdy Jeanette, who had challenged her at the gate, passed with surprising grace across the center of the dance floor, the skirt of her unexpected deep-aqua chiffon gown flowing around her as she sashayed. The beaded capped shoulders and sweetheart neckline performed a magic of their own, making her seem more of a woman, less of a traffic barrier.

"Well I'll be damned," Hugo said, "the Ancient Wall cleaned up real nice."

Evangeline realized the members of the coven had begun working their way forward, no doubt readying themselves for their new leader's arrival.

Les Jumeaux, as Nicholas had always spoken of the pair, passed her hand-in-hand, mirror images of each other in black ruffle-trimmed shorts and sheer beige tank tops over black-sequined bustiers. Without warning, the sister stopped in her tracks, tugging her brother backward. The two froze, piercing each other with their gazes. They were perfectly still, perfectly silent, and still it was obvious they were having a knock-down brawl. After a few moments, the brother gave a slight bow of his head, and the two started back in the direction from which they had come. As they passed Hugo, they stopped and offered him a deep and precisely coordinated curtsy. Then they rose and slipped back toward the exit.

"Marin loyalists," he said, trying to sound nonchalant. Still, in spite of himself, Evangeline sensed Hugo was touched by their fidelity.

A dapper couple she didn't recognize cut across at an angle to position themselves at one of the café tables lining the shadowy walls. A swiveling spotlight caught the woman's hand, betraying a gaudy piece of glass.

Evangeline continued looking from one guest to another, picking each of them apart, setting herself apart. It struck her that she was an outsider, even in this collection of outsiders. Worse than that, she realized she was looking for reasons not to fit in with these people. *Too much him. Too much him.* The truth of Marceline's words dawned on her. She had inherited her father's distaste for witches. For magic. For herself. "I'm getting a drink," she said, already making a beeline to the bar set up in the south transept.

"Not without me, you don't," Hugo called out, rushing to catch up to her.

She stopped just short of reaching the bar, for Alice and Lucy had popped up in her path.

"Good times, huh?" Lucy said, a glass already in her hand. The girl took one look at her and held out the drink. "Here. You need this worse than I do."

"You're right," Evangeline said, accepting the glass and knocking it back. She lowered the glass and looked at Lucy. "Vodka, neat?" she said. "A bit advanced, no?"

Lucy gave her hair a toss. "I wasn't really going to drink it. I just wanted to let Mom think I was."

"Cry for help?" Hugo said from behind her. She turned to see him smirking at his cousin.

"You know what?" Lucy said, hands on her hips. "I'm gonna give you that one. Yes. In less than one week, the whole damned world has gone mad, and frankly, at the moment I don't even know where my mother is."

"Then I'll have what she's having," Alice said, smiling.

"Right?" Lucy said, turning to her, then, "Oh, okay, you win again, but still . . ."

"Why don't you two get out of here?" Hugo said, surprising Evangeline with the true sympathy she heard in his voice. "Wait," he said, reaching into his pocket and pulling out a credit card. "Take this." He leaned in toward his sister. "It's Nicholas's. I've often wondered just how high the limit is. Why don't you two do the testing for me?"

Lucy reached out and swiped it from his grasp. "Anything for science, right, cuz?"

Alice answered with a quiet smile. She nodded. "But we should wait for Gabriel. It would be rude to leave, since he's toasting the last Marin head of the Chanticleers."

Almost as if Alice's words had summoned it, a fanfare from the front of the church caught everyone's attention. Evangeline looked up to see one of the Chanticleers, an older man with the worst toupee she'd ever witnessed, waving his hands. She couldn't think of his real name, but she knew Hugo always called him Perruque after his hopeless, matted wig. "Silence, please," he said into the microphone, his voice too smooth, his elocution a bit too polished. "*Tout le monde, s'il vous plaît.*"

Evangeline scanned the room, confused. Nicholas was surely here, somewhere. She turned back to the front of the bandstand, surprised to see that Fleur had deserted her date and slipped in next to the other coven members onstage. Evangeline hit Hugo's shoulder with her bag, then nodded toward his aunt.

He responded with raised brows and a shrug.

Perruque turned back toward the drummer and gave him a silent signal. The musician brought his sticks down hard on his cymbal, and the sound reverberated through the cruciform, rendering the entire congregation instantly mute.

Perruque put his hands over his ears until the sound dissipated, only then realizing he had slid his toupee to the side. He coughed, adjusted it, and turned back to the mic. "Ladies and gentlemen, it is my great pleasure to inform you I have been chosen to introduce the new head of the great Chanticleer Coven." He raised a hand toward the audience, leading the crowd to turn back. "*Mesdames et Messieurs, je suis ravi de vous présenter Gabriel Prosper.*"

A gasp rose up, and the crowd parted to let Gabriel and his sister pass. Julia led the way, her hair up, her head held high, entirely nude except for the most spectacular emerald necklace Evangeline had ever seen. Gabriel walked behind his sister, fully dressed but in a style of suit that hadn't been in fashion, she would guess, for a hundred years. Their sartorial choices were odd enough, but even odder was the carrying pole balanced across his shoulders.

Her mind flashed to Daniel. His book. The illustration at its center. She turned to Hugo. "We have to get the girls out of here," she said.

"What?" he said, laughing like a total idiot. He turned to Lucy, who was staring at her as if she'd gone mad. But Lucy's contemptuous look melted like a snowflake. She blanched and grabbed Hugo's arm.

"Get out of here. Get the girls out of here, now." Evangeline gave him a shove, but even as she turned around, she knew.

Alice was already gone. She turned, scanning the shadows for her. No trace of her in even the darkest corners of the magically extended space.

"I'll find Alice," Evangeline said, turning toward the others. "Get Lucy away from here. Take her somewhere safe . . ." She paused, unsure of where that might be. "Take her to Bonnes Nouvelles. Tell them I said to let her in."

"But I should help you find—"

"Just go," she said, regretting the harshness of her tone.

"I'm not going without my mom," Lucy said, evading Hugo's grasp and darting across the room to Fleur's side. Evangeline watched as Lucy whispered into her mother's ear. Fleur looked on, concern playing on her features, but she didn't budge.

"What is your . . . ," Hugo began. He didn't finish. Whatever he read in her eyes was enough. "We're in trouble, aren't we?"

Julia made her way over the crossing and climbed onto the stage built over the chancel. She turned—beaming, proud, vindicated—as the lights shimmered over the cascade of emeralds resting on her breasts. Two of the musicians rose to greet Gabriel. Bowing their heads in reverence, they relieved him of his carrying pole and buckets.

Gabriel mounted the steps and stood beside his sister. Guy was the first to approach them, offering Gabriel a jewel-encrusted athame with both hands. The newly crowned king accepted it, grasping the hilt, and then tapped it on Guy's bowed head as if he were knighting him. Guy turned and fell in line between Rose and Jeanette, their square-shouldered sentry in aqua chiffon.

Knife in hand, Gabriel approached Fleur. He stood before her, just to the side, so the audience would be able to see her offering of obeisance. Neither Nicholas nor Vincent were anywhere in sight, which meant that Fleur stood as the head of the Marin family. Her acceptance of Gabriel would seal his power as the new head of the coven.

Gabriel took his time, seeming to enjoy the moment. He held the blade out, waiting for Fleur to lower her head.

"We bow before our new king," Perruque called out.

Fleur spat in Gabriel's face and laughed. She held out her hand behind her, reaching for Lucy. Lucy caught hold of her mother's hand, and with a flash, the two were gone.

Gabriel stood there, seemingly shocked, though something in his bearing suggested happiness rather than umbrage. Evangeline knew Nicholas would never accept an act of open defiance with such grace. Maybe the new leader was just glad to have an excuse to cut another Marin loose, but still his reaction struck Evangeline as another sign something was seriously off. Perruque rushed forward and offered him a handkerchief. Gabriel accepted it, wiped Fleur's spittle from his face, and returned it to its owner, who held it awkwardly for a moment before stuffing it back into his pocket.

The two men stood there for a moment, considering each other. "We kneel," Perruque said once again, "before our king." He braced himself on Gabriel's arm as he lowered himself into a full kneeling position. From there, he smiled up at the coven leader with open admiration. Gabriel took the knife and tapped Perruque's toupee—then, with a quick flick, flipped the blade and cut through the old man's throat.

Julia screamed. The audience began screaming. Evangeline realized *she* was screaming.

Gabriel took the blade and plunged it into his sister's eye. He held the hilt in his right hand, then shoved her body back with his left. Guy flung himself at Gabriel, but the blade sliced clean through Guy's neck, his head spinning across the stage, his body splaying beside it. The crowd pushed back as one, rushing the door, but Evangeline stood frozen. She watched as the two musicians who had relieved Gabriel of his yoke took the buckets he had been carrying and began collecting the blood of Julia and the two fallen men as it dripped from the stage.

Evangeline's heart sank as she saw Alice pushing against the crowd, approaching the gory stage, mounting the steps. Even over the shrieks and screams of those attempting to flee, Evangeline could hear the old witch with the cane approaching Alice, addressing her as Astrid. The girl pushed the crone aside and out of the way, putting herself in the path of the madman's blade. She shouted orders to the sentry who'd confronted Evangeline at the cemetery. The big woman grasped the other woman by the shoulders and dragged her from the stage.

Alice seemed perfectly calm. Perfectly in control. She walked up to Gabriel. Placed her hand on his cheek. He looked down at her, almost lovingly. Alice screamed—a cry of anger, a war cry, not a scream of fear—and dug her fingernails into him. Evangeline felt her knees almost buckle as she watched Alice rip the flesh from Gabriel's face and fling it to the floor.

Gabriel froze for a moment, then turned to the two older witches who were still struggling to make it across the slippery floor. He flung the knife at the sentry, and the blade punctured the back of her skull. She fell forward, toppling the other witch as she did so.

Alice began tearing at Gabriel, shrieking, punching, clawing, but even as she did so, he seemed to grow, stretching to an impossible height, the suit he wore stretching, ripping at the seams, bare bone poking through.

Evangeline's eyes locked on pale skin and a row of gnashing razor-blade teeth. *Babau Jean.*

Everywhere there was pandemonium, everywhere the sound of panicked witches with failing powers attempting and failing escape. Someone, Hugo, took her arm and began to drag her away, even as the glass of the rose window shattered, sending a shower of lead and glass over the hall. She covered her eyes to protect them from the falling glass, but not before she caught sight of three large ravens swooping in, catching hold of the closest witches, pecking them to death with their terrible beaks.

One of the beasts looked up from its carnage. It took one hop toward her, then another. "Join us, half-witch"—she recognized Marceline's voice—"join us." Evangeline felt a rush of pain, a sudden agony as if her own bones were being ripped apart. Marceline cast a hungry glance at Hugo. Evangeline wanted to help him, to protect him, but she felt like she was burning alive from the inside out. She watched as her hands began bending, cracking, black feathers ripping through her skin. The sound of her own screams was terrible.

And then it was over. The pain was done. The world she'd known had fallen away. Everything looked strange. Her thoughts came to her in jumbles. Marceline lunged at Hugo, but her surety slipped into a madness of cawing and screaming when he reached out and slipped Evangeline's chain around her neck and snapped it closed. Marceline, trapped in bird form, began pecking wildly at him. As Hugo leaped back, Evangeline caught hold of his arm and lifted him, rising, clearing the remains of the rose window and taking to the night sky.

# THIRTY

Nathalie had been chatting nonstop—a nervous reaction, Lisette supposed, to escorting a smug ghost and her cantankerous daughter to some as yet unspecified destination. But she fell silent right after the road they traveled swung south and crossed over Chef Menteur Highway.

*Chef Menteur.* The words played in Lisette's mind—the chief liar. Maybe it wasn't a lie, but Lisette sensed something was missing from her mother's story. If only she could silence the screaming in her brain, she'd have a chance to figure out just which piece was missing.

Nathalie held the wheel like she was piloting a ship through heavy storm. Her knuckles had gone white, and Lisette noticed a slight tremble pass through her. Tiny beads of sweat had formed on the driver's forehead.

Without needing instruction, Nathalie signaled, taking an exit from the freeway and heading riverside.

"You know where she's taking us?" Lisette said.

Nathalie nodded. "I can see it in my mind now. It's the old white church. But it ain't a church no more."

Lisette had never spent too much time in this particular part of the city. She recognized the name Almonaster on the street sign, though she connected it mostly to the Pontalba Buildings that flanked Jackson Park. Another left turn led them toward a dead end and train tracks, a sharp right onto a tight single lane lined on one side with double shotgun houses, the other side dotted with what appeared to be light-industrial factories.

Worried eyes rose once again to the mirror. "Ma'am?" Nathalie said, addressing Soulange. "I sure don't mean to pry, and I have all kinds of respect for you, but . . ." Her words stopped, and her hand shot up to her nose. She wiped and glanced down at her hand. Even in the dim dashboard light, Lisette saw it was blood.

"What's wrong? Are you sick?"

*She's a sensitive,* Soulange said. *You're gonna be all right, girl.* The last words were addressed to Nathalie.

"Do you need to pull over?" Lisette ignored her mother.

"Maybe—" Nathalie began.

*You're connected to all this.* Soulange's words came out sharp, causing their already anxious driver to startle. *You think you just happened to be driving a witch yesterday and a mambo tonight?*

"Well, ma'am, it is New Orleans."

Lisette looked back to see her mother staring at Nathalie with a deadpan expression, one she had always sprung on Lisette right before she handed her a tongue-lashing.

"No, ma'am, I reckon you're right," Nathalie said, rushing to save herself.

The woman wasn't only sensitive, Lisette realized, she was smart.

*You know where we're headed, 'cause you're seeing it through* his *eyes,* Soulange said as if she were just now putting the pieces together. *Ah, yeah, I can see it now. He used to feed from your fear. Feed from you. When you were a girl. That bright shining light of yours.*

Nathalie cast a sidelong glance at Lisette, seeming to ask for guidance.

"You do what you need to do," Lisette said.

Nathalie lowered her bloodied hand back to the wheel. "He was gone," Nathalie said, the car slowing to a near crawl as they crept beneath a low overpass. "Just gone. For so long."

*And lately you been feeling your skin crawling at the thought of him. 'Cause you know he's back. That's why you were out there, tonight, looking for Grunch Road. Trying to prove to yourself that Babau Jean isn't real. Even though you know damned well he is.*

"I'm not claiming you're wrong about any of that, ma'am. It's only, I'm not sure you know what you're getting yourself . . . what you're getting us all into. There's something bad . . . real bad . . . happening where you want to go."

*Gonna take a lot of blood for that kind of spell. Rich blood. Blood full of magic. Damned fools and their damned ball. Showing up like lambs to the slaughter.*

"Wait," Lisette said, "what in the hell? What spell are you talking about? Why do you want to go to this church?"

"It ain't a church anymore," Nathalie corrected her. Then, seeming to pick up on Lisette's growing irritation, she rushed to apologize. "Sorry."

"Why did the chicken cross the road?" Soulange said, resurrecting her stock response from Lisette's childhood, something she'd used whenever she grew impatient of Lisette's endless questions.

Twin beams of light—emanating, it seemed, from a bit down the road—rose up into the night sky. A shadow passing through them revealed the largest bird Lisette had ever seen, slicing through the air, effortlessly clutching a full-grown man, kicking his legs, in its talons. The sight made her forget she'd even asked a question.

Nathalie slammed on the brakes, and Lisette, in spite of their slow progress, jerked forward. Eyes gaping at the sight, Nathalie rolled down the window and stuck out her head, craning her neck up at the night sky.

As Lisette's mind balked at the image she'd just seen, the missing piece she'd been reaching for fell into her grasp. "You and Laure Marin. Out there on Grunch Road. Sacrificing your life, her sanity, my heart. To stop Astrid."

Her mother met her gaze but remained silent.

"Why didn't you just take that damned bitch out?"

It infuriated her to see a smile evanesce on her mother's lips.

*Not so simple, my girl,* her mother said.

"Why not? Was her life so much more valuable than your own? Than mine?"

*Astrid may be to blame, but she isn't at fault. Any more than Laure and I were when the Book called to us.*

Lisette felt the shock run from the top of her head to the base of her spine.

*Our history, Laure's and mine, it goes back a lot longer than you could have ever guessed. Back before you "introduced" us. Back even before I met your daddy. When the Book began calling us, we were just girls. We, together, resisted. It wasn't easy. That amount of power. Even muted by the spell meant to contain it, it's intoxicating. But we did.*

*Then something changed. Laure and I couldn't figure out what it was. But suddenly, the Book's call grew stronger. Insistent. Though it no longer wanted either of us. Astrid was the witch it wanted. We had resisted it. We told ourselves that it was because we had each other. That we were stronger, individually and certainly together, than Astrid. But now I'm not so sure. I've come to think that maybe the only thing that saved us was that it wasn't yet the Book's time.*

*So we couldn't just deal with Astrid. We had to protect her. From the Book. From herself. I did what I did because I was afraid. I feared that Astrid might succeed. Worse, I feared that if Astrid failed, you might be next.*

"You thought I wouldn't be strong enough to resist."

*I didn't want its darkness to touch your heart. You have no idea the things the Book asks of you, the thoughts it puts in your head. My death seemed a small price to pay to protect you. Besides, even if it wasn't you, the Book would've moved on to someone else. We did what we had to do to put an end to it. Or at least we hoped we would.*

Lisette was so focused on her mother she didn't notice the vehicle had begun to move again until Nathalie started in laughing, a high-pitched nervous chuckle.

"To get to the other side," Nathalie said, her eyes focused on the rearview mirror rather than pointed at the road like they should be. Lisette began to worry that this night had been too much for the woman. Hell, maybe even for both of them.

*To get to the other side,* her mother echoed Nathalie's words, and only then did Lisette realize their import.

"You're going . . . ," Lisette said, looking back at her mother. She would've slapped her face if she hadn't known her hand would pass clean through it. She would have thrown her arms around her and refused to release her, if only her embrace could hold her.

*My staying on here the way I have. It isn't natural. I didn't cross over when I should've. When I was supposed to. First I told myself it was to keep an eye on Astrid. Then to keep an eye on you, till you got settled. Then the grandbabies came, and I just had to see them grow. And then came Katrina. And you needed your mama all over again. I'm not blaming you, girl. These were all excuses—good ones, maybe—but still excuses. Truth is, I just didn't want to let go.*

*Now I've stayed on so long past when I should've left I'm not even sure I can make it on my own. But there're a lot of witches crossing over tonight. I'm gonna ride home on their coattails.* She fixed Lisette with a sad, somewhat frightened gaze. *I'm never going to get another chance like this. If I don't take it, I might not get a chance again until . . . well, until kingdom come.* She held a phantom hand out to Lisette, then pulled back, seeming to remember that Lisette couldn't actually touch that hand. *You're gonna be all right now on your own, aren't you, girl?*

Lisette gave her mother what she needed, even if she wasn't sure it was true. "Yes, Mama." She forced herself to look her mother straight in the eye so she'd believe it.

Her mother snorted. *You,* she said, *only think you're lying. But you will be. It's time, girl. You know it's true. Your mama has to move on.*

*'Course, first I got to stop Astrid, and I can't do it alone. It might be a battle of spirit, of power.* Lisette knew she'd be useless in a magic fight. *It may be a battle of flesh.* Her mother reached out and let her hand slip through the back of Lisette's seat. *Our only chance is together.*

"I think we're there," Nathalie said, turning back to the wheel. She pulled the car halfway up onto the sidewalk, perhaps to make room for other cars to squeeze by, but Lisette suspected no other vehicles were going to pass. Just ahead, two, maybe three blocks down, Lisette spotted the towers of the old church, lit up like they were the landing strip for the second coming.

A tall man in formal dress dashed past them, slapping a bloody handprint on the windshield as he went. A wave of shouts and screams echoed, and Lisette looked down the road at the mass of people choking the stairs, tuxedos and evening gowns tumbling over each other as their wearers fought their way out of the old church.

"You want me to act as your *chwal?*"

*Do you trust me?*

It wasn't a matter of trust.

Opening yourself up for such a thing meant the spirit riding you had complete control, total access to your every thought, every memory. She hesitated. A moment too long.

"You can take me, ma'am," Nathalie said. "I can help you. If it comes down to knuckles, that is. I'm trained in self-defense."

"We can't ask that of you," Lisette said, her cheeks flushing in shame. "I'm not a coward. I will—"

"I'm alone in the world," Nathalie said. "I can sense you aren't. Besides, I'm guessing it would be a lot less awkward for the both of you."

*She's right,* her mother said, and in the next minute she was gone, hidden inside Nathalie's flesh, speaking through her lips, using her voice. "I understand. There were things I wouldn't have wanted your *grand-maman* to see in me. Just know I love you, no matter what."

"I love you, too, Mama."

"Of course you do," she said. "How could you not?" Her mother's smile rose to Nathalie's lips.

"Are you ready?" Nathalie asked, and answered in the affirmative before Lisette could even think to respond. Lisette realized that her mother had posed the question, and Nathalie had responded, both in Nathalie's voice.

Nathalie undid her buckle and swung open her door. She slipped out of the car, her movements perfectly natural, as if her body had been built for Soulange Simeon to ride. Lisette's shaking hands struggled with her own belt. Nathalie leaned back in, Lisette's mother looking at her through Nathalie's eyes. "You stay here."

"The hell," Lisette bit off the words, "I will." She got her own door open and jumped out.

"My hands are gonna be full." Nathalie slammed her door closed. "I may not be able to protect you."

"Don't try to scare me away, old woman." Fear caused Lisette's words to come out harsher than she'd intended, but she had to admit, their sharpness helped make her point. "I know you too well. If you're thinking about crossing over, you're going to be calling on Legba. He'll protect me."

"Oh, you have faith in Papa now, do you, girl?"

"Yes, Mama, I reckon I do."

"And you're going to honor him again, and the other loa, like I taught you?"

Lisette nodded. Though she didn't speak a word, for her, this was a solemn vow.

A small black dog, a muttsy-looking wire-haired terrier mix by the look of it, appeared, unattended, out of nowhere, and barked at them before running off in the direction of the church.

"Looks like Papa Legba has faith in you, too."

# THIRTY-ONE

Of the witches who'd come, dressed in their finery, pausing to be noticed as they stepped out of their chauffeured cars, a quick estimation of the calf-deep sea of blood and gore pooling around the stage told Alice that no more than a handful could have made it out.

When she looked down at the faces of those left standing, Alice realized they were more than just mirrored images of each other, copied and recopied and spat back out into the world. These mass-produced specters, wading forward to kneel before their king, shared the features of the people whose drug-addled dreams had built Babau Jean's Mahogany Hall replica on the Dreaming Road. Somehow, the old church and his lair—two places that shared no natural connection—had been joined together, just like Nicholas's and Celestin's houses had been fused in the dream that first led her to the Dreaming Road.

Alice stood there, above it all, Babau Jean holding her tight, his hands pinching into her upper arms, forcing her to look on. She sensed that he wanted her to act as his witness, to validate his handiwork, to appreciate his masterpiece. She had a flash of Gabriel, the real Gabriel, seeing him through Babau Jean's eyes. The bogey had fanned Gabriel's long-repressed avarice and pride to trick him and his sister into expanding the space of the church into the Dreaming Road, into welcoming Babau Jean's phantom servants as guests. She had another flash of Gabriel, his eyes wide in terror as Babau Jean skinned him alive just moments before making his entrance as Gabriel. The real man, Alice now knew, was still alive, crammed into a restroom stall in this very building, preserved in agony by Babau Jean's magic.

She hoped, no, she prayed to any force that might be willing to hear her, that Hugo had been spared. He was, after all, her brother. And Lucy. She'd been kind, in her own way. Fleur as well. Her aunt still seemed removed from her, though Alice decided the fault lay at her own feet. Fleur, she'd tried to build a bridge.

She thought of Vincent, grateful she hadn't noticed him among those in attendance.

She thought of Nicholas. She couldn't bear to think of Nicholas. She wouldn't let her last thoughts be of him.

Her attention was drawn to the sight of three enormous ravens, or maybe they were crows. She couldn't determine if these creatures were allies or enemies of each other. One thrashed around in the foul muck, trying to free itself from some kind of chain caught around its neck. The second, still caught up in the frenzy of the massacre but denied further human prey, had turned on the first, cawing and pecking at the weakest member of the trio. The third was making war with the second, but was it trying to protect the collared creature or claim it as its own?

The weakened bird let out a furious caw and began beating its wings. Its protector, Alice now understood, fought off the aggressor as the chained bird rose and escaped through a gaping hole that had earlier that evening encased a rose window. The two remaining crows pecked furiously at each other, the struggle only ending when the beak of the protector pierced one of the aggressor's eyes. A wild screech accompanied the aggressor's rise and escape through the same exit. Alice could feel Babau Jean's growing rage as he ordered the creatures to return, but the final bird simply cocked its head and took to the air, its wingspan seeming to stretch the length of the limousine in which she'd arrived.

But who could really measure, in this space where two worlds had been brought together, the one bent over and folded into the other. The light of one world reflected in the other.

Those worlds were now prying themselves apart, though whether through magical volition or simply each world's separate gravity, Alice couldn't say. Only the monster was likely to know, and she nearly turned back to ask him.

An elderly woman, crying out in desperation, planted herself on her knees on the former church's floor as she grasped at her husband's hands. Alice recognized the woman as one half of the Silverbell Coven and could even see her ring. Her husband was suspended upside down above her. Only half of the gentleman remained visible, his legs hidden by a wall that didn't belong to this space, but to the world that was rotating away from them. The man, whom Alice felt sure was already dead, jerked up, once, twice, a hungry force from the other world having latched onto him. A final tug, and the gentleman was torn in half, his lower body claimed by the other world, his torso falling toward his wife. She reared back in horror, and a glint from her ring glanced off the wall that had swallowed his lower extremities.

Alice wished she were strong enough to share the woman's horror, but her own emotions had shut down. She watched with a detached, clinical eye as the woman went mad. Alice's own cold reason offered distraction by suggesting a solution to the long-forgotten puzzle of Fleur's shoe buckles and how they could have reflected a light shining in her aunt's house in D.C. onto a wall in New Orleans. Alice wished she would have thought to ask her aunt. A shame, really, she hadn't thought of it earlier. She was sure she'd never have another chance to pose the question.

The cries of the sole survivor of the Silverbell Coven were muffled by the dreamers who rose and formed a tightening circle around her.

Alice tried to cry out. To tell them to leave the woman alone, but when she opened her mouth, a loud, cruel laugh pealed from between her lips. Babau Jean controlled her, she realized, had always controlled her. Her own magic had probably never been hers. It had most likely always been in his control. A thought turned in the back of her mind. Keeping her on Sinclair had been the one sure way to prevent both her and Babau Jean from making use of that magic.

She felt a flash of anger at the Silverbell woman, wishing her damned screams would stop. But her anger wasn't hers. It was his. But still . . .

The dreamers backed away, dropping another set of torn limbs into the soup.

Blessed silence.

Then a voice, an all-too-familiar voice began singing in her ear. She knew the mask of Babau Jean had been removed, but she had no need to look back to recognize the voice's owner. It would be easier if she didn't turn. If she could imagine that mask were the monster's true face.

The song, quiet at first, grew as the dreamers, both standing and kneeling before them, joined in. A simple melody, twining into harmony. A descant arose and floated above.

So much magic.

So much magic from the blood. A sea of floating relics from which to draw. Alice was too weak to resist. She breathed in the magic, that delicious, heady perfume.

She used the last of her resolve to clench her jaw, willing silence, but she never really had a chance. She never really had a choice. Her own voice, high and pristine, joined in. To her surprise, Babau Jean released her, knowing, she reckoned, that his power over her was absolute.

The dreamers, as one, stepped back toward the shadows at the edge of the room, the odd angles of their movement showing her that they were following the curvature of the Dreaming Road. Some, Alice faced dead-on. Others hovered somewhat below or above her.

In the space before her, a figure began to arise from beneath the surface of the now swirling blood sea, a head first, then shoulders and breasts. The woman's features were obscured by a blood-reddened cascade of hair, but the necklace she'd first seen worn by the beauty of Mahogany Hall, the same necklace that Julia Prosper had been murdered in, now rested on the rising woman's bosom.

Alice knew instinctively that this woman was not Julia Prosper.

The song grew louder, her own voice straining to be heard. And then came the sound of slamming doors.

Alice's eyes told her that two women had entered the church, but her senses burned with the awareness that her eyes must be lying. An athletic blonde woman led an older, darker-skinned woman into the room, but Alice sensed neither of these women were in control. A flickering showed her that the blonde was merely an envelope, a vessel for a woman—no, a spirit—of great power. A different chant, one just as powerful as her own song, began, its strength offering Alice a spark of hope.

The dreamers' song changed, weakened. The familiar voice that had been leading them lost its luster, turning into the sound of branches scraping a night window. Babau Jean was not all-powerful if he felt the need to hide from these women. With great satisfaction, Alice began to taste Babau Jean's disquiet. It began as denial. *Too much magic to be turned back.* It turned to anger. *That damned Simeon bitch will not stop us again.* But it was only when the second woman stepped around the first and dipped her finger into the blood that Babau Jean's angst changed to fear. The blonde woman stopped, a look of happy surprise spreading across her face, as the older woman began tracing her finger through the air, creating symbols that somehow hung in the very air itself.

The blonde swayed as the spirit that had been within her broke free and fell into the older woman. A bright light burst around them.

Babau Jean grasped Alice again. Did he plan to protect her from the women's waxing power, or would he use her as a shield? As long as they defeated him, Alice did not care.

She looked out, past the bloodstained woman now struggling to rise before her, through the dreamers who began to push back even further, some disappearing cleanly, others in wispy black puffs. The strength of the magic she'd been caught up in began to falter as the dreamers fell away. Soon it was only Alice's voice in duet with Babau Jean's. The rising woman reached out toward him, then dissolved, falling in a shower of red drops.

Alice's vision twisted. She felt herself being tugged backward. And then the world fell away.

# THIRTY-TWO

The morning was warm and beautiful, the humidity, for once, merciful.

It was the Fourth of July. City Park should have been teeming with children, their laughter and cries filling the air. There should have been music coming from the open windows of passing cars, coming from the bandstand, tinny fading cacophonies leaking from the earbuds of passing joggers. But there were no children. There were no joggers. There was no music. There was no sound at all.

Except for the chirping of crickets.

Alice stopped and listened. It was the wrong time of day for crickets, but she guessed circadian rhythms meant nothing here on the Dreaming Road.

"You'll get better at this," Alice heard Babau Jean's whispery voice. She turned to see him stepping out from the shade of an ancient oak. The mask no longer served any purpose, neither to frighten her nor to hide his identity. "Populating a world takes time," he said. "It takes practice. But you'll get the hang of it. The trick is not to try to make them into something. Just hand them a grain. Like an oyster with sand.

Something to believe about themselves. Something to love. Or better yet, feel ashamed of. They'll do the rest."

"Like Daniel," she said.

"Like with any servitor spirit," he said. "But you've come to know the truth, haven't you, Alice? We're all servitor spirits of a kind. The only difference between Daniel and us is that whatever created us thought it would be amusing to leave us bereft of a true purpose. To let us stumble around blindly until we—as if by magic—reveal ourselves. A rather cruel thing to do, I should say."

"I've felt a force calling to me. Asking me to become," she said, "though I'm not sure it's any great creator. I think maybe it's just a mirror held up before a mirror, a reflection convinced of its own consciousness." She knelt and touched the petals of a white lily. They felt so real. The world around her seemed so solid. "I've largely ignored it, anyway. Just gave it enough not to give up on me." She released the petal and stood. "I didn't want it to give up on me. Not completely." It felt good to be entirely honest. "Turns out I, too, am frightened of oblivion."

"And why didn't he give up on you, this creator of yours?"

She paused, considering his question. "Because it knew I was the key to understanding you."

"And do you, my dear? Do you understand me?"

"I think so, though I am most curious about one thing. Something that probably doesn't even matter in the grand scheme."

"And what might that be? We're here now, where no one can harm us, and I'm feeling generous. Go ahead and ask."

She walked up to him and peeled off the bone-white mask, removing also its terrible bottomless eyes and threatening teeth. "Why his face?" She looked upon the smooth skin beneath it, the sparkling dark eyes with their thick lashes, the beautiful mouth, even more beautiful than that of Lucy's friend. "Why Alcide Simeon's face?"

"Why, indeed?" he said, his voice no longer the whisper of branches scraping a night window, but instead a warm baritone, a voice she reckoned must have belonged to the younger version of the sad old man she'd seen holding a silver trumpet. The sensuous lips curved up into a smile. "I'll tell you. I'll tell you everything, but not here. Let me take you to our special place."

Alice nodded. She no longer feared him. Not in the slightest. He had done his worst. He had done it long ago. He had become her father.

She offered the monster her hand, and he took it. Time and space meant nothing here on the Dreaming Road. The next instant, she stood outside "Flying Horses," City Park's century-old carousel. Babau Jean was gone, but she knew he was near. She watched as the carousel's lights snapped on. She pushed through the turnstile and entered the pavilion.

"I do apologize," he said, his voice seemingly coming from every direction at once, though she couldn't see him. "In the common world, your favorite horse has been damaged. Lost a leg, it did. It seemed I should make a few modifications here to reflect the original's form."

Alice circled around until she found the horse. "They call them fliers," she said. "The ones that move up and down." She leaned against the carved animal, wrapping her arms around its neck. It was in her power to repair it, she knew. Perhaps she might, one day, if she couldn't find a way out of here. But somehow she loved the horse all the more for its damage.

She heard a sound like a lever being thrown, followed by a grinding as metal teeth began to tug on the bands that would cause the carousel to turn. Her horse tugged up, out of her grasp. She placed one hand on its hindquarters, then began to walk around the rotating base.

A whistle from Babau Jean's lips swelled into a faithful imitation of the carousel's calliope. She knew the tune. "Over the Waves." The tune had no words, at least as far as she knew, but she remembered singing it to herself as a small girl once. On that occasion, what seemed now a million years ago, he had joined in, adding his gruff and booming voice to her "la la la," catching her by the hands, spinning in circles with her.

She saw him now, standing beside the carousel. She passed him, a youthful representation of Alcide Simeon's face beaming up at her. She kept moving forward, speeding up each revolution. When she next saw him, he had donned the bone-white mask once more. But he was merely toying with her.

It ended in a heartbeat. The carousel stopped as if it had never begun spinning. The lights went dead. The music fell silent.

He had joined her up on the carousel. She could see him just a bit ahead, sitting in shadow on one of the fixed benches, the one he had always occupied in the common world, as he'd called it, whenever she had insisted he ride the carousel with her. He held up a hand and waved her forward. She walked, hearing the tap of her artificial shoes on the boards of the imaginary platform. It seemed so real, as real as any world she'd ever known.

Maybe it was.

She circled around him. Turned to face him.

"Celestin," she said.

His onyx eyes glinted. He ran a hand through his thick silver hair. He patted the bench beside him. "*Viens t'asseoir, ma chère.*"

She slid beside him on the hard bench, keeping her eyes fixed forward. She would've preferred to look upon the face of Babau Jean than at her own grandfather's—no, she reminded herself—her own father's features.

"I loved her, you know, your mother Astrid," he said. She risked a glance at him. His eyes were wide, sincere. "You should know, you were born of love."

"I don't think I care about that," Alice said. "Even monstrous things are sometimes born of love."

"You aren't monstrous. You are far from monstrous. A bit reticent, perhaps, overly tentative, but you are my beloved daughter." He tried to take her hand, but she pulled it back. "I know you don't understand, but everything I've done, I've done to protect you." He folded his hands on his lap. "And to protect your mother."

"We both know that's not true."

"Perhaps not entirely, but as true as it needs to be."

She realized her eyes had adjusted to the enclosed pavilion's shadows. Unreal eyes adapting themselves to an artificial darkness. Would she be able to remain cognizant that all around her was illusion, when her every sense vouched for the realness of this world? Or would that awareness fall away? Alice focused on her own dim features, reflected by a line of mirrors on the carousel's center pole. "So why his face? Why did you steal Alcide Simeon's face?"

Celestin's laugh caused her to turn toward him. "Really? That is your greatest concern?"

"No," she said, "just my first."

"*Bon*," he said with a shrug. "I stole nothing. That was your grandmother's doing. Laure—not really your grandmother, of course, but I suspect due to a lifetime of conditioning, you'll always think of her as such—she was in love with Alcide. Ironic, really, that Laure and Soulange came to be such close friends. But then again, they had a common enemy."

"You."

He answered with a cool smile. "Your great-grandparents—Laure's parents—you must understand that it was a different time. Even if New Orleans had a long tradition of white men forming liaisons with women of color, the reverse was still a sticky issue. Laure's parents would never have allowed a union between the two. So she married me instead. A man of her parents' choosing. A man she never loved. Never even intended to love. She lay with me. She bore my children. But to satisfy her needs, she turned elsewhere." He scanned her eyes, seemingly searching them for any glint of doubt. Alice forced herself to remain neutral, afraid that any display, of either trust or disbelief, might send the wrong signal. "It was your grandmother who sought out Babau Jean, and she who gave him her lover's pretty face."

"Her lover?"

"Yes. Alcide Simeon was her lover," he said, then studied her as if considering what her understanding of that word might be. "Though never in the physical sense." Alice decided his precision on that point sprung more from his own vanity than from any esteem for her grandmother. "A shame, really, the two never had it off together." She could see a smirk form on his lips. "Perhaps if they had, she might've moved on. Instead, she romanticized him, ignoring any of the flesh-and-blood Alcide's faults." The smirk faded. "Alcide showing up at my funeral with his damned horn." A snarl formed on his lips. "You've no idea how it burned when he played it. Just between you and me, I think the bastard almost had me, nearly ripped me out of Vincent's skin, he did. But he's weak. Always was. Never could finish anything unless he had a woman standing over him to make him."

He turned and leaned in, his eyes wide with sincerity. She could smell peppermint on his breath. The same candies he had always shared with her in the common world—the candies she had accepted so as not to hurt his feelings, even though she detested peppermint. "I know it sounds fantastical, but it's true. This is all true. You know of our mad pharmacist and his Beautiful Dreamer?"

She nodded. "I've read a few variations on the legend," she said, her mind turning to the books she'd devoured on Sinclair about New Orleans folklore.

"Oh, the doctor's creation was far more than a legend. Your grandmother and I learned of the creature right before our marriage. A casual conversation with a fellow partygoer about New Orleans and her oddities. Laure never spoke of the Beautiful Dreamer, but I saw the spark in her eyes. I knew all along what she was doing. I watched her. Followed her as she wandered the astral, searching for him. So I made sure she found him. Broken. Monstrous. Tragic. Cowering on the Dreaming

Road in that very recreation of Magnolia Hall you visited. Sneaking out under the cover of darkness to feed on children's fears.

"The Beautiful Dreamer transformed into Babau Jean, the great and fearsome monster, the haunter of children's dreams. I thought the discovery would terrify her. That she'd learn her lesson. Begin to settle down." He raised his brows, as if to say such a reaction was the only rational one. "But no. *La Belle et la Bête*, Beauty and the Beast, it must have seemed to her." He laughed.

"The creature was more than a simple servitor spirit. It was the mask its creator wore to slip into dreams and feed on dreamers. I learned how to ride the creature, to put him on, to make myself one with him. It was the greatest of jokes, really. Your grandmother slipping around, hiding her indiscretions with such care, never knowing that behind the mask of her lover's face was her own husband.

"The next bit came as an accident. Paulina Picot was the first of the Chanticleer Coven to take to the Dreaming Road." His gaze softened as he spoke of the witch. "She was a sad lot, our Paulina. Drab and as weak as water. Her place in the coven was hereditary, otherwise"—he made a motion like sweeping crumbs from a table—"pfff. Not one to miss at all, Paulina, but one day, she did go missing, and someone, I'm not sure who, did, in fact, take notice. It took a while, but a spell led us to her. She'd locked herself away in one of those self-storage facilities—rather amusing if you think about it."

Celestin paused, but Alice didn't react. He waited. Smirked again. Then sighed. "Her body was there, dehydrated, dying. But *she*—her essence—was not. We took the body to the hospital. They put tubes down her throat, tubes up her . . . well, you get the picture. Her vacant form held on for a few days. As her coven leader," he said, placing his hand over his heart, "I was terribly concerned for her well-being." His words dripped with exaggerated sincerity. He leaned back and looked at her through mischievous, narrowed eyes. "That was the reason I gave for staying by her side, day and night. But I was really only curious to see if I could slip into the world she'd created for herself. It was a risk, of course," he winked at her, "*mais qui ne risque rien n'a rien*. I wore the mask of Babau Jean, but to my surprise, she saw me as me. I realized that *I* was her dream. The love she'd given up on knowing. She gave herself to me, and I fed upon her magic as she aged—days, months, years even, all flashing by in what seemed to me to be mere moments. She changed from a drab, middle-aged mouse into a desiccated crone right in my arms, then fell to dust at my feet. I awoke at the sound of the monitor alarm. Paulina was dead. Dead in both her world and the common world. But I was alive. Alive and energized."

He smiled. "I began picking them off, the weaker witches who took to the Dreaming Road. Whenever I heard of a new witch 'missing,' I went hunting. At first, mostly the solitary ones or ones from smaller, weaker covens, but what can I say? I had the taste for Chanticleer. It became a game for me, spreading despondency among the weak. Planting the seed of the Dreaming Road in their minds. After a while, I found we had reached a tipping point, where it was no longer necessary for me to manipulate the others. Escape via the Dreaming Road had become a normalized concept."

"But I didn't choose to come here. And neither did my mother."

"No, but as I've come to understand the Dreaming Road, I've learned there are a few tricks, a few"—he held up his hands and wiggled his fingers like he was about to perform a stage magician's trick—"trapdoors, if you will, between this place and the common world. It takes a lot out of me, of course, but you . . . and Astrid . . . were worth it. No, it's much easier when witches come of their own volition."

"But how could you find them, these witches?"

"Here," he said, sitting up straighter, seeming proud of himself, "is one of the great secrets of the Dreaming Road. All the worlds here seem so different, each built to delight its dreamer," he said, emphasizing each word as if it were its own independent thought, "but they all exist within the same sphere." He paused, Alice intuited, to give her time to consider the point. "And there's only one spot around New Orleans where the Dreaming Road and the common world actually touch."

"Grunch Road," Alice said, remembering, as a small girl, hearing coven members whisper its name. "Where Babau Jean . . . where I guess you killed Soulange, and tried to kill Grandmother."

"I'll let you in on another secret. Really of no import to anyone other than our own acquaintances." He winked. "Laure was already stark raving mad when I found her at the foot of the Dreaming Road." He hesitated, pointing his index finger and pinkie toward an artificial heaven, making a devil's oath. "And Soulange was dead. As dead as dead can be. No. I didn't kill the woman. It was your grandmother who took her life. Part of a spell they used to keep *The Book of the Unwinding* out of my hands."

"But why would Grandmother care? Why would she try to stand between you and your precious book?"

"Because to use the Book, to harness its magic, a man must be without progeny. Magic—the final magic—must fall into a pool without issue. Theodosius, the Book's author—one could almost call him its progenitor—*le salaud fou*, made a few modifications I myself wouldn't have been willing to undergo." He grimaced while miming a tug and a slice. "No, much better to erase one's mistakes than to break one's pencil."

"Erase. You mean murder."

"'Murder was the first act of magic,'" he said, something in his tone causing Alice to realize he considered this a truism. "That is why Laure wanted to keep the Book from me. She wanted to protect her children. Her bastard children she used me to sire."

"But they are your children."

"No," he shook his head, regarding her with severity. "Not at all. They may be of my flesh, but they are not of my soul. No, I know that as Laure lay with me, in her mind, she was giving herself to Alcide. The children she bore, I detest." Celestin made a face like he'd tasted something bitter. "Vincent. *Un vrai fils à maman*, that one, despite his robust nature. I was both relieved and amused when he brought Soulange and Alcide's daughter home to meet his mother and me. No, that one was always his mother's son. Right down to his taste in lovers." A small smile came to his lips. "I enjoyed watching the boy die." He nodded his head, as if trying to make his point. "Really, I did."

Vincent's murder flashed before her eyes, as clearly as if Alice had been there to witness it herself. A moan escaped her, and the look on Celestin's face told her that he realized he'd gone too far by sharing it with her. In that moment, she and Celestin both knew that Alice would always despise him.

"I suspect Laure lied to Soulange," he said, shifting gears. "The woman died without ever knowing the truth of Laure's treachery, though I might decide to apprise her of it now that we've . . . *recon-nected*." He paused, seeming to consider the point. "I've often wondered if Laure simply miscalculated. She destroyed her son's relationship with Alcide's daughter, supposedly for his own good. She took the life—for the most noble of reasons, of course—of Alcide's wife. She sensed my connection to the Book. I believe she might have thought that I, her husband, would be destroyed, or at least significantly weakened by its removal. No," he said, "I can't help but ask myself if it didn't all boil down to Laure still having her hat set for Alcide."

He lifted his hand, waving it as if wiping away a stain. "But that's neither here nor there. She died screaming after years of sharing her mind with someone so much more frightening than our Babau could ever be." He patted her on the knee. "She believed herself to be strong. Believed she could somehow survive the madness she invited into her. But she spent the end of her days seeing the world through Theodosius's eyes. I'm sure of it. The things she dreamed of . . . the nightmares she lived while awake." He laughed. "She was trapped, staring into the darkness. But it was all her own doing. Suffice it to say that if Laure and Soulange hadn't interfered in the manner they did, the Book would have been recovered, and you would've—"

"Ended up here anyway."

"Oh, no, *ma chère*," Celestin's face pinched in on itself as he shook his head. "You would never have been born. I told you that you were made from love. I would have never let you come into the world had I not believed the Book was secured beyond my reach."

"But it wasn't."

He shook his head. "Not as well as Laure had hoped. A book hidden between two realities. She never realized that I and her phantom lover were one and the same. That together we formed a creature capable of channeling magic between realities." He shrugged. Alice was surprised to see what looked to be genuine sadness in his eyes.

"But the book wasn't 'secured.' And I did," she said, "come into the world."

"And that's why I built you this paradise. You must forgive me. I'd intended it for your seven-year-old self, not the beautiful young woman you've become. If you'd just taken my hand when I came for you that first day, imagine all the suffering you might have saved yourself."

"You wanted to bring me here to live and die. In a dream."

"In a beautiful dream. A much better life than Nicholas has given you. Locked away on that icy little island. No, if you had come with me, you would've lived a full and wonderful life. Your every dream realized. Your every hope attained."

"And I would be dead."

"Yes, by now, you would've expired."

"And you would've fed from my magic."

"Yes. It would've been a waste not to."

His expression turned grave. "You're better off here. You are. If you were to awaken, if you were to return to the rest of the family, they would only lock you away again. This time for good."

"Because they believe I'm guilty. Because they believe I've helped you."

"No, dear girl," he said, shaking his head. "None of them would hold you responsible for what's happened. They would lock you away because they believe you're too fragile, yet too powerful, to live freely among them. Just like Astrid." He shrugged. "Nicholas had planned to send your mother to that island of yours. And he would've, too, but I got to her first."

Alice wanted to rail against him, but she couldn't. However much she didn't agree with his decisions, however much she resented and hated the things he'd done, she believed his every word. "But I don't understand. If you come and go along the Dreaming Road, if you can replenish your own magic by feeding off others, what is it to you if magic is fading? Why would you even care about that book?"

"Oh, my dear girl, I don't care about the Book. I never wanted the Book. Your grandmother and Soulange should never have tried to do away with it. It cannot be destroyed, and it refuses to stay hidden any longer, for its time has come. No, if Laure and Soulange wanted to save their children, if they wanted to postpone the end of magic, they should've killed me. The Book sensed the connection I'd forged with Babau Jean." He reached out and took Alice's hand, and she let him. "You see, I was never after *The Book of the Unwinding*. The Book was after me."

# THIRTY-THREE

The morning was hotter than hell, upper nineties already, and the humidity . . . well, at least the rain had finally stopped.

Fourth of July. Jackson Square was teeming with children, their laughter and cries filling the air. Buskers competed for airwaves with the beats streaming from the open windows of passing cars. Evangeline turned, stepping out of the way of a trio of passing joggers, mad to be out in this heat.

Bored tarot card readers and art merchants lined up one after the other along the St. Ann Street walk, tapping on their phone screens or flipping through worn paperbacks, looking up from time to time at passersby.

As Evangeline drew near, a pair of dirty-pretty blond Cajun boys, brothers by the look of them, stopped the arcane French tune they were playing mid-note, then broke out in an old and very familiar Robbie Robertson song. She stopped and gave them an exaggerated curtsy as they sang out her name. She dug a couple of coins from her pocket to drop into the hat that sat on the ground before them, but the nearer man reached out and snatched the cap away, dropping it onto his head.

He gave her a smile. Just a smile. Still . . . the look in his eyes, well, it had been a long time since Evangeline had blushed at anything, but she felt the color rising to her cheeks. She turned and began to walk away, but stopped and looked back over her shoulder at the fellow in the cap. "Sounds like you know where to find me," she said, then turned and merged into a gaggle of tourists flooding into Decatur Street on their way to the Café Du Monde.

She broke with her escort as they went straight to the beignets, and she turned right to find the stairs that would carry her up and over the artillery park. She paused on the platform by the cannon and let her gaze drift out across the strip of parking lots and train tracks to land on the muddy waters of the Mississippi. The river's current, bending and weaving its way through disappearing shores, would soon be carrying Vincent Marin's ashes along—out into the deep, warm waters of the Gulf. It had been Fleur's daughter Lucy who'd followed a clue from his killer and found the body, wrapped in heavy plastic and hidden in an old priest hole built behind a false pilaster in Nicholas's formal dining room. The family had declined Frank Demagnan's offer to see to a "proper burial," but he had his pale hands too busy dealing with the aftermath of the ball to put up much of a fuss.

Although Evangeline had always liked Vincent, she might not have come out today if she'd thought Nicholas would be there. But Nicholas was gone. Just gone. He'd disappeared with such finality that if Evangeline didn't know his ego was too big to allow it, she might have suspected that he, like his wife before him, had taken to the Dreaming Road. Though if what Evangeline had heard about the massacre was true, it looked like Astrid might have had a change of heart. That all the bloodshed was linked to her attempt to return.

Maybe she'd jumped to the wrong conclusion about Nicholas. Maybe she hadn't. Either way, she knew there was no trust between them. Her mother's cohorts were liars. But the thing about a good lie is that it always has a jigger of truth mixed in.

She wasn't the only one unsure about Nicholas and his motives. Some were whispering that Nicholas himself might have had something to do with Babau Jean's murder party. Perhaps it had been an act of retaliation against not only the Chanticleer Coven, but against all the witches of New Orleans for having wounded his pride.

Still, Evangeline could see another possible motive. Perhaps he, too, had experienced a change of heart toward Astrid. Perhaps Evangeline herself had helped push him in that direction.

Others spoke more loudly, and Evangeline feared rightly, that Alice had triggered the monster's arrival. Whether or not she had conjured him willingly was still a matter of conjecture, and probably always would be. Just as Celestin had done before her, Alice now lay in a vegetative state, in the very same facility up near Natchitoches that had cared for her grandfather. Though it was still early days, and a miracle could happen any day, the doctors hadn't expressed much optimism that Alice would ever awaken. Evangeline hated it, but part of her felt it might be for the best if Alice could just slip away quietly in her sleep. It could save a lot of people a lot of pain if she did.

There, at the end of the tiny pier that straddled the rocky shore and jutted out into the river, a figure stood waving at her. Hugo. He had his aunt and his cousin now. But somehow she knew he was still mostly hers—always would be. It was for Hugo, not Vincent's memory, that she'd ventured to the river's edge today. She raised her hand in salute, and descended the stairs.

As she reached the foot of the stairs, a somehow familiar black SUV pulled alongside her, then slid into an empty space. The vehicle's doors opened, and Fleur descended, the driver hopping out with her. "Let me help you with that," the driver called to Lucy, who was riding in the back. "It sticks a bit sometimes." The driver tugged the door open.

"Thank you," Lucy said, then slid out onto the asphalt on shoes tall enough to challenge even Evangeline's most accomplished dancer.

Evangeline was about to greet the mother and daughter when the driver spun around. "Ms. Caissy," she said, "so good to see you again."

It took Evangeline a moment, but her mind flashed back to her ride to Précieux Sang, precisely, she calculated on emotion alone, one hundred and forty years ago, next week. "Nathalie," she said, then reached out to accept the woman's hand. "How are you?"

"Well, you know. Showing up. Diving in. Sticking at it," she said and flashed a bright smile. "Right?"

Evangeline nodded and squeezed Nathalie's hand. "Right. But please call me Evangeline."

Nathalie nodded, placing a hand over heart and giving a slight bow of her head. This girl, Evangeline decided, was a piece of work. If she could handle her liquor, Evangeline might have just found her new best friend.

"Evangeline," Fleur said, "Thank you for coming."

"Of course," she said.

"Ah, wait," Nathalie said, beaming, "y'all know each other?" At that moment, she seemed to remember something. She turned back to Evangeline. "I am so sorry for your loss."

Vincent wasn't her loss, not really, but his death was at least tangential to so many of the personal losses she had faced. "Thank you," Evangeline said, even though the words came out sounding like an awkward question.

Nathalie looked up, peering over Evangeline's shoulder, and a look of surprise bloomed on her face. Evangeline turned to see Lisette Perrault and her family approaching. There was something different about the woman now. She was glowing, if not with confidence, at least with a sense of rightness. She no longer seemed to consider herself a fraud. An older man she recognized as Alcide Simeon trailed behind them, trumpet in hand.

"Ms. Perrault," Nathalie greeted the woman, who seemed just as surprised as anyone to see Nathalie in the mix.

Lisette grabbed her husband's arm. "This is the woman I told you about. The one . . ." She fell silent, looking a bit embarrassed.

Lisette's husband stepped forward, going around Evangeline and grabbing Nathalie's hand. "I'm Lisette's husband, Isadore," he said, "You get tired of that security job of yours, you got a job with me." He pumped Nathalie's hand as she blushed. "We'll talk. The two of us. Afterward."

Lisette's son, one of the prettiest boys Evangeline had ever laid eyes on, came around and took Lucy by the hand. She leaned in and placed a chaste mama's-watching kiss on his lips.

Hell, it looked like everybody knew everybody around here.

"Mrs. Perrault," Lucy said, her voice cracking a bit.

"Miss Endicott," Lisette replied, with a deadpan expression.

"Remy," Fleur said, and the boy looked at her like a deer caught in headlights.

"Ma'am?"

"Thank you for helping my daughter through this difficult day."

"Yes, ma'am," he said, only a little less panicked. He wrapped his arm around Lucy's shoulder, and the two headed out toward the pier.

A younger woman, by appearances Lisette's daughter, came up behind her, frowning. "You're going to let him off that easily? He's been sneaking around with your daughter . . . ," she said, addressing Fleur.

"Manon," Lisette said, swatting her on the shoulder.

"Everyone just lets him off the hook."

"Don't worry, Miss Perrault," Fleur said. "Your brother has more than met his match in my Lucy." Manon's gaze followed the young couple on their way to the pier. "His days of just doing as he will have come to an end." Evangeline noticed the two mothers flashing each other a knowing smile.

Fleur approached and placed her hand on Nathalie's forearm. "I was going to suggest you wait for us in your vehicle, but you seem to know everyone here," she said. "Would you care to join us?"

Nathalie answered with a bob of her head. "Yes, ma'am, I'd be proud to."

They crossed together to join Hugo and the young lovers on the pier. Hugo reached down and picked up the urn that held Vincent's ashes. He came up to Evangeline and placed a kiss on her cheek. She reached out and took him, urn and all, in her arms.

"You okay?" she said.

"Hell no," he said. "I'm stone sober."

"Well, we can do something about that," Alcide said, coming up behind them, offering them a flask.

"Thank you," Evangeline said and took a drink, coughing. "What the hell? Is that even really whiskey?"

"A blend of whiskey and the finest tanker-truck vodka. Does the job, cheap and quick," Alcide said and chuckled, as she held the flask out to Hugo.

Evangeline noticed Lisette was watching closely—an angry, concerned look in her eyes as they narrowed on her father's flask in Evangeline's hand.

Hugo grasped it, then looked down at it, seeming to consider his options. He closed the flask. "I think I need to be here for this. Really be here," he said, holding the flask out to its owner. "But don't go far. Something tells me afterward . . ."

"I feel you, son," Alcide said and smiled. He slid the flask back into his suit pocket and patted it. "Here for you when you need it."

Lisette leaned in and whispered something into her husband's ear. Isadore nodded and began walking their way.

"Alcide," Isadore said. "You play something." He clapped his hand on the older man's shoulder. "Something real nice. Something to put old hurts behind us. Something to honor a good man." Evangeline's heart broke when she saw the way he looked at his wife. She hoped that someday someone would look at her with even half of the love she saw in Isadore's eyes.

Alcide nodded and raised the horn to his lips. He began to blow the purest and sweetest notes Evangeline had ever heard.

At that very moment Lucy flung off her boyfriend's arm. "No, I don't want to do this," she said. Her face was red, angry tears beginning to fall down her cheeks.

Alcide stopped, lowering his horn.

Fleur joined her daughter, reaching out, but the girl refused to take her hand. "Honey, what is it?"

Lucy looked around at each of them, then out at the river's rushing current. "How do we know?" she said. "How do we know this is what Uncle Vincent really wanted?" She turned, for some reason picking Evangeline out of the crowd. "The man who told us this is what he wanted wasn't Vincent. It was a monster, pretending to be Vincent. It was the thing that killed Vincent."

Lisette walked up to the girl and pulled her into her arms, squeezing her tight. "It *is* what Vincent would've wanted."

"How could you know?" Lucy said.

"The bastard took Vincent's heart, so he could know Vincent's true feelings. So he could perform a perfect impersonation of him." Lisette's eyes drifted from Lucy's face to her husband's. Evangeline could tell they were having an entire conversation, without ever saying a word. He nodded. "Besides, a very long time ago, I knew your uncle very well," she said, never taking her eyes off her husband. "In fact, I loved him. Very much. Just not quite as much as I do my husband," she said and paused, giving Isadore a chance to hear the truth of her words. "We may have heard it from the lips of a monster, but this is exactly what Vincent would've wanted." She returned her focus to Lucy. "You can believe that." She nodded in affirmation as she wiped away Lucy's tears. The girl smiled and threw her arms around Lisette, squeezing her tight. Lisette placed a kiss on the top of her head, then turned her over to Fleur's embrace.

Lucy wiped away her tears with the back of her hand. "Okay, so this may be what Uncle Vincent would want, but today is Independence Day. I thought we were supposed to do this on Mardi Gras."

"Oh, *ma chère ma'selle*," Alcide said, lifting his horn to his lips. "That river doesn't care."

# EPILOGUE

"Well, I thought he'd never leave," Daniel's head poked into the carousel.

Alice watched in disbelief as a tiny gray flash of fur dashed past him, bounding up to her. Sugar. The same sweet kitten face, though wizened—miniscule pink nose and peridot eyes still far too large for her face. Sugar put her paws on Alice's legs, kneading her with impatient pats, and Alice lifted the feline into her arms.

"Honestly," Daniel said, "I don't remember your grandfather being such a blowhard."

"He isn't my grandfather," Alice said, as Sugar began rubbing her head against her chin, purring. "You must have heard, he's—" Alice tried, but couldn't bring herself to acknowledge Celestin as her father. Instead she voiced the one thing about him she knew for certain to be true. "He's a monster."

"Sadly, my dear, I've learned there are many unpleasant truths in life, and the truth is, he's both monster . . . and father."

Daniel climbed up onto the platform and reached out, leaning in for a hug.

Sugar twisted in her arms and yowled at Daniel.

"Well, yes," Daniel said. "You were right. You did find her."

The cat made another sound that seemed to defy polite translation.

"There's no need . . . ," Daniel began, but then leaned in, putting his nose almost tip to tip with Sugar's. "Well, all right then, you little fiend, tell me. Now that you've found her, how exactly do you propose we get her home?"

# CHARACTER LIST

## *THE MARIN FAMILY*

**Celestin Marin**—Patriarch of the Marin family and deposed head of the Chanticleer Coven, once New Orleans's most powerful and influential coven.

**Laure Marin**—Celestin's deceased wife. A risky spell worked outside the auspices of the coven led to Laure's commitment to a psychiatric facility for witches. Laure is the mother of Nicholas, Vincent, and Fleur.

**Nicholas Marin**—Celestin and Laure's elder son. Nicholas challenged Celestin to become the current head of the Chanticleer Coven. Nicholas is the father of three children: Luc, Hugo, and Alice.

**Astrid Andersen Marin**—Nicholas's absent wife. A fragile, artistic witch who used her magic to escape the Marin family intrigues, though doing so meant deserting her young children.

**Luc Marin**—Astrid and Nicholas's eldest child, Luc is the likely challenger to his father's position as head of the Chanticleers. He blames his father for his mother's desertion.

**Hugo Marin**—Astrid and Nicholas's middle child. Hugo comes to rely on drink and drugs to mask his own sensitive nature.

**Alice Marin**—Quiet. Introverted. Always watching. The Marin family is hard on its women, and Alice seems destined to follow in her grandmother's footsteps.

**Vincent Marin**—Nicholas's younger brother, Vincent has been blessed with a lack of magic that allows him to lead an independent life of his own choosing. Vincent, unmarried and childless, tries to act as a father figure for Nicholas's neglected children.

**Fleur Marin Endicott**—Celestin and Laure's youngest child. Celestin forced her into a marriage of convenience with a Washington up-and-comer, Warren Endicott, in the hope of seeing Fleur rise to First Lady. As that marriage comes to its dissolution, Fleur is determined to become her own woman.

**Lucy Endicott**—Like a millennial-generation Mephistopheles, Fleur's outwardly superficial and undeniably spoiled teenaged daughter feigns indifference, but always finds ways to improve the lives of those around her.

## THE SIMEON—PERRAULT FAMILY

**Soulange Simeon**—The spell that led to Laure Marin's commitment also caused the death of this once great Voodoo practitioner. Bad blood has run between the families since Soulange was found dead and Laure wandering mad out on New Orleans's haunted Grunch Road. Soulange was the original proprietor of the famous French Quarter Voodoo supply store, Vèvè.

**Alcide Simeon**—Soulange's husband, musician. He blames the Marin family for his wife's death.

**Lisette Simeon Perrault**—Soulange and Alcide's daughter. Following Katrina, Lisette suffered a crisis of faith. Although she runs Vèvè, Lisette no longer practices her mother's religion.

**Isadore Perrault**—Lisette's husband and owner of one of New Orleans's premier landscaping companies. Although Isadore takes pride in having a true partnership with Lisette, he defers to her in matters of religion.

**Manon Perrault**—Lisette and Isadore's elder child, Manon is a no-nonsense self-starter who is currently completing her undergraduate degree in business.

**Remy Perrault**—Lisette and Isadore's teenage son. A visual artist, Remy is preparing to begin college in the fall. Lisette is struck by the similarities between her father, Alcide, and her son.

## THE WITCHES OF NEW ORLEANS

**Evangeline Caissy**—Stereotypes would imply that the solitary witch, a red-headed Cajun, is more temper than heart, but her past has taught her both patience and compassion. A former exotic dancer, Evangeline now runs her own Bourbon Street club, Bonnes Nouvelles, with an eye toward providing for her dancers after their performing days are done. Whether as an enemy, lover, or surrogate mother, Evangeline finds herself connected to each of the Marin men, though she hides the secret of her birth from them all.

**Mathilde, Margot, Marceline, and Mireille**—The sister witches. Having arrived on the banks of the Mississippi before New Orleans became an American city, the four sister witches are New Orleans's first and oldest sorceresses. They are heartless, ruthless, and capable of changing form to meet their needs. Three of the sisters survive; Mireille, the youngest of the sister witches and Evangeline's mother, died after falling for a storefront church preacher and turning against magic.

**Delphine Brodeur**—The sister witches' former servant, Delphine was brought to New Orleans at the age of thirteen, over two centuries ago. With magic fading, Delphine has grown desperate, trying to hold on to her power long enough to exact revenge on her former mistresses.

**The Chanticleer Coven**—Once dozens strong, the moribund coven has dwindled to the Marin family and eight degraded witches: second in command, **Gabriel Prosper** and his sister **Julia**, the vain and punctilious **Monsieur Jacques**, the steadfast and sturdy sergeant at arms **Jeanette**, the elderly and addled **Rose Gramont**, Rose's much younger self-appointed caretaker, **Guillaume (Guy) Brunet**, and a brother and sister duo known as "**les Jumeaux**" or "**the Twins**," who strive to function as a single, indivisible entity.

**Nathalie Boudreau**—Part-time security guard, part-time chauffeur, full-time psychic, Nathalie has a sixth sense that lands her in situations her good sense would tell her to avoid.

**Babau Jean**—Also known as "John the Bogey," Babau Jean is New Orleans's own born-and-bred bogeyman. Go on. Turn out the lights. Face the mirror. Call his name three times. He'll see you.

# ACKNOWLEDGMENTS

Creating a book is a team effort. I'd like to thank Jason Kirk at 47North for understanding that the book envisioned may not quite be the book that gets written. I'd also like to thank Angela Polidoro for, once again, doing all the heavy lifting, Kristen Weber for early input that set me on a better path than I could have found on my own, and my beta readers, including Ermin Federizo Mistica, Pat Allen Werths, and Evelyn Phillips.

Finally, I'd like to thank my loves, Rich Weissman, the world's most understanding spouse, our daughters, Becky and Maddy, and Quincy, the rescue Chihuahua who rescued me.

# ABOUT THE AUTHOR

*Photo © 2017 Mark Davidson*

J.D. Horn, the highly praised and bestselling author of the Witching Savannah series, now debuts a new contemporary fantasy series, Witches of New Orleans. A world traveler and student of French and Russian literature, Horn also has an MBA in international business and formerly held a career as a financial analyst before turning his talent to crafting chilling stories and unforgettable characters. His novels have received global attention and have been translated in more than half a dozen languages. Originally from Tennessee, he currently lives in Oregon with his spouse, Rich.